A SEASON IN ABYSSINIA

A Season in Abyssinia

An Impersonation of
Arthur Rimbaud

PAUL STRATHERN

This edition first published in 2014
by Faber and Faber Ltd
Bloomsbury House, 74–77 Great Russell Street
London WC1B 3DA

Printed by Books on Demand GmbH, Norderstedt

All rights reserved
© Paul Strathern, 1972

The right of Paul Strathern to be identified
as author of this work has been asserted in accordance
with Section 77 of the Copyright, Designs and Patents Act 1988

This book is sold subject to the condition that it shall not, by way of
trade or otherwise, be lent, resold, hired out or otherwise circulated
without the publisher's prior consent in any form of binding or cover other than
that in which it is published and without a similar condition including this
condition being imposed on the subsequent purchaser

A CIP record for this book is available from the British Library

ISBN 978-0-571-31490-4

INTRODUCTION

The Man Who 'Disappeared Himself': An Interview with Paul Strathern

Paul Strathern was born in London in 1940 and studied philosophy at Trinity College, Dublin, after which he joined the Merchant Navy and travelled widely. His debut novel was Pass by the Sea *(1968). His second,* A Season in Abyssinia *(1972), won a Somerset Maugham Award. Later novels included* One Man's War *(1973),* Vaslav: An Impersonation of Nijinsky *(1974), and* The Adventures of Spiro *(1979).*

His non-fiction works have included Mendeleyev's Dream: The Quest for the Elements *(2000),* Dr Strangelove's Game: A Brief History of Economic Genius *(2001),* The Medici: Godfathers of the Renaissance *(2003),* Napoleon in Egypt *(2007),* The Artist, the Philosopher and the Warrior *(2009),* Death in Florence: The Medici, Savonarola and the Battle for the Soul of the Renaissance City *(2011), and* The Spirit of Venice: From Marco Polo to Casanova *(2012). He has also written numerous concise studies of the philosophers, scientists and great writers.*

The following Q&A with Paul Strathern about his inspirations in the writing of A Season in Abyssinia *was conducted by email with Faber Finds editor Richard T. Kelly in December 2013.*

RICHARD T. KELLY: *How did your interest in Arthur Rimbaud begin? What was it about his character that made you want to 'impersonate' him in the pages of a novel?*

PAUL STRATHERN: My interest in someone of great achievement who then 'disappeared himself', so to speak, began with T.E. Lawrence: the Lawrence of Arabia who became 'Aircraftsman

Shaw'. Rimbaud, of course, did much the same. It's an interesting psychology, with elements of disillusionment, rejection of youthful idealism and so forth. And Lawrence's was certainly a curious version of inverted egoism, which had a habit of reverting to its former state – hence his frequent 'backing into the limelight'.

Rimbaud in his later years seems to have had neither the egoism, nor the false modesty, of Lawrence. And none of the game-playing, the schoolboy role-playing et cetera. What he did, he did for real.

RTK: *Your life and your writings have been notably well travelled, and* A Season in Abyssinia *paints an impressively detailed and evocative picture of nineteenth-century East Africa. Did you know this terrain by personal experience before you wrote the novel?*

PS: During the time I spent in the Merchant Navy, the old tramp steamer I was on sailed the Red Sea, called in at Aden and travelled along the Ethiopian coast – all very much the ground Rimbaud covered when he gave up poetry and left France to become a trader. I was there in the early 1960s when Aden was a tacky duty-free port, a flea-bitten outpost of the Empire. But then just over half a century earlier Rimbaud had considered it much the same.

Later, I travelled to Ethiopia with my daughter, and we visited Harar, the city where Rimbaud made his headquarters in the interior. The old city remained virtually unchanged from how it had been in Rimbaud's time, and even from the time of Sir Richard Burton, who was the first European non-Muslim to stay there in the 1850s. Rimbaud seems to have been one of the first, if not the very first, who actually lived there on a permanent basis. On the other hand, there were a few Europeans who passed through as traders, and also an Italian explorer, all of whom encountered Rimbaud.

By coincidence, my daughter is descended from Burton through her mother's side. In Harar there was a resident

French priest who acted as local historian and he was as interested in finding out about Burton as we were in finding out about Rimbaud. His enthusiasm and knowledge gave us access to all kinds of places and information that might otherwise have eluded us.

RTK: *Were you able to find any authentic traces or vestiges of Rimbaud that had survived from the time he spent there?*

PS: There was a rather grand wooden building known in those days as the 'Rimbaud House', a photo of which often used to appear on the cover of French editions of his biography and poems. This proved not to be authentic. It was partly constructed out of leftover railway sleepers from the Djibouti to Addis Ababa railway, which was only started in the late 1890s, a decade or so after Rimbaud had left Harar. However, we were shown where Rimbaud had actually lived – a much more nondescript place with a large dusty courtyard in front of it. A photo of this house, dating from 1888 and featuring a large ostrich, has since been discovered. Peter Porter wrote a poem about the photo, 'Rimbaud's Ostrich', which can be found on the Internet.

Later we travelled down to Djibouti, on the coast, where there was even a Rimbaud Museum of sorts, albeit permanently closed and empty. There was, though, one incident which Rimbaud would have appreciated. The only way we could get into Djibouti from the interior was on a small plane, where we were the sole passengers. The dozen or so other seats were filled with large sacks of *qat*, the local drug of choice, which was flown down to the coast every day, quite legally. When chewed, the leaves of this plant provide a mild narcotic effect. On arrival in Djibouti the regular plane-load of *qat* would be rapidly distributed throughout the town, with sprigs being pilfered at every opportunity. The airport guards and the customs men happily brandished their sprigs while on duty. By the time the *qat* was fully distributed, around noon, everyone was chewing away at their sprig of leaves, and within the hour the entire male population – and some females, so we were told disapprovingly – lay stretched out on beds, or on steps or in doorways, in a pleasant daze. All trade, all activity of any sort, ground to a halt. Rimbaud himself almost certainly partook of this ritual when he was on the coast, and probably when he was in the interior too. He may have given up poetry, but he never gave up drugs.

We also travelled to Tadjoura, which was the old port of the Djibouti region. Rimbaud is said to have started from there with his caravans on several occasions during his voyage into the interior. This meant crossing one of the worst deserts on earth, an inhospitable region inhabited by the Afar, one of the least welcoming tribes on earth. They would attack anyone who ventured into their territory and would cut off the penis of their victim. This would then be hung on a string around the waist. No Afar was permitted to marry unless he could sport such a trophy. Hence, competition was quite fierce.

I did discover one remnant of Rimbaud's time which was still in use. The earliest universally accepted foreign trading currency in this region, and throughout East Africa, was the Austrian silver thaler, the so-called 'Maria Theresa'. This was so trusted that the Arabs and most other traders would accept nothing else. Being suspicious of forgeries, they would scrutinise any proffered coin in some detail. It had to have the image of the Empress Maria Theresa, and it also needed to be dated no later than 1780. Naturally, these coins were in increasingly short supply after Maria Theresa's death. Consequently the British began minting forgeries, taken from an original die, and these soon became more numerous in Africa than the real thalers. In the market in Harar I came across several 'genuine forgery' Maria Theresas and managed to buy one, which I still have on my wall.

Rimbaud certainly traded in the forgeries, and he would store his accumulated coins in a leather belt which he kept strapped to his person at all times, as he had nowhere else safe to keep them. He had learned this lesson the hard way, when someone had discovered where he was hiding his coins. But the weight of this belt – which he wore, as I say, all day and without relief – certainly contributed to his ill health.

RTK: *Which were the literary-historical sources that you found most useful for your research into the life of Rimbaud?*

PS: The Rimbaud biography by Enid Starkie was still the main source in English when I started to write the novel. There were, of course, a number of academic and popular works in French which were far more reliable. Even so, Starkie provides a good romantic angle. The main literary sources, naturally, were Rimbaud's poems, especially *Un saison en enfer* and *Les Illuminations*. My translations of certain sections and quotes are woven into the text of the novel. Though I don't believe in prophecy as such, these proved highly prophetic in a psychological sense.

RTK: *Can you say a little about the decision to alternate between the first- and third-person modes of narration for the novel? Readers who know Rimbaud's work may imagine that his famous 'Je est un autre' gave you a clue. But can you say why you took the notion, what it signified to you?*

PS: Yes, the '*Je est un autre*' idea was, of course, vital. And I switched between first and third person to keep in line with this. I felt that it also emphasised the 'impersonation' element. And the third-person passages stressed the notion that these events actually happened to a real historical figure.

RTK: *Enid Starkie wrote that Rimbaud, aged thirty-three, 'had no curiosity about the fate and the success of his writings, which were appearing in Paris as the work of "the late Arthur Rimbaud".' Were you persuaded that Rimbaud really did come to feel so dismissive of his youthful work?*

PS: He utterly rejected his poetry, and seems to have had few regrets about doing so. I say 'few', because in the novel I try to express his slight – or unconscious – ambivalence on this score. He must have spent quite a bit of time remembering the old days, sometimes with disgust, sometimes with regret, sometimes with wonderment. He knew what he had done – its worth as far as French literature was concerned et cetera. But he had rejected literature as a whole.

1

My life has been a disaster on the grand scale – that I'd better make clear right from the start. A catalogue of my former ambitions would give a Napoleon stage-fright. Art, Ethics, Theology, the Sciences (both practical and occult), even Perception itself, to say nothing of my later efforts at Empire Building, Commerce and Exploration – each of these were at some stage fields which I intended to master. My personality accepted no limits; all that could be conceived was possible. For me, personally. And now, even when I've come to the point where all personal considerations disgust me, I still realise the sublime inevitability of it all. I wasn't mistaken; I was merely trapped. Born trapped. Condemned for the length of a lifetime to play this buffoon Arthur Rimbaud. Yes, it's true what I always used to think when I was a kid: I is another.

In those days, when I was only eighteen, I'd been under the grand delusion for quite a few years that I was a poet. Then one day, in a fit of self-disgust, I remember locking myself in the granary back at home, and writing: *My day is done; I am leaving Europe. The sea air will scorch my lungs; lost climates will tan my skin. I shall return with limbs of iron, sombre skinned, a furious eye: from my appearance I shall be judged as belonging to a mighty race. I shall have gold. I shall be idle and brutal. Women take care of these ferocious invalids returned from hot countries. I shall become involved in politics. Saved . . . Science, the new nobility! Progress. The world is on the march. We are moving towards the Spirit. That's for sure, it's the voice of the oracle I speak. I understand, and, not knowing how to express myself without pagan words, I would rather be silent . . .* So I chucked it in.

But that's all history. Now that same person is thirty-six years old. He's returned from Africa and is lying in hospital in Marseilles. His appearance is that of a cadaverous old man. His eyes are sunk and ringed with darkness, while the horny skin of his face sags over the bones of his fleshless skull like the dark worn leather of an old shoe. His right leg is amputated and his right arm paralysed. Daily the paralysis gains further ground. His sister Isabelle looks after him; and now the small fortune he brought back with him from Africa is almost spent. For increasing periods he is delirious; he speaks of spiritual visions, obscure scientific prophecies, and occasionally of his previous life – as a poet, as a vagabond wandering through Europe, or his years in Africa. Often it is difficult to tell which life he is referring to.

Who would have the effrontery, the lack of any spark of humanity, to mock at a man in such a condition? Only I, Arthur Rimbaud. For you see, I is another.

What happened? How did these juvenile ravings of mine fulfil their prophecy? I'll tell you how –

In August 1880, seven years after finishing his last prophetic poem and abandoning poetry for ever, Arthur Rimbaud was on a ship sailing down the Red Sea. In spite of being ill with fever, he'd still stagger down the gangway at each port to enquire if there was work. He was twenty-five years old and now concerned only with making his fortune. His previous attempts to earn money in Europe, Cyprus and Alexandria had ended in failure. Finally, in desperation he had spent the last of his money on a boat ticket to Aden.

At each port the answer was the same. There was no work for an inexperienced young Frenchman of dubious appearance with no qualifications. Trembling with fever, his mind afire with eerie hallucinations, he would wander through the streets back to the ship and once again lay himself down in the hold amongst the Arab steerage passengers.

By the time the ship was leaving the last of those Red Sea ports, I'd seen, very clearly, a factory instead of a mosque, a pillared building materialise out of three veiled Arab women in long white robes, and any number of ludicrously bizarre monsters, while on one memorable occasion the street-name plaque of a casbah alleyway had struck terror into me as if it were the irreversible verdict of the last judgement itself. I clung to the magic of sanity only by the hypnotism of words, endlessly repeated over and over in my mind. I'm going to be a success. I'm going to make my fortune . . . When I arrived on the quayside in Aden I was broke, devoid of all illusions save for this one redeeming obsession. From now on, what remained of my life was to be dedicated to this business of making money. It was necessary to be absolutely modern.

Looking back on it now, as I lie half paralysed in the luxury of my cosy white-walled hospital room, I can see my state of mind for what it was. Aden was just a godforsaken rock. You can't imagine the place. There wasn't a blade of grass or a drop of fresh water to be had. (They distilled their drinking water from the sea, and it tasted polluted, by chemicals, never quenching the thirst.) The town itself was, and presumably still is, situated in the crater of a burnt-out volcano filled with sand. Razor-ridged walls of rock rose on all sides, looking like the mountains of some long dead planet; and the air, trapped in the crater, shimmered as if everywhere invisible flames were rising into the cloudless blue heavens. Beyond all this there was nothing, just desert.

Rimbaud was discovered in Aden on his last legs by Pierre Vardy, a French coffee exporter, who took him into his home until he had recovered, and then gave him a clerical post in his store at three shillings a day and his keep. Hardly the wage I had expected to earn, even at the outset of my rapid rise to riches. But I had no choice. So my pen, formerly employed in the poetic alchemy of the word, was now reduced to the more mundane, but equally magical chemistry of invoices and inventories. Before my eyes armies of minuscule profit gave battle against the legions of loss. I added and subtracted, balanced and costed, and watched as the figures passed their judgement on these records of enterprises taking place in another world, all the while sitting perched on my stool in the alcove with the other clerks, dipping my quill obscenely into my tiny china inkwell until the boss came in and clapped his hands to announce the end of our daily penance.

Rimbaud soon became dissatisfied with his work.

'You're just fucking me about! Exploiting me!'

'Young man. Arthur. You have a lot to learn out here. Rome was not built in a day.'

'Well this stinking crapheap could have been shat from heaven overnight. You're getting me dirt cheap, and you know it.'

'I have great hopes for you in this establishment, young man...'

What power was it which that man Vardy held over me? That yellow coarse-skinned deeply lined face, always blotched and scratched – he must have shaved himself with a scythe – that fuzz of silver-threaded hair which ran in thin strands from his forehead over the inner baldness of his domed pate, those uneven tobacco-stained fangs which stuck out from between the thin shelving depth of his damp lips whenever he smiled that furtive smile of his, his hairy nostrils, his crouched shoulders, his squat barrel belly pushing out the buttons of his crumpled grey linen tropical suit jacket – how was it that this man managed to keep me? Managed to smile so self-effacingly down at his blotter while I spat out my worst furies, managed to blink his way through my dancing rages (yes, I literally danced in front of that desk of his on occasions) and then succeeded in calmly lighting up his pipe while I grunted into spent silence.

'Young man. Arthur. You have much to learn out here.

Don't worry, I have my eye on you.'

Three months later Vardy set out on a mission to explore the possibilities of trade in the Abyssinian hinterland, and Rimbaud was left in charge of the store. (Still on three shillings a day and my keep.)

Vardy was away for nearly two months, during which hardly a day passed without me going over the draft of my resignation. I took more trouble over that miserable script than I'd taken over the most agonisingly lucid of my precious poems. Those limp dead phrases, those heartless formulas of jargon – 'my resignation' – were stained with even more tears of futility than that final diatribe of self-disgust – my *Season in Hell* – which I'd composed in the granary back at home when I'd first realised that all my hopes, all my pride, all my life so far, had been in vain, deluded, worthless. Because I knew, even as I began – 'Dear M. Vardy, I hereby . . .' – that I was trapped. There was no way out, no other work, no possible method of saving anything more than the miserable pittance that I earned. I was a prisoner in Aden, chained to that godforsaken rock, my unfulfilled ambitions gnawing at my guts as my life ebbed away . . .

Eight weeks later, shortly after Rimbaud's twenty-sixth birthday, Vardy returned from Abyssinia. I was there at his office door, my masterfully banal resignation gripped firmly in my inkstained paw, the minute he set foot inside the store.

Vardy had rented a house inland at the newly opened Abyssinian city of Harar. He had decided to appoint his one intelligent employee as his agent there until such time as his brother, Alfred Vardy, arrived from France to take over as manager. Rimbaud was to get nine shillings a day and his keep, as well as 2 per cent of the profits. His duties were to buy up coffee beans, hide, gum, ivory and musk from the local traders in exchange for some cheap European cloth which Vardy had got himself landed with the previous year. Whenever Rimbaud had collected together enough merchandise, he was to make up a caravan for despatch to Zeyla on the coast, and consequent trans-shipment to Aden. I took my resignation home and burnt it, just as I'd burnt the manuscripts of my poems in the granary back at home – and with that same icy feeling of finality numbing my mind. Once again my ambitions had come to earth, defeated, shrunk to the solid pygmy proportions of reality. Nine shillings a day and 2 per cent of the profits.

However, on the sea-crossing to Zeyla Rimbaud began to see things in a different light. He had learnt more about Harar. No Frenchman had set foot in the place until earlier that year, and he was to be the only European actually in residence. The possibilities were unlimited; it was like some fantasy out of his infantile poems materialised. But this was no winter daydream; this ship with its sails crackling above my head in the last of the fiery night wind was no drunken poetic boat, and that faint outline ahead, transfixed on the horizon by the first twilight of the dawn rising astern like a flock of doves, was no waking hallucination – that was Africa. I was still only twenty-six; I was to be my own master, in the Interior, in an unknown barely-explored place. My fortune was there, waiting to be made. I'd exploit that hinterland for all it was worth, I'd squeeze it to the last drop, I'd exploit myself, night and day. At last, Arthur Rimbaud was to be a success.

From Zeyla, Rimbaud set off inland on the first caravan leaving for Harar. At the edge of the narrow coastal plain, the mountains rose sharply to the inland plateau: a vast barren wilderness. Each night the caravan camped in a small water hollow, and fires were lit. As Rimbaud ate the spicy rice hash that the tribesmen shared around a large heaped bronze platter, the drifting smoke of the fire would blend with the white mist which rose from the water hole, and soon all that was visible under the light star-peppered sky was a smooth-surfaced sea of mist with twists of orange flickering smoke rising from the fires. Amidst the murmurs of the tribesmen, the bells of the cropping camels would tinkle through the silence of the surrounding night.

In the morning at first light the tribesmen would be already up stamping out the grey dusty embers of the fires and loading up the camels. All through the day you simply endured, willing your mind to focus on some distant peak as your horse's hooves clinked against the stones. You could make out no trail and merely followed Youssif, the surly dark-eyed Somali leader, as he picked his way between the boulders, up over the ridges, down along the curving shadowless valleys, while the string of camels carrying the barter and other goods for Harar plodded silently behind.

Each night when the air froze around you and your thoughts became solid once more as your body woke from its heat-induced stupor, you became increasingly possessed by this feeling of inconsolable aching loneliness. What kind of a place lay at the end of a track like this? What the hell ever possessed men to travel day after unending day through such a completely dead world? But you knew, all right. And while you endured, blindly following the nodding robed figure of Youssif as he rode on ahead, you let the heat purge all other thoughts from your mind.

Each morning, before the heat of the day had melted all but the tightening knot of my will, I feasted on the traces of dreams, slaking my thirst with memories of the life I'd left behind me. If I'd have had any tears I'd have shed them, but my eyes were dry and only threads of woollen foam grew at the edges of my lips, glueing them together. And as the desert levelled out into flat dusty rock, Rimbaud's disgust at all he was, all that he had done and been, hardened until it became as unrelenting as the sun that pressed down on the rocky, sunburnt floor of that upper world.

One by one the memories rose and faded. A lifetime draining away against this landscape of mirage. Me, I, my life: that stupid twerp I was. The precocious arrogant fifteen-year-old scholar running away to join the Commune in Paris. Scribbling poems. Blind drunk with the great Verlaine. Off to London. The suffocating fog and the opium dens in Limehouse; the chair-creaking calm in the British Museum; lying on some doss-house bed with Verlaine. Bickering, making up, making love: more poems. Weeping, staggering, drunken Verlaine in that hotel room in Brussels with his smoking pistol doing what his prick could never do. Bang, bang: and I thought I was dead. Verlaine sent to jail. Chucking in poetry for good. Bumming round Europe. Then that final tramp across the snow-bound pass in the Alps to catch the boat for Africa . . . The drunken morning of innocence. Exploits, poems, dreams. No, it was easy enough to give up all that shit. The horses' hooves clinked through the dust of the stony desert floor. Youssif, huddled like a mummy ahead, pressed inexorably on. The running sores on my thighs rubbed against the saddle, the clotted blood chafing the flabby lips of my bruised arse as my horse stumbled forward, its head bowing to the horizon like some abject senile saint . . . And then, when all traces of shadow had vanished, burnt into the ashen earth by the unceasing fire of the sun, then there was only her. And instead of the mirage-blurred desert (no hallucination this, no, dear God no!) my mind's eye would flinch as it gazed once more into her narrow crabbed peasant face with that brown hairy wart on her upper lip, that tracery of bitter wrinkles fracturing the smooth downy skin at the edges of her mouth, and under the male darkness of her heavy eyebrows, the beautiful terror of her cold unflinching brown eyes. And out of the desert furnace around me I would feel the hard field-worked skin of her thick-fingered hands as they clamped my cheeks, forcing my face to look at hers as she searched every line, every mark, every grimy pore – while the beads of sweat grew on my upper lip under the warmth of her potatoey breath and I struggled, with my nostrils flaring, to disguise the contempt which twisted my lips into a smile that could never have arisen from the frozen horror in my guts.

'What is it this time, Arthur?'

'Mother . . . I have come home.'

'Ach!' She shook her head; her crinkled shiny hair

pulled tight from her forehead in that braided rats-tail crown, glistened in the light. 'Such bad, bad blood I see in you.'

And as the desert air turned to fire and the light blinded my eyes, so her face would twist into the knot of my will, and I would feel her inside me, driving me, on. I'll show you, Mother. I'll force you to see what I am. I'll bring back so much gold from this place that you'll want to kiss my feet. And then I'll raise you up, and you'll hug me in your arms . . .

Towards the middle of the third week we came to a high boulder-strewn path which led into a stunted wood. Youssif dismounted and I heard the sound of the late afternoon breeze in the trees become that of a sluice which drowned even the ring of my boots on the stones as I approached. I drank as I've never drunk before, plunging my head into the clear bottle-green water; and then I stood for a long time watching the melancholy golden wash of the sunset ahead. In the distance, near the horizon on a hummock surrounded by green scrubland, was a walled city. We lit fires, and out of the darkness on the black form of the mountains, I saw the faint glimmering radiance of Harar.

Next day the paths were rougher, and we had to travel on foot much of the way. The hillocks were covered with broom and the air was motionless. In the distant sky birds circled, and nearby I could smell – yes, smell! – the water from the springs. And there, rising like a cairn of dun-coloured stones out of the surrounding green countryside, was the city itself, crowned by the pristine white dome of a mosque. It was as if the end of the world lay ahead of me. Here was to be my rented tomb on this earth. Here I would become master of silence, unflinching in my single resolve . . . Silencing the flatulent rhetoric which rose from the festering carcass of his will, Arthur Rimbaud gazed about him in wonder as he entered the city of Harar.

In those days Harar was little more than a small Abyssinian

trading town surrounded by high dun-coloured walls, with ramparts wide enough for the pacing sentries of the Egyptian garrison. Inside was a maze of rutted alleyways running between tall bare walls made of baked mud (together with some more fundamental ingredient, if my nose wasn't playing me up). Occasional gateways gave into round primitive courtyards where veiled native women sat in the shadows preparing food. The little alleyways themselves seemed completely deserted, except for the dogs chained to the gateways, who burst into yapping life as we rode past. The only landmark was the occasional dazzling glimpse of the white dome of the mosque hanging above the rooftops at the end of each side turning.

By contrast, the bazaar quarter with its low-ceilinged mud-walled coffee dens and tawdry booths was packed with yelling traders and the milling drift of the garishly-robed crowds, whose faces ranged from the round shiny pitch black of the Sudanese, and brown-bearded weatherbeaten Somali tribesmen, to the almost pallid lightness of various Arabic features. In the very centre of the city we came to the market place, where the visiting caravaners and merchants laid out their gleaming tusks of ivory, bales of crinkly hides whose unrelenting stench hung over one entire corner of the square, pale hummocks of unroasted coffee beans, and stalls lined with small glass decanters of musk wafting varied auras of sickly fragrance. The square itself was bordered on three sides by a high castled mud wall, and on the fourth side by the long two-storey greystone Governor's palace which towered over the neighbouring ramshackle roofs. The Governor no longer lived there, and the lower windows were all boarded up, giving the place a derelict menacing air. This was the house Old Man Vardy had rented; this was to be Rimbaud's home in Abyssinia.

2

So began my first spell in Harar, a place which is believed by its inhabitants to be modern because every known taste has been avoided in the design and architecture as well as in the layout of the city. Here, as far as I was able to see, you couldn't point out the traces of a single monument to the past. It existed, rotting in its own contemporaneity; its morals and languages reduced to their simplest expression; its inhabitants, who had no apparent need to know each other, going about their daily business in an identical fashion – a vast absurdity inducing in all who endured it an air of solipsist stupefaction.

To begin with I camped out in the main reception hall on the upper floor of the palace, but the novelty of this empty echoing splendour soon began to pall and I moved out into some houri's antechamber down the passage. Here from the window I could survey the market square in all its glory. At the back, my kitchen quarters looked out over the teeming alleyways of the local entertainment district. By way of a change from gazing down on Harar's scintillating world of commerce (my theatre of operations) I would sit in the kitchen quarters during the late afternoons when my work was done, watching as the hooded apparitions roamed through the heavy palls of smoke which always fogged up those back streets at that time of day. Desperately the customers haggled and gesticulated with the child pimps and weird death-in-life painted mummies who paraded their wares like some importuning servants of a death without tears. And as the shadows lengthened, the pitiful howls and humiliations would intensify. The beggars, obscenely uncovered like dogs, would implore on their knees with their tremulous, outstretched hands proffering their pittances at the passing white powder-caked faces which spat down at them from between green-tinted lips. Or a wailing terrified child, her tiny knuckles pressed to her tightly closed eyes, would be held pinned by her master (her father?) while some podgy exotically-ringed hand reached from within a silk-curtained sedan chair to lift her cotton shift, running its caterpillar fingers over her dark tubby thighs.

Half an hour before sunset the curfew bell would toll and the figures begin to filter away into the shadows, leaving only the drifting tendrils of smoke darkening the silent dusk.

At sundown the gates in the city wall were locked and the curfew began. The streets would be deserted, save for the occasional patrol from the Egyptian garrison – and the sick, who according to quaint local custom were always put out into the streets for the night. As darkness came on, the air would be filled with the baying of dogs. Each evening packs of wild dogs were released on the ramparts to keep out the hyenas and lions that lived in the surrounding countryside, and even so occasionally crept over the walls into the streets to rid the Hararis of yet another sick relative.

For me, locked each night in my palace, the sun set twice, the first shadow falling over my watching face as the sun slipped behind the dome of the mosque – a faint skin-pink or lavender shell, a green damask hemisphere, or a harsh charcoal-black shadow, depending upon the light – only to emerge again and then fall a minute or two later behind the distant baked mud ramparts where the tiny silhouetted forms of the leaping dogs bayed against its solid subsiding radiance.

In the evenings, impotent to the charms of my tribal servant girl after what I'd seen from the back window, I'd pace up and down in the darkness for hours on end, feverishly plotting to outwit this hideous fate I'd stumbled into with such naïve intentions. In the solitude of my night-time wanderings through the deserted palace – between the chinks in the upper shutters the vast moonlit emptiness of the walled market square below – my only solace soon became the composing of letters home.

Dear Mother,
After a twenty-day journey across unexplored territory, I finally reached this fabulous city . . .

Dear Mother,
I have been appointed sole agent for the Vardy Trading Co. in this city, the main inland marketing centre of Lower Abyssinia . . .

Dear Mother,
I am alone in this place. There is no competition. I can see that I will soon be able to make my fortune . . .

Dear Mother,
I have plans. Please send me books on iron forging, thatching, glass blowing, candlemaking and brickmaking. Also *The Dictionary of Civil Engineering* . . . These people are primitive and unbelievably backward. If I can establish these simple trades here, I will be master of this place . . . The curfew nights are long and I can teach myself easily from the books you will send . . .

Dear Mother,
I don't intend to stay here very long. I haven't found what I thought I would find . . . But all the same send me the books I asked for, together with *Construction in Metal* . . . also, among the old Arabic papers Father left behind, a notebook entitled *Plaisanteries, jeux de mots* etc. in Arabic . . .

Mother, Mother! . . . Are you impressed by this place, by my wish for these books? When I was a child do you remember how you would spend your hard-earned savings on books so that I could learn . . . learn . . . learn . . . *And then Arthur Rimbaud, the poet, renounced all learning.*

In the mornings at dawn the night-time baying of the dogs on the ramparts gave way to human baying, this time from outside the walls. There the caravans that had gathered in the night, together with the merchants and traders from the outlying districts, would set up a mounting caterwauling chorus until the guard decided, in his own time, to collect the key to the gate from the Governor. And so the market place would fill and my hours of oblivion begin.

How, when you have not one single word in common with him, do you persuade a small hardbitten penny-pinching trader to part with his precious and doubtless purloined tusks of ivory? Those very tusks which are to be the making of his fortune or yours.

After no less than three days of haggling with this whining mouse-cautious caravaner, I finally managed to purchase a consignment of ivory at a fraction below Vardy's maximum price. By this stage I was threatening physical violence, and our particular idots' duel had become the showpiece of the market place. The beggars would gather, slobbering with delight, along with several off-duty troopers from the garrison, and our performance would begin. The novelty of my approach (a total ignorance of accepted method) elicited squeals of delight.

To secure a consignment of hides, I simply hired three strong porters to carry them away into the palace, while I had three other porters lay out in their place my exchange of woven cloth. By the time this particular manoeuvre was complete, the guards had been called. Luckily for me, the trader was loath to part with the cloth I had placed in his possession and the transaction was thereupon deemed a *fait accompli*. But I realised from the mood of the gathered mob that such methods could hardly become accepted practice. I was, after all, the first and only European resident in Harar, and had no wish to upgrade my status to that of being the first European martyr (to capitalism, no less).

So it was that I, Arthur Rimbaud, author of one of the first communist manifestos at the time of the Paris Commune of 1871, was now forced to come to an understanding of the more primitive capitalistic aspects of man's fundamental nature. And not only man's either. These parodies of feather fluffing and ritual bargaining snarls were all too recognisable. How easily they called to mind those opium dream afternoons I'd spent at the London Zoo, watching the rainbow-winged cockatoos and the blue-arsed baboons (living wild in their natural habitat in this part of Abyssinia) as they pranced and backed in their cages, each measuring out its own territory against its neighbour's. In those far-off London days I used to stand on the guard rail with my back to the cages – 'Please do not feed these animals' the slogan at my head – as I harangued the bourgeois gawpers, with their shiny black top hats and candy-laced children, spouting my infantile utopias while snickering Verlaine, pretending to support me, fawned and fumbled and groped me from below. No, neither the Berbers nor the bourgeois, neither the Bourbons nor the Barbary apes, will ever take naturally to the dreams of socialism, it seems. To each his own defended territory.

And what was Rimbaud's territory in this end-of-the-world place, and how did he defend it? Each day I found myself reduced to an ever-deepening sense of solitude, and with it that accompanying feeling of heightened individuality and being set apart, which so soon begins imagining itself on a par with the most dedicated spirituality. When we are reduced to nothing on this earth save ourselves (all other mere delusions foresworn, denied or abandoned) then comes that most enticing delusion of all – self-certainty. Our sense of fate increases with our intimations of Fate, and we learn to control and direct our thwarted desires into the only remaining unassailable territory, where in a final ecstasy of impotence and self-denial we allow ourselves the supreme delirium: a personal destiny. I, Arthur Rimbaud, was destined to live among these people. What did I want with a paltry success in the market place, when with the help of those books – *Construction in Metal, The Dictionary of Civil Engineering* – I could bring a new civilisation to this place, rebuild this entire city according to my own image? I would have riches far beyond the miserly dreams of any peasant mother, and all my failures – my poetry, my prophetic drug-inspired visions, my vagabond wanderings, my corrupted broken love – would each take on meaning as the necessary stages of suffering which precede all true greatness . . .

However, like it or not, even men of destiny have their so-called 'human' moments. With the coming of mid-winter, the nights turned frigid. No letter came from Mother, no parcels of books arrived with the occasional caravans from the coast, and eventually, as night after night I tramped the upper chambers of my derelict palace, I became more and more aware of that tiny figure nestled in the shadows by the fire in the kitchen quarters.

What little I saw of Tahira, my tribal servant girl, was hardly enticing. Her plain delicate-featured face, which she left unveiled inside the palace, remained unvaryingly expressionless as she squatted in the corner sifting the rice and picking with her long fingers at the gobbets of spiced meat she nightly burnt for me over the glowing charcoal bed. In my hunger and irritation I often shouted at her, but only briefly. The fat would sizzle as she blew at the smoking embers in the corner; and then, after I had eaten, she would toast me some muddy bitter coffee before dousing the flames. At this stage the atmosphere would become so acrid with the drifting smoke that the tears would start in my eyes and I'd usually be forced to take my coffee with me to the empty front room, where I'd stand looking out over the deserted market square. When there was a moon I could often make out one of the guards over by the main gate: a crouched figure, squatting in the shadows on his haunches with his rifle propped against the wall beside him. Below his bowed head, between his thighs, the thin red pin-prick of his cigarette would glow as he inhaled.

On that night when I returned to the kitchen quarters I found Tahira by the still-smoking fire, poking at it with her small brush of sticks. The moment I laid my hand on her shoulder (the first time I had ever touched her) she rose without a word. Her flesh was firm under her robes and I let my hands wander over her while the smoke rose blindingly around us in the dim lamplight. Her hand passed gently over my face as soon as she realised what I was doing, and I felt her finger trace the tears down my cheeks. I wanted to tell her that my tears were because of the smoke, but as I opened my mouth I realised that I wasn't capable of explaining such a thing to her. And then suddenly I was overcome by this choking need for tenderness. I laid my head on her shoulder. I wanted to tell her everything, I wanted to explain who I was, what I was doing in this place, what I wanted to become, what I wanted . . . to establish even the most tentative link of shared intimacy.

She stood, limp, her hand resting on my shoulder.

'Tahira?'

She moaned in reply to her name, that little lilting whimper that began at the back of her throat. The way she always replied.

I ground my teeth as my running eyes closed.

'Tahira!' I tried, as tenderly as I could.

She moaned again, appearing slightly uncertain now.

Was I, Arthur Rimbaud, who as a poet had previously discovered the colours of the vowels – A black, E white, I red . . . – I, who had flattered myself once that I had invented a poetic language accessible to all the senses, who had written of silences and of impenetrable nights, who had expressed the inexpressible, now at last to be reduced to this: the crass gutteral of pre-history?

Her black skin and the black shadows were separated only by the red stinging after-vision of the fire in my tears as I blinked.

'Come,' I took her by the arm and laid her down on the skins where she slept in the corner. Her cool hands pressed lightly against my shoulderblades as I parted her robes and then grunted and sobbed out my disgust.

If to have a destiny means that the outcome of one's life can be predicted according to some demonstrable proof, then where Rimbaud's life is concerned one of the more basic axioms of this proof would appear to be that his every humiliation is destined to become a public one. Precisely one week and three sleepless nights of agony after his little lapse from celibacy, Rimbaud was reporting to the commander of the Egyptian garrison asking for a doctor. From Tahira – A so black, I so red – he had caught syphilis.

After a series of sign language conversations, during which I conveyed the nature of my illness in inexplicit general terms, I was finally shown to the doctor's quarters. Here, in a small shuttered room, recumbent on the primitive patient's couch cum operating table and breathing heavily beneath a large rough blanket from under which his bare feet alone protruded, lay the only man with any claim to medical qualifications throughout this entire region of the African hinterland.

I coughed, loudly, several times, and eventually a young tribal servant boy appeared. Without further ado he went up to the bed and scratched the toes of his master, who then awoke, springing to his feet like a jack-in-the-box. It was thus that I first encountered Badjian.

Imagine a small wizened middle-aged Armenian, who after a lifetime of wandering the globe, persecutions and failed enterprises, finally signs up with the Egyptian colonial army as a medical orderly, his only qualification being a certificate manufactured and written by himself in Creole during some previous time of need in the city of New Orleans. This was Badjian, a man who seemed to speak a smattering of every language I had ever heard of, whose unceasing commercial optimism had had him selling Chinese bead fans to the wives of American pioneers as they trekked overland in their covered wagons for the Far West, who had gone bankrupt and been flung into Newgate debtors' jail in London after a scheme for importing garlic on a large scale had foundered at the credit stage, and who had on one memorable occasion cured all the inhabitants in an Anatolian village of some obscure skin complaint by simply coating them in a solution of copper sulphate. (A miraculous cure which had saved his life, for the Turkish authorities had been so incensed at the sight of the entire local population turning blue overnight that they had incarcerated him and sentenced him to death on a charge of subversion.)

While Badjian treated me with various doubtful, and extremely painful elixirs (I drew the line at copper sulphate) he would listen, his kindly knowing quizzical expression occasionally glancing up to focus on some middle distance, as I outlined my own enterprises.

'Arthur,' his hand rested on my shoulder as we sat drinking coffee in his dispensary, 'for seven years I have rotted in this place, despairing of my life. You are like a prophet come out of the wilderness to me. Give me one per cent of your two per cent share of the profits and we will join in partnership.'

'But I'm contracted to Vardy. And besides, you're in the army.'

'Of course. That cannot be changed for the present. I will work for you in a private capacity. We will work together. In the market place I will be your right hand man.'

'One per cent? Is that all?'

'For waking me from the grave, Arthur, I would work for you for nothing. The one per cent is merely to convince us both that I am still a man of business. A force to be reckoned with. Arthur, my friend, our troubles are at an end.'

'Perhaps. But first you'd better cure me of this damn disease.'

'Have no fear. I have studied this particular disease at its source,' he reassured me with bland authority. 'Did you know that syphilis was brought to Europe by the men who sailed with Columbus? It was the American Indians who originally contracted it, but over the years they developed a form of immunity.'

'If you're kidding me, I'll . . .' But I could only laugh as I looked into his lined suffering face, his beady heavily bagged eyes puckering with incredulity that I should doubt his word. There was *nothing* I could threaten him with; in this place I was powerless, completely at his mercy.

'Badjian, what else can I do but trust you?'

The next caravan up from Zeyla brought a letter from Mother.

> My dear Arthur,
> We all enjoyed your letter. Your travels sound very interesting.
> The harvest this year is rather more meagre than I hoped it would be. Windfall Acre and Bottom Meadow can only be used for hay, but we will still make a small profit. Isabelle was out working by the moon to get the last of it all in, because I fell ill in the last week.
> As for you, Arthur, I am so glad that you are at last learning the truth. For so long it troubled me that you would never learn these things. But what is all this talk of expensive books? This foolishness will lead you nowhere. Only by diligence, hard work and saving will you raise yourself up in life. My son, have you not learnt from all your previous follies? Now instead of wasting the money you sent me, I have placed a deposit on a small plot of land, Old Jarricot's, down by Bottom Valley. Land is still our best investment, in these troubled times gold is foolishness . . .

With the letter one small book: *Roret's Handy Manual – A Practical Encyclopedia of the World around Us*. 'To show you, my son, that your mother is not hard-hearted. I am sure this will contain all you really need.'

Also arriving with the same caravan, and no less of a disappointment, was Alfred Vardy, Old Man Vardy's brother, fresh from Dijon to take up his appointment as my new boss. I watched as he was unloaded, prostrate, from the caravan onto a stretcher and carried up the main stairway into the palace reception room. Half an hour later Badjian was at his side.

'He's my new boss, Badjian. Do as you will.'

Badjian fingered various glandular crevices, prised open Vardy's eyelids with his thumbs to reveal an eerie hypnotised stare, and then gazed down the sagging foam-lined orifice which gave into Vardy's throat.

'Exhaustion,' pronounced Badjian, rising to his feet with a sigh. 'He must rest for a few days.'

Such was the exhaustive diagnosis of Harar's expert medical opinion.

For the next week I had Vardy spoon-fed four times a day by Bomba, my new tribal servant boy. (I'd had to send poor Tahira back to her tribe, there was no point in taking Badjian's cure with her still looking after me.) Eventually Vardy regained his strength sufficient for him to be able to sit up and talk for an hour or so each day.

I didn't take to him from the start, but then under the circumstances I don't think I'd have taken to anyone. He was thinner than his brother, and unlike his brother his long silver-stranded black hair disguised no inner baldness. He had the Vardy eyes – large and staring in repose – and several of his brother's mannerisms of speech. I was still 'Young man, Arthur' I noticed, and he had the same habit of stroking his upper lip with his forefinger whenever he was on the point of touching on some topic which he considered to be of importance. The only difference being that his upper lip was covered with a thick brush moustache.

During our conversations I learned that he'd been a travelling salesman around Dijon, whiling away the years and even remaining a bachelor until the day when the summons came from his beloved elder brother. The only unpredictable thing about him was his political views. He considered himself to be an advanced liberal of the modern school: a man of humanitarian principles who welcomed all men as his equal.

'We are all brothers on this earth, Arthur. There are no rewards in heaven for living in misery. One thing I will not tolerate is unnecessary suffering in the name of some mythical deity.'

Outside, beyond the glare that burst like an arrested explosion through the chinks in the shutters, the howling bedlam of the market place rose unceasingly. A fitting background to our invalid's words of wisdom.

'And I warn you, I intend to put my principles into practice in all our dealings with these people.' He plucked a stray bristle from his moustache and twiddled it between his fingers. 'I trust you don't consider my views too advanced?'

I shrugged.

'You have no objections?' he persisted.

'You're the boss.'

'Good,' he replied, fussily rearranging the bed covers about him. 'Now I think it's time I saw the accounts. My brother was none too pleased with the last caravan you sent down. My instructions are that we are to pay far less and consign far more. I hope to make up a caravan in the next week.'

'Mm,' I grunted. We'd see about that.

'By the way,' he began, relaxing deferentially, 'I may be the boss, but seeing as we're the only two Europeans in the city, I do think that we might at least take our meals together. I get rather lonely dining in style up here all by myself.'

'I'm afraid I have to eat alone. Doctor's orders.'

'Rubbish, young man. Arthur, you don't believe in that Armenian quack, surely? There's nothing infectious about me.'

'You may as well know the truth straight away, Vardy.

Loving your neighbour is not the best policy up here. The place is crawling with syphilis. I speak from experience.'

'Really?' Vardy flicked at his moustache with a contemplative frown. 'I see.'

And so Alfred Vardy continued to dine alone in the main palace reception room.

Once up and about, Vardy immediately established his own routine. Early morning exercises at the window, accounts session over coffee, two hours business in the market place before lunch, etc. etc. The model trader, in the true Vardy tradition. Within a month he'd had a local carpenter construct a special table and half a dozen chairs for the palace reception room, and Bomba was ordered to put on a clean robe when serving dinner.

Rimbaud would eat an hour or so before Vardy in his own room; and at night as the dogs howled from the ramparts and Vardy's silver knife and fork (sent up by caravan from Aden) clattered on his plate in the reception room, Rimbaud would be poring his way through *Roret's Handy Manual – A Practical Encyclopedia of the World around Us*.

Iron: a metallic element constituting nearly 5% of the earth's crust, has been smelted since earliest times. To obtain the pure metal the raw ore must first be heated in a blast furnace with coke and limestone. The silica is thus removed in a slag that forms as a molten layer on the surface. Iron is also an essential item in the human diet . . .

From the beginning Rimbaud had saved obsessively, denying himself all but the basic necessities in his effort to accumulate enough money from the small profits to start up on his own. Now, with the arrival of Vardy, even these small profits dwindled. Dijon humanitarianism proved a costly luxury when applied to the traders of Harar.

'Look, Vardy. Either you go, or I do. We're not a charity organisation.'

'But this is only the beginning, Arthur.'

'One more deal like that one you did yesterday . . .'

'I will not descend to common thievery, young man.'

'Then stick to doing the bloody accounts, and let me do the buying.'

After a formal show of reluctance, Vardy finally agreed. So Rimbaud began again on his own in the market place, this time more determined than ever. In the mornings Badjian would assist him – interpreting and occasionally joining in the bargaining – for his one per cent. But the profits still remained low, and Rimbaud soon became desperate, in spite of Vardy's constant encouragement.

'But think of the prospects, young man.'

'What prospects, dammit!'

'Look, Arthur. At the moment we're merely establishing ourselves . . .'

'As a laughing stock. We're getting nowhere!'

'Just give it time, Arthur. It's the prospects that count.'

As a precaution I penned out my resignation on the back of this design for a primitive blast furnace which I had in mind. I'd give things another month, I decided. Already Badjian's cure was beginning to work; I no longer pissed fire, and along with the other delights of the monastic way of life which my obsessive saving had reduced me to, was now added the joy of lurid pornographic nightmares culminating in the occasional wet dream.

'I'm just pissing away my life in this godforsaken hole!'

Badjian sucked his teeth glumly. Pushing aside the jumble of bottles and unrolled puss-encrusted bandages on his dispensing table, he leaned forward on his elbows with a sigh. 'How far are you willing to go, my friend?' he asked, his translucent almond pupils staring out speculatively from under the folds of his hooded eyelids. 'There *are* other methods. Would you be willing to give me a free hand with your merchandise, no questions asked?' I studied the scrubbed wooden top of the table, its surface engrained with the blood and spilt anaesthetics of previous operations. 'Can I trust you, Badjian?'

'Arthur, my friend,' he laid his hand on my shoulder. 'My

dear, dear friend. I foresee ours will be a great partnership.'

'Look, I don't trust you a single inch,' I told him.

'Ah, my friend, such is the nature of all great partnerships.' He gave my shoulder a consoling pat. 'Think it over. If you're interested we can meet in the market place tomorrow. Say a bit earlier than usual, at dawn perhaps, so we can see the caravans coming in.'

That night, still undecided about Badjian's offer, I wrote home to Mother.

Dear Mother,

Thank you for the book. I am sorry to hear about the harvest and your illness. Look after yourself and get well soon. I quite understand your feelings about these matters, but I'm afraid *Roret's Handy Manual* just isn't enough. Out here things are *unbelievably* primitive and one must begin from first principles. So please could you send *at once both Construction in Metal* (price 15 francs) and *The Dictionary of Civil Engineering*. Also, I would still like you to send Father's old notebook entitled *Plaisanteries, jeux des mots* etc. in Arabic, if you can find it. I think it's up in the attic, or maybe in the granary.

I am still living in a very unpleasant and unprofitable way up here, and I shall soon know when I am leaving. I am saving hard and hope in the near future to start up on my own. At present I am contemplating changing my methods. This place is completely uncivilised, apart from the Egyptian administration – which is not all that it appears.

On second thoughts, send *Construction in Metal* to Aden (c/o The Vardy Trading Co).

Your son,
Arthur.

At dawn I went down to the market place. I waited for an hour while the distant ululating chorus of the traders outside the city walls at the main gate gradually rose in volume, and then, just as I was on the point of giving up, Badjian finally appeared.

'So you are agreed, my friend?' he enquired brightly, taking my arm.

'On what?'

'On my plan.'

'But you haven't told me what it is yet.'

Badjian raised his hand in a depreciating gesture. Such mere details could obviously be dispensed with.

For the next few mornings I simply followed Badjian as he perused the merchandise on the incoming ivory caravans. When they had unloaded, Badjian would approach them one by one, inspecting the individual tusks and apparently trying them for weight. He may have sold bead fans in the Wild West, but he knew nothing about buying Abyssinian ivory, that was for sure.

I think it was because I was glad of his company after the long curfew nights, more than anything else, that I went on meeting him; for after the first few days I gave up all hope of his nebulous plans ever materialising. It was during those early mornings in the market square that I came to realise how much there was to appreciate in Badjian. 'Our Caucasian character', as Vardy insisted on calling him, may have been something of a joke with his over-earnest confidential manner towards us two Frenchmen, but I'd seen enough of him to understand the sly intelligence behind the hangdog wistfulness of his more usual expression. Maybe half his stories *were* untrue – although he'd certainly travelled over vast tracts of the known globe, there was no doubting that – but it was the nature of his despair that attracted me most. Long ago, underneath it all, he had come to terms with his own futility. For him, hope was a game one played with a friend. And no matter the result either, apparently. The qualities he had summoned to endure the boredom and misery of Harar were the foundation of his whole attitude; and as we met each morning – he smoking ruminatively as the sun fired the white dome of the mosque beyond – I soon came to realise that where my feelings for Badjian were concerned there was no question of trust. Or lack of it. We'd simply pace the market square, our long stilted shadows falling over the bundles of the porters huddled at the foot of the dark walls as they cuffed away the skinny dogs and muttered and yawned, while with his arm linked in mine we recounted off-handedly our various exploits in the outer world.

'Poetry, my friend?' he enquired, raising his eyebrows.
'Of sorts. Wild, absurd dreams.'
'There is no market for it, I would think.'
'No more than garlic in London.'
'Or chastity in Harar.'
'Touché.'
'A jest, my friend. An idle jest.'

On these mornings he was peculiarly relaxed, a quality I came to recognise in Badjian whenever he was preoccupied with some rash scheme or other.

3

In order to avoid over-exciting himself with undue suspense, and thus exacerbate his already dangerous condition, the invalid Rimbaud in the soothing atmosphere of his hospital room in Marseilles will now relate, in tranquil recollection, the nature of Badjian's plan.

Badjian's Plan

Badjian and Rimbaud would buy ivory with Vardy's barter and decamp for the coast by fast camel. In Zeyla they would exchange the ivory for guns which they would then take by caravan to the Kingdom of Shoa in the North, where King Menelek, who was planning to rise against the Egyptians, was willing to pay large sums for any contraband arms he could lay his hands on. The profits would be enormous, and further gun-running would follow. In a matter of months they would both have made themselves a vast fortune.

'No, Badjian.'

'But why not, my friend? Isn't that what you want?'

'I'm working for Vardy.'

'That imbecile!'

'No, the boss. His brother. I owe him a debt of honour. He picked me up when I had nothing.'

'So, my friend has principles!'

'On the contrary. I just despise petty crookery, that's all.'

Badjian paused, pursing his lips. 'Then I have another plan,' he suddenly decided, and then paused once more.

'Well? What is it?'

'Patience, my friend. All in good time.'

Rimbaud had promised himself that come what may he would leave Harar at the end of the month and take his chance on his own with the small amount he had already saved. Seeing that he had nothing to lose, Rimbaud decided to give Badjian's second plan a chance.

Three days later Badjian began bargaining for a consignment of ivory.

'But that stuff's not fit for shoe horns, you fool!'

'Patience, my friend.' Things were not what they seemed, apparently.

Rimbaud watched suspiciously as Badjian put his plan into action. The trader was somewhat reluctant to part with his miserable ivory – all was well.

The crowd, however, who now always followed the ignorant European and his clown henchman as they went about their daily business, were determined not to be robbed of their morning's entertainment. The urchins yelled and the beggars shook their fists; Badjian raised his price. The trader was being forced to do business.

'Badjian, what the hell are you playing at?'

'Patience, my friend.'

Badjian raised his price once more.

'You're ruining me!'

Rimbaud was now forced to employ physical sanctions upon his partner. The urchins leapt with glee, and two enthusiastic onlookers soon separated the struggling partners.

Whereupon Badjian raised his price once more.

'I disown you! Badjian, we're finished! I publicly disown him! He's nothing to do with me!'

Rimbaud, forcibly restrained, watched as the crowd chanted. With a seemingly frightened air, the trader began to complete the bargain.

As the tears of impotent rage welled in my eyes, I let my head sag onto my chest with a sob. The bastard was ruining me – he was spending every penny of the profit I'd saved.

Badjian grinned surreptitiously at Rimbaud as he clasped the trader's hand to complete the deal.

Rimbaud realised that he had no alternative now but to remain in Harar for the winter.

What this what Badjian wanted?

Yes, I realised with a sickening pang of understanding, this was what Badjian wanted.

Badjian had spent seven solitary years in Harar, and now at last he had a friend, someone he could talk with about his past adventures and unrealised plans for the future. Badjian was pitifully lonely; he had seen his only friend on the point of leaving and realised that there was only one way to stop him.

'Come back, come back, my dear friend, my only friend, come back. I swear I shall be kind . . . We'll live here again, very bravely and patiently.' Verlaine had been in London, dying, writing his last letter to Arthur, who had abandoned him. On my return I'd found that he only had flu.

Was I never to be free, not even here in Abyssinia, to suffer out my miserable existence alone?

'Come back, come back, my dear friend, my only friend, come back. I swear I shall be kind . . . We'll live here again, very bravely and patiently.' But no! Those weren't Verlaine's words, they were mine! It was I, Arthur Rimbaud, who had written those very words to Verlaine begging him to return, not six months later, when this time *he* had left *me*.

What need is it that we have of each other on this earth? This need which can make us sink so disgustingly low, this need which in a moment can make us renounce everything, all pride, everything – just for the company of some other chosen human being?

'My friend, we are rich!' declared Badjian triumphantly.

'My friend, we are ruined.'

'Now, quickly Arthur. We must get the ivory into the palace.'

'You can give it to the beggars for all I care, Badjian. The harm's done now.'

'No, no, my friend. *Quickly!*'

'Enough, Badjian. I can't afford any more demonstrations of friendship.'

'But this is all part of the plan.'

Without recourse to violent language liable to raise his blood pressure (and thus bring this tale to a premature end) the invalid Rimbaud, from the objective vantage point of his hospital bed in Marseilles, will now relate Badjian's second plan.

Badjian's Second Plan

The old Emir of Harar, who had been deposed by the Egyptians seven years previously, now lived in enforced retirement but still carried on a few undercover activities. One of which was smuggling diamonds. These were brought into the city by trusted traders in hollowed-out tusks of ivory. Badjian had been able to spot the right tusks because of their weight. The trader, who would normally never have dreamt of selling his contraband-filled tusks, had been forced to part with them because Rimbaud's business dealings attracted such attention. If he had turned down Badjian's high offer, suspicions would have been aroused. And smuggling carried the death penalty in Harar. So, although he knew his life would be in almost equal danger from the Emir, the trader had been forced to sell.

All that remained now was for Badjian and Rimbaud to extract the diamonds. They would leave the hollow tusks for Vardy. That way Vardy could not claim any dishonesty on Rimbaud's part, merely that he had been an incompetent trader. With the diamonds, Badjian and Rimbaud would set off on fast horses for Zeyla. There they would exchange the diamonds for an enormous consignment of guns, which they would take by caravan to the Kingdom of Shoa in the north . . . enormous profits . . . further deals . . . a vast fortune etc etc.

'Now you have seen what I can do, my friend.' Badjian beamed. 'This is just the beginning. Ours will be a great partnership. A partnership for life.'

'A pretty short partnership, the way you're going about things. We've got to get out of here. You're a madman!'

Barely restraining myself, I watched as Badjian began scraping with a knife at the base of one of the tusks. We'd locked ourselves in the cellars of the palace with the ivory. For the time being at least, we were safe. The cellars, which had at one time seen duty as dungeons, were all but impregnable.

'For God's sake get a move on!'

Badjian picked carefully at the concealed bung in the tusk.

In the hashish visions of my youth I'd seen diamonds encrusted in the heavens, vast crystals releasing the colours of the pure vowels over the groaning mire of the blind circling earth. I'd conceived of ethereal cities constructed entirely out of cool limpid jewels; and in my horror at what I'd feared to be encroaching madness, I'd pressed my hands to my face, only to see the inner night twitching with lightning flashes which revealed a diamond-floored plateau, cleft in two as the earth heaved like the sea . . . In reality, the only diamond I ever remembered seeing was the tiny spark set in the silver of Mother's engagement ring.

'What is it?' I asked Badjian.

Badjian poured the contents of the little hollow in the ivory into the palm of his hand.

'It looks like dust,' replied Badjian, with a perplexed frown.

'It *is* dust! You bastard!'

Badjian peered.

'You great clown, we've been had!'

Badjian raised his eyes. 'If it *is* just dust, we're safe.'

'And ruined.'

'But if it's what I'm thinking it is . . .'

'What?'

'Some sort of . . .' Badjian sniffed.

'*What*, dammit!'

'I don't know. Perhaps some kind of . . . gunpowder maybe. We may have stumbled into real trouble, my friend.'

'Oh my God!' The sweat tingled like acid in my suddenly opened pores. 'How can you find out?' I asked him.

'I'll have to analyse it in my dispensary. Have you got enough money to buy two fast horses?'

Between them, Rimbaud and Badjian hadn't even got enough to buy two fast horseshoes.

While I pondered how I was to escape with my life, Badjian picked open the rest of the tusks. Each one contained the same black powder.

'Badjian, you fucking bastard! I'll wring your neck with my own bare hands! . . .'

Stop! Remember your blood pressure. You'll be in danger of your life if you go on like this. Lying back on the pillows in the calm atmosphere of his hospital room in Marseilles, Rimbaud proceeds to breathe deeply, smoothing his one unparalysed hand over his chest . . .

Now to continue, calmly, with the demise of Badjian's plan.

What did Badjian do next?

Badjian was let out of the side door of the palace, from whence he proceeded with great haste to his dispensary in the garrison, where he began his analysis of the mysterious substance.

What did Arthur do next?

I detached my resignation from the back of my design for a primitive blast furnace and handed it in to Alfred Vardy, telling him that he'd better deduct £50 from my credit because I'd just bought a dummy load of ivory and a real load of trouble. I intended to smuggle myself out of Harar on the next caravan to Zeyla which would be leaving in a few days' time.

And how did Vardy react to this dramatic news?

Vardy did not react to this dramatic news. Because Vardy was not listening properly. Vardy had a problem of his own.

'My prospects, Arthur!'

'Get this straight, I'm resigning. I don't care if I am breaking my contract. You can keep your fucking prospects.'

'Oh, I wish I could be so certain, Arthur. It's all right for you, he cured you.'

What prospects was Vardy talking about?

Not the trading prospects for the city of Harar, but his own private prospects. As the result of an indiscretion with Bomba the servant boy, Vardy had contracted syphilis. Unwisely, he had put off consulting Dr Badjian, and was now in agony.

'You want me to go and get him?'

'*Please,* Arthur. Please! I'm willing to overlook that load of dummy ivory. Or anything else. Please hurry!'

Sensing my advantage, I asked Vardy if I could borrow his pistol (whose previous existence our narrator, in his feverish over-excitement, has omitted to mention, thus reinforcing the adage that these matters should be recollected in tranquillity, or they might just as well not be recollected at all.)

'Take it! You can keep the wretched thing. But for God's sake *hurry!*'

So it was that I called to see Dr Badjian in his dispensary with a loaded gun concealed on my person.

No, I was not planning to shoot Badjian. The gun was intended purely for self-defence.

During the short time since he had left me, Badjian had transformed his sparse dispensary into something resembling an alchemist's den. He greeted me at the door in a state of great agitation, a test tube smoking between his gnarled fingers.

As yet, however, the results of his analysis had proved negative.

Upon hearing of Vardy's disease, Dr Badjian appeared most reluctant to fulfil his medical obligations.

'Bugger him!'

'Look Badjian, he's in agony. Treating him won't change

your bloody magic substance one way or the other . . . Arthur proceeded to bombard Badjian with a variety of arguments, both moral and expedient. '. . . we may not know precisely what we've gone and done; but whatever it is, we've done it. All the analysis in the world won't change that.'

With the greatest reluctance, Dr Badjian finally agreed to do his duty by the Hippocratic Oath (of which, with his particular qualifications, he may well have been ignorant.)

As part of this bargain however, I was forced to one important concession (thus demonstrating once more that the commercial practices of the market place are little more than a crude parody of the crude practices of life itself.)

Arthur's concession: To look after three bottles containing the unknown substance diluted with various mixtures. These bottles were to be shaken regularly both night and day to keep the substance in suspended solution.

'I've got better things to do, my friend.'

'But what am I supposed to look for?' I demanded.

'If they jell,' Badjian shrugged casually, 'then they might well explode.'

'*What!*'

'In which case, we're in trouble,' muttered Badjian: pensive, preoccupied.

'Well, at least I'll know where to look for a doctor.'

'I suppose it *is* quite possible that the Emir might be dabbling in high explosives on the quiet.'

'Is that what you really think?'

'I just don't know, my friend. I have no idea what this stuff is. It could be anything. This isn't really my field.'

A few minutes later Rimbaud showed Badjian into Vardy's room. This at least was Badjian's field, if nothing else.

That night I lay alone by the lamp in my room with Vardy's pistol at my side, listening to each creak in the building. Every half hour or so I gingerly shook the three little bottles, but the solution merely remained liquid and opaque. To distract myself I started once again into my studies from *Roret's Handy Manual*, although I realised that now all prospect of setting up on my own had vanished. These months in Harar had been lost, dead time. A prelude perhaps to some less metaphorical death, if things went on at their present rate. What the hell was I doing here in this place? Was I, Arthur Rimbaud, finally to die, an unwitting cipher in this absurd Arabian Nights intrigue of Emirs and smuggled diamonds which Badjian had dragged me into? Why, the whole thing was insane, incredible. Yet there was Vardy's pistol on the table, loaded; and that nauseous clutch of fear in my stomach, that was real, all right. As I stood at my unshuttered window, I heard, from behind the shuttered window to my right, the rising nightmare whimpers of Vardy. Later, I heard him sobbing, quietly, to himself. Beyond the deserted market place the moonlit white dome of the mosque hung suspended above the roofs of the silent, sleeping city. Had Arthur Rimbaud at last stumbled into that weird land which he had once had inklings of in those drug-inspired nightmare visions of his youth? Or what?

As the night hours passed I shook Badjian's solutions and drank cold coffee to keep myself awake.

Dear Mother,

I am determined to clear out of this place as soon as possible. Owing to various unforeseen mishaps I now have practically nothing saved. Please do not think this is due to any rash spending on my part.

Could you send me news of the work being done on the Panama Canal Project? As soon as that begins, I think I'll go over there. Or perhaps to South America. I hear they are planning to build railways through the jungle and will need men who have had experience of such climates to supervise.

I hope that by now you have completely recovered from your illness. But do rest. Isabelle can surely do the work, and I will send you more money as soon as I can.

Also, could you please send me *post haste* a book on chemical analysis, along with *Construction in Metal* etc. which I hope are waiting for me in Aden.
     Your son,
      Arthur.

Next day I stayed inside, getting the consignments ready for the next caravan to Zeyla, which was due to leave in a few days' time. On this caravan I would leave Harar, secretly, never to return. Meanwhile, upstairs in his bare state room, Vardy nursed his complaint, at the same time endeavouring to complete the accounts in time for the caravan. In spite of the urgency of our separate activities, I knew we were both in fact only passing time waiting for the same thing: the appearance of Badjian.

That day, however, Dr Badjian didn't deign to pay us a visit, and I retired to my room soon after the curfew bell. I stood at my window, doped with fatigue, and watched a scarlet sun set behind the dull mercurial dome of the mosque, emerging several moments later to fall finally below the sharp crenellated silhouette of the ramparts and the tiny leaping shapes of the dogs as they bayed against the dimming sky. Then I lay down on my bed and lit the lamp. I still didn't dare to sleep, and opened my *Handy Manual*. I was now making preliminary studies on civil engineering, together with geology. Ironically, if I was to get a post with the Panama Canal Project or on the jungle railways, I'd probably have to know a fair amount about high explosives. I shook the three little bottles on my desk; if only I'd had those books that were waiting for me in Aden, I'd have been able to find out in no time if that solution contained high explosive, without relying on Badjian's incompetent quackery. As it was, *Roret's Handy Manual* was worse than useless.

Explosives: Materials by which speedy comprehensive chemical action releases a high amount of energy in a single rapid detonation. (N.B. for ethical reasons and in the interests of personal safety and public order, no information on this topic is included in this manual.) *The inexperienced cannot be warned too seriously of the dangers, both physical and legal, inherent in the manufacture of these substances.*

I must have dozed off over this illuminating text, for when I woke the lamp had gone out and my room was in total darkness. I listened as a dog howled on the ramparts, and then suddenly I knew I was not alone. There was someone standing at the open doorway. Checking my initial frozen lurch of panic, I began feeling surreptitiously under the blanket for Vardy's pistol. Without shifting my body I raised the barrel, pressing my finger over the trigger, and called out into the dark . . .

Who was Arthur calling out to in the dark?

Yarousseau.

And who was Yarousseau?

Yarousseau was a French missionary who had arrived that very day on the caravan from Zeyla to take up his post at Harar.

And what the devil was Yarousseau doing creeping about the palace in the dark after the curfew?

'Put on the light, for heaven's sake, whoever you are,' demanded this irritated voice in a raw peasant accent.

'Not until you tell me what the hell you're up to. I might as well warn you, there's a loaded pistol in my hand and at this very moment it's aimed at you.'

The man of God hurriedly, but unfalteringly, explained himself. At the dictates of his conscience, he had been out tending the sick, apparently. 'Please, my good man, please light up the lamp!'

'I thought *I* was going to be the first martyr in Harar, but it looks as if I've got a competitor. You must be out of your mind. They shoot first and ask questions afterwards out there after the curfew. To say nothing of the odd lion prowling about the place.' I lit up the lamp and laid down Vardy's pistol. The tall black shape at the doorway stepped cautiously forward, his robe rustling, and then sat down on the end of my bed in the dim growing light.

'Didn't anyone tell you about the curfew?'

Yarousseau had been fully briefed about conditions at Harar, but felt himself bound to act as the spirit moved him. Considerations of purely personal safety were mere weakness, in his view.

'You must be mad!'

But then from the look of it, perhaps that's why he'd been sent up here in the first place. Rimbaud found himself staring at this large peasant head lolling between a pair of rounded, black-robed shoulders, its bristly pate covered with what was all too obviously the remnants of some Aden barber's inexpert attempt at a tonsure. As Yousseau raised his face from the knotted fingers clasped around the missal on his lap, Rimbaud made out a ruddy-cheeked face with flaring porcine nostrils and thick lips pursed as if on the point of delivering some distasteful kiss. Beneath Yarousseau's perplexed brow, his wide bulging eyes puckered against the light in a distracted, effortful, constipated stare. A typical goofy seminarist, in fact.

'And what do you think you're going to do up here?' I asked him.

'I have come up here to show love to these people.' Yarousseau leaned forward earnestly, pressing his missal to his guts.

Arthur couldn't help but laugh in his face. The people of Harar had already discovered love, he explained: its practice being one of their main occupations. 'Second only to cheating one another.'

'I see you do not know the meaning of the word either,' replied our country lad, arrogant with self-righteousness.

From out of the night, beyond the city walls, there came the distant rasping roar of a lion, answered by an outburst of yapping from the ramparts.

'What possible meaning do you think your precious "love" will have in a place like this?'

'I will give it a meaning,' Yarousseau replied seriously.

'By feeding yourself to the lions after the curfew, I suppose? Hell, wait a minute!' I suddenly remembered – Badjian's bottles! I reached over to the table and lifted them, one by one, examining them and then shaking them. The solutions were still suspended; none of them had jelled.

'What's that, medicine?' he asked. 'Are you sick as well?'

'You're out of luck there, I'm afraid. By the way, are you a doctor?'

'I have done a little training. I've brought equipment with me, and there should be some more coming on the next caravan.'

So Dr Badjian's monopoly was at last broken. I picked up one of the bottles of solution. 'Here, did your scientific training go as far as this? Can you tell me what it is? Not the solution – the substance, I mean.'

Laying down his missal on his lap, Yarousseau accepted the bottle carefully between his dwarfing fingers.

'My life may well depend upon what's in that little bottle,' I told him. 'And yours too.' He needed frightening, this clod.

'I couldn't possibly tell you what it is by just looking at it.' He gave it the full benefit of his bull-browed attention nonetheless. 'What do you mean, our lives may depend upon it?'

'If the substance is worthless and we've been had – then I'm saved.'

'It could be valuable, I suppose.' He held the bottle up to the light. 'I can't judge.'

'Whoever knows its value will probably want to keep his little secret to himself,' I explained. 'At the moment I'm just as likely to end up a pile of bones and guts on the street corner in the morning as you are.'

'Look, I'm afraid I just don't understand what on earth you're talking about.'

I was suddenly exhausted; I'd had enough of this clod. And I still had over half a caravan to consign in the morning.

'Where are you staying?' I asked him.

'I've taken a room in one of the courtyards just beyond the main bazaar.'

'Well, you certainly can't go back through the streets at this hour,' I told him. 'All the patrols will be out by now. Do you want to sleep here for the night?'

'That's very kind of you.'

'Here, you can sleep in this bed. I'll lie over in the corner.'

'But you can't give me your bed!'

'Not a charitable gesture, I can assure you. If anyone's out to get me, they'll murder the person sleeping in my bed. Don't worry, I'll be here in the corner with my pistol.'

'You know, you really are a curious chap. I'm not sure whether to take a word you say seriously.' He shifted as I got out of bed and motioned for him to lie down. 'Have you been long on your own up here?' he asked, unfastening his sandals before sinking back onto the pillow.

'Long enough to take leave of my senses, if that's what you mean. Now turn down that lamp. And give those bottles a last shake for me, will you. 'Night.'

'God bless you, my good man.'

I lay down on the boards in the corner; soon his breathing became regular. I listened, but there was no other sound in the palace. Not even the odd nightmare whimper through the wall from Vardy. Only the occasional long dying howl from the ramparts disturbed the silence of the surrounding night. So now we were to have love in Harar.

Predictably, Vardy was none too pleased at this new addition to our little community.

'But he's had medical training,' I persisted. 'He can treat you properly.'

'And have my prospects ruined in this place?'

'But he'd be curing your bloody prospects!'

Not so, apparently. Vardy now proceeded to enlighten Rimbaud as to his views concerning his prospects in Harar.

Vardy's Prospects in Harar

Africa was like America had once been. A vast unknown, just waiting to be exploited. The prospects were unlimited. As things opened up, Harar would be established as one of the main inland trading centres for the Interior. And as in the New World, Philadephias would grow out of native settlements; pioneer traders would become leading citizens; and similarly, missionaries would become bishops.

'I just don't want to compromise my prospects in any future society at the outset, that's all,' continued the diseased invalid in his most portentious manner. 'One day you'll thank me for what I'm telling you now, young man. Arthur, I'm willing to forget all about that stupid resignation business.' He flicked his moustache self-consciously as his gaze fell to mine.

'That's all very well,' I told him flatly. 'But you know the mess I'm in at the moment.'

'Do you think there's any way of finding out what the substance is? Or what's going to happen?'

'Badjian's supposed to be working at it night and day. And I'm still watching my three little solutions, giving them a shake every now and again.'

'Any change?'

'It's still suspended, if that means anything.'

Later on, I let myself surreptitiously out of the side door of the palace and ran down the deserted alleyway to the back entrance of the barracks. When I arrived at the officers' duty quarters, Badjian was still in the middle of his surgery. I took my place outside the dispensary at the end of the line of ailing troopers. They sat along the bench lolling in the shadows, glum and motionless in their thick, coarse khaki, the occasional ragged bandage tinged like blotting paper with blood or some lurid medicament. From the look of it, Badjian still placed great faith in copper sulphate. One or two were moaning quietly with their heads buried in their hands. The air hummed with flies, smelling of sweat, sharp disinfectant, and a certain unplaceable putrid odour, as if something dead was rotting in the corner. One by one Badjian called in his patients; while in the distance, from across the barren, dusty parade ground in the direction of the troopers' barracks, there came sporadic outbursts of barked unintelligible orders.

Finally, a haggard red-eyed Badjian ushered me into his dispensary, locking the door behind me.

Had Badjian discovered the nature of our mystery substance?

No, he had not, he told me grimly. He had racked his brains, but his every effort had drawn a blank.

'And those solutions I gave you?' he enquired.

I shook my head. 'Nothing.'

We sat in silence at his littered dispensary table as a bugle sounded waveringly from outside across the parade ground.

'By the way, Vardy's pining away for your magical powers. He can't cure himself on faith alone, you know.'

'Ach, bugger him!'

'I know how you feel. But he'd like to see you, at least. It's an old European custom, the doctor visits the patient.'

'Let him go and see the new missionary, if he doesn't like my methods.'

'News travels fast, I see. How did you know we had a new missionary in town?'

'Such news is bound to travel fast, my friend. The whole city will know of our new arrival by now. They will be watching his every move. His life is in great danger.'

'You mean you know about that too? Was he actually seen after the curfew? What happened – did the Governor order them not to shoot at him?'

'What are you talking about? The curfew? The Governor? It will be the Emir who decides his fate.'

'I thought *we* were the Emir's particular concern at the moment. Hell, Badjian, I don't know about you, but I'm

49

worried sick for my life.'

'Your life is safe enough, for the time being.'

'Really? You mean you *have* found out something about that bloody substance?'

'It is unanalysable with the means at our disposal.'

'But Badjian, *someone* must know what it is. Whoever made the stuff. Otherwise how can *he* tell he's not being cheated?' My head sank into my hands as I glowered down at the refuse of bloodied bandages littering the table. How the hell was I ever going to get out of this mess? 'What makes you think we're safe, Badjian? And don't try peddling any shit to me with all your quack talk.'

'Really, my friend. Do you know nothing at all about life in this city?'

'Nothing,' I told him flatly. 'If you must know, I was quite happy in splendid isolation in my goddamn palace before you came along and dragged me into the local underworld.'

Badjian scowled. I could see my manner had hurt him much more deeply than I'd intended.

'So your diseased prick was part of the local underworld was it?' he asked quietly. 'And our partnership?'

I sighed.

'You're certain . . . Are we *really* safe?'

'Of course we are, you fool!'

'I'm sorry, Badjian.' Perhaps it was the sheer weight of emotion which my relief had suddenly unleashed, but I found myself leaning across the table, on pure reflex, and ruffling the curly mane of hair at the back of Badjian's head. 'I didn't mean to be such a bastard, ducky.' I stopped, embarrassed. I hadn't made that gesture for years, not since London with Verlaine, during our day-long, boozy bickering and making-up pub-crawls along the Tottenham Court Road.

Badjian grasped my wrist where it hung, and squeezed it till it hurt, all the while smiling like some sleepy lion.

'My friend, you are living in a world of your dreams. I think.'

There were many things about Harar which my splendid isolation in my palace had prevented me from finding out, it seemed. As Badjian and I sat drinking coffee together amongst the filthy cast-off bandages in his dispensary, while various platoons assembled and drilled outside the window under the palm trees in the dusty parade ground, Badjian enlightened me with his grand saga of our city. I sat, smoking quietly; I was willing to listen to anything as long as it meant that we were safe.

His Story

Seven years previously, in 1874, Raouf Pacha of Egypt had entered Harar at the head of his conquering army. The Egyptians had deposed the old Emir and set up a military governor, who had originally resided in my palace. Thus Badjian had retired from the wars and taken up his post as Health Officer for the province of Lower Abyssinia.

However, as a result of the Governor's somewhat eclectic habits he had found it expedient to move out of the limelight of the palace to some less conspicuous residence up by the mosque. A curiously sensitive action for the representative of a conquering army, but in fact a necessary one.

Before Harar had been taken by Raouf Pacha, it had been a closed city, a world unto itself and its Emir since time immemorial. Its people had become experienced traders and had developed a quaint but strictly observed moral code of their own. The Governor's more cultured moral practices (over which the narrator unfortunately drew a veil) had by their very novelty been a source of deep concern to our more primitively behaved citizens. The Hararis in their timeless isolation had grown fanatic in their rejection of all outside practices. Thus progress in such matters had of necessity to be discreet. Yet gradually and inevitably over the years civilisation had made further inroads into the formerly closed city. And latterly, the advances had begun to take on more permanent form.

First Rimbaud had arrived, to take up residence, then Vardy. And now even a missionary.

'But in such soil, my friend, all alien roots are shallow. The British count this as their sphere of influence now, since they have a hand in Egypt. But in fact Europe does not have any say here yet. If the Kingdom of Shoa revolts in the north, the Egyptians will abandon this place.'

And what would happen then, in this hypothetical future, wondered Rimbaud.

'All the time the deposed Emir is in his palace, watching. Now he has no power, and merely amuses himself by accumulating contraband wealth. And perhaps making a few undercover preparations for the future. But if ever he regained power, he would close this city. And once again it would disappear from the map, back into its own world.'

'So it's just you and your bloody army we've got to thank for our protection in this place?'

'The Emir would only have me killed if he was really desperate. And I doubt if he would ever be so rash as to lay a finger on you. At present his policy is to gain favour. That way, if the Egyptians pull out he'll stand a good chance of being reappointed without any struggle.'

'And what about this missionary? You say he's in danger?'

'A closed city is a pure city,' elaborated Badjian with due solemnity. Our dubious Health Officer had waxed exceeding eloquent during the telling of his historical tale. 'A closed city is free from the decadence of outside civilisation. A living memorial to the One True God. There's no telling how the Emir will react to this missionary. It all depends whether his fanaticism is stronger than his politics. It'll happen quickly, if it happens at all.'

'But meanwhile we're safe?'

'The way I read it. But if anything did happen to this missionary, and it turned out that our mystery substance *was* dangerous . . .'

'We'd just have to flee for our lives,' I broke in. I had no wish to hear our gruesome end spelt out in detail.

'Then our partnership would really begin, my friend.' Badjian appeared to brighten at the prospect of being chased into the desert.

'Begin with what, precisely?'

'Running guns to the North. To the Kingdom of Shoa. There's a fortune there, just waiting.' His fingers reached, closing through the air between us as he spoke.

The fact that we'd have no money, no food, nothing between us and the lions, with doubtless the odd assassin hot on our trail, was not worthy of consideration, so it seemed. Where our partnership was concerned, the golden dream was all.

I groaned tiredly.

'You and your insane plans!'

'My friend,' Badjian began slowly, 'since I have come to Harar I have had my eyes open, and my ears listening.' He paused as his eyes rested on mine, and then shook his head mournfully. 'But to tell you the truth, my friend, I was nothing more than a living corpse until you came along.'

The scuffles and shouting outside on the parade ground had gradually been mounting all the while we'd been talking; but now a bugle blew, and silence descended.

Badjian leaped up. 'The Governor's parade! I'm late, my friend. I must hurry.' He quickly took his jacket and cap from a hook on the wall, and began ushering me out of the dispensary.

'I will come round to see you if I find out anything further,' he called back to me as he started down the passage.

'And what about Vardy?'

'Oh, let him go join a monastery. I'll see, later.'

4

Now that Rimbaud knew he was safe, he saw no point in leaving Harar. Especially while he had practically no savings waiting for him in Aden. Yet it was with a deep sense of misgiving that he stood with Vardy watching the caravan set out for Zeyla. Vardy was now able to get out and about; Badjian's cure was at last beginning to take effect.

From this time on, Rimbaud began to save even more fanatically than before, in his effort to accumulate enough to set up on his own. Working from dawn to dusk he would scour the market place for bargains. He now allowed himself only the scant meals provided by Bomba, avoided the coffee stalls, and took to dressing in cheap native clothes made out of the local cloth. Most of the time he went barefoot. This was now the only way left to him, he realised, if he was ever to make anything worthwhile out of what remained of his life, to redeem the failure of those lost years of poetry, vagabondage and childish visionary dreams. At night he studied, salvaging his previous projects and incorporating them in his new plan.

Rimbaud's New Plan

For Vardy's visions of the future to be realised, in spite of Badjian's gloomy predictions, Harar would have to be linked permanently with the outside world. This way all the Emir's dreams of a closed city would become a thing of the past; and even if the Kingdom of Shoa revolted in the north, the city would not be abandoned. The only answer was a railway up from Zeyla.

Rimbaud poured through his notes on the Panama Project and the various schemes for laying railways through the South American jungle. Any railway to Harar was bound to need similar excavation, and anyone with experience of the terrain and an understanding of the problems involved could well make his fortune in such a project. Tunnelling through the mountains would be the main problem. But far more ambitious tunnels were now being driven through the Alps to keep the passes open for the winter, according to *Roret's Handy Manual*.

Men were digging under the snows, where once Rimbaud had had to dig through the snow itself.

The young Arthur Rimbaud had stood by the customs post at Altdorf looking up to where the curving snowfields wound between the fir-fringed rock faces towards the icy alpine peaks beyond. I'd already tramped half way across Europe; if I was to get through to Genoa in time to leave on that boat for Africa, to start my life again, to redeem myself, to make my fortune, there was only one way. Hitching my pack up onto my back, I started up into the pass.

After an hour or so, the clouds began spilling down the gully ahead. And then I saw that it wasn't cloud, but snow. Suddenly the world of rocky woodlands, high dazzling peaks and distant green valleys below became a soft silent cocoon of flakes. To begin with, I could just make out the roadway where the previous snow had been banked up to head height on either side. In places the wall of snow had collapsed and I had to burrow my way through with my hands. Then the ice began forming in sharp needles on my eyebrows and eyelashes. My hands became like painful metallic objects at the end of my arms and I dug them into the snow as if they were no longer a part of me. My breath became laboured in the rarified air and I found I could hardly inhale enough oxygen into my floundering lungs. The blood felt as if it had frozen in my ears, and through the cavities of my earholes the cold pierced into the very centre of my brain like two solid nails of ice. Arthur, what are you doing to yourself?

Why? Why go on? Rimbaud stumbled forward through the crumbly snow, listening to himself blubber as he lugged his legs like a cripple out of his thigh-deep footholes.

In the isolation of this white abstract world of pain there is a heart that beats somewhere inside you; there are lungs at the base of your throat which choke on this icy air, melting it painfully; and inside the frozen helmet of your skull there is a mind which jars at the blank numbing stab of each breath (like the first shock of raw absinthe in the morning). Your thoughts float, isolated one from the other (blaring out of nothingness, each its own inspiration). That trembling veil ahead is a wall of ice. You clamber, you scramble up to it, somehow. This is a beach of white sand, these are the waves breaking over your head. You are a drunken boat. The inhuman driving screech smooths the surface of your thoughts, planing them away in layers. This is oblivion. You have passed the point of no return now. Your eyes see eddies of smoke curling from the upper edges of the drifts. You are stumbling through flakes of flame and molten boulders of white fire. Then you are wrestling with this solid unyielding element which sings to you. And finally you lie listening to the howl of this angelic choir. This is the music your poems could never sing to. You listen, and the gloss of frozen tears cracks on your cheeks, the choking kiss of fire forcing itself into your mouth. And then it is disgust alone that is forcing you on, keeping you alive, as you spit out Verlaine's sperm. Shouting. You cunt, I loved you! Why, why did we have to bring ourselves to do all that? And the angels answer you . . . No, no! I'm going to get through. I'm going to get to Africa. I'm going to make something out of my life. I'm going to make my fortune. And then the fire is dying. Its blinding whiteness – which is snow, you tell yourself, suddenly waking to this peculiar fact – is turning ashen and dark. Is it night already? Or is my vision failing? The drifting veil of snowflame parts, momentarily, to reveal pitch darkness.

As you lie, listening to the dull uneven drumrolls of your heart, you see that you are on the edge of an abyss. Without realising it, you could have blundered over the edge into that drifting chasm at any moment. You stare down, blearily. Is this the end of the unending farce? Does this futile entity called into being as Arthur Rimbaud simply cease to exist here? The snow veils drift and eddy, forming momentary patterns in the vast swirling maelstrom of chaos. How far have I come? How far have I got to go? How long have I been here? You mouth absurdities as your thoughts reach beyond you, driven by undivined motives.

You remember Eternity: 'Let us whisper the confession of the night full of nothingness. Beyond human care, beyond common urges, you diverge here and fly off as you may. Here is no hope. It has been found again. What? Eternity.'

You choke, your bile dribbling as the words of your poem mock you. Is this what you've been blundering towards all the time? Every minute of your life pressing on to this? Your head sinks into its hollow of whiteness, your staring eyes fixed on the speckled delirium beyond . . .

I woke from some howling unrecallable dream into silence. My eyelids unglued. My vision pierced the darkness in fragments. I was in some white mountainous world of night and silence. And there ahead was a light. The monastery on the other side of the frontier. I was saved!

This flickering consciousness in a kernel of being watches as its monstrous possessor breaks through this crust of smooth snow, erupting into life like some long-buried fossil. Hands claw at the night. It totters through the frigid silence with the mindless persistence of some groping beast driven unwillingly onto two legs by evolutionary powers beyond its control. Finally it reaches the door, and peers through the grille into the light.

A voice filters swimmingly from within, questioning.

In answer, the beast's lips part, the ice tearing the numb flesh. 'A – I – A.' *Africa. I am going to Africa. But only in its mind can it will the words; its cracked lips and frozen palate can only form the vowels.* 'A – I – A.'

The door opens. Onto a red glow in the darkness. Black. Red. Black. The beast is saved. Charity will nourish it, and it will drag itself on to Africa to give birth to the dreams whose power alone woke it to survival in that upper world of ice.

I stood at the window to my room looking out into the night over the silent city. Behind the empty market place rose the dome of the mosque, a dull lustreless bubble of whiteness under the clouded starless heavens. No, there was only one way to prevent Harar from becoming a closed city again. A railway. Making use of all the most modern methods, with a tunnel through the mountains. I returned to my table and began sketching a rough outline of the journey I'd covered up from Zeyla. The mountains. The plateau. The wilderness. The desert . . . But the journey had been so long. There was so much I found I could no longer account for. And try as I might I could fix no definite order to my random memories. Nothing seemed to follow. Did that wilderness of stunted trees come before or after the desert? . . . What on earth had I been thinking of during those long days?

I was still racking my brains when I heard someone approaching along the passage. Instinctively I blew out the lamp and reached for Vardy's pistol. I wasn't taking any chances, in spite of what Badjian had told me. But as the footsteps came up to my door, I recognised them as Bomba's. He knocked and I called him in, laying down the pistol and striking a match.

What the hell did Bomba want?

As often as not Bomba wanted nothing more than a romp. He'd frequently steal things in the most flagrant circumstances just for the sake of the chase. Vardy was all too ready to take the bait. Arthur would listen as they pounded through the upper apartments, slamming doors, Bomba scampering and giggling while Vardy shouted after him like a schoolmaster. Even after the little lapse which had led to his unfortunate illness, Vardy had still insisted on retaining Bomba.

'As a matter of principle, Arthur. I'm having Badjian treat him as well.'

'But he'll only go and get it again.'

'In which case I'll have him cured again. The boy knows no better. I'll have Badjian inspect him once a month.'

At the end of the chase Vardy would lead a squealing Bomba by the ear back to the state room, and there Bomba would be ceremonially beaten.

'For his own good, Arthur. I'm training him.'

So, to the sound of Vardy's slipper on his bare bottom, Bomba would learn his lesson.

With Arthur, Bomba was more circumspect, always rather afraid of the gruff, taciturn manner adopted by his more solitary master.

'What do you want, Bomba?' I asked, as he stood grinning playfully at the door.

Bomba came forward and gingerly laid his hand on my shoulder.

'No, Bomba! Get out! Back to your room.' I slapped away his hand.

He leapt back, sniggering shyly, the smooth skin of his thigh breaking from between his parted robe. He'd obviously only just got out of bed; he had nothing on underneath.

'Off you go!'

Bomba hesitated.

'What do you want, for heaven's sake?'

He frowned, trying to repress his shifty smirk, and then beckoned me forward.

Uncertainly, I rose to my feet as he started towards the door.

'What is it?'

He came back and reached forward to take me by the arm.

I caught his wrist.

'What?'

He wriggled, sniggering nervously as he pushed me away with his free arm.

I grabbed his other wrist.

'*What do you want?*' I snapped agitatedly, while he wriggled in my grasp, giggling, thrusting himself against me in his efforts to break free. Through the thin cloth of my native smock I felt his limbs pressing against mine. Half playfully he bit at my shoulder and I released his arm, grabbing at his neck. I was embracing him, pressing him to me. For a moment he stopped wriggling and I felt my erection rising between us. With a little snigger he waggled his hips, and then began pressing his hands against my chest, trying to free himself. As my breath caught in my throat, my hand ran down his back, pulling him against me, clutching at the smooth mould of his buttocks.

'Bomba! No!'

He was struggling frantically, urgently, but without any real effort to break free. He appeared to be trying to lead me out of the door into the darkness of the passage.

I stumbled out after him as he led me by the hand, down towards the kitchen quarters. Once inside his room I drew him to me again, panting as I pressed my body against his, smoothing my hand inside his robe over his bare hips. He was still wriggling, giggling, apparently trying to say something between biting playfully at my shoulder, my hands, my neck. I took his hand and drew it down over my stomach.

'*There, Arthur. Your little magic wand, hard as ivory.*'

'*No, Verlaine. Stop!*'

'*I love my little pear, my beautiful little pear.*'

'*I love you too, but* please! . . .'

'*I'm going to eat my little pear.*'

'*Oh, God, what are we doing? I love you, Verlaine. Oh, I love you.*'

Arthur trembled as he took Bomba in his arms.

What am I doing?

You want him. You want him. At this moment you want him more than anything in the world.

But what if he's diseased?

You don't care. You don't care if you rot in Harar for ever.

You want him now more than anything . . .

What do I want?

This semi-naked figure giggling insinuatingly, struggling playfully, wriggling. This hot breath against mine, this cheek against mine, the smell of his hair in my nostrils. This robe slipping from these narrow shoulders, parting across the milky hummocks of this firm chest. This smooth thigh pushing between mine. These arms entwined in mine, these hands playing over my back, half frantic, half pressing as this robe falls away and my hands smooth over these hips down to the curve of these thighs . . .

You want this.

In the absence of all else.

But in the darkness there are voices, calling. Howling. Discordant.

Rimbaud froze, listening.

And Bomba's wriggling became purposive action, dragging Rimbaud to the window.

Below, in the darkness of the alleyways, Rimbaud gradually made out the robes of a crowd clustered at the corner. Baying. Wrestling. Then, from further up the alleyway, came the dull pounding of boots. A patrol was moving in, at the run. The crowd parted, scattered against the walls. And then Rimbaud saw Yarousseau, kneeling by some fallen body, his arm raised against the rain of blows. They were beating him to death!

Without waiting a moment more, our hero ran down the passage to his room, pulling up his trousers as he went. There, from the midst of the exact still life laid out beneath his burning lamp – three bottles of cloudy solution, and a pistol lying amongst some scrolls depicting diagrams of tunnels, various engineering projects and an incomplete route map – he selected his weapon. As he ran downstairs, he checked with his fingers to see that it was loaded.

By the time our hero had arrived on the scene the air was alive with the wailings of the fallen and the occasional hollow wooden clunk of an Egyptian rifle butt making contact with a Harari skull. The curfew patrol was clearing the alleyway.

After a display of tedious heroics *(which the narrator, in his present invalid state, is in no mood to elaborate upon)* Rimbaud found himself standing over his stricken rescuee.

Tableau Vivant: Honour defending Love
Our hero, improperly buttoned at the front, waves his pistol inexpertly at the scowling Egyptian officer whose hand rests uncertainly on his holster. Background: to the left a ring of troopers, butts raised, some subduing the angry mob of natives, whilst those nearest stand in hesitant support of their officer. To the right, our loving man of God kneeling beside the pitted wall, his outstretched hands resting on some obscure bundle of woe as his face turns upward pleadingly, the dark dribbles of blood streaming over his cheeks. A scene rendered aesthetically bearable only by a minimum of *chiaro* and almost total *oscuro*.

Jiggering with panic, I began dragging Yarousseau to his feet. The crowd were yelling, throwing stones now, threatening to break through the cordon any moment. I shouted, waving my pistol at the officer, and he slid his hands quickly away from his holster. Yarousseau lumbered against me, his head sagging onto my shoulder. The clod weighed a ton! I glanced quickly to my side, steadying him with my pistol hand as I slipped my other arm around his waist. Although my glance took only a fraction of a second, not even time for the officer or any of the soldiers to move forward, a lightning-clear image of what lay behind us, at our feet, imprinted itself on my vision. It was one of the whores. She was lying awkwardly spread-eagled against the wall. One half of her face was still young, smooth-skinned and delicately featured, but on the other side it was as if the skin had slipped. The white of her eye protruded from her drooping eye-socket and the sagging slit of her lip cut into the bloated pox-festered skin of her cheek. Only a few whisps of hair remained on her skull, and her robe, which was torn down the front, had fallen aside to reveal a withered bosom, wrinkled like scrotum skin, which she was attempting to cover in a pathetic gesture of modesty with the long graceful fingers of her hand. As the image repeated itself in my mind's eye, I saw, in the unblemished side of the girl's face, the features of Tahira.

'We can't just leave her, Arthur!'

'Like hell, we can't.' I stumbled forward, dragging Yarousseau with me. But it wasn't Tahira, I knew, merely one of her tribe.

And so, as the crowd parted before him, our gun-toting hero made his exit, dragging the cumbersome deadweight of the unwilling man of God from the scene of his would-be martyrdom.

As the botched work of art is consequently accommodated by the botched theory of aesthetics, so the gratuitous act inevitably gives rise to the endless wranglings of a gratuitous morality.

'What right had you to leave her behind?' stormed Yarousseau, now much recovered, sitting on my bed with a twist of bandage circling his head like some ragged fallen halo.

'What the hell do you think you were up to out there in the first place!' demanded Rimbaud.

'That's got nothing to do with it!'

'It bloody well has! Why do you think they called the guards?'

Thus, from two diametrically opposed positions, the bargaining begins and the ethical transaction gets under way. Eventually, as emotions cool, distinct similarities begin to emerge.

'If you must know, I was perfectly happy working away up here at my notes, until you went and woke up Bomba. Is it absolutely necessary for you to go prowling the streets at night?'

'I believe it is, Arthur. You see, before I volunteered for this mission, I lived for a number of years in the mountains in an enclosed order . . .'

'But you got ideas. Renunciation wasn't enough for you. You wanted to change the world. Oh yes, I know your type all right.'

'I became aware of the spirit,' Yarousseau continued firmly, his head resting on his hands, for all the world as if he were conducting some private conversation with his Maker. 'A power of which you are probably not aware, Arthur.'

'What!' Who the hell did this country bumpkin think he was? I, Arthur Rimbaud, who had seen visions of eternity, whose poems had described the landscape of hell itself – unaware of the power of the spirit?

'What on earth do you know of the power of the spirit, you clod?'

'I feel it, deep within me. More sure even than my faith.'

'A kind of insane self-certainty which overcomes all opposition?'

'In a manner of speaking, yes.' In a broad peasant accent, aye.

'A profound conviction of one's own destiny?'

'Precisely.'

'The supreme delusion, in fact.'

He looked up. The understanding yokel patronising his favoured sheep. 'You speak as if you have been aware of these things too, my good man.'

'I was, once.'

'And what happened?'

'They wrecked my life. So I gave them up. Along with all other mere dreams.'

'But why?'

'Because I am who I am.'

'That is pride, my good man. As well as being blasphemy.'

'On the contrary. You'd have me surrender the one thing

I have – myself?'

'That way alone brings release.'

'From *what*, dammit! From Harar? From all this wretched suffering? From these driving needs? From these insane ambitions that make us what we are?'

'From it all.'

'Hell no, you poor deluded clod! You too inhabit this fucking city. You too suffer. You too have ambitions for that precious 'power' of yours, be they ever so bloody selfless. Take a closer look, Yarousseau.'

'I confess, certain things do remain.'

'In me, nothing remains . . .'

'But you just . . .'

'. . . but this thick-skinned buffoon I was born into. And with him I intend to make my mark on this world. To change it, according to my own ideas. I'll use him like a blunt instrument if I have to. But you'll never get me to renounce him. Buffoon though he may be, he's the talent I was born with. Bury yours if you will Yarousseau, but for God's sake be aware of what you're doing.'

'My good man, your pride has betrayed you back into the world again.'

'So you and your precious power are going to redeem the world, are you? You wait, you clod. With my so-called pride I intend to make a new world. A better world, a world fit to live in. What on earth can you tell a diseased whore in a language she doesn't understand?'

'Love, my son.'

'You'd teach love to whores? And you tell me *I've* got pride!'

Rimbaud and Yarousseau sat in silence; the bargaining was now complete, apparently. Although what precisely had been the nature of the transaction, and what exchanged, remained a mystery – even to the participants. Perhaps it was this feeling of being cheated that led Arthur to inflict a further little down-to-earth truth upon his agricultural friend.

'Listen to me, you bloody clod. Your life's in danger. Get out of this city while you can. I'm not talking about martyrdom now, I'm talking about cold-blooded murder.' So Rimbaud explained to Yarousseau his plight in Harar, as Badjian saw it. '. . . the Emir may well be after your life, Yarousseau.'

Yarousseau listened, nodding gravely. Here, there was no bargaining.

Next thing, the ivory market slumped. There was nothing to be had beyond the odd overpriced shipment of rubbish. After several days, Rimbaud was approached by one of the traders. Was Rimbaud willing to sell the ivory he had bought with Badjian?

Rimbaud certainly was. But it's hollow, he began trying to explain. The trader either knew, or didn't care. He eventually paid Rimbaud even more than Badjian had paid for the stuff.

I'd redeemed my savings!

Rimbaud's revised Plans (in the light of his redeemed savings)

He'd stay in Harar for the winter in an effort to double his savings, and then leave for Aden. There, he'd try to get some backer interested in his project for a railway to Harar. Once he'd interested one backer, the money would come pouring in. He'd buy as large a share in the project as he could, and then take over superintending the actual construction, along with a qualified railway engineer. That way he'd have a regular salary and a growing investment. With savings from his salary he'd finance caravans from Harar, thus maintaining his position there as an established trader. Then, with the railway boom, he'd make his fortune. Further investments would follow, and in a matter of years . . .etc etc.

But this meant living in Harar permanently.
Did I really care?

Living in Harar, Rimbaud had lost the habit and even the taste for European life (assuming he'd ever had one.) In fact, the combination of saving-induced asceticism and Harar itself had practically cured him of a taste for any life whatsoever.

But what about that little lapse with Bomba?

This had struck at the very roots of Rimbaud's conception of his life in Harar. Rimbaud knew now that he could no longer live independently, alone. He would have to share his life.

But who with?

Not Bomba, that was for sure. Rimbaud decided that in a few weeks' time he'd buy another servant of his own, a tribal virgin this time. They were cheaper. He'd teach her to cook and look after him. Perhaps he'd even marry her if she gave him a son. Then when the time came he would send his son to France, to get a proper education, in engineering and the new sciences. His son would be able to come back and one day take over Rimbaud's business empire.

Why not budget for your funeral, while you're about it?

I turned down the lamp and buried my face in my hands. Did it have to be like this? Was there no room at all in my life for any feeling?

A moment's weakness, a diseased prick.

What had it ever meant?

Verlaine. A wrecked life. Corrupted love. Dreams. Madness.

Had it ever been any different?

Remember Henrika, wearing that silk scarf and her best brown and white check cotton dress (so out of date that it probably hadn't been in fashion since some time in the previous century)? How she'd clung to your arm as you'd walked together through those nondescript London suburbs, the sky overcast and the warm south wind heavy with the smell of the wakening winter-ravaged market gardens and withered meadows. Then she'd stopped in front of a sheet of water left after the floods and pointed out some tadpoles;

but beyond, behind us, the factory with its screaming mechanical saws and belching pall of soot-raining smoke had always been there, following us at the end of the road.

By that time the farce with Verlaine had been ended and he'd been locked up in jail in Brussels. I was alone, working as a drudge in that box-making factory in south London. How could you have known, Henrika, that in the mind of that shy sulky French boy in his scruffy dungarees there lurked an ogre who dreamed of the fire-storms of hell? Your little wifely arm dragged like a chain of sanity on mine, the world you described as ours was suffocating me.

And so now, resident at last in a hell whose banality outshone even his most ambitious nightmares, Rimbaud was dreaming of buying himself a little Harari Henrika, and having a half-African son who would follow in his father's footsteps. Tears of self-disgust welled into my eyes in the darkness.

As a result of my warning, Yarousseau decided to leave on a mission to the Gallas tribes in the East.

'I just looked in to ask you if you wanted to come with me, Arthur.'

'*What?*'

'I'd like a companion. And you know the territory.'

'I've only passed through it. Just the same as you. I'm no expert.'

'Then you don't want to come?'

I thought for a moment. 'You'd travel by the Zeyla caravan route?'

'Yes. I intend to stick as close to it as I can.'

The mountains. The wilderness. The desert. I could map out the route for the railway. 'What would you want me to do?' I asked.

'Just keep me company. I thought you might be interested in a holiday. Aren't you due for one? How long have you been up here?'

Almost a year gone, and still only dreaming. But this way

I could get the tribesmen to show me the less steep passes. Search out supplies of wood for the sleepers. Ask about the winter rains, about hostile natives and tribal territories.

'We'd be gone a month,' continued Yarousseau, 'but that wouldn't be too long, would it?'

A month's salary out of my savings. No profit from the first two winter caravans.

'I think we'd get on well together, Arthur.'

'No. There'd be no profit in it. I'd have to eat into my savings.'

I'd buy that virgin instead.

Three days later I saw Yarousseau off at the city gates. He had a horse, and a mule to carry his belongings. Under his broad-brimmed black hat his face was burnt lobster-red, while his robes, already gone shiny, had begun to fray at the edges. As he started forward, the canteens of holy water clanked gently around the mule's arse.

'It's not too late, Arthur. You can still come if you want.'

'Not bloody likely.'

'Please, my good man, watch your language. This is the start of a holy mission.'

'Look after yourself, bumpkin. Good luck! You'll need it.

'I shall trust in God's will. Farewell, Arthur.'

The poor clod! He was going to a certain death, and I think he knew it too. Badjian had told him that it was suicide to travel out in those parts without a gun, but no matter how we'd raged at him he'd still insisted on going unarmed.

That night, for the first time since I'd abandoned poetry, I took up my pen to compose a purely imaginary piece. A letter to Yarousseau's superiors.

> It is with a feeling of inconsolable loss that I write to inform you of the death of Father Yarousseau on a mission to the Gallas tribes. Harar now has its first martyr. Up here, news of Father Yarousseau's death was greeted with indescribable scenes of grief. The market came to a standstill, and was finally closed for a week as a mark of respect

for the beloved departed. The Emir himself, although not yet converted from the errors of his heretic faith, has declared a season of public mourning to be observed by men of all creeds for this man of God who was the first to bring the light of Love to Harar.

Already Father Yarousseau's name is a by-word for love in the tiny alleyways and estaminets of the quarter behind the palace where he did so much of his work. To the European community he was a great solace in this lonely heathen place, and I need hardly tell you that the courteous sophisticated understanding presence of this prince of the church will be greatly missed at our receptions and public functions. As for his Works, I would particularly like to mention his succour of M. Vardy through the vagaries of his unfortunate recurrent illness, and his administration of the last rites to our illustrious senior citizen Dr Badjian. Even more miraculous (and I can assure you that I do not use the word lightly here) was his conversion of the notorious Arthur Rimbaud, whose spectacular vices and corruptions had become a by-word throughout Lower Abyssinia. M. Rimbaud, a changed man, has donated his ill-gotten fortune to charity and is now contemplating retirement to a life of renunciation and penance.

As my pen writes for the people of Harar, I find it only proper that I should modestly veil myself in the anonymity of one of their number.

    Yours faithfully,
     A loyal citizen of Harar.

PS. A vast punitive expedition, a crusade no less, is at present being mounted to subdue the wretched Gallas territory and recover the remains of our local martyr. And even as I have been writing these words, I have learnt that the Emir has already begun preparations for transforming the market square into a holy place, in the midst of which will be placed a shrine to Father Yarousseau.

Rimbaud blotted the letter and placed it in his drawer, along with his notes on tunnelling, engineering, incomplete route maps, sketches for blast furnaces, railways through the South American jungle, canals through the Panama, unfinished letters to Mother, calculations of savings, drafts of his resignation etc etc.

5

'It's a primitive form of gunpowder, Arthur.' Badjian had at last discovered the nature of our mystery substance. 'The Emir is evidently preparing for the future. As we should be, my friend. Have you thought any more about our little gun-running expedition to the Kingdom of Shoa? You must have a fair bit saved by now, surely? And in a few months' time I'll be due for my end-of-service bounty. The day I get that we can start,' Badjian continued, enthusiastic as ever, as we sat sipping sherbet water together in his dispensary. Outside, beyond the open window, the parade ground was empty – a sunbaked sandy wilderness criss-crossed with little whirling cones of wind-driven sand.

'You'll have to go on your own I'm afraid, Badjian. I'm staking my future here.'

'In Harar? Are you crazy? As soon as Shoa revolts in the north, the Egyptians will just pull out. And you know what'll happen then. The Emir will simply banish all foreigners and close the city. It'll just become like some enclosed monastery.'

'Not if I can help it.'

'But the Emir is a fanatic, Arthur. You think I am telling you a myth about this gunpowder from the Interior?'

'Of course not, Badjian. I believe you.'

'Why, the Emir's probably got enough stashed away by now to send half of the city sky high.'

'But don't you see, if there's a source of gunpowder in the Interior so much the better. It can be *used* – to *our* advantage.'

'How?'

'Building bridges. Excavating tunnels. I intend to build a railway up from Zeyla. That way trade will be established once and for all, and no one will be able to close the city.'

Badjian sighed, exasperated, patting the flat of his palm against his forehead. 'My friend, you just do not understand. This place is only held by force of arms. All this trade, it is nothing. You owe your very existence up here to the garrison alone. Which reminds me,' he sprawled forward earnestly across the unusually clean table, 'I must warn you. There can be no more games of bravado for you and your European friends. Your performance the other night with your missionary friend was not well received by the Governor. Breaking the curfew, resisting arrest, pointing a pistol at an Egyptian officer – these are serious offences. My influence is not unlimited, you know.'

'Don't worry, Yarousseau's gone now. It won't happen again.'

Badjian shook his head, with a faint despairing smile. 'And so now we are to have a railway. What for, Arthur? What *for*?'

'To open up more trade with the Interior. To establish civilisation up here.'

'But there is no more trade. You can see for yourself what comes from the Interior. Bits and pieces. A little bit of gunpowder, a few horns of ivory. What kind of civilisation do you think you'd establish with that?'

Badjian's views on the prospects for the future in Harar were a great blow to Rimbaud's confidence. His railway, and all his hopes, he began to see, were nothing more than idle dreams. He'd wasted a year of his life in Harar, and what did he have to show for it? – a miserable sixty quid's worth of credit in Aden, according to his latest calculations.

'Arthur, young man. I'd like a word with you.' Vardy fluffed his moustache as he closed the ledger on his desk. 'I've been meaning to talk to you for some time.'

'What about?'

'About your behaviour.'

'What behaviour?'

'You're beginning to worry me, you know. Just look at yourself – what do you see?'

A ravaged-faced staring-eyed barefoot desperado in a native smock and frayed cloth trousers. 'A failure.'

'Nonsense, young man. You're no failure.' The idea was unthinkable. 'What you've got to do is learn to relax a little more, enjoy yourself, take a broader view of life.'

Vardy was desperately lonely, starved of human company. Vardy was pleading with Arthur to come out of his shell, to involve himself with people a little more. To live, no less. Instead of locking himself away in his little room all the time.

'I know you don't care too much for my type Arthur, but ignoring me won't make me simply disappear. With a bit of give and take we could make our time up here so much more pleasant for ourselves. After all, we all depend upon each other in this life. Why can't we simply admit it and be friends?' Harar could be a happy place, where people enjoyed themselves.

'Is that why you came up here? To enjoy yourself?'

Vardy caught the look in my eye, and coughed, lowering his gaze to the closed ledger before him. 'By the way,' he continued, in a more abrupt tone, 'I'd like you to load up that ivory for the next caravan. You know, the hollowed-out stuff we got lumbered with.'

'I've sold it,' I told him evenly.

'You've *what!*'

'It was no use, and I got a good price for it.'

'*On whose authority?*' he suddenly exploded. 'What do you mean – *sold it!* That wasn't your ivory to sell. We *need* that ivory. You get out into that market place and buy it back at once!'

'Buy it back yourself. It was junk.'

'I can't send down a caravan with no ivory! What kind of a caravan would that be?'

Suddenly I saw it all. How could I have been so blind?

For Vardy a caravan consisted of certain pre-ordained goods. Which could vary slightly, in quantity and quality. But if it didn't consist of basically the same goods in basically the same quantities, then it simply wasn't a caravan. So that was why we'd kept back that consignment of first-grade coffee beans till the mould had got at it, why he'd forbidden me to buy any more hides when the traders were bringing up caravan after caravan from the Interior of beautifully tanned stuff, why he'd insisted we saddle ourselves with all that rotten gum which they'd only sell in bulk.

'You bastard! You've been *ruining* me!'

Without further ado, Rimbaud handed in his resignation on the spot.

Three days later, I took the caravan for Zeyla. To hell with the whole idea of Harar, it could remain a closed city for all eternity as far as I was concerned.

I took my leave of Badjian at the city gate.

'You have taken the right decision, my friend. There is nothing here. Write to me and I will join you. I have only a few months of my term to go now.' He mumbled something about gun-running and his precious Kingdom of Shoa, and we parted. I don't think either of us really expected to see each other again.

A week or so later, as the caravan passed across the plateau, I signed to the Somali leader to ask some passing tribesmen whom we'd encountered if there was any news of a stranger travelling with a mule off the caravan routes. The tribesmen retired a short distance away and gibbered amongst themselves, squatting so that their loincloths brushed the rocky floor, their spears pointing in a circle up into the sky. Eventually their chief came back and started drawing something in the dust at the caravan leader's feet. Apparently a 'devil-djinn' had passed through these lands on horseback a few weeks beforehand, and they had been frightened.

What had happened to him?

As soon as they had discovered that he was a 'devil-djinn' they had led him far into the desert and left him there 'so that he could talk with the sun'.

Poor Yarousseau. The least I could do was send off that obituary letter from Aden.

6

Am I getting any better? I no longer know what to think. Will I ever be free again? Am I to remain in this wretched hospital room for the rest of my life?

Africa. All my thoughts are directed towards that one objective. If I can get back to Africa, everything will be all right again.

But the paralysis is gaining ground. Each time I try to move any part of my body around those paralysed limbs it becomes more difficult. My only hope is the pain. As long as I can feel it in all my limbs I know that I can recover them. They are not dead. I must fight. All the time. Must keep that pain alive. Pain is life. . . . But it's beginning to dull my mind now. I've started to lose all sense of time. Yesterday – or was it the day before? – I thought the sun was rising out there, but as I watched that lurid red sky it slowly grew darker.

During the daylight hours, Isabelle sits knitting by the bed, telling me stories about life at home with Mother on the farm. When the pain becomes too much I lie back on my pillow, cursing, cursing, with all my strength. At the first sound of my obscenities, Isabelle stops. And then for hours, or days – or years, it sometimes seems – there is only the click-clack of her knitting needles.

The Treatment. Act 1, Scene 1.
ISABELLE: Today we have a surprise for you, Arthur.
DOCTOR (*producing some metal contraption, with straps*): Your new leg.
ISABELLE: Shall we try it on?

DOCTOR (easing the patient upright). That's better.
ISABELLE: Now be sure to say if it hurts, dear.
DOCTOR: That's right. You hang on. I'll ease it over the stump.
ISABELLE: Keep still, Arthur! It's not hurting you, is it?
DOCTOR: He has to be able to feel it. You can feel it, can't you? . . . No, the stump's not dead.
ISABELLE: Don't wriggle about so!
DOCTOR: Oh dear, it doesn't seem to fit. There's not enough for it to grip onto. Perhaps the stump has swollen. Part of the healing process, I expect.
ISABELLE: What's going to happen now?
DOCTOR: Don't worry, we can always alter the fitting. (*Letting the patient take hold of the contraption.*) That bit there.
ISABELLE: ⎫
DOCTOR: ⎭ Arthur!

The patient, having raised the metal contraption above his head, starts striking about him, finally flinging the contraption away from him with a grunt. It hits the far wall and falls to the floor with a clatter.

What can I do in Africa with only one leg?
They can change the fitting, they said so.
I will learn to use that leg, even if the pain drives me mad.
I will. I will!

Arriving back from Harar, I met Old Man Vardy on the quayside at Aden.

'No ivory this time?' He poked his stick amongst the bundles which had already been winched ashore.

'M'sieur Vardy, you don't seem to understand – I've resigned.'

'Yes, yes, young man, Arthur.' He leaned down to feel one of the bales of hide, rubbing the skin between his fingers. 'I presume you'll be putting up at the store?'

'That's very kind of you.'

'You can start work at your old position next Monday. Take a few days off, enjoy yourself for a bit.'

I laughed in his face. I had other plans. I wasn't going to end my days rotting in that joint.

'I'm looking for other work, Vardy.'

He straightened up slowly, pushing his battered Panama back over his balding pate, and fixed me with what I presume he considered to be a kind, fatherly eye. 'Young man, Arthur, there *is* no other work.'

And bugger him if he wasn't right! There was nothing. For several days I tramped about buying expensive rounds of drinks for various dead-beat agents and drunken know-alls in the hotel bars around Steamer Point, but by Monday morning I was back at my old desk. God's fucking teeth!

And how were the prospects in Harar, Old Man Vardy wanted to know.

There were no prospects in Harar.

'And why not?'

History may repeat itself, but at present the narrator is a very sick man and has better things to do with his time. In those days, however, I felt different. To avoid scratching away with my pen at those bloody ledgers, I was willing to waste half a morning describing to Old Man Vardy the various intrigues and possible uprisings etc threatening Harar.

'Nonsense, young man. You're far too alarmist in these matters. You may have inside information, but down here we can see it all from a broader perspective. I don't think the whole region would be affected if Shoa went up.'

'The Egyptians would pull out. You can't deny that.'

'No. I agree. You've a point there.'

'And if the Emir takes over, Harar will become a closed city again.'

But this was sheer fantasy. Such things just didn't happen in this day and age.

I began to wonder: had I thrown in my hand too soon? After all, what was Badjian, what were his opinions?

At night, Rimbaud would pore over the two new books which had been waiting for him in Aden. Mother had sent him *Construction in Metal* and *The Dictionary of Civil Engineering*.

List of projects (stimulated by these books and various stimulated minds in the bars around Steamer Point) which at one stage occupied Rimbaud's mind during the following months while he worked in Aden: Panama Canal. Tunnels under the Alps. Railways (South America, Harar, Siberia). Gold rushes (Australia, East Indies). Gun-running (Shoa). Ship salvaging (Cape of Good Hope). Opening up Marco Polo's overland route to the East. Suicide.

As the months passed, Rimbaud's old ascetic habits lapsed. The prophet returned from the wilderness is liable to find even a small town in a burnt-out volcanic crater on the edge of the desert at least slightly stimulating. And expensive. Rimbaud's desperation mounted as his savings dwindled and the collection of empty whisky bottles grew in the corner of his room.

On Thursday evenings I would dine with Old Man Vardy and his new French wife. A fascinating, truly French experience in this withered English garden of Aden.

Emelia Vardy was a real floozy. God only knows where the Old Man had picked her up. She'd receive me at the door dressed like Lady Macbeth in some third-rate Paris flea pit. Her long scarlet varnished fingernails would nip my biceps as she showed me in to the Old Man amongst the china, chintz curtains and antimacassars in the drawing room. And then she'd sit perched on the edge of the velveteen sofa, her dark eyes glowering vacuously (she must have been short-sighted or something), occasionally rising and pulling the bellcord to summon the maid for a short muttered consultation on the state of the cooking, while the Old Man hummed and hawed over his aperitif. Emelia Vardy had a flabby slack-lipped sensual face, which naturally settled into a sulky frown, until the Old Man considered it time to drop business and include her in the conversation. Cackling like a harridan she'd then shriek out her pleasantries, waving away the Old Man's pipe smoke with a bat-like hand. By this time the black ribbon round her neck would have begun to slip and her cheeks would have flushed to the same colour as the scarlet ribbons she knotted in her flowing black hair. Over dinner, her wide mouth (made up like a bayonet wound) would begin leering as she offered the steaming vegetables with much laying on of hands. Flinging herself about in deep-throated chortling abandon, her boots would bang into my calves under the table.

'And what are your plans for the future now, young man?' Vardy would inevitably ask, puffing out his smoke signals over the brandy as we sat round amongst the china ornaments once more.

'I've written to the *Société de Géographie* to see if they'd like an article on Harar. After all, I was the first man to live there.'

'The first *civilised* man,' chimed in her ladyship, emphasising her point with a delicate pat on my knee.

'I hear they pay well for articles about such places,' I'd continue.

Or: 'I've written to Paris to see if anyone's interested in financing an expedition to the Interior.'

Or: 'I had thought of setting out on a mission to Shoa.'

'But that's gun-running territory, young man.'

'You *are* a desperate man,' simpered the lady of the house, demurely lowering her mascara blackened eyelids. 'How terribly exciting!'

'Yes, gun-running,' I replied, holding the Old Man's eye, steadily.

'I'm not sure I approve, Arthur.'

'Or maybe slave trading. I've heard there's good money

in it, now that they're trying to clamp down.'

'What, shipping little virgins across the desert for all those nasty fat sheiks in their harems?' Emelia Vardy was in her element, wincing with delight. 'More coffee?' She leaned over my shoulder, brushing her fat tit against my ear. 'I think you're secretly a bit of an adventurer, you know.'

'No, Emelia dear,' Old Man Vardy struck up another match. Puff. Puff. 'Arthur's no adventurer, are you young man?'

'No. I'm here for the money.'

Vardy shook his head. 'No, no. That's not it, either. Not by a long shot. I know your type, young man. All these big plans, all these fantastic ideas. I know my Arthur, Emelia.' Puff. Puff. Suck. 'It's glory he's after. You want to make a name for yourself, young man, don't you? I can read you like an open book.'

'If I make a name for myself, it'll be for a profit.'

'He used to be a poet back in Paris. Did you know that, Emelia?'

Her ladyship was quite overcome. A real live poet in her 'salon'! At her scarlet fingertips, no less.

'I told you never to mention that, Vardy!' The wine, the greasy *pot au feu*, the brandy, that prick teasing bitch – and now this. The last straw. 'All that art shit is dead and done for. Dead, I tell you. A thing of the past . . . I told you . . . in strictest confidence . . . childish dreams!'

'Calm down, my dear.'

'Take your hands off me!'

'I hit the mark, all right.' The old fool chuckled. 'Poetry, exploring, making railways. Fame, Arthur – that's what it is, isn't it?'

Was I, Arthur Rimbaud, just going to sit here and be jeered at by fools?

'Take my advice, young man. Get yourself a nice bit of skirt like I've done, and forget all about these childish dreams . . . where are you going?'

I slammed the door behind me and blundered into the

darkened hallway. I was still fumbling amongst the coats when her ladyship came out, carrying a lamp. She closed the drawing room door behind her.

'Now that wasn't very polite, was it? If you go on like this I won't be able to ask you back, you know.'

More laying of hands. I stood, trembling, my mind clouding with lust as she ran her fingers over my flushed cheek, smiling insinuatingly.

'Were you really a poet?'

'I, I . . . Don't touch me!'

She was close to me now, her face lurid as leprosy in the dim light. I could feel her breath on my cheek, her sharp sweet perfume catching in my nostrils. The flame of the lamp trembled as she playfully pouted her fat blue lips. 'What's the matter?'

'I've got syphilis.'

Her eyelids flickered, and then she leered. 'You really are just a little boy, aren't you? In spite of all this desperate man act. Don't worry, I don't frighten that easily. I'm not one of your little slave virgins.'

'Leave me be!'

'Don't get excited, now, here's the door. I'm letting you out, if that's what you want.' She simpered as she drew open the door. 'So my wild man wants to become famous and carve a name for himself.'

Once, bored on my first Sunday morning in Africa, I'd wandered outside Alexandria and come across the ruins of the temple of Luxor. Sitting in the shade, for want of anything better to do I'd carved my name on one of the pillars, which then only had its lintels visible above the desert sand. Now, so I hear, they've excavated that temple and those lintels stand sixty feet above the ground.

Unknown to Emelia Vardy or himself, the name of Arthur Rimbaud was already carved in the sky, his cultural vandalism a riddle for the passing scholar in the desert.

However, rotting in Aden with my savings dribbling away, I wasn't interested in any wilful defacing of history. I hadn't got time for immortality; I was twenty-seven, I'd just pissed away another year of my life, I was desperate.

Dear Mother,
I am back in Aden. Thank you for the books *Construction in Metal* etc. This knowledge will be very useful to me in any country where there is no information whatsoever. I have various plans . . .

But what could I say? The *Société de Géographie* wasn't interested in the articles of a mere exporter's clerk in Aden. I had no influence and no written qualifications, no backer would ever invest in any expedition led by such a nonentity; and I hadn't got anything like the capital necessary to finance any gun-running project inland to the Kingdom of Shoa. One by one, all my plans had come to nothing.

Dear Mother,
I have no further plans. I have decided to accept M. Vardy's offer and return to Harar on a two year contract. This time I shall have a clerk of my own and be working independently of M. Vardy's brother. Besides trading, I shall be expected to mount a small expedition into the Interior to the south of the city to explore prospects for trade. My salary has been increased, and if I work hard – and I have learnt to work hard in Harar, Mother – I shall be able to save a considerable sum by the end of my contract.

Thanks for all your letters which were waiting here for me in Aden with my books. I'm glad to hear about your riding school project. I'm sure it's the best thing for those fields, and with prosperity increasing in Charleville I am certain you will be able to make a go of it.

Poor Isabelle, I can hardly imagine her now. So the little sister I once knew has now become a young girl, a marriageable lady. I hope her riding accident doesn't affect her prospects – I'm sure that her suitor will understand that she must rest to ensure a proper recovery.

Also, along with Father's old Arabic notebook *Plaisanteries et jeux de mots* etc – where could it be? the cellar perhaps? – could you send me the companion volume to *The Dictionary of Civil Engineering* – that is, *The Dictionary of Military Engineering*.

Your son,
Arthur.

7

On arrival at Zeyla, Rimbaud heard that the Kingdom of Shoa had revolted in the North. There were rumours of an Egyptian defeat, and although fighting was still several hundred miles to the north of Harar, no one could say exactly what was happening there. By helping unload the barter from the ship with his clerk, Sottiro, a rather green gangling lad who strongly objected to being made to do manual labour, Rimbaud managed to get his merchandise onto the monthly caravan for Harar, which happened to be leaving that day. Also on the caravan, Rimbaud noticed among other things a string of donkeys laden with empty coffins. Natural disasters such as war were obviously only an added incentive to the Abyssinian trading instinct.

Next day, Rimbaud returned to Aden to inform Old Man Vardy of the new state of affairs. With that barter already on its way, Old Man Vardy's reading of the situation would be a foregone conclusion.

'You'd better go straight back and try to catch up with that caravan, Arthur. You must know yourself, young man, that merchandise is worth a fortune. I'm sure this war is all alarmist talk. Harar will be quite safe. But whatever you do, don't risk that merchandise.'

Rimbaud returned to Zeyla to find his clerk on the tail end of a glorious binge which had accounted for almost his entire month's salary in advance. Something of an achievement considering the local prices of what passed for wine, women and song.

Forcing his way through the knot of spectators which

had gathered outside the local grog den to witness this spectacular marathon draw to its close, Rimbaud edged into the seat beside his clerk, gracelessly declining the favours offered him by the assembled ladies of the house.

'What the hell do you think you're playing at, Sottiro?'
'No t'going tr Huarah. Fuck Harar! Hva drink!'

Exercising an unusual display of tact, Rimbaud joined Sottiro in a drink. If I went back to Harar with no clerk, I'd be forced to work for that imbecile Alfred Vardy again, I realised.

With an air of only partially convincing conviviality, which he obviously found great difficulty in maintaining, Rimbaud proceeded by subtle and devious means to try and reason with his clerk.

Rimbaud's subtle and devious suggestions as to why Sottiro should accompany him to Harar.

– The war was mere alarmist talk. ('Fuck the war! Bang! Bang! Peeeeyouwong! You're dead!')

– There was a fortune just waiting to be made in Harar. ('Shust spenta fortune miself, actulair.')

– Things were even cheaper in Harar. ('Rearlee? I got it off this lil tart f'nuffing. She *loves* me! Donyou duckie?')

– In Harar, Sottiro wouldn't have to rely on the charity of professional ladies, he could buy a little girl of his own in the slave market and have her all to himself. ('Higgit! Higgurp! Oooouarrgh! . . . Shorry. Awful mess. Did it go over your trousers?')

– By the end of their two year contract in Harar, they would both be rich men. ('That's goodidea. A goo-ood i-dea. Why dun we go there then?')

After a somewhat clumsy midnight bathe in the local camel trough, Rimbaud helped his clerk onto the back of a horse and set off at once down the trail for Harar. I was in no mood for any second thoughts.

From the start of the journey, Sottiro merely functioned.

He neither spoke, nor showed any sign of life, rocking in his saddle like an automaton, his hands resting on his thighs with the reins dangling free. My questions remained unanswered as his half-closed eyes gazed forward into the empty distance. This behaviour I considered quite natural while it was still dark, and even understandable in the dim greyness of first light; but when the sun rose from behind the mountains, its pink light flaring across the plateau while the sand shifted filmily in the dawn breeze like the waves of some huge barren ocean, and there was still no sign of life from my travelling companion, I began to have my doubts.

Hangover? Guilt? Misgivings? Fatigue? While the heat of the day rose, I found myself surreptitiously studying his lean lank-haired skull as it nodded regularly at the end of his long swan's curve neck. What was going on in there?

He wasn't even wearing a hat, just a thin white shirt and his narrow striped clerk's trousers, the ends folded inside his socks. His pointed patent leather shoes, somewhat the worse for wear, dangled negligently through the stirrups, banging against the belly of his plodding horse. As the heat grew, and my head began to throb with the effects of the previous night, I found myself envying Sottiro. This boy was a marvel – he could ride through anything!

Towards the end of the first week, Rimbaud and Sottiro began to cover better distances, and Rimbaud soon abandoned the idea of sleeping by the regular water holes. At the end of the day, too exhausted for conversation, he and Sottiro would sit in the silence of the desert around the twisting smoke of their little fire as they chewed at their lentils and bully beef hash, guzzling their fill of lukewarm water from the goatskins. At night, Rimbaud would fall asleep watching the occasional shooting star flare noiselessly across the heavens, disappearing behind the high black silhouette of the mountain peaks which rose on either side of the desert trail, while Sottiro's regular breathing sounded beside him. Somewhere to the north, beyond those mountains, Yarousseau had met his end.

As the days passed, Rimbaud pushed up their daily average. This appeared to have no effect on Sottiro, who merely grunted in reply to Rimbaud's questions. There was still no sign ahead of the caravan with their barter.

'Well, with a bit of luck we might be there by tomorrow,' I told Sottiro as we sat around the flickering fire. It was after midnight, and in my exhausted state I'd hardly bothered to let the lentils boil for more than a few minutes. They were like pellets of shot, floating in the tepid stew of stringy salt beef.

'Tomorrow?' grunted Sottiro. 'But you said it took over twenty days.'

Conversation at last!

'We've been hurrying on a bit. Didn't you realise?'

'Nope.'

'Sottiro,' I leaned forward, raking the embers. 'Are you all right?'

'Yep.'

'I mean, you haven't got a grudge against me, or anything?'

'Nope.'

'Don't you ever talk, except when you're drunk?'

'Not much.'

I nodded. 'Quite right, why waste words.' I poked at the last fizzing sparks that had sprung up in the breeze. 'How are you finding the trip?'

'Fine.'

'Is it anything like you expected?'

'Nope.'

'Look Sottiro, are you sure you're all right? I mean, you don't wear a hat or anything.'

'I'm tired.'

'Sottiro, tell me. You *are* all right, aren't you?'

He yawned and stretched, and then lay back. I'd given up

all hope of him replying, when suddenly he blurted out: 'Arthur, you do know what you're up to, don't you?'

'Why, of course, Sottiro. Don't you worry about that.'

'I mean, I . . . I.' He was stuttering, as if making the effort to talk were draining him of all energy. 'What you said . . . about Harar, all that . . . it is true, isn't it?'

'Don't you worry, I'll make it true.'

'Two years. I'm giving you two years. I'll follow you anywhere, I'll do anything. I won't fail you. But you did promise me, at the end of two years . . .' He was still lying on his back, as if speaking to the heavens.

'At the end of two years we'll be rich. You see.'

The silent passage of a shooting star made a fitting astrological background to Rimbaud's confident prediction.

'You know what I'm doing, don't you?' continued Sottiro (now beginning to irritate Rimbaud slightly with his insistence). 'I'm giving you two years . . . I'll kill you, if this is all for nothing.' Sottiro's voice sounded devoid of all emotion, with that deliberate even finality of utter conviction.

Rimbaud lay in silence, finally turning on his side to face the last warmth of the dying fire. So now he was to be held responsible for his dreams. With his life, no less.

Next day we made slow progress, and I decided to press on through the night. The faint edges of the new day were already rising by the time we were approaching the walls of Harar. As we ascended slowly up the trail I could hear the murmurs of the waiting caravans around us in the gloom. The occasional camel bell tinkled and several of the traders were already up, huddled around small fires, wrapped like mummies against the chill while they sipped at their coffee. As the dawn rose behind us, casting a sudden spectacular light over the hillside, I made out the laden wagons, gilded wooden poles and embroidered canopies of the tents flapping gently like bunting in the breeze. Finally, just before the gate itself, we came to a string of donkeys loaded with empty coffins. At last we'd caught up with the caravan, and our barter.

Had Harar changed during Rimbaud's months of absence?

As he led his clerk into the city, Rimbaud's nostrils (fresh from the clear night air) breathed in once more the unique odour of the alleyways, his ears (for so long attuned to the silence of the wilderness) heard once again the rising hymn of commerce in the bazaars, and his eyes (dulled by the emptiness of the desert) feasted themselves at last on the cornucopia of treasures which littered the market place. Neither Vardy's new America nor the enclosed monastic city which Badjian foresaw with so much gloom and apprehension had yet come into being. Harar had not changed.

That afternoon, after unpacking, Rimbaud led his clerk on a conducted tour of the sights of this, the jewel of Lower Abyssinia. Sottiro loped silently at his side, occasionally peering with suspicion into some low den. Finally, Sottiro passed judgement.

'This place is just a dump! We'll never make a fortune here!'

'What did you expect? Gold lying in the gutters? We've come here to do business.'

'Well, when do we start buying?'

'There's no immediate hurry. Making a fortune takes time, you know.'

'You're not going to get out of it that easily. Where's the slave market?'

'Look, you can't just charge into these things. And besides, Old Man Vardy doesn't deal in slaves – not yet, at any rate.'

'I want that slave girl! You promised me!' Sottiro appeared to be getting quite agitated: a not particularly welcome sign of life.

'Is that all that kept you going across the desert?'

'You promised me you'd get me a slave girl, and then we'd make our fortune.'

'Just like that, eh?'

'I warned you.' Again that same deliberate, even tone: the implacable voice of the threatening child. 'I'll kill you if you don't.'

So off we went to the slave market to spend Sottiro's second month's wages in advance. After looking over the wares for half an hour or so, he selected a chubby little Gallas virgin. When the deal was done, Sottiro's long sullen face creased into a sly grin of satisfaction.

'Well, she's all yours,' I told him.

'And I can sell her back when I've finished with her?'

'Whenever you want to. Wait till the market's right and you might even make a profit on her.'

'Really? You mean you can even make a profit on girls up here?'

'You can make a profit on anything, if you try hard enough. Now come along, they're not going to wrap her up in a parcel for you.'

We started back to the palace.

'Arthur,' Sottiro turned to me with a pensive confidential air, 'I thought you were going to be a hard boss, I must admit. But I can see now that underneath it all you're really quite a decent fellow.'

I grunted, non-commitally.

Sottiro laid his hand on my shoulder. 'I'm sorry I threatened to kill you back there in the desert,' he continued, waxing jovial now, 'I can see now that it wasn't really necessary. We'll easily make a fortune in a place like this. They really are primitive up here, aren't they?'

Gently I removed his hand from my shoulder. He could keep his out of place charm for his little bundle of joy. I'd noticed the large curved dagger in its embroidered sheath hidden amongst his belongings when he'd unpacked that morning. Without further comment I led my gangling, overgrown child accomplice up the stairs to his room in the palace and left him to try out his new toy.

Would you end up by behaving like this? Buying yourself some little virgin in the market place? Or would perhaps a little boy be better? Sickened at the touchingly human scene which he had just witnessed, Rimbaud swore to himself that this time he would live entirely alone in Harar. His days of love were over. (*For ever, Verlaine. Never again, damn you.*)

That night, Vardy entertained Rimbaud and Sottiro to dinner in the state room. A state room transformed – in one corner at least. In this section of the desolate echoing splendour of former glories, the floorboards were now overlaid with rush mats, and by the door was a pool of blood red carpet, tastefully bordered with white silk tassels. The bare wooden chairs had been covered with cloth (green check: Vardy Trading Co, best barter) in delightful contrast to the table, which now also sported a cloth (red check: Vardy Trading Co, second best barter). Whilst on the wall behind the head of the table, above two crossed polished scimitars, hung an oil painting of Old Man Vardy, executed in the very latest impressionist style. Our budding interior decorator obviously had a definite talent in this direction. Either that, or the new style now served merely as a cloak for bungling ineptitude.

(*'Are we meant to accept these ravings as art? M. Rimbaud, whoever he may be, is certainly no poet – in spite of all M. Verlaine's protestations to the contrary. To be absurd is in the scope of everyone.'*)

'I thought a few civilising touches were necessary,' remarked Vardy, beaming with pride now that he could show off the fruits of his months of solitude. 'Local primitive, with certain up to date French flourishes.'

Sottiro was highly impressed; and as Bomba, clad in rustling new robes, served the meal (the same damp brain-sized dollops of rice and spiced gristle as ever) I could see that Vardy was likewise impressed with Sottiro, who had dressed for dinner in a tie and sprouted a set of effusive mannered gestures which he obviously considered appropriate to the occasion. I only wondered how Vardy would take to Sottiro's recent acquisition from the bazaar.

However, I was soon to be spared further suspense on this burning issue. When we'd finished our meal and were sitting over coffee, there suddenly arose from the direction of the kitchen quarters a series of high-pitched shrieks, interspersed with what was all too recognisably the sound of someone being beaten. Vardy frowned and began looking about him as if he'd just shifted his arse into a splinter poking up through one of his precious new covers, while Sottiro affected an expression of utter bewilderment, glancing over at me.

We listened as the sounds came closer, and then the door burst open to reveal Bomba dragging in the biting, wild-eyed, writhing figure of Sottiro's little bundle of joy. Sottiro immediately leapt to his feet, but made no further move as Bomba pushed her over towards Vardy. She fell in a crumpled whimpering heap at Vardy's feet.

The poor girl had apparently been found by Bomba scraping food from the dirty dishes in the kitchen; and Bomba, obviously unaware of her status, had taken her for a thief. I explained to Vardy who she was, while Sottiro fumbled with his chin, gazing up at the portrait of Old Man Vardy.

'I see,' replied Vardy, slightly put out. 'Well, I suppose it's only natural that a young man should want company in a place like this.' He turned to Sottiro, who lowered his gaze, still fingering his chin indecisively. 'But you're going to have to take her in hand, young man.'

'Take her in hand?' Sottiro was genuinely baffled.

'What he means, Sottiro,' I explained, in as understanding a tone as I could muster, 'is that she's not just going to lie in bed all day waiting for you to get a hard on.'

'But I thought . . .'

'Even slave girls need food.'

'Quite, quite,' replied Vardy, now definitely embarrassed at the turn the conversation had taken (in such civilised surroundings, too). 'She'll have to learn her duties,' he went on, 'take a turn at the cooking and give Bomba a hand. All that kind of thing.'

'Oh, I see.'

The girl continued sniffing, while Bomba simply stood there, hands on hips, glowering.

'But Arthur,' Sottiro turned to me appealingly, 'you never told me!'

He was actually trying to shift the blame onto me!

'Perhaps I assumed too much,' I began. 'The purpose of a slave girl is to supply *all* your basic needs. You do have other ones, I hope?'

'So she's a sort of servant, as well?'

'That's the great thing about Harar, Sottiro. Every day you're up here you learn something new.'

Vardy coughed. 'Young man – Sottiro, isn't it? – I understand how you feel. Perhaps Arthur didn't explain these things quite fully enough. We all have our needs, and I for one believe in respecting them. Every man has his own way of life. But you do have responsibilities too, you know. There's soon going to be quite a little community up here. We're just the pioneers. So it's vital that we establish a decent way of life. A norm. Upon us depends the whole future of this place.' This was an advance on the old Dijon egalitarianism – had Vardy been turning over the grey matter during his long hours of solitude? 'It's us pioneers who set the standard, young man.'

Vardy turned to Bomba, raising our hapless slave from her snivelling abjection with a helping hand. After a perfunctory attempt to put her at her ease, he told Bomba to take her away and give her something to eat. Bomba gloomily obeyed.

Sottiro, who had been watching every move with deep suspicion, turned to Vardy as the door closed behind them. 'But I only wanted,' he began, glancing morosely in my direction, 'Arthur promised me . . .'

'Quite, quite, young man.' Vardy was positively preening

himself in his new fatherly role. 'In fact I'm glad this has happened. If we're to establish a realistic norm up here, we must take into account *all* tastes . . .'

'Including the normal, I should hope. The poor kid only wanted an honest to God . . .'

Vardy irritatedly waved down my irrelevant interruption; he was in full flight now. '*All* tastes. But decently, and in a civilised manner. Without certain definite standards, God only knows what kind of Babylon our little community would grow into.'

I listened as he waffled on to an open-mouthed Sottiro. 'The Norm' was all too recognisably Vardy's – but where on earth had he picked up all this talk about standards?

'Things don't seem to have changed much,' I finally interrupted, unable to take any more, 'in spite of the fact there's a war on.'

Vardy coughed once more, visibly unsettled by my utter indifference to his little lecture. 'Yes, yes. A war . . . But I think everything's pretty much under control up here. After all, it's only in the north that things have really boiled over. And it's always been rather primitive up there, so I hear.'

'Badjian never thought so. He reckoned it was a case of repression. And bloody savage, at that.'

'By the way,' Vardy fluffed at his moustache, still keeping an eye on Sottiro, who was playing the fascinated audience – presumably in an attempt to re-establish himself. 'Our Caucasian character has gone to ground. I haven't seen your friend Badjian for a couple of months now.'

'Really?'

'Several weeks after you left he resigned his commission. He's living up in the north of town, so I hear. He doesn't hang around the market place any more.'

And what was Badjian up to now, I wondered. All his predictions about Shoa had proved right enough – what of his little vision of the future of Harar? 'Have they found a replacement for him?' I asked, 'or is our occupying army now operating without the benefits of modern medicine?'

'I hear he still calls in. Apparently they just can't find any replacements at the moment. The war, I suppose. Here,' he leaned across confidentially, 'I did hear a rather juicy bit about him a few days ago, though. Do you know what? He's been seen slipping in through the side door of the Emir's harem.'

'Badjian?'

'Yes. Rumour has it that the Emir has gone and got himself a dose of the local disease.'

'Oh?' remarked Sottiro from the other side of the table, still playing the fascinated listener. A taxing role in view of his utter ignorance of the subject under discussion. 'The local disease? What's that?'

'Syphilis, young man,' murmured Vardy, in a voice just above a whisper. 'The place is rife with it.' I received a stern cautionary glance. 'Now perhaps you'll see why we need to observe certain definite standards.'

Sottiro looked at him with a pinched frown of incomprehension, an expression which was already becoming something of a regularity on the noble Italianate features of my second-in-conmmand.

But Vardy didn't deign to lower his standards sufficient for him to repeat the word a second time.

'Civilis?' muttered Sottiro enquiringly, his features still creased with befuddlement.

'*Syphilis!*' I yelled at him, unable to restrain myself a moment longer. I could see that I was going to have to encourage my clerk's morose silences; Sottiro incommunicado was a source of positive joy, compared with this performance.

Vardy reacted to my yell as if the splinter had just sharply reasserted its presence through the lining of his chair. And then I heard the patter of feet in the corridor.

Bomba appeared grinning at the door.

'No, no, Bomba. Go away!' Vardy waved him off with an aggravated flourish. 'Arthur, please!' he turned to me. 'We are at table.'

Then we both noticed Sottiro, whose head had sunk to the table. He appeared to be fumbling agitatedly with something below the tablecloth. 'Oh no,' he whimpered, and then looked up, baring his teeth in what seemed to be rage. 'Arthur, I'll *kill* you!'

'Calm down, young man, Sottiro. What on earth's the matter?'

'Kill you! Kill you!' Sottiro was beside himself, his face twitching with fury.

'Don't worry, Sottiro,' I began, as forcefully reassuring as I could, 'your slave girl was quite clean. She was a virgin.'

'What?' he hesitated. 'Was she?'

'Well, you ought to know.'

Again, that pinched frown. 'Yes,' he muttered, gazing into the middle distance as if he were performing some great feat of memory, 'I suppose she must have been.'

'Young man, Sottiro, you're going to have to learn to curb your rash ways. I do wish you wouldn't act on impulse, so. You can't afford it. Not up here. You'll tire yourself out in no time in this atmosphere. By the way,' Vardy turned back to me (if he twiddled that moustache of his much longer he wouldn't have a hair left in it), 'talking of tiring yourself out, reminds me. We're not on our own up here any more. Forgetting our Caucasian character, that is. We've got a new addition. He's a funny, tired old chap. Pleasant enough, though. And got a mind of his own, too. He's called Grimes; he's an Englishman. You must have a talk with him some time, Arthur, he's a very intelligent man.'

'What's he doing up here?' I asked.

'Trade. The same as us.'

'So we've got competition.'

'Arthur, why must you always look on the black side? Can't you see, this is the beginning. Harar is on the map, now. It's opening up. Fortunes are going to be made out of this place in the next few years.'

Sottiro, now that he had recovered, was all ears. 'Fortunes? In the next few years?' He leaned forward, earnestly.

'About how much do you suppose someone could make in the next *two* years?'

'Two years?' replied Vardy, mystified at being pinned down to such exactitude.

'Yes. Two years.' The scintillating exchange continued apace. 'That's how long I'm staying up here. I want to make as much as I can in two years,' explained Sottiro seriously. This was definitely his subject – no need to feign interest here.

'Young man, Sottiro, by that time I hope we'll have cured you of your rash ways. After a couple of years you may well find you want to stay up here for good.'

'Can't you just give me an idea?' persisted Sottiro. '*Approximately* how much?'

But Vardy was not to be committed to the actual. 'I know you clerks like to have these things all laid out in facts and figures, but accounting isn't everything. The benefits I'm talking about aren't all just cash profits.'

'But Arthur promised me!'

'Like the little slave girl, eh?' Vardy chuckled. 'Don't you go telling Grimes that's all you came up here for. He'd throw a fit.'

So that's where Vardy had picked up all this talk about standards. Obviously there'd been rather more to his evening of domestic bliss than sewing up his precious covers and dabbing away at Old Man Vardy's portrait.

To forget, to impose, to approximate, to compromise, to bargain, to live, no less: the mad sing in unison. As ever. And the collective fiction of those persuaded of their own reasonable motives is written in the transactions of bedlam. So Rimbaud returned once again to do business in the market place at Harar.

All my juvenile plans come to nothing, I would return home after my summer wanderings across Europe. Weary and starving I would tramp back across the fields towards the farm. But in my absence the old familiar landmarks would have assumed this alien patina of unfamiliarity. The green growing fields of spring had long since been reaped, the stubble burnt or ploughed back into the earth; the high grass in the hedgerows had turned yellow and strawlike, crackling underfoot so that when I closed my eyes the sound of my boots became that of pressing wind-driven flames; and the brambles, twisting out over the dry caked mud of the footpaths, contained only the occasional black withered berry. The bitterness bit through the sweetness leaving me thirsty, and the tiny pips stuck in my teeth. The haystacks had grown around the farmhouses, and the sheep were sheared and coughing. What I recognised, I somehow no longer recognised. Only Mother, her face set, her eyes searching my face as she held my head at a distance between her harvest-coarsened hands, would remain the same.

Business as usual. And so the daily bargaining in the market place began once more.

That night Rimbaud declined Vardy's offer of 'a place at table', although he was assured that a place would always be kept for him 'for when you have at last come to understand the necessity for these social commonplaces'. Sottiro, on the other hand, took up the offer with alacrity, Rimbaud noticed.

Whatever insanity it was that Rimbaud found himself surrendering his daylight hours to, he was determined that the nights should remain his.

When Mother and Isabelle had gone to bed, I would take my lamp across the yard to the granary and settle down to my poems, shivering as a dog barked occasionally from one of the nearby farms, setting off a chain of distant barkings across the fields into the night.

In Harar, as the dogs barked into the night on the ramparts, I studied *Construction in Metal* and *Practical Chemical Analysis* (Mother's latest concession). The latter was of particular importance now. And not just for analysing the contents of any hollow ivory I happened to find myself landed with, either. The techniques I could learn from it would be of inestimable value on my planned trading expedition to the south. Although the area was still uncharted, and indeed unpenetrated as yet by any European explorers, I had good reason to believe it was rife with possibilities. And possibilities far beyond the banalities of simple 'trading prospects' (the sole redeeming feature of all Africa in the eyes of Old Man Vardy.)

No, my dreams of opening up Harar with a railway had merely been scratching the surface, I realised. I'd been living here like a blind man, merely studying techniques which would have guided me in my blindness. Tunnels, cuttings, embankments, excavations — what were these? How could I have failed to see? Nothing other than the techniques of mining. If I could only see the ground I covered on that expedition through a miner's eyes, then the earth was mine, and all that I could find in it.

Painstakingly I noted through the chapters on geological analysis, while in my imagination I conjured up, with the aid of those solid earthbound words, pictures of ore-bearing terrain. Tinstone territories, blue clay mountains and ridges of lode-bearing ore cleft by seams of metallic crystal, rose before my mind's eye. I learned the methods of distinguishing Galena from Black Jack and Lead Glance. The simplicities of copper mining gave me great hopes: the natives themselves would be wearing worked ornaments if there was any of that about. They might well have been picking at the surface of huge underground fields which had been lying since the earth's beginning, waiting. Where silver and gold were concerned, my hopes were less sanguine. They both occurred in natural form and were likely to have been discovered and exploited well before I happened along. Still, I determined to keep an eye open for the appropriate ores and found myself once again imagining such landscapes. The glint of silver in a high face, or the flicker of gold in the bed of a mountain stream — such were the wildest dreams of my long nights, interrupted only by the occasional sudden outburst of yelping from the ramparts. The jackals and lions were on the increase that season, and the dogs were more restless than ever.

I made a list of the necessary chemicals I would need for my analysis and wrote post haste home to Mother.

> ... don't worry, Mother, I know enough now to tell Fool's Gold from the real thing. I shall travel those southern territories with only certain fixed things in mind. You see, now that I am beginning to understand the exact constitution of the elements that are in the earth, I will soon be able to detect at a glance which ones are valuable. But it will of necessity remain largely guesswork until you can send me the appropriate equipment and substances – otherwise in my sampling I may well be forced to load myself down with God only knows what amount of worthless stuff.
>
> I have great hopes, Mother, but don't hold open too many expectations. My hopes have been dashed too many times now for me to be able to afford to commit myself to any rash optimism. I am well aware that for the most part I will be travelling over barren, worthless terrain and merely making contact with primitive natives for the purposes of opening up trade. The events of the last few years have taught me resignation, and I know that as for the rest – these hopes which I cannot rid myself of – they have only the remotest chance of materialising. I am living an extremely simple life, saving even more scrupulously than ever before, and slowly my small fortune increases ...

However self-denial, like self-abuse, renders no sense permanently blind. Even in Harar, that crass end of all appetites, Rimbaud was to find, as many a fasting rapist or saint serving out his time had found out before him, that tastes once evoked linger as long as life itself. Emelia Vardy's *pot au feu*. Mother's blackberry curds. Isabelle's lapin biscuits fresh from the oven. English stout: harsh and creamy, tasting of the mould of old wooden barrels (*ah*,

Verlaine, those days in the Tottenham Court Road). Oysters: flavour of the sea itself (gnarled empty shells scattered over the pub table amongst the pint pots as you read your poems . . . Nevermore. Memory, memory, what do you want of me? . . . We were alone together, walking in a dream . . .) All these, and others, rose again to intoxicate Rimbaud as he attempted once more to pare his life down to his one single resolve.

Fleeing from the smells of camel dung and rotting ill-cured hides in the market place, I would indulge my deprived hunger with the wafting odours from the gruel dens and sweetmeat booths of the bazzaar.

. . . we were alone together, walking in a dream, our hair and thoughts in the wind.

Why am I forced to remember these things?

Do you recall our old ecstasy?

No . . . No!

Does your heart still beat at the mere mention of my name?

No, Verlaine. Here I must live in oblivion. Here I am discovering new ecstasies, new sciences, new names.

'Hello there!'

'Who the hell are you?'

'Grimes is the name.' And so the name takes on flesh.

My hand was grasped by this tall, broad-shouldered character dressed in long baggy khaki pants and a khaki shirt whose short sleeves stuck out like pennants. On his head he wore a battered, broad-rimmed green felt hat whose shadow obscured his face.

'Didn't you hear me calling? You walked right past me. I was just snatching a bit of luncheon in one of the local pot houses.'

I nodded perfunctorily as he gestured to his empty table. So now life in Harar was going to be enlivened by this scarecrow. I followed him back to his table and took a seat. Just the sort who would impress Vardy – right down to the polished leather of his obviously home-made boots.

'Care to join me in some lung hash?' he asked, laying aside his hat now that we were in the shade of the awning. His face was puce beneath the whispy sweat-plastered crinkles of his thinning grey hair and his corrugated blotchily-freckled forehead. The lines scouring his rough skin fanned out from his scowling flesh-wrinkled eyes like a drooping pair of whiskers, and the lower half of his long heavy-boned face was dominated by the slack-skinned droop of his mouth: a deep downward-curving scar, like on a death mask. The whole impression was one of ugly violent appetites, barely contained.

'Try some,' he began hoarsely, indicating his wooden bowl of lung hash, 'it's surprisingly good.'

Craving after exotica though I may have been, the sight of those white rubbery strips, spongey with pores, floating in that green watery sauce, was enough to still all my appetites.

'You were the first man up here, I understand,' this Grimes went on, speaking between large spilling jaw-grinding mouthfuls. 'That's what I admire. The pioneer spirit. Vardy told me all about you. Self-reliance, that's the thing.' He chuckled away to himself at some private joke, carving his spoon around a morsel of floating offal as he drained the green sauce. 'And a good show you made of it too, so I hear.'

'Good show? I saved *nothing*! I left this place as good as broke.'

'I'm not talking about business. I mean what you made out of your life up here. It's all too easy to go to pot on your own in a place like this.' Those white bulbous gobbets swimming in the gradually subsiding tide of bilious sauce: I'd seen them somewhere before, I could swear it.

'You do have to set yourself certain definite standards,' I hazarded.

'Exactly!' I'd hit the mark all right. Grimes beamed – a broad, vicious, wistful expression: not unlike that assumed by the larger gorillas. 'That's what I always say . . .' Standards to the right of them, standards to the left of them: I listened as Grimes went on to demonstrate the truth of his preliminary remark. Vardy must have lapped it up '. . . a man's no better than a savage unless he restricts himself according to certain definite standards.'

'That's tripe!' I suddenly recognised the foul mess; I'd seen it served in the pubs along the Tottenham Court Road.

'*What?*' The gorilla scowled, leaning forward as if on the point of scratching under his armpits. 'Tripe?'

'That lung hash – it's tripe. Isn't that what you call it in England?'

His face creased into an even more intense frown, and then his lips parted to emit the true gorilla call. Grimes was laughing. 'That's another thing I heard about you from Vardy. Sense of humour. Very good! Very funny about you and that missionary chap!'

'What – Yarousseau? What about him?'

'Keep those missionary wallahs in their place. I quite agree.'

'He happens to be dead. If you consider that a joke . . .'

It was, apparently. Enough to choke him on his nauseating tripe.

'Look,' I began. 'I'll have you know Yarousseau was a very close friend of mine.'

The essential ingredient of all bad jokes, the hilarious misunderstanding, now unfolded itself. 'You mean . . .?' 'I mean . . .' 'But I meant . . .' '*Oh!* I thought you meant . . .'

Sparing himself further agonies of Anglo-Saxon humour, the narrator will now extricate the facts from their hilarious setting.

The Resurrection of Yarousseau

Rimbaud's letter announcing Yarousseau's untimely decease at the hands of the unconverted had caused a great stir in ecclesiastical circles, and in no time an emissary had been despatched to Harar to gather more details. He had arrived unannounced and immediately run into 'our senior citizen Dr Badjian' apparently risen from the dead. Badjian had read through Rimbaud's letter proclaiming his death, and been completely baffled. Seeing references to Vardy's 'recurrent illness' he'd immediately suspected that Rimbaud had kept the whole truth back from him, that Yarousseau had been fighting a losing battle trying to cure both Bomba and Vardy of syphilis while they both reinfected one another. Bewildered, and more than slightly curious, Badjian had allowed the priest, a middle-aged rather intense, excitable Spaniard, to persuade him to take them both down to 'the quarter behind the palace where Father Yarousseau did so much of his work', where Yarousseau's name had apparently 'become a by-word for love'. The priest had been horrified on seeing the brothels, and even more disturbed at Dr Badjian's familiarity with their inmates – many of whom were regular private patients. There'd then followed a slight misunderstanding between them. The priest had wanted to be shown the shrine which had been set up to the local martyr, Yarousseau; and Badjian, assuming he meant the local Moslem shrine, had taken the hapless priest there. The priest had been aghast, almost losing control of himself by now, as he began to understand what he thought had happened. So this explained Yarousseau's protection from the Emir, who was 'not yet converted from the errors of his heretic faith'. Yarousseau had been converted to the unspeakable Islam! Which meant that 'the notorious Arthur Rimbaud', Yarousseau's most famous convert, must have been converted to Islam too! And what of M. Vardy, whom Yarousseau had treated for his illness? What faith was M. Vardy now, the priest wanted to know. Had he too been converted by this devil in disguise? Badjian was by this time completely at a loss. He had no idea *what* faith M. Vardy held, he told the priest. Immediately the priest had asked to see M. Vardy – perhaps it wasn't too late. Resigned to the curiously excitable ways of this man of God, Badjian had led him to the palace. There the priest had burst in to find Vardy in the middle of his early morning physical jerks, prostrate, doing press-ups on the state room floor, and immediately assumed the worst. Another lapsed Catholic bowing to Mecca. Yarousseau must have been the devil incarnate – worse still, he'd been a Moslem missionary. The entire European community had become Mohammedan overnight.

And what was Badjian's faith, the priest had finally demanded. Badjian's reply had apparently been noncommittal, with a hint of Moslem affiliations for professional military reasons. But he had been born a Christian, he added, as far as he could remember. That did it. The place was obviously a hot-bed of lapsed Christians – seething with apostasy. Yarousseau's departed soul must be excommunicated, the facts transmitted in full detail to the hierarchy.

The priest had stayed three days in the palace, avoiding all contact with Vardy, busily scribbling away at his report. And then, on the morning when the caravan he intended to take down to Zeyla had arrived in the market place, who should he see on the end of it but Yarousseau – his robes in tatters, delirious, waving a canteen of holy water, after having been found in the wilderness by one of the outriders, more dead than alive.

In a rousing ceremony before the gathered crowds, the priest had excommunicated Yarousseau on the spot, calling down on God to exorcise the devil and damning him with the curse of the Almighty.

Eventually Badjian had come to the rescue and taken Yarousseau back to his old room. The priest had apparently followed them at a distance, and eventually summoned up the courage to enter the devil's quarters. There he'd found Yarousseau on his knees before the little altar he'd set up in the corner, praying to God for his deliverance from the wilderness. What kind of a devil was this Yarousseau? The priest had fled in terror of his life.

Finally, two days later when Yarousseau had recovered, the priest had called to see him, determined to extract an explanation and confirm Yarousseau in his excommunication. After a series of heated misunderstandings (of a decidedly un-English and unhumorous character) Yarousseau had convinced the priest that he was still a Christian, and always had been one, and that in fact he'd merely been away on a mission to convert the Gallas tribes. Was he, the priest, perhaps muddling Yarousseau with someone else, Yarousseau asked him. Further 'continental' misunderstandings ensued and the priest had finally come to the conclusion that Harar was a city of the devil, a place of evil spirits not fit for any Christian. Yarousseau had been re-baptised and despatched forthwith on another mission to the Interior, warned to stay well clear of Harar except for the purpose of making contact with the outside world. Thereupon poor Yarousseau, hardly recovered, had set off once more into the Interior, complete with donkey and canteens of holy water, while the priest, after registering his disgust to a bewildered Vardy, had left on the first available caravan for Zeyla.

Rimbaud's conclusion: Yarousseau was dead. For sure, now. No man could expect that miracle in the wilderness to be repeated a second time.

'On the contrary,' replied Grimes, 'I hear he's down south near the Ogaden somewhere. He comes in once every few months to collect his mail. I think he was in a couple of weeks ago, now you come to mention it.'

Rimbaud's revised conclusion: Miracles could not be expected to become the norm. This supernatural routine couldn't guarantee a life indefinitely.

'It's my guess,' continued Grimes, 'that he's holed up in some friendly little village, just sitting it out.'

There and then, Rimbaud decided that whatever other purposes he might accumulate for his projected expedition to the south (along with trading, establishing business contacts, prospecting, excavating, furthering his scientific researches etc etc) the prevailing purpose would be to search out Yarousseau. And bring him back. Alive, if possible. Rimbaud's thoughts broke the surface with the traditional liturgical refrain. 'What have I done? I've got a life on my hands. I'm the one who's to blame for all this.'

'I'm afraid I don't agree with you there at all,' Grimes began fanning his overheated face with his large green felt hat. 'Those missionaries are the ruin of any decent place. You carve your little niche at the back of beyond, and then what do they do? Move in and try to show you up. No, once they start to arrive it's time to leave.'

'So you're not staying long up here?'

Grimes sighed, heavily. 'No, young fellow, I'm too old to be moving on again now. This place is my last chance. I'm here for good. If I make a pile, I may go back to the old country to die. If not . . .' He rested his hat on his knees, nodding meditatively, finally coming to life with a wistful grin accompanied by a rueful shrug. 'That's why I appreciate the standard you set up here. Make this place a place where a man can be what a man *can* be – not just some haven for the misfits of this world. I've seen them, I can tell you. Not that I'm a puritan, young fellow. Don't get me wrong there. I was capable of letting my hair down with the rest of them, when I had some. When there was occasion for it, that is. And I'm partial to the odd snifter or two of the local hooch of an evening, I'll give you that. It's just that I think it's essential that one preserves oneself.' If the Harari firewater and Grimes' face were anything to go by, pickling himself would have been a more accurate description.

'You've no idea exactly where Yarousseau is?' I allowed my thoughts to surface once more.

'Haven't a clue. Down south somewhere, that's all I know. Grimes mechanically acknowledged his partner's complementary obsession. 'That fellow's contact with the outside world is pretty tenuous.'

I'd have to ask around the caravans. Anything coming up from the Interior.

'Talking about contact with the outside world,' remarked

Grimes, fanning himself once more. 'How's everything getting on out there these days?'

'Same as ever,' I replied. I was still trying to place myself in Yarousseau's shoes. What would he do? The first trip had taught him his lesson – he'd obviously know this second time that it was mainly a matter of survival, enduring as best one could.

'Same as ever? Come, come, young fellow. There must be more to it than that?' What did this haw-hawing gorilla want now? 'I believe that in a place like this it's essential to keep a link with the outside world,' he continued, undeterred. 'On your own you can start to lead yourself up the garden path with all manner of strange ideas. It's only contact with civilisation that keeps you normal. Besides, there's no real escaping from it, everything concerns you in the end these days. One way or the other. Why, we might all be at war without knowing it. If we didn't keep contact, that is.'

Rimbaud sighed, scowling morosely at the passing throng. 'You think so? Contact with the outside world doesn't seem to have done poor Yarousseau much good.'

8

It was inevitable, I suppose, that there were going to be problems where the accounts were concerned.

'But what's the point of putting down the price you *didn't* pay?' insisted Sottiro; where extra work was concerned, this boy was willing to fight to the last gasp.

'Because that column is my estimate of the standard price.'

'Why on earth put it down in the accounts? It only shows you've been cheated.'

'It's the only way I can tell if I'm getting better. If I get overcharged on one load, I know then that I have to make it up on something else.'

'But what have Harar standard prices got to do with the prices the stuff will fetch outside? They're what you use to judge the profit.'

'The Harar standard prices matter to *me*!' This was my final word. 'Now get cracking!'

To work off my irritation I returned to the cellar and began heaving bales out ready for the next caravan. Gradually, as the sweat started to drip from my face and the stench of hides began getting into my clothes, my hair, my skin even, my anger dissolved. How could I expect the boy to understand all the foibles of my own particular piecemeal accounting system straight away? Why, it had taken *me* time enough to evolve – partly from bits picked up here and there during my old odd-jobbing days around Europe, partly from snatches of garbled know-how I'd acquired during my spells at the Vardy store in Aden, and partly from my own mental processes as I'd estimated, calculated, threatened, cajoled and harangued in the market place. Without those accounts – my own particular accounts – in mind as I bargained, I knew I was lost out there amongst those thieving bastards.

I began lugging out the gum bales onto the trolley, dragging them load by load up the ramp towards the yard. If it was still as hard as this for you, doing your second spell in this place, how must it be for Sottiro, only just arrived here?

'*My life is worn out. Time now only for frantic deception. To amuse oneself dreaming of fantastic universes, complaining and bickering with this charade of a world . . . You who claim that the sleeping dead can dream marvels, seeing the cast-off vestments of truth itself in their graveyard fevers, how do you account for this slumbering which is called mortality?*'

For you this hell was familiar territory. (Hadn't you been about Sottiro's age when you wrote those words?) Panting, I rolled the last barrels of coffee up the dim causeway towards the light. Give the lad a chance. Show him what happens, explain the business to him, let him see what it is he's accounting for.

'Sottiro, you're free!' I burst in on him as he sat, pen poised, brow furrowed, over the mystic rows of hieroglyphs. 'For the rest of the day you can come and watch me make a fool of myself in the market place.'

He looked up, narrowing his eyes suspiciously.

'You might even be able to help me out,' I added, by way of encouragement.

'Oh no, that's your job.' No one was going to trick our Sottiro into overloading himself with work, that was for sure.

'I just thought that if you saw what was involved you might have some idea as to how we can simplify my rather crummy accounting methods.'

'Simplify them?' His eyebrows rose, quizzically.

So Rimbaud introduced his clerk to the practices of the market place at Harar.

'You know, Arthur,' began Sottiro, as we made our way past the caravaners' pitches, 'I think I'm going to enjoy myself here. It struck me only just now, these are probably going to be the best years of my life.'

Perhaps I'd underestimated Sottiro's resources where life in Harar was concerned. Around us the descant of discord was rising to its mid-morning apotheosis amongst the fluttering booths and crowded stalls.

'Arthur,' Sottiro caught my elbow excitedly, 'this is how I always dreamt it would be.'

The landscape of my worst nightmares, no less.

'A city like this, Arthur, with nothing to hold us back!'

Utopia at last!

The counterpoint catcalls of the crowd suddenly swelled into one vast multi-throated roar as they surged forward. With tears of sheer joy dribbling unchecked down his cheeks, young Arthur Rimbaud had been carried on down the street. Before him the backs of the crowd scrambled up over the barricade, and then he too was pulling at the rubble of cobblestones, clambering. A fleeting glimpse of a turbulent river of heads before him, and then he was being swept on, down, on down the street until the houses on either side gave way to the vast resonant plain-song ocean of the Place de la Bastille. The echoing intensity of the voices around him flared out amongst the liturgical choruses from the far-flung corners, and then gradually the dissonances coalesced into one pulsating, multitudinous accord.

'*Vie – la – co – une – mune – vive – la – vie – une – vive -- la – com – une – vive – la – commune!* Vive La Commune! *VIVE LA COMMUNE!*'

Dumb, his voice no more than the rasping in his inflamed throat, the throbbing from this vast cloud of sound borne aloft by a hundred thousand tongues blurring in his eardrums, its icy electric edges pressing down over his skull, Arthur saw, through tear-blurred eyes, beyond the waving, seething turmoil of heads, banners, pikes, rifles, sticks, fists, shoulder-carried women and brandishing swords, the arms of the distant orator raised patiently above his head, as if surrendering at gunpoint.

After an ecstasy of chaos – all words splintered into a foam of gutteral fragments – the roar ebbed, swirling into silence as the voices of the people subsided into their throats.

'Citizens of Paris!' The fragile reedy voice danced at the end of the wind, threatened at every moment by the undertow of murmurs. 'Citizens of the Commune! Communards! Paris is ours!'

The thunderous breaker of sound burst as the orator flung his torn red shirtsleeves into the air. The breeze fluttered through the enormous red flag behind him, unfurling it, so that for a moment the orator's red shirt became a part of it, with only the whiteness of his tiny upturned face standing out against the rippling background, which curved in a billowing arc over the distant roofs like some lurid blood-red rainbow reaching into the sky.

The roar dashed itself into discord, subsiding, raggedly.

'. . . all that we want. Nothing can stop us now, fellow communards. The barricades are manned against our enemies, who surround us . . . but we must remember, we have enemies within . . . who will . . .'

The tide turned, surging forward on a violent waving breaker of anger, the banners sweeping against the empty sky . . .

Now where had Sottiro got to? I turned to find him standing several paces behind me, gazing apparently in openmouthed rapture at the spectacle of the assembled citizens of his utopia. However, as I approached him, I saw that Sottiro's attention was in fact focussed on one particular figure whose appearance stood out even in this bedlam of scrummaging motley. Rimbaud's eyes boggled as he caught sight of Badjian striding towards him through the crowd.

Gone was the old tired army khaki, and in its place a shining black suit edged in broad gold facing, complete with gold epaulets. The impression would have been halfway between that of a Balkan Admiral-of-the-fleet and a ringmaster in a third-rate German circus, if it hadn't been for the cut of the suit. Obviously it had been run up from some tribal cloth by a local tailor who had never seen a European suit and had been forced to follow Badjian's specifications. Unfortunately, after seven years garrisoned at Harar, Badjian's notion of elegance had diverged somewhat from the course of European high fashion, with the result that what he was now wearing would probably have offended all standards of accepted taste throughout the length and breadth of Europe, or indeed wherever cloth was turned into suits.

Badjian stood, posing proudly, as I gazed in awe.

'My civilian uniform,' he informed me, holding out his arm for me to feel the cloth.

'You could only get away with it in Harar, Badjian!'

'Perhaps, my friend.' He was definitely offended by my lack of appreciative enthusiasm. 'But my business is in Harar. And here one has to cut a figure according to local tastes. Besides, I have seen similar things. In Paris, for instance, suits like this were once very much the fashion.'

'A discontinued line, I can assure you . . . By the way,' I continued, 'you must meet my clerk. Sottiro – Badjian.' I introduced them. Badjian's spirits revived slightly as he shook Sottiro's hand. Sottiro was visibly spellbound by such a display of magnificence in the market place of Harar.

Turning to me with a flourish, Badjian started forward. Sottiro followed, his eyes glued to this spectacle of sartorial parody as Badjian self-consciously assumed the necessary cuff-shooting elegance for his role.

Which still retained its deeper cutting edge, however.

'I am sorry if I disappoint you, my friend,' he began, with an air of shifty sharp-eyed coolness, 'by my continuing presence.'

'Don't take it to heart, Badjian. We all have our tastes.

But this was apparently another of those misunderstandings – without which life at Harar, or life on the stage of the traditional French bedroom farce, or even life at the grand international conference table, would not be what it is. Rimbaud was of course referring to Badjian's spectacular appearance: a matter of purely fashionable taste. On the other hand Badjian, so it transpired, was referring to Rimbaud's celebrated letter to Yarousseau's superiors, in which Rimbaud had rather prematurely announced the disappearance of senior citizen Dr Badjian from the face of the earth: a matter of slightly more ethical tastes.

'It was only a joke, Badjian. It didn't mean anything. Nothing personal.'

'Nothing means nothing, my friend,' replied Badjian solemnly. 'I am surprised at a man like you . . .'

Badjian's words tailed away into the surrounding hubbub, and the two of us continued in silence on our leisurely amble through the market place, accompanied at an admiring distance by Sottiro (still taking discreet perspectives of this new-found wonder of Harar).

And why had Rimbaud returned to Harar, Badjian eventually wondered, with something of his old nature now returning to enliven his manner.

'I came back simply because there was nothing else. Everything came to nothing.'

But hadn't Rimbaud considered Badjian's plans for Shoa? (Gun-running to the North, business with King Menelek, vast profits, further business . . . fortune assured, rich men etc etc.)

'You seem to forget there's a war on, you bloody oaf.'

Yet this only increased the stakes, it seemed.

'What, risk my neck trying to make quick profits out of some desperate tin-pot king? You've got a hope, Badjian.'

But there was so much more to gun-running under the present circumstances than mere quick profits. Here was the chance of a lifetime for anyone enterprising enough (or rash enough) to involve himself in the whirligig of changing fortunes. Didn't Rimbaud realise the balance of power in the whole of Lower Abyssinia was now at stake?

'I know, Badjian.' Here, at least, Rimbaud was one step ahead – armed as he was with several differing appraisals of the situation: Badjian's earliest outline of future possibilities, Old Man Vardy's more worldly perspective from the vantage point of Aden, Alfred Vardy's somewhat quietist domestic viewpoint on the spot, and Rimbaud's own understanding of the conditions necessary for the realisation of his latest scientifically inspired dreams. Rimbaud had concocted his own plan, he explained.

Rimbaud's plan

Rimbaud's fortune lay in Harar, or nowhere, he had decided. And he wasn't going to be cheated out of his last chance by any bunch of revolting savages. He had sent home for the latest edition of *The Dictionary of Military Engineering*. As soon as it arrived, he would make plans for the defence of Harar and take them to the Governor. The city could easily be defended by a mere handful of men, if necessary. Napoleon himself couldn't defeat science. Why, Rimbaud would defend the city single-handed if need be.

'Then you will be defeated by the oldest method of all, my friend. In the same way as the Emir's plan for a closed city is doomed. You must realise . . .'

Badjian's new appraisal of the scene (in the light of recent events).

King Menelek of Shoa was the popular hero of the moment, the people's man. Harar would only remain under Egyptian control, or a closed city (or even a city defended single-handed by scientific methods) for as long as it took Menelek's representative to reach the gates. Since the passing away of the old closed city, the people of Harar had come to understand the possibilities of freedom for the first time in their history, and at the mere call of Menelek's name they would rise to a man. The Egyptians, or the Emir (or the man of science) would be deposed, and then Menelek would appoint his own Governor, together with a completely new hierarchy. Here was where Badjian came in – for the transfer of power would guarantee that whoever held a position in the new hierarchy was bound to make his fortune. The men who would make up this new ruling order would require but one qualification – that they had shown themselves to be Menelek's friend against the Egyptians (or whoever else held Harar).

'Well, that rather rules you out, Badjian, doesn't it?'

'And why, my friend?'

'I'd have thought ten years' service with the Egyptian army would have been disqualification enough.'

Badjian flicked the dust from his cuffs with disdain. This was evidently a mere trifle.

Badjian strolled on in silence, giving time for the irresistible force of his argument to sweep away the last vestiges of opposition in his apparently unmoved companion.

'So, when do we start for the North, my friend?' began Badjian impatiently, after a suitable pause. Instigators of irresistible forces could hardly be expected to contain themselves for long.

'No, Badjian. I can't do it.' All my plans, my hopes for my scientific analysis, my search for Yarousseau. 'If you must know, I'm setting out on an expedition to the South.'

'But if we go North, think of the rewards, my friend. One day Menelek will need men like us to run the city for him.'

'No, I'm staying down here. In Harar I know what's what. I know what I am . . .'

'And what is that, my friend?'

'A failure at present, I admit.' I gazed at him grimly. Such admissions didn't come so easily any more. 'But here whatever I'll be will be of my own making. I'm not tying up my plans with any Menelek, even if he is all the things you . . .'

'Whoever spoke of tying anyone up? What is there to lose? Do *I* look tied up?'

Hardly, in a suit like that. But it was time to change the subject.

'I hear on the grapevine that the Emir requires your professional services these days.'

'Is that so? And what did you hear, my friend?'

'That he's got himself a dose of syph.'

Badjian caught the look in my eye, returning it with his old sleepy-lion expression. 'Our New World disease knows no restraint, Arthur. True, he has a mild infection. Requiring a prolonged course of treatment. As a matter of fact, we've got to know each other quite well. He is a man of considerable charm, in his own way.'

'So the doctor is taking no chances.'

'None whatsoever. One must always allow for accidents. Especially where recurrent diseases are concerned.'

'And the course of syphilisation is fraught with accidents?'

'Exactly,' Badjian guffawed appreciatively, linking his arm in mine in a confidential manner. 'Arthur, my friend, it is so good to have you back. You must realise that but for you I would still be a mere nothing. The day when you arrived up here was the beginning of a new lease of life for me.' Instinctively Rimbaud found himself tensing. Was he alone responsible for this transformation? Or what was it that had changed our easy-going Causasian character of old into this flashy unknown quantity? (Whose presence was still holding Sottiro's close, undivided admiration, Arthur noticed.)

'So you're still intent on denying me my little trip to the North?' Badjian persisted.

'Why don't you go on your own, if it means so much to you?'

He would, only too willingly, he explained. But there was just one snag. The Egyptians, who were diverting all their funds to the war, were no longer in a position to pay their officers any retirement bounty. 'So I have no money to buy guns. Like yourself, I have only my small savings.'

The implication was clear. Only our combined resources would be enough.

'No, Badjian. I'm going South.'

Badjian sighed, shaking his head, before turning to include Sottiro in the conversation, clapping a friendly hand on his shoulder. 'So you're going to be leaving us soon, I hear?'

Sottiro, overcome by such lordly attention, mumbled some vague reply.

Badjian turned back to me, letting his hand drop from Sottiro's shoulder. 'Do you know anything about that part of the Interior?'

'No,' I replied. 'Practically nothing. Why, do you?'

'No,' he shook his head, ruminatively pursing his lips, 'me neither . . . But I do know a man who might be able to help you. He has travelled much in these parts. A fine man,' he eyed me knowingly, 'who may well be of assistance to us all one day.'

And what was Badjian springing on me now?

Badjian lowered his voice, although it was obvious Sottiro wasn't listening. 'This man I am telling you about is someone whose star may well rise. From the northern sector of the heavens.'

'A man who has contacts with a man of the people, perhaps?' suggested Rimbaud.

Badjian could only cough at such a blatant suggestion, as the people of the market place pressed in around us.

9

On the next caravan from Zeyla, beside his usual quota of barter Rimbaud received a small packet and a crate. The first contained *The Dictionary of Military Engineering*. The second he had a porter carry down to the cellars. At last his long-awaited chemicals had arrived!

That night, when the others had retired to bed, Rimbaud crept down to the cellars with his lamp and began prising open the crate. The inside was crammed with ball after ball of screwed-up brown wrapping paper. How typical of Mother! Cautiously he began unfolding the first ball of paper, taking great care so as not to spill any of the chemicals inside.

But there were no chemicals inside. There was nothing inside.

And two dozen balls later (with slightly less care being taken for spilling contents) there was still nothing inside.

Rimbaud began pitching in at random, and eventually his burrowing hands came across a smooth bottle-shaped parcel.

Containing one bottle. Of Absinthe. And a note. 'To tame The Wild Man of Harar. Fondest wishes, Emelia Vardy.'

'The cow! The bitch! The whore! The cunt! Fuck! Fuck! Fuck! . . .'

At this point, Rimbaud's rage as he danced in his tiny lamplit cellar passed into the realms of the inexpressible, his gutteral yells transcending all mere verbal meaning.

Breaking finally into a sublime, and absolutely inexpressible silence, Rimbaud stood in the cellar of his derelict palace, breathing deeply as he gazed down at the bottle of

Absinthe clutched in his fist. On the label, rising against the cloud-dappled blue heavens above the maker's name, the arch of a rainbow curved up from one cluster of gold medallions, plunging through a ceiling of embossed cumulus, before descending to a similar cluster of gold medallions on the other side.

'Arthur! It's rainbow time!' Verlaine giggled, tracing his finger waveringly over the label of the bottle along the line to which the inner level had sunk. He sprawled forward over the table, combing his fingers through his beard as he clumsily refilled Arthur's glass.

Beyond, the sun was glittering through the bramble-entwined lattice at the end of the café garden.

'Now is the time of the sublime assassins!'

'Arthur, not here! Sit down!'

'Now that we have vapourised the soul's chemistry this poison will flow through our veins until the sickening codas of the ultimate cornet. All discords unite to form the harmony of nothingness! At last we have achieved the derangement of all senses! Let us now . . .'

'Sit down, for God's sake! The manager! . . .'

'I thirst only for the utmost imagination, beyond the freedom of all mortal unreality. The locked universe . . .'

'You're spilling it!'

'. . . is smouldering in a riot of perfumes, pigs' trotters, smegmatic pearls and managerial incompetences . . .!'

'Don't worry, m'sieur. We'll pay for it.'

'. . . whose complexity defies even the mechanics of damnation, the lunatic magic of judgement intoxicating the archangels of delirium as they bawl like babies through the cocksucking boudoirs of the unfrocked divine ham Aphrodite . . .'

'What did you want to go and get us chucked out for?'

'I am arrived from forever, and . . . am . . . going . . . I'm going to be . . .'

'Not there! In the gutter, you fool!

'Ugh! . . . Where can we get something solid to eat? . . . I just feel like some ordinary scrambled egg.'

Rimbaud unstopped the cork, and sniffed, closing his eyes to the dim lamplit gloom of the palace cellar as he inhaled.

'The bitch!'

He rammed the cork back into the bottle and flung it away from him. It clunked against the stone floor, rolling through the scattered brown clouds of unwrapped wrapping paper.

For a long moment he stood, irresolute, trembling slightly. Then, scrabbling amongst the paper, he found the bottle, picked up the lamp, and left, locking the door behind him.

'Arthur, I know you don't care about *your* appearance,' began Sottiro cautiously.

'What's wrong with my appearance?'

'Nothing. Nothing at all. Those native smocks and woollen trousers can look quite nice. On the right sort of figure.'

But Sottiro didn't have the right sort of figure, apparently.

'You want to get yourself a suit made, is that it?' I asked.

'How did you guess?'

'Like Badjian's monstrosity, I suppose.'

'You mean you don't mind?'

'For all I care you can go around in a rainbow-coloured loincloth. So long as you don't expect me to accompany you about the place.'

'But that's fantastic!'

There was just one slight drawback. 'How the hell do you think you're going to pay for it? As it stands at the moment, you're still four weeks wages in arrears for your little slave girl.'

Sottiro frowned, drawing the feather of his quill down the side of his cheek. 'What's the limit, Arthur?'

I shrugged; he'd obviously set his heart on it. 'This is. The absolute limit. After this, not a penny more on credit. Nothing.'

'Nothing more, Arthur. I promise.'

But as it turned out, there was one further snag. Badjian was very reluctant to disclose to Arthur the address of his tailor when he heard what Sottiro wanted. Badjian didn't fancy having his sartorial supremacy rivalled by a mere clerk. However, after a series of delicate negotiations, during which Arthur acted as go-between, it was eventually agreed that Sottiro's suit should be of a different coloured material, have a degree less gold facing, and under no circumstances epaulets. Badjian had his position to uphold.

So, every afternoon, an hour before the curfew bell, Sottiro would finish work and go down to the bazaar for his daily fitting.

Several days later, Badjian entertained me in his new room up in the northern sector of the city. Here he introduced me to a certain Ras Makonen, the man who could tell me about the Interior.

'Down south, beyond the mountains, it is very remote. No caravans pass through those parts. It is said to produce good hides, and some gum too. And I have heard tell there is excellent musk to be had at the far limits of the region, on the banks of the River Web. But no traders can be bothered, it is all so distant.'

I listened, stifling a yawn. This was just market place gossip. I could have told him more myself.

With a cool smiling politeness, that betrayed absolutely nothing of his feelings, Ras Makonen rambled on. His light skin, long straight nose and dark deep-set eyes, I'd recognised at once as Shoanese. There was a small community of them living by the north gate; several of the caravans which traded along the northern routes were manned by Shoanese who lived in Harar.

So this was the man who according to Badjian could well be of assistance to us all, whose star was due to rise 'from the northern sector of the heavens'. Badjian hovered in the background, delivering sherbet water and laying out cakes, suspiciously solicitous.

'And there's no quick way through the mountains to the South?' I asked, when Ras Makonen dried.

'There are rumoured to be ways,' he continued, in his flat gentle manner, bowing his head as he spoke. It was obvious he considered me excessively polite, and in the traditional manner was going through the game of discussing what he considered to be irrelevant topics, before I at last brought up the real topic. But what *was* the real topic? I glanced over at Badjian with a meaningful glare. He'd got me here under false pretences, the bastard.

'Badjian,' I called across to him, when Ras Makonen had finally lapsed into bored silence. 'Our friend here knows nothing about the South. Why, he doesn't even pretend to.'

Badjian raised his hands, wincing like a conductor whose orchestra has just struck a crashing discord.

'Please!' He turned immediately to Ras Makonen, relaxing with great effort. 'Arthur spends his curfew evenings pouring over books.'

Ras Makonen, I could see, was more than faintly embarrassed at Badjian's performance. 'You read?' he began.

'A bit.'

'It must be very enjoyable.'

Surely he wasn't interested in my studies in chemical analysis?

'I intend to do a bit of surveying when I'm down South,' I continued.

'And you read about these things at night?' He sipped at his sherbet water, waiting for a reply: now no longer bothering to conceal his utter indifference.

'Yes. I've got a few plans.'

'Yes, Arthur,' Badjian leaned forward, glowering at me intently, 'so you were telling me just a few weeks ago in the market place. You were talking about some book or other you were going to get. A Dictionary of Military Engineering or something, wasn't it?'

Not a feature moved on Ras Makonen's impassive face, but I knew there and then that we'd at last moved on to the real reason for my visit.

'Yes, I do have a book on Military Engineering. It arrived

the other day, as a matter of fact. Why, do you want to borrow it?'

The book itself was a compendium of the most verbose and undigested jargon I'd ever come across. I could hardly understand a word of it myself, without constant reference to my companion volume, *The Dictionary of Civil Engineering*. With Badjian's knowledge of written French, and Ras Makonen's knowledge of military operations (if any), they'd probably be able to decipher no more than half a dozen of the historical entries between them. And I somehow doubted if their interest lay in Trojan Horses or Hannibal's elephantine difficulties while crossing the Alps.

'You will let us see it?' asked Ras Makonen, genuinely surprised.

'If you want to.'

'That is very kind of you. I did not know you were our friend.'

I looked across at Badjian. Now what was I letting myself in for?

Badjian smiled. 'Arthur is very generous,' he turned to Ras Makonen. 'But Ras, you must understand, this is an extremely valuable book.'

'I am willing to pay very highly for such generosity,' Ras Makonen nodded to me courteously.

It was too late now. And besides, why shouldn't I make some cash out of that worthless tome of jargon?

'I'd just like to make this perfectly clear,' I began firmly. 'Badjian knows where my sympathies lie in these matters. I just want Harar to remain open for trade.'

'And so it shall,' replied Ras Makonen.

'I take no sides. I'm simply here for my own gain.'

'Arthur is being modest, you will understand, Ras,' beamed Badjian. 'This is European practice.'

'Look Badjian, I've no intention of becoming involved.'

'But you *are* involved, Arthur. Up to your neck. As soon as you set foot in this city you became involved.'

'I'm just concerned for myself. I only came here to save

enough . . .

'You saved Yarousseau.'

'That was different.'

'Not in the eyes of some, Arthur.'

'What do you mean?'

As a result of Rimbaud's doing, explained Badjian, Yarousseau was now free, out of reach. Of those who might prefer to see him more permanently removed from the scene. 'And besides, you were the first man to stay up here. The first outsider. Can you blame Harar if it sees you as responsible for each new addition to the European community? No, Arthur, you may think you're just working for yourself – but in fact you're responsible for more up here than almost any man but the Governor.'

During the long curfew nights Rimbaud continued with his studies, which were now becoming increasingly difficult. On his own, with no access to outside reference books, his notes had begun to drift more and more into regions beyond his practical experience. Only in a world constructed entirely out of his imagination could he attempt to visualise the vast but subtly precise abstractions which he persevered so hard to comprehend.

To this were added further difficulties, of a rather more down to earth nature. Working through the night, I'd grown quite accustomed to the sounds through the wall from Vardy's room – the nightly tapping out of his pipe on the windowsill; the less regular blundering in the dark in the early hours, followed by the soft hiss of his relieving himself into his chamber pot; and even, on rare occasions, the faint high tremolo of an unsuppressed sob. Sottiro, however, from the other side, was a different matter altogether.

After dining with Vardy in the state room, Sottiro would invariably retire early to his room; and then, from his side of the wall, my studies would be serenaded by my clerk's truly amazing feats of stamina with his slave girl. Nightly, to the accompaniment of the orchestrated whines and screeches of his long-suffering bed (of fewer and fewer nails) Sottiro's agonising croaks and the ululating death rattles of his loving partner would ring out across the empty market square. Mingling doubtless in the lower alleyways beyond with the less convincing sighs and whimpers of abandonment rising from the sick, laid out for the night along the walls outside the courtyard gates. The jackals had been increasing lately, and with them the lions, and it was no longer a rare sight when I passed along the high walled alleyways on my way to the main gate in the morning, to find a shredded blood-stained shroud and bared white ribcage amidst a litter of spilling gut scattered over the baked mud in front of some still-barred courtyard gateway. The scavenging dogs would lope off at my approach.

In the early hours, when I had finished my studies in chemical analysis, I would leaf through my *Construction in Metal*. This was still the mainstay of my hope, I realised. The Interior had only remained unexploited because it had remained inaccessible. If I was to find anything at all worthwhile down there, then I was going to need the most modern methods of transportation to get it out. Which meant a railway. While I studied into what remained of the night, the jackals would howl outside my window, from beyond the walls, and occasionally a lion would roar, closer. The dogs would explode into a cacophany of yapping on the ramparts. One could never be really certain, from simply listening to the sounds, whether the disturbance came from within the city or not. In the next room Sottiro might groan to life enough for a few minutes of creaking rhythmic consciousness, and then the night would be silent once more.

As the silence mounted to a singing in my ears, and I matched my work from *Construction in Metal* to my notes from *The Dictionary of Civil Engineering*, or even my earlier plans from the old *Handy Manual*, only one distraction remained. On the window ledge, casting its dim shadow across the moonlit wall, stood Emelia Vardy's bottle of Absinthe, its green shoulders silvered with a glowing sheen.

For a river of this size in such terrain, Rimbaud read on, *a bridge with two struts is required, as shown in fig 1. After excavations on either bank the supports of thin calves and thighs encased in black stockings the suspensions resting in each socket her breasts plump and white in her cupping bra for the upper deck to pass from the near bank as she runs her hand over my cheek . . .*

'I'm not one of your little slave virgins, Arthur. You won't have to teach me anything.'

'No, Emelia!'

. . . the surface soil must first be excavated and banked up on either side . . .

'Are you afraid of me, Arthur? Look!'

. . . to ensure that while the track is laid, her breasts falling loose, her hands unfastening her stays, easing her panties gently over her round thighs as her eyes brazenly stare into mine . . .

'No! You cunt! I detest you! You disgust me!'

If the terrain is such and it is impracticable either to drain or circumvent the waterlogged area, the tracks must be laid directly over the marsh (see fig 2) by an embankment or elevated way. Great precaution must be taken to ensure that there is no tidal flow or movement of water across the intended path of the track which is rooted, stiff as a poker, between his thighs as he presses against me, his hands caressing my shoulders, passing down over the main body of the marshland to whatever depth is required . . .

'Ah, Arthur! My little wand of ivory!'

'Verlaine! You dirty old bugger!'

'My little pear!'

. . . the shored-up embankment, in this case, must not deviate from the upper course of his beard tickling my chest as he presses his lips to my nipples, his hand moving over my thigh and each sleeper must be secured in its bed as well as being harnessed to the track, for any movement of his hands gently around the individual sleeper will cause vibrations . . .

'Gently, Verlaine!'

'Arthur!'

... the constitution of the bed is all important as he presses his face to the pillow and my hands will find that rough chippings on their own are not enough as they encircle his body, passing over his stomach to maintain the brace as I press myself into him, ensuring that the locomotive rides between the globes of his buttocks his hand around mine as I ease the pins on both sides simultaneously to maximise in unison ...

'No! *No!*'

(A jackal howled beyond the walls.)

... for this it is necessary to clear the undergrowth to a distance of at least ten feet on either side of the track ...

(One by one the dogs howled back.)

... pressing on through this grunting tremulously ...

'Faster, now!'

'Gently! ... Oh, *now!*'

'Oh, my darling!'

Against the silence of the night, the bottle stood on the window sill, its green shoulders silvered with a glowing sheen.

On the next monthly caravan I received a letter from Mother.

Dear Arthur,

I am afraid I have some bad news this time, my son. The riding school is not working out as I had hoped. In spite of the fact that riding is becoming more and more popular, and many of the townsfolk have horses of their own, they are now learning to ride by themselves, without experienced instruction. Apart from the fact that we suffer, this is a foolish and dangerous practice and has already resulted in several accidents. One poor boy may well have been maimed for life.

Our riding school, I am glad to say, has a record of no accidents whatsoever. But if things continue to go so badly, I will be forced to close down the school next month. This I hardly dare contemplate for the effect it will have on poor Isabelle. Since she recovered from her accident and her broken engagement (the man was a complete wastrel and ne'er-do-well, I later discovered) she has spent all her time helping down at the stables. She will, I fear, find this further disappointment very difficult to bear. Still, it will soon be harvest time and she will be able to lose her worries in hard work, I hope.

As for all this talk of chemistry – I am surprised at you, Arthur. I cannot bring myself to waste so much good money on all these worthless trifles. Old Courbet is probably going to put up one of his fields for auction – the one next to the riding school – so I am keeping your money aside for that. Should there be any left over, I will send you some of the cheaper items on your list.

I am so disappointed in you, my son. I thought you had learnt your lesson. And then suddenly in the midst of all my difficulties with the riding school (they are cheating me over the accounts, I know that) I receive from you this further list of extravagances. I hardly know what to think. You have been away so long, Arthur, that I sometimes find myself wondering who you are now. What kind of person has my Arthur become? Do you know yourself?

But do not worry, I have your best interests at heart, my son. Eventually, when you have learnt what it is to be a man, you will thank me.

Your fond

Mother.

Rimbaud could rely on nothing. No equipment. No chemicals. Not even any books. From now on, he realised, his studies would have to be self-sufficient. At nights, he redoubled his efforts, regularly working long into the small hours. Lamp oil was now his only extravagance. However, as if Sottiro and his little endurance tests weren't enough, I now had to contend with Grimes.

The insinuation of Grimes

Primary condition: Grimes sitting alone at night in his nearby courtyard over his 'regulation tot'. The sound of mournful toneless songs drifting across the empty market square. 'Faw those in pear-ill awn the sea . . .' 'Land of Ho-ope and Glawree . . .' Saturdays, double tot. 'Nellieee *Deeeen! . . .*'

Secondary condition: Grimes invited to Vardy's dinner parties – in no time becoming a regular fixture. Gorilla guffaws from down the passage.

Tertiary condition: Grimes decides that the state room in its present state is being wasted. What a place for a club room! A centre, where the Europeans of Harar could meet each other, play a round of rummy, exchange views on the topics of the day etc. Vardy enamoured.

The limit: The evening hours filled with the constant sound of hammering and sawing. Grimes, the self-sufficient man, a confident carpenter of sorts, constructs large lop-sided tables and uneven chairs in 'European' styles. Vardy, overwhelmed, sets to work covering these rude constructions with choice examples of his own needlework. Sottiro, press-ganged from arduous domestic duties of his own, put to work as dogsbody – planing planks of rough local wood, sweeping shavings, unravelling balls of wool, etc.

Beyond the limit: Grimes and Vardy form a delegation to seek out further assistance. Perhaps, thought Vardy, Arthur might give a hand white-washing the walls of the state room.

'Like buggery, I will!'

Grimes, poking a finger, idly turning over the covers of the books on Rimbaud's desk. '*Construction in Metal, Practical Chemical Analysis* – I say, what's all this?'

'Selfishness. Pure selfishness.' In the opinion of Vardy. 'Why, here we are slaving away to make something worthwhile out of this place, and all you can do is lock yourself away with your miserable books.'

'*The Dictionary of Military Engineering* – you've got quite a collection here, young fellow.'

'After all, it's for your good as well, Arthur.'

' "Chapter Seven: The Modern Siege". Fascinating stuff!'

'We'll never attract anyone up here unless we provide the rudiments.'

But rudiments of this nature held little interest for Rimbaud. 'Get the hell out of here, both of you! *Before I throw you out!*'

Next night, I was interrupted early by another knock on my door.

Enter Sottiro, clad in his new suit.

'I knew you'd want to see it, Arthur.' Sottiro drew himself up to his full height, resting his hand gallantly on his hip.

I suppose I should have realised that Sottiro would never content himself with any slavish imitation, even of Badjian's spectacular design. Sottiro had been inspired by further ideas of his own, which had resulted in what could only be described as a coat of many colours. The shiny Shoanese black cloth of Badjian's suit had been supplemented with a broad blazer facing of embroidered Gallas cloth, while the trousers were lined along the outer seams with strips of blue felt of the sort the Hararis usually employed as decoration for their camel harnesses. I watched while Sottiro strode up and down my room, obviously enamoured with his new appearance.

'Well?' He finally came to a posed halt.

'It's original, I'll give you that.'

'Come on, Arthur. You're not an old stick-in-the-mud, are you?'

'But what on earth's it *for*? You can't go prancing about the market place in a thing like that.'

'I thought I might wear it for dinner. Or in this new club we're making. Put a bit of life into the place. After all, Vardy's old dull-as-ditchwater-suits and Grimes' flabby pants don't exactly set the place alight.' (My homespun efforts at fashion were obviously beyond all comment.) 'Don't you think it's a good idea, Arthur?'

I shrugged, unable to restrain a grin. 'Yes, why the hell not!'

Sottiro was delighted. 'I always knew we were two of a kind, Arthur. Underneath it all. You can't pull the wool over my eyes. All this business about studying at night – I know what you're up to. You and your bottle of Absinthe. How about a little drink? Just to celebrate the new suit.'

'*No!*'

'All right, there's no need to bite my head off! Drink it all yourself, I don't care.'

'If you'd have looked a little closer on your snoopings, you'd have seen that I haven't touched a drop.'

'Why not? You've opened it. Are you saving it for something? What the hell's it for, if it's not for drinking?'

What the hell *was* it for? 'I don't know.'

'I suppose you keep it to remind you of your old Paris days. Vardy was telling me you used to be a bit of a poet.'

'Was he now? Put it down. Yes, if you must know, I keep it to remind me of the old days.'

'Oh yeah?' Sottiro replaced the bottle on the window sill, grinning slyly. 'There's no need to peddle that shit with me, Arthur. I'm not like those other two fools. I know where you got this bottle from, all right.'

'Oh? Where?'

'She gave me one too, once. That's one of the reasons why I volunteered to be sent up here. I didn't fancy getting the sack over that old cow.'

'I thought you came up here for the money.'

Sottiro shrugged. An expressive, almost sophisticated gesture in his new attire. 'You should get yourself a little slave girl, Arthur. It's much nicer that way.'

Several days later, Badjian came round to collect *The Dictionary of Military Engineering* for Ras Makonen. In exchange he gave Rimbaud a little leather money bag containing the equivalent of sixty pounds in Harari exchange tokens. As much as all the money that I'd saved so far during my entire time in Abyssinia.

'Badjian, what are you up to?'

'Me?' Badjian put on an expression of innocent incomprehension that might just have passed for acting in the third rate London music hall where he'd probably first seen it. 'I am making money for you. Is that not what you want?'

Badjian left, and Rimbaud stood at the window of his room, fingering his chin, watching as Badjian hurried away across the empty market square. The curfew bell was tolling, and gradually the darkness of the night began to deepen the dusk.

Whether it was something to do with the acquired sense of sophistication brought on by his new suit, or simply lack of interest after his exhausting efforts at interior decorating, I couldn't tell, but for the next few days there was an almost uncanny silence from Sottiro's room.

On a sudden impulse of goodwill I decided to give Sottiro the bottle of Absinthe. He opened his door to my knock, dressed in all his finery.

Had he taken to sleeping in the thing? Perhaps this explained his new found abstinence.

'Here,' I held out the bottle, 'a present.'

'Why, thanks Arthur.' He glanced behind him, raising his finger. 'Sh! She's asleep. Shall we go to your room?'

'I'm working. You drink it all. It's yours.'

'*Please!*' he whispered frantically, 'Not so loud! She's asleep.'

'What's the matter? I thought you liked her awake.'

'Arthur,' he rested his hand lamely on my shoulder, 'if you only knew. She's *insatiable!*' His whisper hissed down the dark empty corridor.

'As I've noticed. The wall is rather thin.'

'Is it?' he asked quickly. 'You mean you can hear?'

'I can't very well help it.'

'Then you know what a life I lead. Honestly Arthur, it's terrible.'

'But I thought that was what you wanted.'

'I do,' he replied slowly, with an air of reproach, 'sometimes.'

'Well you should learn to say no. Like you did to Emelia Vardy.'

'I know. But you see . . . Well, in the end, what else is there to do up here? I just find I give in.'

'Well in that case you'll be pleased to hear what I've got to tell you. I've decided we can't hang around waiting any longer. My equipment's not going to arrive anyway. We're going to start out on our expedition next week. You'll be free of her for a whole month.'

'*What!*' he exclaimed, all pretence at whispering dropped. 'You mean I can't take her with me?'

'Sottiro, we're going on a dangerous expedition into unknown territory. Never crossed before by Europeans. We're not going on a holiday.'

'That's a shitty trick!' he exclaimed, his voice trembling with anger. Even in the dark I recognised the reappearance of our difficult friend, the thwarted child. 'You dirty doublecrosser! Here, you can keep your bloody bottle!' He thrust the bottle back into my hands and reopened the door behind him, slamming it in my face. Almost before I'd settled down to my notes the floorboards were creaking once more, as energetically as ever.

Rimbaud stood at the open window of his room gazing out over the darkened city towards the white moon-fired dome of the mosque.

What the hell was I doing with my life up here?

Rimbaud's last hopes now lay in this place. His science, his engineering, his plans for opening up the Interior, his hours of idiotic bargaining in a barely comprehended language – all these depended on Harar. And yet life in the city was as uncertain, more uncertain, than ever before. The war was going badly in the North, the Egyptians were still rumoured to be on the point of abandoning the place, and now Badjian was dragging me into his bloody intrigues.

Rimbaud stood, fingering the bottle of Absinthe, glowering grimly down at the rainbow label. He'd given up everything. And for what? He'd made a mess of his life. Daily the failure became more confirmed. More irreversible. Absolute.

The icy terror played soft-fingered over my guts as I sighed. There was no point in fooling myself any longer. The ectoplasmic mist of my breath drifted out into the cold night air, and I shivered, my lips parted, my teeth bared.

But who could Rimbaud call out to from the pit of his lonely self-imposed solitude? He raised the bottle above his head.

One swing of his arm and the bottle would be shattered, the air awaft with those familiar fumes of aniseed as he held the splinter-necked weapon in his fist. Above the imploring innocence of his trembling wrist . . .

Rimbaud stood, his eyes closed against the darkness, his muscles tautening, his breath deepening.

'Hello there! I'm just on my way up.'

Below the open window, Rimbaud made out Grimes slinking across the market square for another night's hammering at his bloody club room.

'You cretin, don't you realise! This place is finished. We're going to have to clear out at a moment's notice!'

But Rimbaud's words merely reverberated silently in the endless silence-choked chambers of his skull. Charged. Unspoken. Grimes was already inside, banging the door closed behind him. Muttering his commonplace thoughts up the stairs.

Couldn't they see? It was all doomed!

Blundering clumsily out of my room down the passage, I knocked on the club room door.

'Look,' I began, as the faces peered up from their various tasks, 'don't you realise . . .' No, why should I ruin their dreams. 'Here, you can have this bottle of Absinthe for your damn club room.'

I placed it on the cloth-covered table. As I closed the door behind me, I heard the first surprised exclamations of approval break the silence within.

In my room I lay on my bed watching as the flame slowly burnt down the wick of the lamp, its oil finished. The sooner I got out of this dream world the better. I'd leave on my expedition, get through the mountains to the south, and open up that Interior. Badjian was right, his was the only way. On the proceeds from my expedition to the South, I'd break my contract with Old Man Vardy and go gun-running to the North. One expedition. Followed perhaps by a quick slaving run up country on the return journey. (Slave trading was where the real money lay – at least that was what Badjian had hinted. And he ought to know.) Then I'd get myself a French wife and set up somewhere else on my own. There must be other Harars, other alternatives . . .

The precocious scholar, dissatisfied with all learning, had run away from school to join the Commune in Paris. Disgusted at the reality of his hopes, the boy-wonder poet had dedicated his life to grappling with the magical sophistries of the Unknown, to deranging his senses and becoming a visionary. His perception shattered by drugs, his vision hallucinated, the perverted degenerate had abandoned poetry for ever and set off to tramp round Europe. Finally, the down-and-out vagabond had left home for the last time, his future life dedicated to just one thing. The making of his fortune. And where had this led me? To Harar . . . The roar of a lion rasped through the night air, dying. Close by. I listened as the dogs yapped into life on the ramparts. Another triumph for Harar's sick cure; that lion was inside the walls, I could tell, by the relative distances of the dogs barking from their separate points in the encircling night.

But where now? Another Paris? Another city taken over by the Commune? Another non-existent visionary world? Another Europe? Another Harar? . . .

Rimbaud, now thirty years old, with the skin of his face already drawn, sun-wrinkled and leathery as that of a man twice his age, his hair now almost completely grey, lay in the darkness of his room in the all-but deserted palace at Harar. Darkness blurring into invisible darkness as the tears welled in his eyes.

'*What kind of person has my Arthur become?*'

A failure, Mother.

A broken spirit in a tired clapped-out body.

The first man to live in Harar.

About to be the first man to penetrate the hinterland of Lower Abyssinia . . . Yet another unknown . . . I will be setting out into territory which no European has ever seen . . . I, Arthur Rimbaud, will be staking my claim where no man has ever set foot before me. Discovering what men have only guessed existed. Mapping a land of which men have only dreamed. Naming the unseen, tracing the course of the unknown. Turning the dream into reality. There perhaps at last I'll be able to make myself into something! Oh, I will. I *will* . . .

Sleep, you poor dope, you're just wearing yourself out.

But no sooner had Rimbaud dispensed with the contents of Emelia Vardy's first parcel than a second one arrived. Containing half a dozen silk shirts: scarlet, yellow, lime green, peacock blue, patrician purple and violent violet. 'To the poet who seems to have forgotten how to write. Is just a word, simply to let me know that you're still in the land of the living, too much to hope for? All yours, Emelia V.'

This time I felt nothing, not even a flicker of irritation. I'd been expecting nothing else – and besides, this was no seductive bottle of Absinthe. Silk shirts for Arthur Rimbaud, I ask you! I slung them into the corner of my room. Torn into strips they might be useful as caravan tags or bandages, or even handkerchiefs.

Within a week Rimbaud had despatched his consignment caravan to Zeyla and assembled all the essentials for his expedition to the South. With the added cash from the sale of his *Dictionary of Military Engineering* he had hired a string of a dozen mules and bought some large leather panniers. This wasn't just going to be a simple trade prospecting expedition. Any rifts exposed to the surface whose appearance even vaguely matched with the mental pictures he'd formed from his notes on soil analysis, he intended to excavate – for general samples, or even simply for the particular sample and whatever of value it might contain.

As the day of their departure approached, Sottiro sank more and more deeply into his old silent ways: an ominous reminder of his previous mode of travel – as well as of certain still unfulfilled financial promises. That fancy knife of his was obviously still hidden away somewhere amongst his belongings.

When the day finally arrived, I was up well before dawn and had the mules fed, harnessed and strung out across the yard even before the traders outside the gate had begun their first ululating chorus for the keys. After checking that everything was loaded, I went and banged on Sottiro's door – for the fourth time.

'We're leaving the minute the gate opens. *So get cracking!*'

He grunted something, and I heard his footsteps padding across the bare floorboards.

After rousing Bomba and getting some coffee and something to eat, I went downstairs and led the mule train out into the market place, where the first of the porters were already huddled around their makeshift fires in the dying darkness.

I was standing underneath Sottiro's window, with my hands already cupped to my mouth, on the point of yelling up to him for positively the last time, when I suddenly became aware of this dim featureless shade towering beside me at my elbow.

'*Who's that?*' I shied away, stumbling back against the

rump of one of the mules.

Without a word this tall shrouded figure leaned forward, helping me upright.

'What the devil! Who are you?' I demanded.

The sky was still a faint cobalt blue, tinged with light only at the silhouette edges of the market walls beyond. I could just make out the white bandaging of a turban around its head as it stepped back, wrapping itself once more in its long grey robes.

'I have come to bid you farewell on your journey.'

Peering forward, I recognised Ras Makonen.

'What the hell do you want?' I snapped sharply, my heart still blundering against my ribs. 'Creeping up on me like some bloody ghost!'

'I have been watching you, but you did not seem to notice me,' he replied gently.

'Who told you I was setting out this morning, anyway?' I asked him, still peering forward. The light was increasing moment by moment, but I could still only just make out the faint outlines of his features. Beyond him, the black clusters of the porters around the fires had obliterated the dancing flames, leaving only the pulsating glow which flickered up against the shadows of the walls. In the distance the ululating yells from outside the main gate were beginning to rise, insistently.

'I think it was Badjian who told me you were leaving,' he replied, after a few moments.

Badjian couldn't have told him, because I hadn't told Badjian what day I was leaving. But then I suppose he could have guessed easily enough from market place gossip.

'Why the sudden interest in my movements?' I asked him, my nerves steadier now.

'Because you are going South, to the Ogaden,' he replied, still in the same gentle, courteous manner.

'Really? You didn't seem to know much about the Ogaden when I asked you the other day.'

But this was not the full reason for Ras Makonen's little

social call, apparently.

Ras Makonen's interest in Rimbaud's Expedition to the Interior.

Back home in Shoa, Ras Makonen had been a trader himself. A year ago, he had come across a sample of some musk 'whose fragrance exceeded that of all others I have ever smelt.' This musk, so he had been informed, came from a small town called Imi on the far banks of the River Web. (*On the other side of the Web? But that was the back of beyond. At the furthest limits of the Ogaden.*) He had come to ask Rimbaud a favour. Should Rimbaud obtain any of this musk on his travels, even the smallest amount, he would be only too pleased to buy some. At any price Rimbaud cared to name. (*But what was so special about it?*) It was possible his memory had been deceiving him, Ras Makonen explained, but the fragrance of this particular musk had been enough to make him set out on a trading mission from Shoa south into Lower Abyssinia, in the hope of finding some more. He had only got as far as Harar when the uprising had taken place in Shoa. Secret orders had reached him from King Menelek that he was to remain in Harar and act as Menelek's undercover representative. When the time came, and King Menelek ruled all of Abyssinia, Ras Makonen was to be appointed the new Governor of Harar. (*Was he mad? This information was worth more than a man's life. Why was he trusting me like this? Or was he just trying to involve me even further in his goddam intrigues?*) So he had never obtained any of his priceless musk, Ras Makonen continued, and none of the traders in the market place had even so much as heard of it.

'Is it *that* good?' I demanded.

'Do not raise your hopes. I am not even sure if it is there any more. The sample I was given had been sealed for many years.'

'How do you expect me to tell if I've found it? What does it smell like?'

Ras Makonen smiled broadly, but in his usual polite, almost expressionless manner. It was now quite light and the embers of the fires under the market place walls were being stamped out by the porters. The sparks rose in fountains under their feet.

'Only to a man who knows it,' replied Ras Makonen eventually, 'is it possible to convey that one knows it too, I think. It is exceptional. You will certainly recognise it, should you come across any.' He laid his hand on my shoulder. 'You will do me this favour?'

'If I can,' I shrugged. It was all so bloody vague. But then if he really was willing to pay for the stuff, it was worth keeping in mind. Ras Makonen had doubled my savings once already. He'd financed a good half of the expedition, if he did but know it.

'Farewell my friend, I wish you luck on your travels.'

I watched as he walked away across the market place. By now the stalls and awnings were going up, their canvas walls billowing gently in the early morning breeze. Outside the main gate the distant chant of the traders waiting for the keys had risen to a harsh pulsating roar, like the war cry of some deep-throated ogre. Was that all Ras Makonen had come to see me about? I listened as the roar beyond gradually quickened in pace. No one in their right senses went risking information that was worth their life in this place with a mere trading acquaintance.

(But hadn't Arthur too once unthinkingly risked his life in this place? For Yarousseau. And what had prompted Arthur, no stickler for etiquette, to go and see Yarousseau off on his expedition to the Interior?)

I leaned on the rump of the ass beside me, watching as the tall figure of Ras Makonen disappeared amongst the stalls. I felt curiously moved. And then suddenly I became aware of a deep, multiplying sense of apprehension. I'd gone to see Yarousseau off to what I'd thought was a certain death.

From intimations of fleeting reality, to confrontation with blatant appearance.
 Enter Sottiro, immaculate, in sartorial abortion.
 'No, Sottiro,' I told him firmly. 'No.'
 'But why *can't* I wear it?'
 'This isn't a fashion parade. We're setting out on an expedition to the Interior. Unknown territory. There's no knowing what we may come across.'
 'Then it doesn't really matter how I dress, does it?'
 'I'm not concerned with the social niceties . . .'
 'Oh yes you are. You've got it into your mind what an explorer should look like, and . . .'
 I was trembling, barely controlling myself. He'd done his utmost this morning, had Sottiro. *'Take it off!'*
 'And what do you suggest I should wear instead?' Sottiro was obviously all prepared, his face set: the wilful child.
 'Anything! I don't care what you wear. But not *that!*'
 But Sottiro hadn't got anything else to wear.
 All his other clothes were worn out.
 Rimbaud wore his native smock, why shouldn't he wear his suit?
 Sottiro wanted one good reason why he shouldn't wear his suit.
One good reason why Sottiro shouldn't wear his suit:
 It'll wear out.
 Shrink in the rain.
 The colours will run.
 The colours will fade in the sun.
 Some cannibal might take a fancy to it.
 It wouldn't blend with the terrain – he'd be a sitting target.
 It would get dirty, torn, burnt, chewed by wild animals, struck by lightning etc etc.
 'Wow! I never realised so many things *could* happen to a

suit.'

'Okay, now get upstairs and get changed.'

'No.'

'Why not?'

Sottiro hadn't got anything else to wear.

All his clothes were worn out.

Rimbaud's smock . . .

One good reason etc etc.

In desperation Rimbaud lunged forward, but Sottiro was too quick for him. Dodging under a mule, Rimbaud's clerk evaded his master. To the glee of the gathered crowd, Rimbaud gave chase. Up one side of the mule train. Under the lead mule's belly. Down the other side of the mule train. Gaining ground.

Then Sottiro was fumbling at his pack, which was strapped to the back of the end mule. As Rimbaud leapt towards him, Sottiro held out his knife, panting, his hand shaking.

The crowd in ecstasies. These European performers were capable of such breathtaking realism.

His mind blank with anger, Rimbaud stood his ground.

Should he assert his authority by producing Vardy's pistol with all the swash-buckling bravado expected of the leading role upstaging the flashy villain?

In the first act?

Of a saga that was to lead its main protagonists into the heart of darkest Africa?

Such lengthy productions require pace, suspense, the gradual revelations of character under increasing stress, intrigue . . .

Rimbaud stomped off into the palace, leaving the villain to entertain the mob . . . In a matter of minutes our hero returned clutching Emelia Vardy's shirts in his fist.

'Here. You can have these to wear.'

Sottiro lowered his knife, reaching forward gingerly. 'Silk! . . . How much for?'

'For nothing.'

'For *nothing?*'

'A gift – to show how much I value your services.'

Sottiro resheathed his knife, taking the proffered shirts, rubbing them against his cheek. 'They *are* real silk! Do you mean that, Arthur? Just because you don't want me to wear my suit?'

'Yes.'

'But why don't you want me to wear my suit?'

'*Because I don't like it!*'

'I thought that was all.' Sottiro nodded, smiling: the child, victorious, with his new presents. 'At least you're honest.'

'What do you mean?'

'Because that's all there ever is, isn't there?' Sottiro watched as his master frowned. 'I mean, there's really nothing more to it all, is there? – only likes and dislikes. Everything's just a matter of taste in the end, isn't it?'

I listened: the roar at the gate had reached its crescendo, splintering into various discordant yells. The keys had obviously arrived.

'Come on, Sottiro. Stuff those shirts into your pack. You can change as soon as we're outside the gate.'

Sottiro clambered up onto his horse, and the first European expedition into the hinterland of Lower Abyssinia started forward on its way across the market place of Harar. The waiting crowd parted to let Rimbaud through, leading his horse and the mule train behind him. Over the market place the whistles and catcalls pierced the air as Sottiro emerged, on horseback, dressed in all his finery. So after all that, he'd still got his own way! And Emelia Vardy's shirts into the bargain. Either this boy had a genius for getting his own way, or Rimbaud's much vaunted will-power, so much in evidence of late, had ceased to function – in any effective capacity.

10

'*Forward . . . That's right . . . Now balance . . . Remember to keep a hold . . . Forward . . . Remember . . .*'

The patient stumbles forward another pace, placing his metal leg in front of his balancing foot.

'*Forward . . . Remember . . .*'

Another pace. The patient stumbles forward again, his limbs oiled with sweat, the stub of his amputated leg ringed with fire in the clamp of his artificial leg. With a near orgasm of agonised effort the patient drags his artificial leg forward in front of his balancing foot.

'*Forward . . . Remember . . .*'

I'm going to get there! It's going to work!

'*Forward . . . Remember . . .*'

Only by enduring this core of suffering will I burn out all my weakness.

'*Forward . . . Remember . . .*'

'A – I – A!'

'Now you must rest, Arthur. You mustn't wear yourself out.'

'I'm not wearing myself out!'

'Oh, but you are, Arthur. You must rest now.'

Is it beginning to work at last? Am I really getting better? . . . As I lie in bed, Isabelle arranges the flowers over by the window. Fresh pink sprigs of bougainvillea. The air is filled with their light clear scent: their own original perfume. I have her take them away as soon as they begin to stink. That heavy cloying odour which they give off when the flower is dying nauseates me.

Poor Isabelle, what does she think of it all? A brother she hardly knows, a lined wizened little old man returned from a place called Africa, lying in hospital in this huge hot city where the ships hoot and set out under a cloudless azure sky for distant exotic places beyond all possible experience. She's never been away from home before, never left Mother, never even slept under a different roof from her, except for those few nights when Mother left her alone on the farm to look after the harvest while she went back to Charleville to auction off the effects of the riding school. 'I was so sad, Arthur. I wept over the ponies most of all . . .' She talks like she used to when she was a little girl. She is working it all out for herself, perhaps for the first time. Marseilles and a sick brother are like a yardstick: her life can now take on previously unrealised values. '. . . and all day as I was gathering in the harvest, bending down with my hand-scythe, I could see my tears falling amongst the stubble.'

But now there are no tears. Perhaps it's the fact that she doesn't weep which gives me most hope of all. If she wept for her little ponies, then surely she wouldn't be able to hold back if she knew her brother was going to die?

And each day we go through it again. 'Forward . . . Remember . . . Forward . . . Remember . . .'

But the paralysis is still gaining ground. I know. Each morning when I wake at first light I run my hands over my body. At the outer limits of those limbs they're cold. Numb. Dead . . . What's happening to me? Is there really any hope?

'Arthur, are you listening to me? . . . I have something to tell you. The doctor has decided that you must have a course of treatment. Only if you are willing, of course. He says it will help to give you back the use of your limbs.'

'What is it?'

'Only if you are willing, of course.'

'What is it, woman!'

'A sort of shock, I think. He says it's this new electricity. Something to do with science. He says it may be rather painful, but . . .'

'Is it the only way? Won't it happen naturally? Is there no other hope?'

'Oh Arthur, you musn't talk like that.'

Pain, my only hope. As long as I can feel it. All else: all care, all love, all patience, pity, understanding – all these I've lost. As the agony increases, all feeling for them is burnt out of my mind. I no longer understand anything but suffering.

'Are you willing to go through with it, Arthur? It will help you to walk again.'

Forward ... Remember ...
Forward ... Remember ...
I will. I will!

The first European Expedition into the hinterland of Lower Abyssinia left the market place at Harar by the side gate and started into the network of winding empty mud-walled alleyways which led to the main city gate. At the courtyard doorways the dogs yapped, dancing against the tug of their chains as we rode past, the string of mules stepping slowly out behind us. At one of the closed doorways lay the grey motionless shroud of what appeared to be a sleeping sick man, his head resting against the doorpost. Only as we approached did I notice the bloodstained midriff of his robes. The white ribbon of his gut trailed out over the clenched fist at the end of his dangling arm; and below the hem of his robe, between his bare splayed knees, the lurid glossy spill of his entrails spread over the dust like some hideous miscarriage. The whole front of his body had been eaten away, leaving only the ribcage and the occasional visible white vertebrae of his spine.

Slowly, as the days passed, Rimbaud's expedition pushed further into the barren rocky highlands of the Interior. Beside him, Sottiro nodded forward, comatose and silent in his sweat-blotched scarlet silk shirt, his head jerking at the end of his neck to the movement of his horse. Behind them, the mule train picked its way along the valley floor through the drifting cloudlets of risen dust, while on either side the scrubbly rock faces rose steeply to the sharp high ridges.

So at last you find yourself in the barren wilderness of all your hopes. But in your mind's eye, you have these pictures. Imaginary landscapes, rife with lode-bearing seams. And as you screw up your eyes against the blinding light you try to match these pictures you've formed in your imagination with what you see around you. But they do not match.

And then, after another week of travelling you realise that you are lost. The trail should have branched to the west to take you round those distant blue peaks which lie to the south, but you are still heading directly towards them. On the other side of those peaks is the Ogaden, but you have been told that there is no direct way through. In trying to match the pictures in your mind to this barren territory which you find yourself crossing, you have somehow missed the way.

But you see no point in turning back now. As long as you can follow this direct trail, you will press on. Perhaps there is a direct way after all, you tell yourself. If you can discover a new way through, then maybe you can open up the whole of the Ogaden. Possibly even get as far as Imi.

Eventually you come to the foothills. The trail is little more than a track now. And then, at the end of a day's journey, you come to this green rocky gully with a spring seeping out of the rock face and forming a round pool. You tether the mules and light up your camp fire. As the sun sets behind the ridge to the west, the smoke from your fire drifts out through the still silent air over the surface of the pool. While your companion sleeps, you sit up looking out over the black glassy water. The smoke from your fire now hangs in a thin flat veil over the gulley, and below this filmy veil there are wispy curls of mist rising from the pool. This is the end of the track. You are now completely lost, you realise.

I neither knew nor cared where I was any more. My stomach was hollow, my knees weak, my mind light and singing with hunger. As I sat on the curb I scratched at my hair, pinching at my skull for the lice.

The crowds were still spilling down the street from the Place de la Bastille, chanting.

'Vie – la – co – une – mune – vive – la – vie – une – vive – la – com – une – vive – la – commune! Vive la Commune! VIVE LA COMMUNE!'

It was getting dark. I just wanted to sleep. Dragging myself to my feet, I stumbled on as the crowds filtered away around me. Eventually I found myself in this wide deserted boulevard. Most of the houses were boarded up. Skirting down the side alley, I climbed over a wall into some dark garden heavy with the scent of flowers. One of the shutters was already off its hinges and the window smashed. After carefully kicking out the last flakes of glass, I heaved myself in.

As soon as my boots landed on the carpet, I froze. At the far end of the room a solitary flickering flare cast veils of leaping light over the walls. There was a marble fireplace and a row of dim gilt-framed paintings above the glinting glass front of a cabinet. From the shadow-webbed ceiling hung a dark-hearted chandelier, icy with the glimmer of reflected light. The flare appeared to be tied to the leg of an upturned table, and on the floor, at the edges of the glow of immediate light, were several bottles. As I peered, I made out various dark figures, their hollow-eyed faces turned towards mine. There was this insistent rustling. Whispering. Together with what sounded like a group of men straining to lift some heavy object. Then a clock-like repetition of hiccups, followed by a long self-perpetuating spasm of coughing.

'Who goes there?'

'I . . . It's only me . . .'

'Ach, it's only some stray kid.'

The faces around the flare turned back to the light, mut-

tering to one another. From somewhere in an upper storey there came a hoarse wavering yell followed by the tinkle of smashing glass.

As my eyes became accustomed to the gloom I made out at my feet the body of a soldier, his uniform half torn off his back. Suddenly he grew two extra naked limbs which kicked out of his jerkin. An arm reached out from under his, moving over his shoulder. And then the face of this girl turned out of his hair to look up at me. Surreptitiously I backed against the wall, feeling below me, and sat down, crouching in the shadow. Beside me were a pair of heaving hairy-creviced buttocks and a white breast cupped in a dark-fingered hand.

Then I saw in front of me the smeared face of some old hag who seemed to be gnawing at a bare thigh. Her wild straggly grey-streaked hair fell in fingers over the white skin of the thigh, combing it as her head nodded. I watched as a hand reached from out of the darkness, pulling the hair back from her face. She looked up and I saw the shiny points of reflected light in the dark sockets of her eyes as her gaze fell on mine. For a moment she simply stared, like an animal disturbed while eating. And then I saw what it was she was eating . . .

'Where did you come from, little boy?'

Behind her a figure sat up, emerging into the dim light as a National Guardsman, his uniform peeled open from his neck to his crutch. The hag's dangling breasts hung down over his thighs, screening his large erect prick as she rose, craning towards me through the flickering gloom.

'What are you doing here, little boy?' her cracked voice called over to me, lisping slightly.

The National Guardsman began fumbling under the folds of her tattered skirt, but she slapped his hand back. Various other shapes began rising, emerging into the light as heads, dishevelled torsos, reaching arms. A bottle clinked, and then from somewhere down below in the cellars I heard the steady, regular sound of bottle after bottle smashing. Above, *in the upper regions of the house, a voice began to howl as if in some final agony of desolation.*

'We've got a little eavthwopper!'

The hag's bony face creased into a leering open-mouthed smile, her tongue playing over her lower lip beneath three goofy spread fangs.

'A little boy who wanth to thee more than ith good for him!'

I pressed back against the wall, edging away as she peeled the National Guardsman's groping hand from her breast and began crawling towards me.

'What do you want, little eavthwopper?' Her breath stank brassily, of wine, garlic and vomit. She pressed her face close to mine, the hanging flaps of her breasts swinging in unison beneath her arms. With an almost girlish gesture she parted her straight straggly hair from her face, tossing it back over her bare scrawny shoulders.

There were other heads now, behind hers. Figures, emerging, rising to their feet. Unashamedly uncovered. Staring down.

'What thall we do with him, boyth?' The hag reached forward, running her coarse-skinned fingers over my face. 'Thuch a curiouth little boy.' Her tongue pressed against her goofy upper teeth.

Someone spat, there were sounds of laughter, and from somewhere in the dark the hiccups started again.

'What do you want, little boy?' Her finger began prodding my chest, and then her other hand was running over my thigh.

My terror snapped. I flung myself forward, pushing her away from me, my fingers pressing into the cold putty of her breasts as she shrieked. Clawing, scratching, biting. I kicked, struggling as I felt other hands grasping me. Then I was being held, pinned, my calves and wrists crushed against the floor. A circle of faces peered over me, their features looming in the light. Above them appeared the rising flames of a torch. I screamed, screwing my eyes closed, frantically struggling. But my body could only strain, pinned at its limits.

When I opened my eyes, I saw the old hag's face rearing towards mine, grimacing, thin-lipped. She spat, and I felt the gob of spittle land on my cheek, dribbling over the side of my lip. I smelt the stink of garlic and tobacco juice. Behind her head, I saw the other heads part, and the torch leaned forward through the darkness. It was held by a huge naked guardsman, his thighs towering like pillars, his long circumcised prick dangling from a cave of darkness. His chest and tiny head receded into the darkness above.

'What thall we do with him, boyth?'

I heard voices, calling, high above me. The old hag threw back her head, cackling, cupping her flopping dugs in her hands and bouncing them. Another hand reached down to pull at my shirt, but the hag quickly slapped it away. 'Thoppit! He'th my little boy!' Then she was pulling at my belt, leering up at me, waggling her tongue between her lips, as the voices lowed with delight.

'Thall we give the little boy a thwill?'

I heard someone belch. And then the sound of spewing in some far corner. The faces around me, above me, were bowing in and out of the light, giggling, leering. The air suddenly smelt of Absinthe.

Then the hag had my trousers open, her rasping fingers picking at the tiny bulbous spout of my prick. She began stroking it, wheedling it, nursing it like some tiny animal, while the shrieks tore the darkness above me. Gradually the feeling welled through my loins as I watched, struggling, yelling every obscenity I could think of.

Slowly my prick grew.

And then other hands were reaching for it. I screeched with pain as the hag slapped at the other hands, her flat breasts swinging. They were fighting over me, clawing, scratching at my groin.

I closed my eyes, shrieking.

And then there were only her hands, plucking at it. My

prick was tiny again, my balls throbbing with pain.

'Don't you like me, little boy?'

I felt her breasts trail over my stomach, and then my prick was covered with something warm and wet, playing with it. I opened my eyes. Below my waist bulged the grey-flecked hummock of her head. I could feel her tongue, licking, her teeth pressing against my limp flesh. My prick tingled, aching. Finally she looked up, her tongue still poking between her lips.

'Tho you don't like me, little boy?'

She spat up at my face, her neck jumping forward like a snake's. I felt the spray splatter over my cheek, my chin, my neck. She leered, her eyes narrowed, as the spittle dribbled from the corner of her lip.

My chin was juddering as I whimpered.

'You cunt! You cow! You bitch!'

She flew at me, scratching at my cheeks while I wrestled, pinned. Then I was smothered. The others were trampling on me, pulling at her. The struggling continued, fitfully, and then stopped. I yelled – I was buried, suffocating.

Next thing my limbs were twisting in their sockets. They were turning me over, laying me face downwards on some damp cushions. I heard a rising chorus of yells. Then the sounds began blurring in my eardrums. Something solid landed on the back of my neck, and as I frantically twisted my face out of the cushions I felt two limbs pressing either side of my head and the hissing rustle of skirts in my ears. I smelt the cheesy stench of fetid underclothes. The old hag was bouncing on my head, yelling. I wriggled frantically, my lungs straining to inhale. At last inhaling. The hot nauseating mushroomy stench of her cunt.

I was swooning, while my lungs retched for breath and the distant chorus of yells dissolved beyond me.

Returning, deafeningly.

The sudden stab of pain burst like a shock through my body and I bit in a spasm into the suffocating folds. The cut-

ting edge of fire plunged into me, splitting my arse.

But even as the pain blurred, spreading through me in a cramping wave, I felt my prick start, aroused, pressing into the cushions. While this rod of molten iron began burning through me, working its way into me, violating me.

The hag was bouncing on the back of my head again so that the yells blared and receded, blared and receded, Truncated obscenities and cries. This pair of hands grasping at my ribs, this wiry tickle playing over the cheeks of my arse. And still this exquisite unbearable root of pain working into me, pushing rhythmically into my innards.

I could breathe, my prick was alive, straining at each thrust as I trembled on the point of release, and this pain cut into my nerve-endings, tautening my limbs with an agonising, tremulous excitement . . .

I was swooning, the agony drifting into numbness as my climax came, and melted . . . the pain went on, driving into me, at a distance . . . and then I was floating, released . . . I could feel nothing. Nothing pressing down on top of me. Nothing inside me . . . A dull numb ache, a shiver of cold . . . Silence. Darkness . . .

I was naked, sticky, stinking of Absinthe. As I moved I felt a stab of pain in my arse. The first grey light of day was filtering through a tall, broken window. Beyond, trees, a lawn. My arse was cracked, crumbly, pain-blotchy. Withdrawing my tentative hand, I saw blood on my fingers.

Around me, semi-naked bodies, motionless and grey, spreadeagled. A man's head lolling back, its mouth hanging open. Snoring. An old hag, flat on her back, arms circled above her head, skirts pulled up over her front, her legs splayed – a fallen ballet figure. Petrified, in grey stone. A thick-fingered hairy hand cupping her hideous wound.

Arthur Rimbaud gingerly pulled on his cold damp absinthe-stinking clothes. Silently he hobbled across the room. By the window he picked up a half-empty bottle of absinthe and put it to his lips. The spirit clawed into his stomach, pressing out its emptiness, glowing. Rimbaud heaved himself up through the window, giving a little involuntary cry of pain as he pulled up his legs. Dumbly, he stumbled forward across the dew-still lawn. While the sunlight filtered into the empty streets, he passed through the suburbs and finally came to the barricades.

'*Halt!*' *The ragged National Guardsman advanced, lowering his bayonet when he saw that it was only a boy.* '*Where d'you think you're going to, son?*'

'*Home.*'

'*Where's home?*'

'*Charleville.*'

The soldier stared glassy-eyed down at the boy, his nose wrinkling, his lips parting as he yawned, silently. '*All right, off you go. Back to Mum where you belong . . . Hey, wait a minute, why are you limping? Y'hurt?*'

The boy nodded.

'*Where?*'

'*Inside.*'

With a derisive snort, the soldier waved the boy on. '*Fuckin schoolkids.*'

Rimbaud stumbled down the road towards Charleville. Mother would be there in the kitchen, bent over the stove. And as I came in through the door, she'd turn. (How many times had she turned to rest her eyes on mine as I stood on the threshold, home once more? How many times must I return to this?) She'd brush her fingers on her apron as she approached me, her shoes ringing on the flags. And then she'd be holding my head, her damp floury hands pressing against my cheeks as she looked into my eyes, searching.

'*What is it this time, Arthur?*'

Her coarse wrinkled shiny hair, pulled tight from her forehead in her braided rats-tail crown, would twinkle in the light as she shook her head at my muttered words.

'*Ach!*' *Her brown eyes, hard and unyielding, fixed on mine.* '*Such bad, bad blood I see in you.*'

She'd push me away from her. '*Why, you're filthy! You*

stink! Just look at you! . . . And what's all this? . . . Bits of filthy paper . . . Poems, you say? What poems? Filthy dirty. What does this say? 'My poor heart dribbles at the stern. O abracadantic waves bathe my heart that it may be cleansed . . .'

It was pitch dark in the gully. The smoke from the flickering fire at my side was still drifting out in a dim settling veil over the surface of the pool. But underneath it I could distinctly see these tiny waves, fanning out in concentric ripples, through the darkness, across the pool, towards me. I listened. I could hear the tinkle of water. There was something drinking on the other side.

An animal?

I picked up the pistol lying beside me and crept silently around the edge of the pool, ducking behind the boulders, peering into the mist in the direction of the tinkling water. Then I saw this dark solid shape. It was a man, drinking.

I raised the pistol, steadying the cold metal of the barrel in my other hand.

But why shoot him? He obviously wasn't an enemy, or he wouldn't give himself away so easily. He'd probably been attracted by the light of the fire. Perhaps he was another traveller, like yourself. No one lived in this territory.

But how was Arthur to communicate with this unknown figure in the dark without frightening him off?

Crouched and shivering in the hedgerow outside the town, the young vagabond Rimbaud had listened to the owl hoots of the vagrants calling to one another in the woods across the valley. Rousing himself and pressing his chilled fingers to his lips, he had hooted back . . . Eventually he had found his way to the circle of bearded tramps sitting around the fire in the clearing.

I cupped my hand to my lips. 'Who-oo!'

The tinkling of water stopped. The last ripples fanned out across the surface. I could see the glow of the fire, a misted pulsating pinkness, its brilliant molten reflection slipping quite clearly along the black ripples under the bank of smoke.

I watched as the figure rose slowly to his feet. He was a Negro. As he stepped cautiously forward, crouching slightly, I saw that he was entirely naked. He had a spear, but he appeared to be only resting it on his shoulder.

I blew softly, once more: 'Who-oo!'

Steeling myself, I rose to my feet, still pointing the pistol.

As soon as he saw me, he straightened up and moved towards me through the parting tendrils of grey mist. He'd obviously never seen a gun before.

He came up and stood before me, silently. The mist drifted around us. Then his hand reached forward and rested lightly on mine. His cold fingers touched my wrist, his palm resting on the barrel of the pistol. But before I could panic, he spoke. His voice was deep, and curiously toneless. It was a tribal tongue which I didn't recognise. When I didn't reply, he spoke again, his voice robbed of all resonance by the mist. He took his spear off his shoulder and pointed towards the mountains, raising his feet as if he were marching, and then held his head on one side, looking at me.

Did he want to know where I was going?

'Anywhere, beyond . . .' I gesticulated up in the direction of the dark outline of the mountains. 'Ogaden?' I tried, shrugging.

No response.

'Imi?' I tried again, hopefully, enunciating both syllables slowly and clearly.

I heard him sigh, or maybe he was simply cold. 'I-mi?' he repeated it slowly, as I'd done.

'Imi.'

'Eye-me!' He recognised it! Again he sighed, or shuddered. I pointed with my free hand to my chest and then towards the dark form of the mountains. Immediately he did the same, and then pointed to me, holding his head on one side again.

Was he going there too? Or was he offering to lead me there? Or was he simply trying to be friendly?

Eventually I led him back to our camp. Almost at once he lay down, crouching up close to the fire, and fell asleep. I sat watching him, my pistol on my lap. There was always a chance that he knew a way through.

I must have fallen asleep, because next thing I knew it was dawn. The Negro was standing at the head of the gully, looking down at me. As soon as he saw I was awake, he raised his hand, and then motioned with his spear towards the peaks. I quickly loaded up the mules, and then shook Sottiro awake.

'You mean you're going to let him guide us? Just like that? When you can't understand a word of what he says?'

'Yes.'

'But what if we get lost?'

'What would you say if I told you we'd been lost almost since we set out?'

Sottiro would say nothing, apparently.

Pausing for only as long as it took Sottiro to change into the last of his rainbow assortment of silk shirts, the expedition started forward up the gully.

For two days we followed the Negro, making slow progress up through the foothills and into the mountains. At night he would share our meal and then sleep by the fire. He seemed to know a way, all right.

On the third day, he led us up to the head of a high boulder-strewn valley, and then we were forced to dismount as he led us along a ledge which wound up the side of the towering blue-peaked mountain.

I peered ahead, puckering my eyes against the light. High up above, the narrow line of the ledge climbed around the mountain along the sheer face of the rock towards the wrinkled snow-flecked blue ridge.

From the highest point in the clear blue heavens the cataract gushed out, its spilling white-foamed torrent leaping into the air beneath the shimmering arc of a rainbow, before subsiding, with a gradual unfolding finality, into a huge, elastic slow-motion curtain of spreading spray. The roar of the waterfall reverberated between the wide sheer rock faces, charging me with a sudden pulse of fear that seemed to run through me like the very blood in my veins.

The spray splattered in drifting veil-like waves along the ledge from the fringe of the waterfall. I saw the Negro disappear along the ledge as if into a mist, first losing all colour, then becoming a mere shadow, a shade, a blur. Nothing. Next moment the white veil was hissing over me. I stumbled forward, peering ahead through jewel-obscured eyes, and made out the bent form of the Negro waddling on, his arms shielding his head, his spear poking in front of him, as if he were advancing to do battle with some unseen giant beyond.

I turned to see the shadow of my horse loom behind me through the mist, and as the spray drifted I caught a glimpse of the leading mules. They were simply plodding forward along the narrow ledge, heads bowed, abject and unthinking. Sottiro was obviously still pushing them on from behind. He hadn't rounded the corner yet and seen what lay ahead. Rimbaud found himself grinning over the gulf of sheer panic which had opened inside him.

At my next step, the drifting torrent of spray suddenly parted to reveal the path moving through an eerie, luminescent twilight along the edge of the vertical drop. Above and all around the water formed a thundering canopy; and below it the rock face had become bulbous with dripping lichens and hanging drapes of slimy green weed. At the end of the ledge, there was a creeper-covered fault in the rock. Below the glistening green leaves was a low narrow diagonal cleft of darkness: the entrance to a cave. I saw the Negro duck into it, vanishing immediately in the inner darkness. I stumbled forward, pausing only to retrieve the dangling lead rein of my horse.

But as I approached, sliding my feet over the green slimy surface of the ledge like an inexpert skater, I realised, with a sudden spasm of apprehension, that the entrance to the cave was too small. The mules would get through all right, but never a horse.

There was nothing else for it, I decided on the spur of the moment. We'd come all this way, there was no going back now. I went up to the horse, pulled the pistol out from my pack, cocked it, and poked it behind the horse's ear. The horse shook its head, lightly, snorting. I held its muzzle, soothing it, and pulled the trigger.

The horse bared its teeth, nibbling at the bit. Nothing had happened; the cartridges were damp. The horse turned its head, pushing its muzzle into my shoulder. I dug the pistol into my belt as my head sank, bowed, against the side of the horse's face. The constant unfurling explosion of the water beyond roared through my mind, obliterating all thought as I gritted my teeth, my fingers clawing into the matted dampness of the horse's mane.

As I shoved, the horse reared up, stumbling on its back legs. Its front hooves kicked into the rock face beside me. And then I was pushing with all my strength at its subsiding body. I heard it whinny as its hooves landed with a clatter on the slippery path. Yet almost as soon as its hooves had touched the ground, it reared once more. This time I heaved my shoulder against its rib cage. But now its body was falling towards me. I flung myself forward as the horse's body banged against the rock face above me. Its hoof stumbled onto my arse as I lay on the ground. At first I thought I was being crushed, my whole pelvis on the point of crumbling. And then, suddenly, the weight shifted. When I turned from the rock face, I saw the horse, wide-eyed with panic, its teeth bared, its whinny lost in the roar of the torrent, pawing frantically at the air above me. Its back leg kicked for a hold, scuffling; and then, after a moment's statuesque poise, it began to topple, surprisingly slowly, over the edge. Its legs splayed out as it fell, turning on its back, its straight extended limbs spinning through a slow arc as it tumbled against the exact subsiding lace of the torrent. And then it was gone.

Along the ledge, the lead mule stood, snorting clouds of condensation, its eyes blinking, bedraggled, unmoved. I got to my feet, snatched at its dangling lead rein, and limped forward. My hand was smudged with blood I noticed as I yanked the mule on through the cave entrance, backing into the dimness.

It wasn't until Rimbaud turned to face the darkness of the cave that he remembered that the horse had been carrying his pack. Ahead in the roof of the cave he saw a narrow opening giving onto blue sky; the silhouette of the Negro moved across it, leading the way. His pack containing all his personal belongings . . . But what did Arthur Rimbaud, vagabond of three continents, want with packs of personal belongings? They contained nothing of any value. Rimbaud watched as the other mules began stumbling through the dim glassy light of the entrance. Nothing. Nothing of any value whatsoever. Rimbaud steeled himself as he turned to pull the lead mule forward into the darkness, to which his eyes were now gradually acclimatising. His limbs were suddenly weak; he could feel the strength draining out of his legs. In his pack there had been his book of analysis. His geological studies. All his chemical notes. Rimbaud stumbled forward, stamping the circulation into his legs. Now he had nothing to go on. Only what he could remember. What he could dredge from his mind.

Glancing back he saw Sottiro, carrying his pack over his shoulder, emerge through the entrance against the dull beady brilliance of the waterfall. With a final stamp Rimbaud started forward again. All around, and in seemingly distant chambers high above him, the darkness was alive with the insistent flurry of pressing, singing whispers: the amplified roar of the waterfall. Peering forward through the gloom, he made out the silhouette of the Negro as he passed once more in front of the hole in the roof of the cave. The floor of the cave was sloping upwards. Gradually, as he picked his way forward, Rimbaud became aware of the dimensions of the cave: that tiny hole up there was the way out! Moving on into the growing light as the whispers surged and eddied through the unseen chambers around him, he saw ahead what appeared to be a well-defined path.

The mules followed behind him, snorting, their harnesses clinking, the clatter of their hooves echoing precisely through the blurred whispers. When finally Rimbaud reached the opening, which by now had grown into a large patch of empty blue sky, the Negro was waiting for him. Below, Rimbaud saw a gentle green slope running down in the brilliant sunlight into a vast open plateau of waving grass. The Negro came up to his side, gesturing, holding his open hand forward. 'Ogaden,' said the Negro, nodding.

11

Rimbaud's expedition followed the Negro down into the rolling plateau of waist-high grass, which shifted around them, hissing in gentle waves as they passed. Once or twice in the late afternoon Rimbaud thought he saw the scattered specks of grazing herds on the distant slopes, but they appeared to be untended and wild. That night the expedition camped by a waterhole, and the roar of lions rose out of the grass as it breathed in the night breezes. Next day Rimbaud dried out the ammunition, and when they stopped at midday he tried out Vardy's pistol, firing it into the air. The explosion receded over the empty hilly plateau in a long blurring echo, unfurling between the gentle slopes. The Negro simply stared at him, resting his chin on his knees. So he obviously did know about guns!

For three days they tramped from waterhole to waterhole, the Negro apparently guiding them through the trackless grass by instinct alone. There were no landmarks and the mountains receded behind them in the shimmering heat haze. Then on the fourth day they came to a small grass hut village by a stream. The bare-breasted women sat at the entrances to the huts weaving grass mats on simple looms as the naked pot-bellied children scampered in the sun. No one seemed particularly surprised at the arrival of the first European Expedition to penetrate into the heart of the Ogaden. Eventually a wrinkle-faced grey-haired old Negro leaning on the shoulder of a milky-eyed blind youth came out to greet them. He welcomed the Negro as a friend, calling him Ayif, as far as Rimbaud could make out.

There followed the traditional primitive meal, at which

the uncivilised habits of the strange natives were surreptitiously scrutinised. Conversation was difficult, since these oddities of the earth didn't appear to speak any known language and seemed to be interested only in a substance called Imi, and something which smelled, highly, to judge from the clumsy gestures of their absurdly-dressed, dyed-skinned leader. The hosts, however, proved sufficiently tactful, ignoring the possible implication that their chief guest might be referring to them. The only thing to do was sell him something and speed him on his way before his companion with the roving eyes, dressed in the rather fetching violet chestcloth, began putting ideas into the heads of the younger virgins. The men would probably be back from hunting soon and might resent such close scrutiny of the anatomy of their future brides by this spindle-shanked freak who probably had a prick as long as that of a wild ass.

Accordingly, the dour mask-faced leader was shown to the hide-curing huts. Here he continued his strange performance by behaving as if he'd never seen such hides before. In a most uncommercial manner, with gestures of childish delight, he began fingering the skins, exclaiming, and rubbing his cheek against the fur (obviously sniffing for any improperly cured patches). The extraordinary man seemed to be in raptures, like a foolish young virgin after being chosen at the bride-picking ceremony; and he immediately offered to buy the lot. In exchange he offered some fine-woven cloth covered in curiously simple repetitive designs. It wasn't a very good colour pattern, but then some of the younger gad-abouts might take a fancy to it.

With an almost provocative lack of ceremony, the pale-skinned trader simply accepted the first offer, loaded the skins onto his mules, dumped the cloth in the mud where the goats shat, and began preparations for starting on his way once more – while his violet-clad companion stood about making curious one-eyed blinking motions and contorting his face at the sniggering group of thirteen-summer virgins. And so the brief and rather distasteful visitation was over.

It would make an interesting story round the fire, and some of the brighter sparks might even make a song and dance out of it. These uneducated natives would be worth a laugh, even if their plain cloth wasn't up to much.

For the next four days, the expedition pressed on across apparently uninhabited territory. As far as Rimbaud could make out from the Negro, Ayif, the journey to Imi would take them a week. But on the fifth day, Sottiro started to develop some kind of rash. Within twenty-four hours his skin had begun to swell in livid blotches and he soon became too ill to walk or even sit upright in his saddle. With the aid of Ayif, Arthur constructed a makeshift stretcher which could be strung between two mules, but by the end of the day it became obvious that Sottiro could travel no further, for the time being anyway.

Why the hell had I saddled myself with this oaf? I should have left him behind in Harar.

Rimbaud sat beside the smouldering embers of the camp fire, listening as Sottiro's groans rose in the darkness beside him. We'd made slow progress, but still we couldn't have been much more than a day's journey from Imi. What the hell was I going to do now?

Back in the barn at home, drained of all tears, the music of his abandoned misery moaning out of him, Arthur Rimbaud had added the final words to his last poem. 'And so now I must bury my imagination and my memories. I am given back to the earth, with a purpose to pursue, and wrinkled reality to embrace . . . Let's go! . . . I have seen hell; I might even have died there . . . and now it will be permitted to me to possess truth in a body and a soul.'

Let's go!

Rimbaud got up and went over to the packs. Taking out the pistol and tearing a leaf from the account ledger, he scribbled a quick note. 'Pressing on to Imi for help. Stay where you are, Arthur.' After surreptitiously depositing the pistol and the note beside Sottiro, he began to load up the mules, stringing them together. As an afterthought, he left the last two still tethered. They'd act as a landmark. What the hell, there was nothing else he could do. He might just find some help in Imi. As well as that musk.

Crossing to the other side of the fire, Rimbaud shook the dozing Negro.

'Imi, Ayif.'

Without a word the Negro rose and picked up his spear. Rimbaud followed him into the dark, leading the mules behind him.

The dawn grew slowly to our left, pinking the opposite hills. The strips of cloud on the eastern horizon blazed with inner gold, their radiance gradually dimming the exact crescent of the moon, obliterating the last zodiacal patterns of the stars from the paling blue of the upper heavens. Ahead, Ayif pressed on, a dark featureless silhouette.

It was the middle of the morning by the time the rain clouds began darkening the sky. Out of the shifting whispers of the grass, I heard this constant high-pitched hiss growing on the wind. And then the rain swept over us, bouncing like clouded marbles in the dry dust for several seconds before spreading in a muddy pock-marked sheen across the surface of the earth. Within minutes the mules were bogged down.

After heaving and cursing till his strength almost gave out, Rimbaud eventually lost his temper and began battering the lead mule with his fists as it tottered, its hooves squelching deeper into the mud. Why now, damn you! Rimbaud raised his face to the clouds, yelling with rage as the rain plastered his hair over his face. Ayif stood, propped on his spear, expressionless, while the tears of rain coursed down his cheeks. His skin suddenly appeared quite blue.

With a final spasm of rage, Rimbaud kicked at the lead mule. His boot caught its hind leg. He saw its leg shudder with pain as it tried to pull itself free of the mud, and then it was toppling, its load spilling from its side. Rimbaud heard the snap, like that of a dry brittle stick, even through the heavy hiss of the downpour. As he watched, aghast, the mule sagged onto its haunches, the white splinters of its bone breaking through the skin of its hind leg. Vainly, it tried to pull itself upright with its bent forelegs.

The pistol! Where was the pistol! Put it out of its agony. But the pistol was with Sottiro. Oh God, what have I done? The mule twisted on its front legs, still trying to raise itself, its head bowing dumbly with effort.

'Oh God, Ayif. How can I put an end to it?' I was on my knees in the mud, my hands resting on the mule's straining neck. 'I didn't mean to. I didn't.' The mule's head nodded, reaching forward. 'I promise I didn't!' But I was talking to myself; Ayif could never have heard me through the rain, let alone have understood me. The mule's ears flickered instinctively at my yelling voice. 'Oh God, Ayif. I hate myself! I *hate* mySELF!'

When I raised my head, Ayif was standing before me. I saw him crouch down in front of the mule, and then suddenly I felt the mule stiffen under my hands. As I got up from my knees, I saw Ayif withdrawing his bloodstained spear from its front. The beast convulsed fitfully, and then sagged, a gush of blood spouting from the wound left by Ayif's spear. Slowly the pulsing of the gushes lessened as the blood spread through the muddy water of the hoof pools.

'Imi!' I finally yelled at Ayif, pointing forward.

The rest of the mules were still tethered to the carcass. I'd leave them; they wouldn't stray.

Ayif started forward, expressionless as ever, and I tramped after him. By late afternoon the sky had begun to clear ahead. The rain softened, and eventually stopped. The sun was now setting fierily amidst towering black clouds, its rays flaring over the distant grey hills to the west. There was still no sign of Imi.

I stumbled on, my clothes hanging heavily on my body. Ayif began to look round at me as the dusk thickened, but I motioned him on impatiently.

'Imi!' I shouted at him, heaving my boots free of the

sticky mud. His feet squeezed through the mud ahead.

As darkness came on I made him quicken his pace. He was tired, I could see. And now that we'd abandoned the mules there was no food or water.

Eventually, without warning, Ayif sank to his haunches. I stood over him, breathing heavily, and then subsided beside him.

'How far?' I asked, gesturing determinedly. 'Imi?'

He nodded glumly, pointing ahead.

'How *far*, dammit!' There was no going back at this stage. I had three gold Napoleons in my pocket. Enough to buy as much musk as I could carry, and maybe even hire another mule. Only that musk could justify my journey now... And besides, there was still Sottiro.

I got up, and motioned for Ayif to start. Reluctantly he hauled himself to his feet and loped forward. I strode on as fast as I could. The mud was less sticky now; already the wind was drying it out. Ayif was lagging behind, I noticed. I motioned for him to be quicker. It couldn't be that far now. Ahead, the clear starry night was disappearing behind a rising band of woolly darkness; there was more cloud on the way. I listened for the rain, but could hear nothing above the light shifting of the grass all around and the dull, cloddish monotony of my footsteps and my rasping breath. Ayif's bare feet were silent behind me. As the clouds approached, I turned. And then stopped in my tracks. Ayif was gone.

Rimbaud stood, while the black wind-torn edges of the cloud-bank moved over the stars above him. Now he was alone. Utterly alone. Lost.

'... *and now it will be permitted for me to possess truth in a body and a soul.*'

Gradually, as the blood charge of Rimbaud's terror mounted, the darkness became absolute. Now there was only going on. To this place he knew existed. He had been told it existed. Somewhere. Out there. Beyond the darkness. Imi. You're mad. This is madness. But Rimbaud knew himself to be now beyond the sanity of all reasonable alternatives. Only in the possible existence of this saving madness was there any hope.

With a swallowed whimper he blundered forward, blinding his awareness to all that whispered and seethed around him in the darkness. For an hour or so, as the sweat melted over his limbs, he stumbled on, his footsteps growing shorter as he felt the strength draining from his body. Then he was staggering. Forward a pace. Sideways a pace. Forward a pace. Backward a pace. Around the barely supported hollowness of his stomach. As the darkness itself began to shift, undulating about him. I felt my pores open, prickling, as my skin appeared to freeze. I clawed at the spiralling darkness as I fell, and then my eyes were grinding into the damp unyielding earth. Blind, visionless. My awareness receding to a minuscule point. Extinguishing.

There was a moon, and an archipelago of stars. The grass was shifting about me like the sea. Then I became aware of this other sound. Duller, thicker, more earth-resonant. As if things were falling out of the sky around me. Objects of some kind, not too heavy. But there were no shadows falling against the stars. Then the sounds stopped . . . The low distant growl of a lion. Immediately the grass was alive with leaping, fleeting shapes. Dancing around me, over me. I sat up. And as the vertigo spun through my skull, I saw the rising form of an antelope twitch away from me in midflight. I watched as the dark shapes bounded free of the grass in long gliding leaps. And then I lay down again, resting my cheek against a cool rustle of grass.

The sun was up, but not far above the horizon. I could move. I could crawl. My head parting the grass. Behind me the endless rolling plateau under the cloudless sky. A faint blur above the horizon: the blue-peaked mountains.

Rimbaud continued crawling, mechanically, uphill. Thoughtless. Aware neither of tiredness nor strength. Only the rustle of the breeze in the grass passed through his mind. And then there was no more grass breaking about his forehead.

Below, the receding muddy cliff fell sheer to the brown churning rapids of a river. Which curved away from him. On the far bank, way beneath him, in exact miniature proportions: tiny white-washed cube houses, curving alleyways, *people!* in coloured robes, palm trees, a white domed mosque and a high thin minaret – Imi! . . . Rimbaud watched as the tiny figures moved below, going about recognisable business. The women washing clothes on the banks of the river. Men bargaining in a small market square. That wide brown foam-flecked expanse of rushing water below: the Web. There was no way across. Or down, as far as he could see. He scratched at the dry crumbly earth with his fingers and threw a handful over the picture before his tear-blurred eyes, watching the dark specks fall, tumbling away, scattering. And then he crawled back into the grass . . .

As he lay, the heat of the sun pressing into his face, he became aware of this faint smell of perfume on the air. *No Imi, no musk*, he realised with a calm sensation of utter finality. Forget it . . . He sniffed. Again. It wasn't his imagination. The smell was coming from somewhere nearby. Over there. Rimbaud turned on his side, pressed himself up from the earth, and began slowly crawling forward. His head swimming as this fresh delicate fragrance feathered his nostrils. At its centre, a heady richness which was somehow thick and sensuous, without cloying. Reminding, of so many sweetnesses. And yet awakening, rising, for the first time.

Like the first icy lift of opium in the veins, releasing.

Like the delirious rasp of an orgasm.

Like a crystalline chord, splintering.

Like . . .

Ras Makonen laid his hand on Arthur's shoulder. 'Only to a man who knows it, is it possible to convey that one knows it too, I think.' Rimbaud crawled forward through the grass, drawing the smell into his lungs. And then, as it grew stronger, he became aware of another smell, which seemed

to come from the heart of it: richer still, but more all-pervasive. Nauseous. As he approached, Rimbaud recognised the stench of putrifying flesh.

The grass parted around Rimbaud's head, and before him he saw the reclining awkward-limbed carcass of a deer, its skin torn open from its neck to its rear flank. The flesh had been chewed away and the grass all around was flattened.

Even as the flies rose from the carcass in a droning cloud before his dreamy eyes, leaving a teeming tracery of insects, Rimbaud recognised the skin of the animal. It was identical to those which he'd bought from the old man and his blind boy back at the village. So they were musk deer skins!

Rimbaud lay at the edge of the flattened grass breathing in the smell of musk couched in the heavy, choking odours of putrefaction; and then, as he felt the saliva well around his tongue, he understood. Food! He heaved himself forward and began picking at the flesh with his trembling fingers, tearing it away from the bone in long pink rubbery strips. The insects scurried at his fingertips. And then he was chewing. It was cold, and slimy, with the salty taste of blood. He swallowed it, in lumps, his lips drooling with saliva, pausing every now and again to savour the rich gamey tang which pervaded its spongy rawness. Eventually, he lowered his head and began gnawing the flesh free of the flanks, his teeth nibbling at the hard glossy surface of the bone . . . After eating his fill, Rimbaud lay back in the grass and fell almost immediately into a deep sleep.

The shadow passed across my face. My eyes blinked open. It passed again. The sky above me was alive with these ungainly winged patches of darkness, swooping, rising . . . Vultures! I sat up quickly and felt the flies rise from my caked tickly cheeks, buzzing above my bloodied hands. But as I rose to my feet, steadying myself, my head muzzy and pounding with the heat, I could feel the strength in my limbs. Pulling back the skin on the haunches of the carcass,

I tore off three long strips of flesh and shoved them into my pocket. Spitting into my hands I rubbed them clean of blood, and then wiped the caked blood from around my lips with my damp palm. The shadows of the vultures were curving across the grass. Ahead I could see my flattened track zigzagging back up to the cliff edge, and then meandering away in a series of long winding curves in the direction of the faint shadowy mountains on the horizon. The sun was still high; I had several hours of light. With luck I might be able to make it back to the mules before nightfall. I'd sleep there, and then ride back to Sottiro.

Finally as his shadow began to lengthen in the golden light, Rimbaud made out the dark shapes of the mules on the hillside in the distance. By the time he drew up to them he was stumbling once more with weakness, placing one foot in front of the other as he tottered forward with glazed eyes.

Two mules lay savaged, their cargo of skins shredded, ruined; and the carcass of the dead mule with the broken leg was bloated and stinking. He couldn't sleep the night here; the lions would return for the other mules. It was a miracle they were still unharmed: at least four loads of skins were saved. Rimbaud stood, gazing blankly into the growing dusk. The remaining mules stood frisking amidst the flies, shaking their ears and craning towards him, suspiciously. What nightmare had those eyes witnessed? Then Rimbaud noticed. The swollen carcass of the lead mule had lost the lower half of its broken hind leg, and there was a long trail of flattened grass stretching down the slope into the dusk. The live mules had dragged those three carcasses over half a mile . . . Rimbaud untied the lead line from the carcasses and clambered up onto the first mule. The others followed in line, as the advance party of the first European expedition into the furthest reaches of Lower Abyssinia started back on its attempt to reach base camp.

If I could just keep going.

As the night passed I chewed at my strips of meat, sucking them, placing them over my eyes. Their cool sliminess roused me. When I dozed off, propped in the saddle, the mules would stop. Several times I came to myself with a start, straining my eyes open, peering into the darkness, steadying myself on the saddle. I'd kick the mule forward, and we'd be on our way once more.

As the first light grew over the grass, illuminating the landscape in a vague filmy blue, I began to get uncontrollable spasms of shivers. The mule started frisking beneath me as my knees shook and my heels banged into its flanks. Eventually, it took to breaking into unpredictable short-distance trots, forcing me to snap out of my comatose state and cling with a sudden tensing of muscles. Finally, still shivering, although the sun was already hot on my face and forearms, I made out the two black blurs of the mules I'd left with Sottiro.

Or two flies.

Or two spots before my eyes. Slipping over the blurred landscape.

Two mules.

Dead or alive? . . .

Alive. Baring their teeth, as if about to bray.

And Sottiro, squatting by a pile of twigs. Apparently recovered.

'Arthur! So glad you're back. I thought you were never going to make it!'

His face, double-imaging before my glazed stare.

I fell forward, slithering out of the saddle.

'By the way Arthur, could you light up this fire for me? I haven't quite got the hang of it yet.'

Rimbaud subsided onto his knees in the grass, toppling, asleep even before his face hit the ground.

12

After a day's rest Rimbaud decided to set off to the west. That way, he calculated, they would eventually join up with the regular trading trails and he'd perhaps be able to do some business in an attempt to redeem the time he'd lost. Also, he'd be able to try and fulfil the other main objective of his expedition. He would see if he could find out where Yarousseau had gone to ground after his banishment from Harar. And whether in fact he was still alive.

After five days' journey to the west, they came upon a small caravan trail which led to the north. This was obviously the way round the blue-peaked mountains. Soon they came to inhabited territory, and at night Rimbaud would camp, often in the company of other caravans, by some lonely village oasis, eating with the heads of the families in the cool night air of the courtyard around the well. The women would sing and the men play on their flutes, while the water tinkled in the darkness under the palm trees along the irrigation channels.

When I calculated we were only a week or so distant from Harar, I began asking, amongst the usual trading enquiries and questions about the terrain, whether there was word of anyone like myself who had lived – or possibly was still living – anywhere in the region.

The villagers would frown.

Like me, I would gesture, indicating the colour of my skin.

But by this stage my skin was burnt as dark as theirs.

A man with features like mine, I tried to explain, tracing

my fingers over my face.

But my face was lined, and more coarse-skinned than ever now. And as I explained, I knew that to the young men I was describing an old man, to the old men an ugly one, to the rich traders a poor trader, and finally, to the poor traders, something quite beyond their usual experience. Consequently, it was from the poor traders that I first began to pick up hints that Yarousseau's existence was known of in these parts. Where, precisely, they could not say. But they had heard tell. To the east, they thought. In one of the valleys to the north of the blue-peaked mountains. But that took me in a complete circle! I'd been there, I told them. No one lived there. They would shrug. There were a few hidden villages. I would have to ask.

As Rimbaud progressed slowly north-east through the villages which lay in the foothills of the blue-peaked mountains, occasionally buying a consignment of gum or hides, he began recognising, in the faces of the different tribal families, various prevailing features. The set of a pair of eyes, the narrowness of certain cheek-bones, the straight line of a nose. Where had he seen those eyes before? That nose? As the days passed, Rimbaud found himself increasingly haunted by this face which he could never quite visualise. And every face he saw seemed to remind him of it in some obscure way.

In his loneliness, as he endured the hardships of the journey, Rimbaud found himself deriving a peculiar comfort from this face which he could never quite see, but knew existed somewhere at the back of his mind, just beyond the reach of his recall. And as it tantalised him, it also comforted him. It was a presence, a solace in the empty wilderness, a feeling of warmth in the cold night. He found himself talking to it, telling it his hopes, his fears, confessing to it the deep, almost sensual melancholy which gradually seemed to possess him as he progressed further and further on his travels. This had been the journey which was to realise all his hopes, but he knew now that it was just another journey, like so many others he had undertaken in his life. Perhaps it would always be the same. The unknown, the new, the unrealised, would always take on the features of hope, only to withdraw into some further realm the moment their originality became real, endured, corrupted by the commonplaces of crass experience.

And then, one evening, he came to an oasis, and there was this face. All the features were there! The old toothless hag smiled up at him as he rode up on his mule towards the gate. This was the face that had been there at the back of his mind. And there it was again, in the features of that bearded man coming across the courtyard to meet him, and in that young girl standing at the far doorway. Each one had this same face. With exactly those features. Immediately Rimbaud knew the face that had been with him on his journey. Tahira! His tribal servant girl. He'd sent her back to her village after she'd given him syphilis. This must be Tahira's village!

Then, as he sat in the courtyard with the village headman, Rimbaud saw her, standing over by the well. She was staring at him, frozen, open-mouthed, as she leant over the wall of the well, a stone pitcher under her arm.

The village headman bent forward and tapped Rimbaud's hand. Did the foreign traveller wish to buy any hides?

Yes, he would do business, Rimbaud indicated.

When he looked back, Tahira had drawn her veil over her face. Now he could only see her eyes.

Tahira! For so long I have been talking to you. For so long you have been my only comfort.

She looked away, setting the pitcher down beside the well pail. Then she looked up again.

Tahira, will you come back to Harar with me? Will you share my life?

What is your bid, demanded the village headman, indicating the hides that had been laid out in front of them.

Rimbaud perfunctorily indicated his price.

Could you teach me not to loathe myself, to find comfort,

or even love perhaps, where I have found only self-disgust and contempt?

The village headman indicated his price. The bargaining had begun.

I would have you cured, and then maybe you would bear me a child. A son whom I would educate. A son who would redeem the ruin I have made of my life.

Rimbaud scratched out his higher price in the dust.

I would teach you to speak French. We would live together. If Badjian can cure me, then surely he can cure you too?

Abruptly, the village headman indicated that the bargaining was over. He was old, he did not like bargaining. He would accept the foreign traveller's price. Did the foreign traveller want anything else before he went on his way?

Raising his finger, Rimbaud pointed to Tahira, who immediately turned and began lowering the bucket into the well. I would like to buy her, indicated Rimbaud.

She is no good, indicated the old man, turning down his mouth in contempt. But he had others. Younger. More comely virgins. Which this one definitely was not. This one was something of a bone of contention, to judge from the rapidly rising passion of his gestures.

I don't care. I want her, I indicated. How much?

But she is married, indicated the village headman, to one of my sons.

Tahira raised the bucket and began pouring out the water into the pitcher. She was looking at me now, her eyes gentle, perplexed, questioning.

But her husband does not want her, continued the old man with a gesture of dismissal. She is yours if you want her. Take her, I give her to you with the skins. We have made a good bargain. She has caused nothing but fighting amongst my sons.

With a curious feeling of exaltation, which was all the more forceful for being so outside his present experience, Rimbaud helped Tahira up onto his mule and led her away towards the camp outside the oasis where his mules were tethered. Tahira rode beside him in the dark, without a word, as Rimbaud blinked, peering ahead into the night through his damp, blurred eyes.

Sottiro was naturally incensed. 'You selfish bastard! You go and make me spend a month's wages on some fat little nymphomaniac, and then you won't even let me take her with me. And then you have the cheek to go and buy one for yourself. For nothing!'

However, when Tahira started cooking the meals Sottiro's attitude underwent a slight change.

'You mean she's going to look after both of us?'

'Of course. I won't take any unfair advantage. She'll be sleeping on her own till we get to Harar.' If he'd only known why, he'd probably have left the expedition there and then.

'You know,' he went on, 'perhaps it wasn't such a bad idea taking her on. After all, if they were giving her away for nothing it would have been rather rude to turn her down, wouldn't it?'

The prospect of edible meals and no further spells of cooking duty appeared to have cheered Sottiro up more than anything so far on our travels. He had long since tired of his role as the best-dressed explorer in the heart of Africa.

Throughout the day, Tahira would sit on her mule, her veil drawn up under her eyes. Rimbaud would walk by her side, occasionally smiling up at her or resting his hand on hers. Sometimes, towards the end of the day, Rimbaud would begin talking to her, telling her his thoughts, much as he had done to himself before he had found her, before he had realised who it was he was talking to. Tahira's eyes would smile as she looked down at him. They still had no language in common.

Eventually they passed into the barren valleys to the north of the blue-peaked mountains. Here the sides of the ridges contained pockets of stunted trees and were often scarred with landslips; scattered boulders and banks of rubble lay on either side of the narrow trail. Rimbaud soon found himself studying the terrain as they passed further up into the higher valleys. The boulders were of the same rock as before, but they were often split along curving faults. The rock faces revealed by the landslips were seamed too, Rimbaud noticed, frequently appearing like some huge sculpted freize (a triumphant procession, or battle perhaps) which had been abandoned by the artist just before the figures had begun to emerge into any permanent determinate shapes.

The eagles drifted high above the fallen rubble of the landslips, gliding in wide decelerating swoops against the folded seams of the rock faces, swooping occasionally like released arrows. Their wide feathered wings would bat against the grass, or flutter, phoenix-like in the heat blur, as they emerged from the stony wilderness. Then they would rise once more, mounting into the air in a long steep curve, some dark twitching shape grasped between their talons.

Yes, Rimbaud decided, there could well be something of value in these mountains. As he unpacked his spade and sample pannier from the mule, he scoured his brain for the pictures he had constructed in his imagination from the pages of his lost analysis notes. But still nothing matched. Evidently this landscape was something he hadn't foreseen, for it definitely contained ore of some kind, he saw as he began hacking away at the rubble with his spade. The ring of his metal spade against the stones echoed between the rock faces, and then he started back to the mules, bowed down under the weight of his filled pannier.

As we passed through the scattered tribal villages, I continued to ask after Yarousseau. By now I'd begun to recognise various persistent features in their gestured replies. Yes, I was not the only man like myself in these parts, they told me. There was another. Who had never been here, but was always in some further place. They had heard about him. He held a position of authority in one of the upper tribes. He was their god. But yes, he was definitely a man. Like me? No, I was not a god. I was a man the same as he, but not a god, apparently. This god brought the rains from across the mountains with the blue peaks. No, they had never actually seen this man-god. But they had met men who had claimed to have seen him. Yes, they assured me patiently, his appearance was in many ways exactly the same as mine. And like me, he spoke a soft tongue of his own. He spoke to the blue peaks in his own tongue.

Day by day, as we moved through the highland valleys, the details became more consistent. By now the villages were poorer. These were the tribes of settled grazers, I learned, who had only settled down to live in these villages a few seasons previously. The valleys had then been fertile and a good home, only now the rains had not come and many of the tribes were on the point of reverting once more to their old primitive nomadic ways. But in the mountains there was a man-god, a rain-king, who would bring this season's rain, they assured me, though many of them hardly appeared convinced by their own words.

Eventually we came to a small grass hut village, where the lean cattle stood awkward and stick-legged or lay on the grassless baked-mud valley floor with their bones poking up under their loose hides. Here the black-skinned furrow-browed chieftain leaning on his stick of office told us that beyond the head of the valley was the large plateau valley where the rain-king lived. Was this really Yarousseau? Had the old man actually seen him? Yes, he had seen him; but his eyes were dim now, he could not describe him well. He had seen the god-king's shape. He was tall.

Two hours later Rimbaud led his expedition around an outcrop of boulders, and there below was the plateau valley. On the hillside, facing the blue peaks beyond, was a large grass hut village with several ribbons of smoke trembling up into the fiery dancing air. Below in the valley, a large herd of cattle lay dotted about amongst the sagging yellow sun-dried grass. As the expedition descended into the stifling windless air, crackling noisily through the dried grass underfoot, Rimbaud saw that most of the cattle, who appeared to have scattered and settled at random, were all too visibly on the point of death.

The Meeting

Scene: A primitive grass hut village in darkest Africa. The entire native population is gathered around as the explorer leads his expedition into the large central clearing across the fissured baked-mud surface of what appears to be a dried-up pond. The explorer stops before the main grass hut, outside which are two posts bound together in the form of a cross. Half a dozen tall blue-black warriors clad only in ragged loincloths stand with raised spears barring the entrance to the hut.

The explorer mimes his opening question before the silent warriors as the silent crowd stares.

Is this the village of the man-god? Where the rain-king lives?

For several moments no one moves.

Then there appears at the doorway of the hut a tall priest dressed in frayed robes, his face thin and haggard, his skin burnt lobster-red.

EXPLORER: Yarousseau!
PRIEST: Arthur!

The warriors part, and the priest and the explorer stumble towards one another. They greet in the traditional French manner, embracing one another, placing their cheeks each against the other's, calling each other's name several times.

PRIEST: Good heavens!
EXPLORER: You old bastard!
TOGETHER: What on earth / the hell are you doing here?

Etcetera.

Further introductions follow, in the more formal French manner. The priest shakes the hand of the explorer's clerk and the explorer's concubine. The crowd press forward, murmuring, as the priest bids his guests be seated. The warriors erect a canopy, and then usher the crowd back to a respectful distance.

As the priest and the explorer converse, the explorer's concubine sits silently beside him. Beside her sits the explorer's clerk, who does not listen but carries on his own silent conversation with several of the nearest female members of the audience, using international gestures of interest and admiration. His advances meet with little more than the odd, odd glance. The members of the crowd are only interested in the doings of the two leading characters.

The explorer, after apologising about some obscure misdemeanour which appears to have taken place some time prior to the present action, begins to recount his travels.

The Explorer's Tale

A typical explorer's tale, full of the usual exploits, descriptions of fantastic places, near loss of life, the woman of his choice sold to him free of charge, penetrating insights into the nature of the human condition etc etc.

The crowd, as crowds will, soon become restive at this unintelligible monologue. A side interest in the dubious activities of the explorer's clerk develops. Comments are passed assessing the abilities and virtues of the explorer's concubine. These mutterings come to an abrupt halt, however, as the priest begins to recount his exploits.

The Priest's Tale

The priest began by gratefully accepting the Explorer's apologies concerning his obscure misdemeanour, explaining that the explorer's actions were the will of God, as far as the priest was concerned. The obscure misdemeanour and any subsequent feelings of guilt were a matter for the explorer's conscience alone. However, as a result of this misdemeanour, the priest went on to explain, he had been banished from Harar. (The explorer accepts these remarks with a certain lack of patience, together with what would seem to be references to the priest's appearance: old hat, no need for dirty linen in public, etc.)

After being exiled from Harar, the priest continued, he

had wandered for nearly a fortnight from village to village, attempting to spread the Word to large curious audiences of tribesmen. Inevitably, both on the public stage and in the private hut, his words and deeds had been met with blank incomprehension, eventually bringing him almost to the point of despair. At each village they had given him food as a reward for his exertions, and put him up for the night. Often including in this generosity a little bedwarming example of thoughtful local hospitality. Temptation indeed for a young man of God in the prime of life. After a night of fervid prayer for deliverance from the temptations of the flesh, accompanied as often as not by active resistance, the exhausted priest would be led to the trail and sped on his way.

What could he do? There was no sickness for him to cure, and nobody seemed to want him (with the odd carnal exception), let alone understand him. He had finally decided to go and fast in the mountains in a last despairing attempt to discover God's will – at least where he was concerned.

And what had God wanted of him? After prolonged fasting and prayer, the priest had come to understand that the spirit should expect nothing on this earth. Nothing beyond reliance on its own strength. Which was the will of God, apparently. For him as well as for all men.

But how had he become a god, the explorer had persisted, rather impatiently. Patience, was the priest's answer, the explorer must give the man-god time. All things happened in God's time.

Continuing in his own time, the priest had described how on his way down from the mountains, the man-about-to-become-god had foolishly mislaid his mules one night in the valleys. Two days later, exhausted, his food finished, his holy water drunk, the priest had mounted the far ridge. (*All eyes turn as the priest points.*) From there he had seen this, his first village since he had taken to the mountains. Overjoyed, he had run down the hillside.

Also, he had run because he had seen a storm coming up the valley he had just crossed. He had arrived in the village, his tattered cloak flowing in the breeze, the rain literally pounding his footsteps. To complete the picture, nothing less than a blinding flash of lightning followed by a crack of thunder that had sounded as if the sky was splitting in two. Thus, clapping his hat to his head in the breeze, the new rain-king had entered the village of Jiba. The Jibanese had been without rain for six moons.

'You old fraud!'

Yarousseau shrugged, ruefully, picking at his inflamed stubbly jaw with his thick, broken-nailed fingertips. 'I wonder, Arthur,' he remarked, surprisingly gloomily.

'Well, aren't you satisfied? You must have them eating out of your hand. They've all seen the light by now, surely?'

'Have they?' Yarousseau was shaking his head. 'I sometimes wonder just what light it is they have seen . . .'

'You mean to say, after a cluster of miracles like that, you still haven't managed to convert them?' The explorer appeared almost indignant.

'Oh yes. Nominally. In God's eyes they are all His children. I am instructing them in the faith,' continued the priest, still somewhat preoccupied, as if somewhere in his words there lay an answer to his problems, 'I teach them the Lord's Prayer. Each morning, before they leave for the fields, we go through it, line by line. They chant out the words after me in the dusk as the morning light grows. All of them, the whole village. Gathered out there just as they are now. And then the sun rises. When we make a mistake we go through it again. Until their voices no longer falter between the words and we all get it right. This used to be the greatest time of my day. Possibly, I used to think, the greatest time in my whole life. All those voices rising out of the shadows before me. And then, several months ago now, I suddenly heard them as if for the first time. "Hallowed be thy name. Thy kingdom come," they chanted, "Thy will be done." Their eyes were all focused beyond my raised hands, above my head. They were watching the sun come up from behind the peaks. It was then I realised that it wasn't just them who didn't know what they were doing, or what they were saying. I didn't either. And those words which I'd known almost as soon as I could speak, were suddenly utterly alien to me. "Thy kingdom come. Thy will be done." I realised that I had no idea of what they meant. That I'd never really had any idea of what they meant. That all of it, everything, was simply beyond our understanding. That these people chanting in the dim light were no different from those others chanting in the dim light of the nave back home in the monastery. We none of us knew. I felt then as if a terrible abyss had opened up around me. "Amen," I heard them say, and wait for me to dismiss them or make them say it again. But I couldn't, I could only stand there struck dumb by this awful feeling that never, anywhere, would I be at home on this earth ever again. That there would never be any tongue I could call my own, that there would never be anything I could ever know. That all my life I was condemned to be lost, wandering the face of the earth amongst other lost people. People who were unable to recognise how deeply they were in fact lost. I don't know how long this sense of utter desolation remained with me, but the next thing I knew the square was empty, with only the shadow of the cross falling across the dried-up waterhole. The sun was already rising in the sky and they'd all gone out into the fields.'

All the while Yarousseau had been speaking, Rimbaud had noticed the warriors creeping forward towards them from the edge of the crowd. By now they were squatting directly in front of them, staring forward intently into their eyes. They were so close that Rimbaud could even feel their breath on his face. His nostrils flared with revulsion at the intimacy of their personal odours. Tahira and Sottiro had begun backing apprehensively into the long shadow cast by the canopy in the rays of the setting sun.

'Back!' ordered Rimbaud sharply, waving his hand.

But the warriors didn't move, or indeed appear to take

any notice. They were hunched forward, their shoulders dimpled with muscles, squatting. Their stomachs bulged over their loincloths as they breathed, peering stonily.

'Get back!' Rimbaud waved his hand imperiously, noticing the black flick of its reflection pass over the shininess of the nearest warrior's eyes.

'No, Arthur. It's no use.' Yarousseau restrained Rimbaud's arm.

'For God's sake, what do they want? Order them back. Aren't you meant to be the god around here?'

Yarousseau sighed deeply, lowering his face into his hands. 'Oh Arthur, I was so hoping it wouldn't come to this.'

'Why, what's the matter?'

'Why tonight, of all nights!' Yarousseau raised his face from his hands. 'Arthur, I'm afraid that wasn't the whole truth, what I told you just now.'

'You mean there was no sunrise? No Lord's Prayer?'

'Oh yes. There was that all right. But that's only the end of it.'

The Beginning of the Truth, according to Yarousseau

The Lord's Prayer was an act of self-justification. As well as being a prayer in thanks for deliverance after the long night's ordeal, Yarousseau explained. For at sunset, on various appointed nights, the man-god would be subjected to his ritual interrogation to find out why he didn't bring any more rain. All night Yarousseau would lie pinned by the warriors beneath his cross, while the warriors took it in turn to chant at him in the darkness, and then place their ears to his belly as if listening for an answer. They wanted him to make rain, they explained. Yarousseau had tried protesting to them that he had no such powers, but it was no use. They had seen him do it once. And now they were desperate for more rain.

Only as the first light grew beyond the peaks would they release their rain-king; and then Yarousseau, light-headed from lack of sleep, would recite the Lord's Prayer with them once more. They would chant as fervently as ever, but Yarousseau knew that afterwards they would go out into the fields to throw their magic sticks, staring for hours on end at the far blue peaks. It was from there that the rains came, apparently.

By now the faces of the warriors were pressed right up against ours. We were breathing each others' breath.

'For God's sake, Yarousseau, do something – or I'll suffocate!'

Yarousseau shook his head calmly, decisively.

How could he go on behaving as if they just weren't there? 'Well, if you won't . . . Get back! Get out of it!' I lunged forward, pushing at the shoulders of the warrior in front of me, but it had no effect. He was as solid as a statue. He merely stared, his eyes searching mine, as I backed, stumbling to my feet. 'I can tell you, Yarousseau, if I were rain-god in this place . . .'

'Heaven forbid!' The clod was behaving as if the whole thing were some kind of joke! Or maybe it was just my behaviour.

'Can you do *nothing!*'

Again, he simply shook his head. But with an air of gentle sadness now. 'Arthur, what *can* I do?'

'Use your power. You're not the local god for nothing, are you?'

Still he sat there, facing them. It was almost as if he was speaking to them and not to me at all. 'But that's just it, Arthur. I have no power . . . Once, perhaps, I naïvely believed . . .' He sighed, his breath flickering the eyelids of the warrior before him. 'But not any more.'

'I've got a pistol. Do you want me to get you out of here?'

'No, Arthur. My fate is here, now.'

'So you're on your bloody martyrdom kick again, are you?'

'My fate is their fate, Arthur.'

'What, you'd entrust yourself to their little magic sticks? At the mercy of God knows what misunderstandings?'

'That's what I'm afraid you'll never understand, Arthur. You see, I no longer believe that their misunderstandings are any more mistaken than my own.'

'I despise my wisdom more than chaos itself; in order not to carry my disgusts and betrayals through the world, I have managed to erase from my mind all human life,' so Arthur Rimbaud had understood as he sat in the granary tearfully scribbling out his last poem. His 'Season in Hell'.

Abruptly taking his leave of the priest, the explorer signalled to his two companions, took up the reins of the lead mule, and led his expedition through the silent crowd into the long shadows of the grass huts, and out towards the open hillside beyond.

That night, while I lay on the slope above the village in my sleeping sack listening to the inner whistlings grow in my mind around the steady thumping pace of my heartbeat, I gradually became aware of a faint rising moan below. Its flat plaintive chant swelled and receded through the still night as my blinking eyes painted layer after layer of darkness over the brilliant stars. Beyond, below, the distant moonglimmer of the peaks rose against the clear cloudless sky at the limits of my vision . . .

Throughout the night the moans rose, and fell . . .

In chorus now. Falteringly. In response . . . There was light, growing. The voices rose, and fell: finally.

'A-men,' I recognised.

And then a single strident voice pronouncing some indecipherable blessing.

The sun had risen beyond the exact jagged silhouette of the peaks.

'I've come to bid you farewell,' the priest called out as he stumbled up the slope in his ragged robes, his Bible clasped to his breast.

The explorer had already loaded up his mules and was stamping out the ashes of the camp fire. Around on the slopes the villagers were out tending their sick cattle in the morning sunlight, while up on the ridge a group of warriors appeared to be throwing sticks into a dustbowl.

'I can't stay long, I've got sick call in a few minutes,' the priest wheezed, visibly tired after the short climb. His eyes were puffy and narrowed against the light, his manner vague and rather jerky, although he was obviously trying to be brisk and friendly towards his temporary parishioners.

'So you're still at the old curing the sick bit, are you? Have you got any equipment with you?' The explorer went on kicking through the ashes as the priest stood, beaming blearily.

'I've got a few bits and pieces. I do as best I can.'

The explorer stepped out of the ashes and turned dourly to face his visitor. 'Would you be able to give that little cunt over there a clean bill of health?' He nodded towards his concubine, who was already seated on a mule.

The priest suppressed a frown, his eyelids flickering. 'Why, what's the matter with her?'

'Last time I fucked her I got syphilis. Does your medical experience stretch that far?'

'Arthur, are you deliberately trying to provoke me?'

'No. It just happens to be the truth, that's all.' The explorer shrugged offhandedly, his face remaining expressionless. 'I can't help the way things are – any more than you apparently can . . . Oh, forget it! I'll get someone to do it back in Harar,' he snapped with a sudden burst of irritation.

'No, Arthur, I'd like to do something for you. If this is all, then I'll be quite happy to oblige the poor girl. I suspect in Harar they might just tell you what they think you want to know.'

No, Badjian would tell me the truth as well, I knew.

After a few minutes forceful persuasion, the explorer's concubine allowed herself to be led down to the village to be examined by the priest. She returned with the priest several minutes later, her face clouded, her cheeks flushed; and the explorer then set out on the five-day journey down the trail across the foothills back to Harar.

Tahira had been clean, cured somehow, or at least as

much as I was. As much as could be determined by the methods available.

13

Harar was as good as civilisation itself. Those blank mud walls rising out of the scrub; the maze of inner twisting alleyways where the courtyard dogs leapt over the rutted baked mud, yapping at the end of their chains; and finally the bedlam of the market place in all its glory, overlooked by the solemn derelict facade of my very own palace – I was home!

Sottiro, who had insisted on dressing for the occasion, beamed down graciously from his mule at the faces of the assembled curious who had gathered to watch the return of the first European expedition into furthest Abyssinia.

News awaiting Rimbaud on his return:
- The war against Shoa was going worse than ever for the Egyptians. Harar could still be abandoned at any moment.
- The Do-it-yourself European club room in the palace had at last been completed.
- A parcel from France: containing one children's encyclopedia, *Wonders of the Modern World – Illustrated*, and a note 'I do hope this will do, Mother.'

And what had they seen on their travels, the assembled European residents of Harar had both been anxious to know. Over dinner in the new European club room Rimbaud watched as his clerk – in filthy finery – regaled Grimes and Vardy with superlative descriptions of the wonders of the Interior.

Rimbaud's only contribution had been a mention of some mysterious musk.

'A scent, eh?' Grimes peered forward, brow earnestly furrowed as he ground his teeth on Bomba's celebration dinner hash: the higher ape seeking to grasp this experience beyond its experience, or perhaps some elusive grain of spice trapped in a cavity. 'Which smells better than any other stuff you've ever come across, eh? But you didn't manage to bring any back with you?'

'Anyone who could get that stuff out could make a fortune for himself,' I told him.

'Are you sure it isn't just you, Arthur?' Vardy twiddled his moustache with a sceptical air. 'I'd like to judge for myself first. Don't set your heart on it, Arthur. You know how suspect musk can be, commercially speaking.'

Rimbaud retired early to his room. Where he found Tahira waiting for him. As he sat on the edge of his bed, plunged into a deep gloom at what had become of all his hopes – for the expedition, for the Interior, for Harar even, now that it had become reality once more – he felt Tahira's hand play over his back.

'A-ur? A-ur?'

'Tahira.' He smiled faintly as he turned to face her.

She took his hands and squeezed them, her eyes holding his as she pressed his palms against her breasts.

'A-ur?'

'*Arthur*, Tahira.' Rimbaud corrected her, instinctively. And then, hardly aware of what he was doing, Rimbaud's hands began parting Tahira's robe. Next moment he was pressing his face into the soft smooth flesh of her breasts.

Slowly Tahira sank back, drawing him against her, as her cool hands began peeling off his clothes, releasing him. Her robe fell away and her thighs parted beneath him.

'A-ur!'

'Tahira.'

'Ah! Ah! . . .'

Outside in the night, beyond the pressing whimpers of

Tahira's breath, a single dog howled, long and waveringly, from the ramparts.

The Ogaden skins had remained undamaged by mildew on the long journey, I found when I unloaded them in the cellar. There'd be no need to recure them. So perhaps, balanced against the cost of those missing mules, I might in the end just make something out of the expedition. It wouldn't eat into my savings at least; but then on the other hand, it was just so much time lost. Still.

Each evening, after dinner, Rimbaud began giving Tahira simple lessons in French.
'I am Arthur . . . You are Tahira . . . This' (a sweep of the hand at the bare lamp-shadowed walls and night-darkened window) 'is Harar.'
'I . . . am . . . Arthur.'
'No! No! . . . *I*' Hand on chest. 'You.' Finger pointing. 'You say: "You are Arthur".'
Tahira's hand clawed at the air indecisively. 'Yousay. You-are-Arthur.'
Night after night, Rimbaud would go through the objects in the room.
'This is the light . . . These are my books . . . wall . . . night beyond window.'
'This-is-the-light. Those-are-I . . . Arthur-books. Wall. Nightbeyondwindow.'
And finally. 'Yooowl! This is the sound of the dogs.'
'Yooowl!' Tahira would repeat, giggling. This was the signal for the end of the lesson.
As Tahira slept, Rimbaud would work at his table.
Rimbaud's dilemma: To try and copy out as much as he could remember of his analysis notes (lost with all his personal belongings in the waterfall), while his memory was still fresh –
Or: to make out a report on his expedition for the Société de Géographie.

Rimbaud's reasons for choosing the latter: There was no time to be wasted. The Egyptians might well abandon Harar at any moment. He was getting older, and still he hadn't even begun to make any real money. A report to the Société de Géographie could bring in cash. Possibly, if the Société were suitably impressed, they might even finance him to undertake some real expedition – after all, he was the only Frenchman who really knew this part of Africa. That way he would no longer have to rely on Harar. He would become an explorer. Undertake some spectacular expedition right into the very heart of Africa. He would become famous. A household word. He would become rich, his fortune assured . . etc etc.

There'd be time enough to try and remember those old analysis notes later.

Dear Mother,
      I am back from the Interior. There was little profit in it, I'm afraid. However, I am submitting the report of my expedition to the Société de Géographie and have high hopes here. I am the first European to have penetrated those furthest regions of Lower Abyssinia.

You say you do not know what has become of your Arthur, that you no longer recognise him. Would you recognise me as Arthur Rimbaud, the famous explorer? For that is what I may well be on the way to becoming. But if this is to be the case, Mother, I will need far more than the small children's encyclopedia which you have sent me. I know how difficult things must be now that your riding school project has folded up, but you must allow me to judge these things for myself. *Wonders of the Modern World – Illustrated* may be very well for those who want to read *about* explorers . . .

In the evenings before her lessons, Tahira would leaf through the coloured pages of my children's encyclopedia, fingering the glossy pages in awe. The first time I'd found her looking at it, she'd been staring at a coloured illustration of an erupting volcano, the book held upside down in her lap. It soon became her favourite possession.

It wasn't until he'd been in Harar for a few weeks that Rimbaud met Badjian and Ras Makonen in the market place. Badjian, resplendent as ever, commiserated with Arthur over the total failure of his expedition, while the three of them strolled amongst the stalls.
'It wasn't *that* much of a failure!'
But Badjian had good news, he assured Arthur. King Menelek at last controlled all of Shoa, and now had further ambitions for Lower Abyssinia. Also, *The Dictionary of Military Engineering* had been very well received by His Majesty. (So that's where it had got to!)
Badjian continued, out of earshot of Ras Makonen, bending down closer to Rimbaud's ear as he pretended to inspect some ivory on one of the stalls. 'You will be pleased to hear that the Emir has at last been cured of his unfortunate disease. A most grateful patient, Arthur.' Adding, as Ras Makonen drew up beside the stall, where the trader had stepped forward and begun demonstrating his wares, 'This is the man, Ras, who once sold Arthur some hollow ivory.' – It was too! The very man! – 'But I soon cured Arthur of such childish mistakes.'
As Badjian pretended to inspect his ivory, the trader nodded, deferentially: a cool, murderous grin frosting his features.
'But how come he's still alive?' protested Rimbaud. 'I thought you said the Emir would have him bumped off after what we'd done?' Badjian's eyebrows almost met his hairline at the enormity of Rimbaud's unrealised indiscretion, while Ras Makonen frowned quizzically beside him.
'And what had you done?' asked Ras Makonen puzzled.
Badjian quickly ushered the two of us away from the stall, guffawing hollowly: the forced chuckle of the ham stage

villain. 'Poor Arthur, he didn't know who he could trust when he first came up here.'

'Until I met Badjian, of course.'

But no irony was too heavy for Badjian. 'You see how it is, Ras?' Badjian linked his arm in Ras's as he guided him on his way. 'That was before Arthur came into partnership with me. A partnership that has a great future,' Badjian glowered meaningfully in my direction, 'if all goes well, Ras.'

Ras Makonen nodded, understandingly.

The drift of Rimbaud's thoughts: Should the Egyptians abandon Harar and Menelek gain control, with Ras Makonen appointed as Governor, those who had shown themselves to be Menelek's friends in time of need would be rewarded accordingly. There would be great opportunity for making vast profit out of the ruin of those who had not shown themselves to be possessed of such foresight.

On the other hand, should the Egyptians abandon Harar and the Emir gain control, those who had shown themselves ... etc etc, with similar vast profits.

Badjian was evidently making plans to ensure that he came into both these apparently mutually exclusive categories. And most important of all, Badjian obviously had sufficient influence to ensure that Rimbaud could be included in both these categories as well.

But why should Badjian take such pains to include Rimbaud in his plans? Sentimental ties of friendship from earlier less ambitiously devious times? Loyalty to their much talked about partnership? (A somewhat dormant activity, of late.)

Neither, Rimbaud quickly realised. Badjian had included Rimbaud in his plans because Rimbaud had established trading links with Aden, an absolutely dependable outlet to the outside world and its markets. Because Rimbaud was open to persuasion that his interests were above considerations of mere principle.

Rimbaud was gullible; Rimbaud could be used for anything.

Rimbaud's instinctive reaction: I won't be used like this. Get out of all this intrigue while you can, Arthur. You don't know what he's up to – it might lead anywhere.

But Rimbaud now realised that as long as he remained dependent on Harar for his plans, his future was at the mercy of Badjian's intrigues.

'My apologies, Ras,' I began, coming to myself. 'You must think me very insensitive. I'm sorry, I forgot myself.'

Ras Makonen craned forward, his face peering past Badjian's as we strolled on, linked either side in Badjian's arms. 'I am afraid I do not follow you,' replied Ras Makonen, frowning slightly.

'I forgot to tell you about your Imi musk.'

'So you have some for me?'

I shook my head. 'I got within sight of Imi. But the Web is impassable. At least at present.'

Ras Makonen nodded philosophically.

'But I think I smelt the stuff,' I continued. 'It's . . .'

Like the first icy lift of opium in the veins, releasing . . .
Like the delirious rasp of an orgasm.
Like a crystalline chord, splintering.
Like . . .

I raised my hands in an expansive gesture of despair, a gesture slightly hampered by Badjian's linking arm. 'What can I say to make you believe I actually . . .'

'I believe you,' Ras Makonen smiled. 'It is truly unbelievable, is it not?'

Badjian frowned at me, meaningfully, questioningly, as Ras Makonen raised his face smilingly to the sky.

Next morning I was up before dawn. The Zeyla caravan was due with the new barter I'd ordered from Aden. There was a cold wind in the market square, and I went over to join a group of porters around one of their fires. Two of the circle edged aside, making a space for me, and I squatted in silence with the others, warming my hands as the flames crackled and spluttered through the tangle of heaped brambles. In the distance, from outside the main gate, the baying of the caravaners calling for the keys had just begun: a low palpitating drone, mounting, as the faint blue light dissolved the darkness. The wind eddied about the market place, whipping up the dust into hissing scurries, and the smoke fanned around the circle of dim faces. I felt the tears prickle in my eyes as the choking clouds broke over me. The porters were hopping on their haunches, chafing their limbs against the cold. I noticed one or two of them grin to one another as I began copying their actions. I was still the eccentric of the market place: no merchant was ever up at this hour, let alone warming himself around a porters' fire.

Gradually, as the bowl of steaming coffee was passed around, the muttered conversations began. I listened intently – this was one of the reasons why I'd taken to coming to the fire. Here the gossip of the market place was exchanged: the Shoanese caravans were going out and not coming back: the Emir was smuggling again: rumours of drought were coming in from the south.

Much rain in the Ogaden, drought only this side of the blue mountains, I chipped in, pronouncing deliberately. This was also my chance to pick up more Harari. I'd learnt my lesson where bargaining in the market place was concerned: ignorance was another luxury I could no longer afford.

Then, from the other side of the fire, I heard a voice reply. No rain in Ogaden now, I understood as the porter spoke, River Web has dried up and gone into mountains . . .

But suddenly he was silent. All their faces turned to peer up, beyond me.

'I do believe it's Arthur, isn't it?' The voice of Grimes sounded out over the assembled company.

The ball of brambles was collapsing, settling in on itself amidst the ring of white ashes as the flames leapt free from the fire. All faces avoided Arthur's as he glanced about him. With a limp, offhand gesture, Rimbaud took his leave of the company and rose to address his fellow European.

What the hell did Grimes want of Rimbaud at such an unearthly hour?

To tell him that his face was black, apparently.

Rimbaud spat into his palms and began wiping his smoke-darkened face.

'You're only making it worse,' Grimes guffawed. 'Looks like warpaint now.'

Most of the stalls were already up in the market place, and in the distance the yell of the caravaners at the gate had risen to a rhythmic, ragged roar. Rimbaud beckoned one of the watersellers across and began splashing his face clean as the waterseller poured the water from his little tin cup into Rimbaud's hands. Meanwhile Grimes, dusting the angular protuberances of his khaki shorts and shirt-sleeves, began his customary variations on a meteorological theme.

Bugger the weather! Why the hell didn't he come to the point, wondered Rimbaud as they began strolling around the empty sector of the market place where the outside traders set up their stalls. 'Bugger the weather! Why the hell don't you come to the point?' Grimes liked a man who was forthright and to the point, so he explained to Rimbaud. He believed in calling a spade a spade. He had no time for shilly-shallyers. Plain speaking was what he believed in. Straight to the point, was what he always said.

Rimbaud found himself speculating as to what this point could be. Aloud. And in his own inimitable plain speech. Without so much as a mention of spades, shilly-shallyers, forthright men etc, etc.

His companion in the tasteful shit-brown outfit informed him that he was going to be blunt. That he wasn't going to mince matters. That he did have a very important matter on his mind.

By which time the strolling pair had completed the circle and were once again passing the flickering ashes of the porters' fire. The chant at the gate was still rising; the keys were obviously going to be late today.

The minute the keys arrived at the gate, Rimbaud would have to go, he explained. 'So, for God's sake . . .'

Rimbaud's companion decided to cut a long story short, to go right to the heart of the matter, man to man, etc.

The heart of the matter (in language that avoids plain speech, unminced matter, blunted being etc.)

Sottiro's suit – which was a downright disgrace.

Some kind of pimp's mess kit.

Like the livery of a third rate Neapolitan brothel-keeper.

Making a laughing stock of us all in the eyes of the locals.

The beginning of the end of all decency.

Intolerable lowering of standards.

Worse than going native.

It was a matter Arthur should look into
> cut out
> stamp down on
> put an end to
> nip in the bud
> put his foot down on

The whole thing boiled down to one factor: the absolutely deplorable influence of Our Caucasian character. 'That Badjian should be run out of town, if you ask me. It's all his doing really.'

'If you don't mind, Badjian happens to be a friend of mine.'

But Badjian was apparently no friend
> up to no good
> a downright disgrace
> dressed in some kind of pimp's mess kit
> Neopolitan livery etc etc.

And so they completed their third circle past the ashes of the burnt-out fire.

With Rimbaud interrupting to express the opinion that his clerk's private life was his own affair. And that Badjian's affairs were a matter for his own conscience.

'You don't mean to say you actually approve:
> of that suit he wears?

of Badjian's influence?
of Badjian's shady dealings?
of what sort of place Harar was likely to become
if this sort of behaviour continued?
Was Rimbaud really sympathetic towards these things? Was he, *honestly*?

Rimbaud was luckily spared any compromise (aesthetic, ethical or logical) which his answer might have involved him in. The roar outside the walls had risen to its crescendo, and was now subsiding. The gates were open.

Abruptly Rimbaud took his leave of his companion in cloacal-coloured attire. He'd had enough of plain speaking, unminced matter etc etc.

The caravan from Zeyla contained the barter stocks I'd ordered, together with a small package.

Had mother relented? Were these my chemicals at last (which I now so desperately needed to analyse those samples of ore I'd brought back from the Interior and simply dumped down in the cellars)?

The package contained a bundle of brightly coloured second-hand clothes reeking of scent. And a note.

I'm sure even the wild man of Harar will find that bare primitive tastes begin to pall so quickly without a few civilising graces. I only hope your little Tahira fits into these things as well as they fitted their previous owner. Now perhaps you'll learn what it's like to be forced to imagine the details of a wild life which you so long to hear about. Will you never write to me, Arthur?
We all think of you so much down here.
    Tenderest wishes,
        Emelia.

Rimbaud flung the parcel into the dust, and stormed into the palace to find Vardy.

'What the hell do you mean by passing on the details of

my private life to your brother's bloody wife?'

Vardy had meant no harm, he assured Rimbaud, backing in his seat as this wild man waved this crumpled piece of paper under his nose. Vardy had merely mentioned Arthur's recent acquisition in passing, as a joking aside in his last letter to his brother Pierre. He had in fact simply wanted to reassure his brother as to Arthur's intentions. 'Pierre has always been a bit worried that you might just disappear off into the Interior one day without a word. He's terrified of losing a good man like you, you know.'

Rimbaud stomped out of the club room, speechless with rage, his fist still brandishing the crumpled piece of paper.

14

Anything left in the market place was always considered fair game for the scavengers. By late afternoon, as the stalls were being dismantled and the last of the local caravans were threading their way out through the gates, the scavengers would be moving through the sea of daily refuse, picking over the discarded piles of straw, boxes, torn cloth, palm leaf wrappings and animal dung, while the porters, in a long line, swept it all towards the billowing smoke and blackened walls of the incineration corner. I was quite prepared to see anyone wearing Emelia Vardy's cast-offs. Anyone, that is, except their intended recipient.

Who greeted me at the door to my room that evening dressed in some scarlet silk and black taffeta monstrosity.

'Tahira! Where the hell did you get hold of that?'

Arthur was the porters' friend, Tahira explained, her long thin limbs rustling the folds of taffeta as she gestured. One of the porters had seen him drop his parcel, and had kindly delivered it to his room.

'Arthur not like Tahira?' she finished, her eyelids raised, her face pleading. She was standing framed against the window, her thick hips and sturdy straight-limbed stance rendered subtly awkward – like an actress who can't act – by the crumpled flowing lines of the dress. She smiled, faintly, uncertainly, as she patted at the beribboned bulges. She had the thing on back to front.

'Arthur not like Tahira?'

'But why don't you want me to wear my suit?' Sottiro persisted, standing his ground by the loaded pack mules as

the expedition prepared to start out.

'Because I don't like it!'

'I thought that was all. At least you're honest.'

'Why?'

'Because that's all there ever is, isn't there. I mean, there's really nothing more to it, is there? – only likes and dislikes. Everything's just a matter of taste in the end, isn't it?'

Tahira had her back to me; and although there was no sound, I could tell from the defeated sag of her shoulders and her bent neck that she was weeping.

'Oh, Tahira!' I placed my hands on her shoulders. Her body was limp, abject; she stank of Emelia Vardy. 'Of course Arthur likes Tahira.'

She turned, her heavy eyelids squeezing the teardrops from her eyes. She already had the front (the back) undone. I trembled as I ran my hands over her shoulders, forming them around her breasts as she pressed herself against me. And then my face was buried in the dark perfumed rustle of taffeta.

Easing her shoulders, she shrugged herself free of the dress while my lips passed over her skin. The lingering fragrance rose in my nostrils as I felt her hands pressing under my clothes, over my skin, down.

Rimbaud lowered her onto the bed, shaking, his eyes pressed closed, his teeth gritted. Wrenching off his clothes, he pushed her thighs apart as the taffeta crumpled beneath him, its brittle softness parting around his prick. He heard her gasp as he thrust himself into her, and with a quick spasmic burst of energy vented the sudden charge of his lust on the treacly insinuating smile that rose before his mind's eye.

'Emelia!'

'Arthur!'

'You bitch!'

As I lay, panting, quickly spent, my teeth still gritted, my face pressed into a soft, crumpled cloud of perfumed underskirt, I felt Tahira's hand smooth over my back, pressing.

For a moment or two she continued trying to move under me.

'No, Tahira.'

Her hand lessened its pressure, lying flat and lifeless against my skin.

'Arthur?' she enquired gently, after several minutes' silence. 'What is emelia?'

'What?' I snapped, abruptly rising from my thoughts.

'Emelia. Arthur say emelia.'

I sighed, my breath shuddering; already the surface of my skin was cold.

'Arthur,' continued Tahira, after another long silence. 'Tahira like Arthur. Tahira like emelia with Arthur. Emelia good with Arthur.' She chuckled softly, smoothing my goose-pimpled skin.

But I knew. It was the first time she hadn't got anything out of it.

From then on, in the evenings Tahira would take off her robes and change into one of Emelia Vardy's cast-offs. As she repeated her lessons by the dim light, I would smell the dying fragrance of Emelia's perfume.

'These . . . are . . . matches . . . Now, remember?'

'Yes, Arthur. Tahira remember . . . This-is-the-lamp. These -are-the-matches. This-is-the-wick. This-is-the-glass-cover. We-light-the-lamp-in-the-. . . Tahira forget.'

'Dark! Dark!'

Gradually, as the evenings passed, the smell of Tahira's body took possession of the dresses, stifling all other lingering fragrances in the lamplit dimness.

These now existed in Rimbaud's imagination alone.

Within a few weeks I'd finished a draft report of my expedition to the Ogaden. Putting it aside, I immediately started to re-sketch my old lost chemical analysis notes from memory. There were large and vital gaps, I knew; but with the help of the mental pictures of likely terrain which I'd formed in my imagination prior to setting out on the expedition, I managed to remember far more than I'd expected. Those pictures had remained clear in my mind. The more so, I realised, because I had in fact seen nothing which resembled them (and thus distorted them) on my travels.

In between times, when my memory dried up, or my thoughts were disturbed by the barking of the dogs from the ramparts rising to a pitch at the long unplaceable deep-throated roar of some nearby prowling lion, I would turn back to my report of my travels in Lower Abyssinia, amending various descriptions, searching for words the better to convey the actuality of what I had seen. I intended this report to convince the Société de Géographie of my suitability to be appointed as an officially sponsored explorer. Systematically I set about obliterating all the unconscious poetry which had slipped out whenever I'd forgotten myself; this had to be a scientific document.

In the end, as a guide, I forced myself to imagine I was writing a trading report to Old Man Vardy. But even trade requires the enumeration of possibilities, sees hopes, the development of resources, all the poetry of potential profit, I soon realised. More cancellations, more blotches. And then I became aware – while I penned those words as if to Old Man Vardy – who in fact those words would have been intended for. Anything I wrote to Old Man Vardy would obviously reach that cow Emelia's eyes. Unwittingly, my words had been performing for this audience too, implying their author – I am he, you bitch, he who has actually seen these things, he who can do without you, you prick-teasing cunt.

In despair, I began scratching out word after word. But what was going to be left? How could I show these scientific flatheads what I had actually seen, without conveying who I was – or at least, who I didn't want to be? How could I present myself to them as an explorer of the future, and at the same time as a scientist, a dullard like themselves?

Eventually I found myself leafing through my *Children's*

Encyclopedia (Tahira's property now). *Wonders of the Modern World – Illustrated.* E for Explorers. There was Livingstone, Burton, Paulitschki. Behind each of these dour lividly highlighted portraits, I tried to imagine the man himself. Missionary? Megalomaniac? Empire builder? Misfit? Adventurer? Outcast? Scholar? Madman? What had driven them into Africa? What had they been searching for? What dreams had possessed them? Why had they chosen to impose themselves on this place? I stared down in the dim flickering light. Who were they – to the world – that the world accepted them, encouraged and aided them, egged them on? Then suddenly I knew, as I slammed the covers of that child's dream book closed, exactly how I should present myself, how I should write to those scientific dullards, on whose condescending interest I relied for all my hopes. I picked up my pen and began writing my report out anew, every description, every line, every word, addressed as if to Mother.

The palace cellars: a dank, stagnant-aired passage of chilled fungoid smells. L-shaped. Heavy-doored chambers leading off the inside of the L. In the furthest chamber: piles of skins (Harar and Ogaden), two rotting panniers of damp unanalysed ore samples. A figure, muttering to himself, bending, heaving, between two hurricane lamps. Silhouettes focussing, unfocussing: scattering webs of darkness over the dark stone walls.

Rimbaud checking the last of his Ogaden skins for mildew as he loads them up in preparation for the next caravan to Zeyla.

Footstep-scrunch echoes along the passage, approaching. Enter, a third lamp. Behind it a hollow-socketed, moustachioed skull, peering: Vardy.

Social greetings exchanged. Brightly. Gruffly.

Vardy sits himself down on a pile of skins, setting his lamp at his feet.

'Well Vardy, what do you want?'

More talk of plain speaking, man to man, etc (see Grimes) as Arthur begins moving the bales of skins.

'Shift your arse, Vardy, I've got to check that lot.'

Vardy rises to his feet, lifts lamp, and perches himself on next bale.

Variations on a theme of Grimes continue, with tentative hints at main theme.

'You'll have to shift again. I'm checking that lot as well.'

'Look, what *aren't* you checking?'

'That lot over there.'

Vardy settles tentatively on a mouldy pannier of ore. 'Now look, Arthur. Let's stop playing games . . .' etc.

The Heart of the matter (Vardy's version)

Grimes has a point etc . . .

'Look, if you've just come down here to pester me with more of that nonsense about my clerk and his rainbow suit, then you might as well bugger off and stop wasting my time. Now, if you don't mind, I'd like to shift that lot.'

Vardy rising, agitatedly. Tentatively inspecting the seat of his pants for damp ore. 'But you just said you weren't checking this lot.'

'I'm only shifting it.'

Vardy remains standing as Rimbaud pulls at the rotting, spilling panniers of damp ore.

To come to the point etc. Vardy's objections to Sottiro's suit:

Grimes objected to it.

It was totally lacking in taste.

It wasn't the sort of thing we wanted in Harar at all.

It was symptomatic.

It was, not to put too fine a point on it, decadent.

What sort of place did Arthur want Harar to become?

Arthur wanted Harar to become a place where everyone went about their own business. Without poking their noses into affairs which were none of their concern. A place, in fact, where simple Dijon humanitarian principles learnt to stick up for themselves.

But the importer of Dijon humanitarian principles to Harar was more concerned with the future now, it appeared. 'This kind of behaviour reflects on us all. Our whole way of life up here. Would you want to be seen going about dressed like that? . . . Would you, honestly?'

'Look, he happens to be a rotten clerk. I know that, I'm the one who has to put up with him. So why the hell shouldn't he dress like a rotten clerk? Getting him all dolled up like some Bourse lackey isn't going to change matters one jot.'

'So you're just going to let things go on like this, are you? Let the place turn into some kind of Babylon. Is that what you want?'

'You know what I want, Vardy.

'What, precisely? Just to make money? Then you should realise that your interests lie in putting a stop to this kind of thing – before it queers the pitch for all of us.'

'Who said I was just interested in making money?'

'Then what else do you want?'

'You to shut up. Now bugger off!' Rimbaud began scraping handfuls of unanalysed ore samples off the floor and stuffing them into the rotting panniers. They wouldn't hold much longer – the seams were splitting. He'd have to find somewhere else to store them or this muck was going to start damaging his skins.

'You know the trouble with you, Arthur? You just don't care about Africa.'

There were bound to be repercussions, I knew. For the next few days I studiously avoided both Vardy and Grimes. Even going to the extent of doing some of my business in the stalls outside the main gate when I knew Grimes was about in the market place. Outside the city the merchants paid no gate tax and one could sometimes pick up the odd bargain or two. It all depended on what kind of mood the Egyptian officer at the gate was in when he assessed the tax on one's purchases. Late afternoon was the best time, when he was getting ready to pack up. But it meant hanging about. And this was to be my undoing.

'Hello there! Been looking for you all over the place.' Rimbaud sullenly acknowledged his khaki-clad fellow European, and prepared for the worst.

But Grimes had something else on his mind now, besides Sottiro's appearance. 'Ever seen one of these before?' Grimes unstrapped a small black box from his mule. 'It's what they call a camera. First one you've seen out in these parts, I expect.'

One of the wonders of the modern world, no less. And introduced to Harar by Grimes. Rimbaud grunted, curtly.

'It shows things exactly as they are. A miracle, really. When you come to think about it.' But Grimes' interest wasn't only in the theory of the matter, he explained, coming to the point (etc). He wanted a picture of Rimbaud. For the club room. 'You know. First resident of Harar. Explorer of Lower Abyssinia. That kind of thing . . . I'd like to take pictures of all the founder members of the club. Put it all on record, so to speak. But you're the one I really want. The pioneer of it all.'

'Really?'

'Come now. This is no time to be modest. I want you down for posterity.'

Grimes just couldn't conceive of anyone not wishing to subject his appearance to the gaze of posterity. Fumbling at his mule pack, he drew out a collapsible wooden tripod.

'Now, let me see. We must have a suitable background.' He glowered about him, pursing his lips speculatively at the rocky scrubland. 'The sun's over the city right now, so you'll have to stand back there.' He pointed to a small outcrop of rocks over by a hummock of brambles.

With a shrug, Rimbaud followed Grimes' finger and took up a suitable posterity-inclined stance on one of the lower rocks, while Grimes set up the tripod, affixing a black cloak to the back of the camera.

'Marvellous things, these cameras, you know,' his muffled

voice boomed out from under the little black cloak which was now draping his shoulders. It was as if this spindle-legged object had suddenly learned to talk, as well as sprouting a shifting khaki-shorted backside. 'They record the truth. So you can see what it was *really* like. If you can get it into focus, that is.' A short period of silence, during which the five-legged animal appeared to be suffering from some kind of posterial irritation. 'Of course, it's the end of all art. You realise that, don't you?'

'And why's that?' asked Rimbaud, shifting his pose. Was Grimes actually making the picture in there, or what was he doing?

'Well don't you see? We won't have to rely on any of those damned artists to show how things are any more. We'll have these things. Hold yourself! I still can't get the wretched thing to work. It's all so dark in here.'

'Perhaps if you took off that robe thing?'

'No, no! That's essential. Has to be kept dark so that only the right bits of light get in.'

'And where do they come from?'

'From *you*, old chap. That's what makes the picture. Reflection. The light from you . . . I'm damned if I can see a thing, you know.'

The hairy black legs of the box-headed monster shifted once more and began pawing the dust.

'There's a hole in the front, is there?' asked Rimbaud.

'There's a lens. Which you have to focus. But I'm damned if I can even find the thing.'

'A lens? Where?'

'In the front!' The box-headed monster shuddered, as if it had sneezed. 'Of *course!*' Grimes emerged from the black robe, wild haired, his lined livid face glistening with sweat. Carefully he reached forward and removed a black disc from the front of the box. Behind the disc was a gleaming lens. 'You might have told me before, old chap,' he added, reproachfully.

'But how was I to know?'

'What do you think I was doing under there?'

Rimbaud refrained from replying, and Grimes dived back under the black robe once more. 'Ah, *that's* it! Perfect, Arthur. Perfect! Just hold that pose.'

I watched as the monster twitched, and then became still.

'No one coming, is there Arthur?'

'Where?'

'Don't *move!*' Grimes yelled. 'Nothing coming between us, that's what I mean. No natives. Nothing walking about just out of range.'

'Not that I can see.' Several curious urchins were giggling over by the stalls, but otherwise the whole performance had attracted surprisingly little attention.

'Hold it, Arthur!'

'What?'

'No, no! Just stay as you are.'

'Are you still taking it?'

'Don't speak! Don't say a word! . . . Now . . . Hold it! . . . Ready? . . . *Are you ready*?'

'What for?'

'That's it!' Grimes emerged once more. 'That's it, Arthur! We've got you down for posterity now.'

'It's all finished, is it?'

'Absolutely.' Grimes began stripping off the black robe from the box and dismantling the tripod.

'Where's the picture?'

'Steady on, Arthur. That has to be developed. At the moment the picture is sealed in here, in negative form. There's some kind of chemical process that I've still got to read up in the instructions. I should have it ready for you in a few days, though. One for you, and one for the club.' Grimes began strapping the collapsed monster back onto his mule.

'Now I've only got to get one of your clerk, that Sottiro fellow of yours.'

'I'll send him along tomorrow afternoon, if you want. He's due for a few hours off.'

'That's very kind of you.' Grimes lowered the box carefully into its case. 'And, ah, by the way – make sure he's properly dressed, will you?'

'I'm afraid the only thing he's got is that coat of many colours. Why, will it affect the light?'

'What light?'

'For the camera.'

'Oh, good heavens no. I told you, this thing can make a picture out of anything. It take things exactly as they are, no matter what.'

'In black and white?'

'Yes, exactly, in black and white.'

'Then it'll have to take a black and white picture of Sottiro in his rainbow suit, I'm afraid. That is, unless you prefer the naked truth.'

When I ran across the next caravan from Zeyla in the market place, I found a letter for me. Forwarded from France. The address of home obliterated by Mother's crosshatching. Only the name remained – Arthur Rimbaud Esq – in the original hand.

Verlaine's!

The howling shell of Rimbaud's surroundings fell away . . .I. Agape. Speechless.

As the world withdrew. Disengaging from this wrinkled, imploding speck of sentient loss.

And then, in a blink, returned. A cacophony of sensations simultaneously hammered into place around me.

Rimbaud looked up to find himself standing in some primitive market square with the sun blazing down on mud walls, a gaudy row of booths, native merchants gesticulating. Noise. Light. Colour. Indecipherable complexity of seething sensations. Two trembling, dark-skinned hands (*his own!*) deliberately tearing this white envelope in half. Tearing again. Pausing, as this fragment detached itself before his eyes.

are you doing now? What are you

you become? Who
you are selling penny jewels to the crazy
natives? You
seen in Russia, America, China
a legend, you realise. Your fame is
lifetime
famous in Paris, Arthur. The name you
always we long to know
the voice of the future for some
us all. If you

The trembling, dark-skinned hand turned over the crumpled piece of paper. The blinking eyes read:
poems. All this out of your
theories. They've named you
about yourself. Details of me
But now I have
bosom of the One True Church
God is my
now
my appeal in vain. But do tell us
so much longing
I wondered. What has become
you.

The fragment settled gently, floating away across the dusty square in the breeze.

Rimbaud grunted, shook his head abruptly, and walked on across the market place to begin the day's business.

Also on the caravan was a small box of chemical samples. Mother had at last relented!

That evening I finished my report for the Société de Géographie on my expedition into the Ogaden; I'd send it by the return caravan. Now I was free for my chemical researches. I'd already completed all I could remember of my old lost analysis notes, and together with them and my new box of chemicals I retired to the cellars to begin my analysis of the soil samples I'd brought back from the

Interior.

Locking the door behind me and setting the lamp on a pile of hides, I began tipping the damp, unanalysed ore out of the rotting panniers into little heaps on the stone floor. Rimbaud was shaking with excitement.

An excitement whose tremors are felt even now. And must be avoided at all costs if this tale is not to be cut short by catastrophe. The invalid Rimbaud will thus resort once more to techniques guaranteed to dispel excitement in all but those for whom information alone is an intoxicating stimulant.

The Results of Rimbaud's Chemical Analysis.
There were no results to Rimbaud's chemical analysis. One by one his tests revealed nothing. The acids fizzed, the gases rose, and the lurid muddy precipitates trickled across the stone floor. There was nothing of any value in any of Rimbaud's samples as far as he could detect from the primitive means at his disposal.

Conclusion: He would have to construct a few simple apparatuses for more exhaustive analysis. He would have to collect more samples. To the east, the west, the north, Abyssinia was still barely explored, its properties unanalysed.

Rimbaud sat watching as the acid solutions slowly dribbled from the neat rows of samples down the crevices in the stone floor. When their paths met they would hiss violently for several seconds, the bubbles twinklingly reflecting in the lamplight, before continuing on their course.

Rimbaud's continuing meditations on a theme of scientific research:
Supposing all his explorations revealed nothing of any value anywhere in the whole of Abyssinia? What then?

Then he would be in a position frequently encountered by all great scientific researchers. He would have drawn a blank. *He would have failed. There'd be no point in any of his grand exploring schemes. His life would be in ruins.*

Etc . . .
Failed?

What course would he adopt if he were a great scientific researcher?

Why, he would study the results of other great scientific researchers. Hunting for clues which they had overlooked.

What works of other great scientific researchers did he know?

He had read of a Russian, Mendeleyev, in his *Wonders of the Modern World*. According to this fund of wisdom, Mendeleyev had said that all the chemicals of the earth could be split into elements. That these elements could be listed in a Periodic Table.

Had Mendeleyev overlooked any clues? Had he realised the full significance of what he was doing?

He had not, in Rimbaud's view, realised the full significance of what he was doing. (Gimlet-eyed, Rimbaud peered forward into the darkness, resting his chin in his cupped hands.) Mendeleyev, like all modern scientists, had missed the point, Rimbaud found himself realising.

How had Mendeleyev missed the point?

Mendeleyev, like all modern scientists, had discounted the work of previous centuries of research in the parallel field of Alchemy. But Rimbaud, with his unique knowledge of both the occult and the practical sciences, could see that Mendeleyev's Periodic Table was just what the alchemists had been looking for throughout the ages. (Albeit, without realising it.) If this table listing the fundamental hierarchy of the elements could be combined with the time-honoured processes of alchemy, it would mean the liberation of all matter. The transmuting of worthless stuff into gold would be seen to be just a part of a whole cycle of possible changes.

Conclusion: If Rimbaud couldn't make his fortune out of this, then he'd make his fortune out of nothing.

Course of Action: Send home at once to Mother for a book on Mendeleyev's theory. Make a list of every alchemical process he could remember.

It had been easy enough reconstructing those laborious notes on chemical analysis which I'd lost in the waterfall – remembering my previous studies in my old labour of love, Alchemy, would be child's play by comparison.

Rimbaud hugged his knees up under his chin as he found himself remembering his studies back in the library at Charleville when the school had been closed by the Prussian war – how he had poured through *Les Clefs des Grands Mystères*, *L' Histoire de la Magie* and the *Dictionnaire Mytho-Hermetique*. In those days his studies in Alchemy had been for a different purpose: to invest his poetry with the strength of magic, to give it the added power of occult meaning so that his visionary words could at once be themselves and yet at the same time contain the necessity of the secret locked within them. I had discerned how beauty itself could at the same time be made to contain the mysterious formulas for transforming base metal into gold. Oh, what a fool I'd been! If that was true of words, how much more true would it be of these chemicals themselves. No poem ever turned into gold.

Conclusion: Rimbaud's whole life had been spent missing the point.

– Creating poems which contained the secrets of the universe.

– Deranging his senses in order to see the visionary world.

– Rearranging the elements of his former failed poetic self to create this new man he had become.

Who, now, at last, had understood.

What Rimbaud had been trying to do to himself, his senses, his talents, he should have been doing to the world.

Combining { The hierarchy of the elements (Chemical)
The processes of changing the elements (Alchemical)

Which would mean that –

The elements of the earth could be changed. Split and refused.

All things would thus be seen to be relative. Relativity

alone would be absolute.

All matter – the entire world – would be subject to the will of man alone.

All man's dreams could be interpreted. Into reality.

Nothing would any more need to be what it is.

There could be an end to all want, all suffering.

All men could be equal.

Rimbaud's long, open-mouthed breaths rustled through the silent vaulted night of the cellar around him as he gazed up wide-eyed at the crusted scallop of imperfect darkness which enclosed his vision.

More immediate conclusions: With this process Harar could be made self-sufficient. Rimbaud could make his fortune, achieve fame, etc etc.

Rimbaud watched as the muddy solutions drained away, seeping through the cracks into the foundations. At last he'd be able to give his life a meaning. A purpose sufficient to all his hopes. An object beyond all his wildest dreams. Leaning down, he blew out the lamp and then crept out of the cellar, locking the door behind him. Edging his way up the stairs so as to avoid the creaking boards, Rimbaud made his way to the landing. Vardy and Grimes were still muttering together in the club room. The fools, let them bicker away about their prehistoric standards. All that shit about 'taste' and 'values'. My new discovery would render them all redundant. Why, I would revalue the values of the very elements themselves! Rimbaud eased open the door to his room. Tahira whimpered in her sleep as he got into bed beside her. For a moment she trembled and kicked, convulsing in some nightmare, and then with a sigh she moulded herself against him. Rimbaud lay, listening as the distant baying of the dogs on the ramparts died into the silence of the night. Beyond his feet, at the window, the white dome of the mosque glowed, dull and leprous, under the weak misted gold of the half moon.

I am getting better now. My strength is returning. This

new scientific treatment of electric shocks they are giving me is beginning to work. Though the after-effects have blurred my nerves to such an extent that I can no longer sleep, it means that I now have the nights to myself. And in the early hours when I sense the first light of day will soon be approaching, I begin my experiments.

First I warm my limbs and measure the decreasing frontiers of my feeling. (Still the paralysis seems to be creeping up, infinitesimally. But it can't be – it must be my imagination.) Then I crawl in the darkness to the end of my bed and take up my metal leg. As the light grows, I ease it on over my stump . . .

Yesterday, I managed to balance myself upright. Alone!

Today, I took my first agonising pace.

Agreed, I collapsed back onto the bed. But it's all coming back. I am remembering how to use my limbs again. I am learning to move! On my own. Of my own accord . . . Tomorrow, I will take another pace. Unaided. My responses are returning. Deep inside me, the old reactions are re-awakening.

Tomorrow. And tomorrow. And tomorrow.

I will. I will.

On my own.

I am learning to walk again.

By the time Isabelle comes in, I am back in bed. Neither she nor the doctor are aware of my experiments. I will learn to walk without them.

Forward . . . Remember. Forward . . . Remember. In my imagination I rehearse the first steps of my recovery.

15

Reports soon began reaching Harar of the worsening famine in the Interior to the south. Still the rains had not come. The wells were drying up, the crops withering, and the fields reverting to the wilderness – according to the trickle of refugees who now came into Harar each morning with the caravans. They were the lucky ones; only those with relatives in the city were allowed past the gates.

So it was that one morning the old man who had sold me Tahira, accompanied by his five sons, arrived at the palace. The oasis had dried up, he explained, and he had come to stay with his relatives. Which meant me, I discovered.

Rimbaud wasn't sure.

But Vardy was delighted to be of assistance, and said that they could take the empty room at the end of the passage.

Grimes remembered similar circumstances in India . . .

Sottiro, after appearing not to notice, started making remarks about the smell.

Rimbaud decided to cut his losses by employing the old man's sons as his permanent porters.

Tahira began by avoiding them like the plague; but within three days they had her cooking for them. One of those sons was still officially her husband, Rimbaud realised.

Gradually I was forced to admit to myself how precarious my hold on Tahira was. I had only bought her. (Not even that; I'd been given her, as a goodwill gift, in part exchange for a consignment of half-cured hides.) The old man and his sons were her people; they would always have a power over her which I could never touch.

Now, each evening as I taught her and she went over the words she had remembered, her manner became more withdrawn, her face blank, her eyes mournful, mute and pleading, as she gradually receded into herself.

'What's the matter, Tahira?'

'Matter?' She frowned: a pinched stare. 'What is matter, Arthur?'

'Tahira is sad. Arthur does not know – why?'

'Matter. Matter . . .' She clung to the word, repeating it as her face splintered, her chin trembling. And then she was sobbing, burying her face in the taffeta folds of her dress.

I sat down beside her, placing my arm around her collapsed juddering shoulders. But I could do nothing to persuade her to uncover her face as she sobbed, her cries stuttering incoherently out of her shaking body. Gritting my teeth, I rested my face on my hand, my fingers pressing into my eyelids.

The pores of darkness shifting.

Gradually Tahira subsided against me.

'What is it, Tahira?'

She sniffed, her face still buried in the black taffeta folds. 'Arthur . . . Oasis not dry. All is untrue . . .' And then she fell away from me, twisting free of my arm as she toppled sideways onto the pillow. I watched while she drew her knees up against her belly, the gentle grating donkey bray of her sobs sawing into me. What the hell was the matter?

Eventually, long after Tahira's sobs had sunk into the heavy regular sighs of sleep, Rimbaud picked up the lamp and returned to his desk. Half-heartedly he began sifting through his re-written analysis notes, occasionally filling in a gap with some remembered formula. *How can I keep you? How can I make you mine, Tahira?*

Rimbaud found himself remembering all the promises he had made to himself (*to you, Tahira, but you had never understood them*) when he had seen her standing by the well back at the oasis. How he would teach her French. How they would live together. How he would give her a son . . .

And what had I done about all those promises?

All a man could do. If she didn't have one up the spout by now, it wasn't for lack of trying.

Rimbaud clenched his jaw as he stared down at her dim, rounded sleeping figure (knees drawn up under her chin, head bent, encauled in the silky transparency of her dress) growing out of the vague edges of the light cast by his lamp.

Was this love – this incubating knot of feeling, this inkling of the pangs of loss – love?

'Tahira, I . . .' But who would hear? . . . 'Bear with me, ma petite.'

As the reports of the famine became more widespread, my thoughts increasingly turned to Yarousseau. What had become of him out there? He was long overdue for a visit to Harar; already there were two letters waiting for him in the club room. Had the villagers finally understood that their rain god had no powers? What would they do when they realised that he was only a man like themselves?

Vaguely Rimbaud considered the idea of setting out to rescue his friend. But this was mere dreaming. To mount an expedition, even a small one, would have meant borrowing from Vardy or Grimes. And as it was, with all the added expenses incurred by his relations coming to stay, Rimbaud was already eating into his precious savings. Added to this, the famine had begun to affect trade, and he had begun staking his wages as down payments to secure regular consignments from the caravaners. It was the only way to get them to do business now; it was a sellers' market.

At night, Rimbaud began the long process of reconstructing from memory all the alchemy and magical studies of his youth. (Mother would hardly have sent me a children's primer on sorcery, even if I'd had the cash to pay for it.)

I was descending the stairs into the cellar, carrying a lamp. Suddenly my strength seemed to blunder out of me. Forwards. I crumpled, my face lurching on ahead of the light, into the darkness. The pain was sudden, sharp, stunning, And then I was lying there watching as the silent viscous blue flames spread over the step beneath my eyes, the light sparking in the fragments of shattered glass. And pinpricks of sliding stars peppering my vision. The flames spilled tremulously over the lip of the step, down. Isolating into puddles. And the spiral of vertigo uncoiled in my skull . . .

Huge bare feet dancing in the flames. Which parted about their heels. Voices. The old man's sons . . . I was being carried, down . . . and laid out on the stone floor, in pitch darkness . . .

Voices. Light. Shadows. A wicker chair, I recognised, from the club room. Creaking as they heaved me into it. Raising me, up. Carrying me. Into light . . . Pulling the cover of my bed around me as I breathed, deeply, sheathed in my cold sweat-dampened clothes. You're ill; you're suffering from strain, worry, something mental, I told myself, quite lucidly. And then nothing . . .

When I awoke, it was night. I was shivering, an icy sweat dribbling from every pore, my mind seared with the aftervision of this nightmare of dazzling rainbow-tinted snowscapes under the singing phosphorescence of rippling stars.

London. Limehouse. The Chinese opium dens with Verlaine. That's where I'd seen those skies before . . . *This is the tomb where you intend to destroy me with enchantments. I, hidden. I, revealed. The flame rising again to defy all redemption. Pride, fired. With the vision of the ultimate ice-age of all wisdom. A universe consumed, shimmering, encauled in the form of its own extinction*, I had written later, when I had eventually returned home, trembling with mortal dread as I retraced the voyage of my soul through the territories of its undoing.

But now I knew what these ravings meant. These fevered nightmares of mine, which drew their images from those earlier visions, could be used. In those visions of mine were hidden the secrets of the magic processes. Mendeleyev, with his list of all the elements, had only described the world as it is; and those old alchemists, without fully understanding the world in which they lived, had simply had inklings of what the world could be. By combining the two, I, Arthur Rimbaud, would discover the ultimate logic of all truth!

Conclusion: In delirium, truth – in magic, logic. Another sick man smiles in the darkness, his mind sharpened by the pain of his one-legged half-paralysed body as he contemplates the stronger, more complete body of his former self and its African truths from the distance of his cold-sheeted bed at the edge of Europe. Such are his only amusements in the sleepless night when the world sleeps around him.

And as the pristine darkness of the night gradually dims, one aging man rouses himself to face the new day, fumbling in agony as he draws on his artificial leg.

In the light of an earlier dawn, another younger man scribbled at his desk, still trembling with weakness as he copied down his dreams. And then, with a sigh, began estimating his financial position, balancing advance payments against the consignments still needed for his next caravan. I'd have to risk the last of my savings on this caravan, and then just see what happened. The market couldn't get worse.

In an effort to regain his strength, Rimbaud abandoned his habitual ascetic ways and started buying meat in the local dives, breaking into his remaining money, frantically gorging himself on anything that took his fancy. All in the desperate effort to keep his flagging energies alive.

Ivory. Hides. One more consignment of coffee. And still no gum . . .

As the days progressed, his fever gained a stronger hold. Often he found he couldn't walk unaided. The old man's sons would support him as he bargained, rasping out his offers. Finally helping him to his bed when he slumped, silent, the sweat dribbling down his face.

It's mental. It's all in the mind, he told himself. But as

Rimbaud raised himself, his elbows gave and his face fell back into the pillow.

There were periods of light, followed by periods of dark. As far as I could tell. Days followed by night. Nightmares from which I woke, screaming. Then days of ethereal calm.

Was that Badjian against that night-darkened window? Ras Makonen standing above me?

Grimes? Vardy? Is that you?

The night-darkened window . . .

The distant murmur of voices rising from the sunlit market place . . .

Night again. The bed, cold. 'Tahira!'

She hadn't been sleeping there for days, I suddenly realised.

'Here, swallow this.'

Vardy, sitting on the side of the bed, spooning bread and honeyed goat's milk into my mouth. 'I do believe you're getting better!'

'Tahira!'

'No, try to swallow.'

Beyond Vardy, the floorboards, empty. Tahira's clothes gone.

She's gone back. . .

Below the window the drift of murmurs from the unseen crowd in the market place, bubbling across the square like the waves of the sea. The call of the traders, the cries of the soothsayers . . .

Yarousseau! . . . What's happened to you? Where are you?

Rimbaud's thoughts unwound as gradually he subsided once more into the territory of his obsessive nightmares.

Fire. Darkness. The multiplying trivia of horror.

'I must try and stay awake.'

'I do believe you're becoming almost human.' Vardy, gently easing another mouthful of honeyed goat's milk

between my lips.
 The room light, rigid.
 'Thanks Vardy.'

'More? Best to get down as much as you can.'
 'No thanks, Vardy. I'll only be sick.'
 The room lamplit. Aglow. Cosy. Beyond the window, dark.
 'You shouldn't be up at this hour, looking after me.'
 Vardy shrugging, sheepish.
 'Thanks Vardy.'
 'It's nothing. I'd only be lonely on my own.'
 'But you've got Grimes, haven't you?'
 Again a shrug, this time dismissive. 'Grimes is company.'
 Arthur reaches out his hand and lays it on Vardy's arm. 'I'm sorry. I used to despise you. But now I think I see . . .'
 Vardy gently removes Arthur's hand, smiling glacially. 'You must sleep now.'
 Darkness.

Then day. Then night. Separate. Routine. Regular feeding. By Grimes, now.
 The reassembling of reality. Harar. Abyssinia. The war in the north. The famine in the south. The slump in the market.
 'I must get that caravan off, Grimes.'
 'You shouldn't be bothering your head about . . .'
 'Get Sottiro!'

Rimbaud explained to his clerk their financial position. 'If our consignments aren't fully made up and ready for the next Zeyla caravan, we're done for.'
 They needed coffee. Gum. Anything. As long as the price was right. But especially gum.
 Rimbaud gave Sottiro a list of maximum prices. 'One penny above these prices – *on anything!* – and I'll have your guts for garters.'
 'Don't you worry, Arthur.'

Rimbaud made Sottiro drag the bed over to the window. Where he sat, leaning on the sill, watching as Sottiro marched out into the market place, resplendent in all his finery, followed by the old man's sons.

Within the hour they were carrying back a large consignment of gum.

'At half price?'

'Yes, Arthur.'

'How the hell did you do it?'

'I bargained with them.'

Rimbaud poured over the accounts: they might just break even.

Next day Sottiro bought 2 tusks, 3 sacks of coffee and half a dozen barrels of gum.

'But these prices are fantastic!'

'We'll make our pile, Arthur, don't you worry.'

'You bastard! You're cheating me! You must be!'

'Arthur!'

'I'll be checking every single thing when I'm on my feet. Remember that.'

'Well you bloody well go ahead and do that then, you ungrateful bugger!'

Next day, Sottiro didn't bother to visit Rimbaud after storing his purchases in the cellar. Rimbaud had counted them from the window as they were carried in by the old man's sons. Nine barrels of gum. Six sacks of coffee. A dozen bales of hide.

'*Sottiro! Sottiro!*'

No reply.

The bastard's ruining me! The last of my savings!

After he had been fed, Rimbaud waited until everyone was asleep, and then eased himself out of bed. The gum barrels were always marked with the purchase price. If he could only get down to the cellars he could find out how much Sottiro was cheating him.

But by the time he had crept as far as the top of the stairs outside the clubroom, his strength had given. With a sigh he slumped against the wall, subsiding, setting down the lamp with a clatter as his head lolled. His eyes disengaged, swooning. Then, as he sat gasping at the edge of the pool of light, he heard a rustle on the stairs below him. Someone was coming up. The rustling stopped.

'Bomba!'

No reply.

'Who's there?'

He was shivering now, his back pressed against the cold stone wall.

'Help me up!'

The rustling began again, ascending. And then he saw Tahira's face at the edge of the light, looking down over him. Her eyes puckered against the light as she instinctively drew her robe across the lower half of her face.

'Tahira!' Arthur craned forward. Silently she withdrew into the darkness, her eyes wide and staring now. '*Tahira!*'

Rimbaud listened as the door of the old man's room creaked open at the end of the passage, and closed behind her.

'Help! For God's sake, *help!*'

The resonance of his voice died through the silence of the darkened palace. Then he heard a grunt, followed by a series of shuffles, from inside the club room. A moment later he saw a vague light growing under the door.

'Help!'

'I say, Arthur! What are you doing out here?' Grimes set down his lamp, and quickly began hauling Rimbaud to his feet.

In an aura of tobacco and heaving boozy breath, Rimbaud was unceremoniously dragged back to his room. Rimbaud listened in the darkness as Grimes grunted along the passage to retrieve the lamps. There wasn't a sound from the other rooms. The bastards! I'd yelled enough to waken the dead.

Grimes set the lamps down and plonked himself on the

chair beside Rimbaud's bed.

What on earth had Arthur been up to? No fit state. Gadding about at dead of night, etc etc.

But what had Grimes been up to at this hour in the club room, wondered Arthur.

Grimes, more than a little befuddled, explained that he had been having a go at this wretched developing. Photography. Arthur's picture, in fact. But he was damned if he could make head or tail of the thing . . . There was this damned negative, the undeveloped thingumijig. Some chemical process. But it was all magic to him. 'I do apologise, Arthur. But I rather think your picture's going to be something of a failure.'

'You sound as if you've been mixing the processes. It's a matter of developing the negative first, and then fixing the image. At least that's what it said in my encyclopedia.'

This was news indeed to Grimes. Whose mind was beginning to wander now, after the effort of response. Arthur sat back, drawing in the alcoholic fumes.

'Would you like me to have a go at it, Grimes? I've got nothing better to do stuck up here all day.'

Grimes grunted out of his bemused state. 'What? Yes, yes. Very good idea. I *see!* Yes, that *would* be a good idea. Very kind of you, Arthur.'

In the vague chiaroscuro of the lamps, Grimes' features had softened so that he appeared almost as he must have done some thirty years earlier: gaunt-faced, earnest, extrovert. Stinking drunk.

The younger man could have been mixing for a fight, Rimbaud realised, where the older man was in fact doing nothing more than grapple for his thoughts. Which Rimbaud heard himself listening to.

With all the brusque certainties of manner dissolved, there was now only a man. Who had, it seemed, made a mess of things. 'A frightful mess, Arthur. When you come to look at it. I . . . where was I? Am I detaining you?'

'Whatever possessed someone like you to come up to

Harar, Grimes?'

'India. Upper Burma and the Shan States.' Grimes was still wandering in some labyrinth of his own making. 'A fresh start. Obscurity in Siam. Bangkok, same mistake again.' The geography of some distant eastern empire sighed out with the fumes: its more banal factual history thankfully obscured by befuddlement.

Grimes stopped, frowning into shadowy age.

'Right you are, then. You develop it for me.'

Next morning, Grimes brought in the chemicals and developing trays.

'It has to be done in the dark. You do know that?'

Rimbaud knew.

'Do you want me to explain . . .'

'No. That's all right.'

'I just thought I'd better point out . . .' Coming to the point, etc. Grimes was himself again.

Rimbaud too. 'Okay Grimes, off you go. You've obviously got business to do.'

'On the contrary, Arthur. I'm almost redundant.'

'What do you mean?'

'You know how things are. What with the famine and the nasty turn the war's taken, I've got my caravan made up a whole week in advance. Good prices, too. The traders have gone all panicky, unloading stock left, right and centre.'

'You mean the prices are down?'

'Well down. Didn't you know? I thought that was why you'd sent that clerk of yours out. To clear up while the going was good.'

'Are they down to half prices?'

'Come, come Arthur. Not *that* much. But a good twenty per cent, I'd say.'

Rimbaud watched Sottiro set out into the market place. He didn't even bother to turn and look up when I shouted.

Rimbaud counted the day's haul. A dozen barrels of gum.

Seven sacks of coffee beans. Five tusks.

Next day: More. And hides. Where the hell was he getting the money from?

The bastard! He must be getting it on credit!

Next day: More ivory, more hides . . .

Rimbaud glowered. His eyes narrowed. Thoughts, murderous.

The negative lay among the chemicals, undeveloped.

Enter Grimes, morose, chewing his lips with agitation.

'What's the matter, Grimes?'

Grimes begins to explain . . . '*What is the matter?*'

Grimes continues his explanation . . . '*What*, for God's sake?'

Grimes comes to the point . . . 'Yes, I know. He's cheating me.'

Grimes explains . . . 'No?'

Grimes continues etc . . . 'If you're still on about that bloody suit of his . . .'

Grimes etc . . . 'What do I care about his business methods? So long as he's not cheating me. *Which he is*, I know.'

Grimes etc . . . 'They called the guards? *Twice!* When?'

Grimes etc . . . 'No one told me.'

Grimes etc . . . 'He's working for me. Not Badjian.'

Grimes etc . . . 'Of course I'm sure. That's only market gossip. Just because they *dress* alike . . .'

Grimes etc . . . '*What* methods, for God's sake!'

Grimes etc . . . 'He can't be any worse than *they* are.'

Grimes etc . . . '*What!*'

Grimes etc . . . 'Who, precisely?'

Grimes etc . . . 'But they're all my best contacts!'

Grimes etc . . . '*None* of them will deal with him?'

Grimes etc . . . 'Only under threat of what?'

Grimes etc . . . '*What* to do with Badjian?'

Grimes etc . . . 'They want all outsiders barred from the market place? Who said?'

Grimes etc . . . 'Why? Just because of . . .'

Grimes etc . . . 'How *can* I do anything? Look at me!'

Grimes etc . . . '*I know* he's my responsibility. But I'm a sick man.'

Grimes' conclusion: Things had got out of hand. His last chance to make good, his last chance in life, was being ruined. So many times he had had success within his grasp. In the palm of his hand. At his fingertips. Back home on the farm. In society. In London. Abroad, on his own. And always the same bone of contention. The spirit of the thing. Which previously, not to put too fine a point on it, he'd taken into his own hands, onto his own head, with guts, a heart to do it, a mind to see it through. Because he couldn't stomach seeing the whole show fold just because of human weakness. But now he was in no fit state, too weak, beyond his grasp . . .

Rimbaud's conclusion: Things had got out of hand. His last chance to make good, etc. Ditto . . .

Their only hope: Vardy.

Their joint conclusion: As a man, Vardy just hadn't got it in him. Sottiro wouldn't pay a blind bit of notice.

Rimbaud pondered, loins tingling with desperation.

. . . and Sottiro started into the market place, swaggering, smacking the gaudy seaming of his trousers with an ivory fly whisk, as the old man's sons strode behind him. They no longer sloped, Rimbaud noticed.

The porters and merchants parted before Sottiro, silently. Bargaining ceased and all heads turned to stare whenever he passed.

Later in the morning the porters began to form in small groups, Rimbaud saw. As they muttered, they would glance up at his window, only turning away when they saw Rimbaud's face. They never came when I called now; hiring the old man's sons had long since put an end to my days of learning Harari round the fire.

An hour or so later, the calls in the market place began

subsiding, trade visibly coming to a halt, as the crowd started to congregate around the central stalls, hushed. Then they were parting to reveal Sottiro, followed by the old man's sons, each loaded up with merchandise. Sottiro was strutting, positively revelling in the sullen silent stares.

For a moment he paused, gazing slowly about him, smiling faintly. And then he began pushing his way into the crowd, brusquely waving them out of his way with his newly acquired ivory fly whisk. The crowd folded aside – a veritable Red Sea before this Moses of the market place. Eventually Sottiro came to a halt in front of a half-empty stall.

'Here, you,' he yelled to the owner, a cringing old skinflint who I'd crossed swords with many a time – a hard bargainer, who knew the value of his stuff all right, but who had often kept the odd consignment of high quality hides aside especially for me when he knew I had a caravan to make up. 'Here, you. You said you hadn't got any good hides yesterday.'

The man whinged. He still had no good hides, he indicated.

'Well, it so happens I've got some here that I've decided I don't want.'

Sottiro called one of the old man's sons forward. 'You can have this lot. At a price. I need the cash, to go on trading.'

The old trader shook his head. He didn't want to buy.

But Sottiro ordered the hides to be put down regardless. And then quoted a price: a fantastic price.

The old trader raised his face to the sky. He didn't want to do business.

Whereupon Sottiro advanced, poking his fly whisk threateningly into the man's face.

The crowd stood, silently watching, as the old man raised his hands, shaking his head.

Sottiro repeated his offer: exactly. *He obviously intended to get that price!*

The old trader continued shaking his head, peering round

appealingly, visibly frightened.

Sottiro shouted, poking out his hand. (As Rimbaud began fumbling under his bed.)

The old trader whimpered.

Still Sottiro shouted, threateningly, poking his hand out for the money as if the deal were already done. (Rimbaud opened the box.)

The old trader cringed, almost into a ball, rocking himself from one foot to the other, pulling at his fingertips in agitation.

Sottiro continued, poking out his hand

as I gazed down the barrel of Vardy's pistol, my finger resting against the cold metal of the trigger guard.

'Money! Money!' *He stood, poking out his hand, repeating the words again and again as if in some frozen hysteria.* 'Money! Money!'

Rimbaud's lips mouthed his words. *His* words!

'Money! Money!' I repeated, flatly, insistently.

Verlaine stumbled forward into the room, slobbering, weeping drunk, staggering. And then I saw he had a pistol in his hand.

'So you want to leave me, do you?' he blurted out, his shiny lips blubbering.

'Money! Money!' The young Arthur Rimbaud backed against the wall, even as he heard his voice, toneless, hard, demented. 'Give me money!'

'S'you wanner leave me, jew?'

Verlaine was fumbling behind him, turning the key in the lock, his legs crossing one another as he leaned, grabbing for the chair. He sank onto it, slewing sideways, the pistol still pointing at the end of his outstretched arm. It was almost as if he were beckoning me.

'Ser yer wan'leaf me, jer?'

He was steadying his pointing arm with his other hand, his face streaked with tears, the spittle from his open mouth dribbling out over his beard, hanging in a loop as it caught in his lapel.

'Money! Money!'

'For th'fare home? Is zat isnit?'

My hand was cold against the cold wall, but I could feel the sliminess of my sweat as my hand moved, pressing back against the wall's unyielding solidity. The warm dampness of my piss trickled down the inside of my thigh. I could see his finger on the trigger: it was trembling.

He belched, toppling sideways, but somehow still keeping the gun pointing at me. And then, as he slumped forward in an effort to regain his balance, I suddenly felt myself drift out of myself . . . That shabby nondescript Brussels hotel room was immediately something else, and yet at the same time something intensely, horrifically vivid, as if its actuality had been unmasked before my eyes while I hovered beyond it, staring. The white porcelain jug in its bowl on the table in front of the cheesy lace curtain draping the window. My open suitcase lying amidst the churned folds of the unmade bed. The books scattered on the floor, fanned in an arc where Verlaine had kicked them out of his way. And the frayed flower-patterned mat stretching across the bare floorboards from his feet to mine. Verlaine was wiping his beard on his cuff, the spittle lining the cloth of his jacket like a dewy cobweb.

'Y'really? . . . No, Arthur. No!'

'Money! Money!' I replied mechanically, tonelessly, the words breathing out of me. My other hand was still held out: some disembodied upturned claw.

'Arthur . . . really?' he sobbed.

'Forever. We're finished.' I heard myself speak, quietly, firmly, distinctly. 'Forever. Get that into your thick skull. Now give me the money.'

I could still feel the outer limits of my body. My toes in my shoes, my jiggering calves, the warm dampness creeping down my trouser leg, my icy wet palm pressed against the wall.

Verlaine coughed, snivelling, gibbering. There was a

crack, not very loud, and a little yellow flash. I felt my wrist yanked back through the wall. Verlaine was falling forward. There was another crack and another little yellow flash from the pistol as his head fell forwards towards me. My ears suddenly began singing. Verlaine was weeping, crying out, crawling towards me. I looked down. There was blood dripping onto the floor at my feet. My wrist was bleeding.

Then Verlaine was pressing his face into my groin, hugging at my thighs.

'Oh, Arthur. God! Oh God! What have I done?'

I could feel his chin moving against my prick as he toppled off balance. Then the blood from my wrist was running over his ear, trickling down his neck onto his collar.

'Oh God, Arthur. Oh God. Shoot me!'

Then he released me, and I watched as he began crawling about the floor. Finally he got hold of the pistol. He was holding it by the barrel, pushing it into my unwounded hand.

'Shoot me. Kill me. Put an end to it.'

I felt my fingers close around the barrel. It was wet and slimy. By now my wounded hand had begun to throb. It felt as if it was in a vice, and at each throb as if someone were trying to yank my arm out of its socket. I raised the pistol. I could feel the giddiness beginning to tug inside my skull.

Verlaine was on his knees in front of me, staring up at me, his beard covered in a fine lace of spittle. For the first time I became aware of the pervasive stench of absinthe. I watched as he clasped his hands. He was praying, imploring me. I held the gun away from me, pointing it down. He was saying something, gibbering, but I couldn't hear him for the rushing in my ears. His eyes were red-rimmed and the streaks of tears had gathered dust and filth so that he looked like some weird painted savage dressed up in European clothes. For several moments I stared at this utterly alien face; and then I was peering down along the barrel at the end of my arm, pressing the trigger. The book jumped at my feet, as if it had been flung across the floor, and the pistol leapt in my hand. There was a wide, diagonal groove in the cover of the book and I could see the inner white of the pages. Then my head was sinking, and once again I was staring down the barrel, all strength draining out of me.

Rimbaud blinked. The crowd down below in the market square was parting. Sottiro emerged, brandishing a small leather purse in his fist. The old man's sons, bent down with merchandise, followed as Sottiro strutted towards the palace, his eyes narrowed, beaming. Rimbaud watched, open-mouthed as Sottiro passed beneath him, beneath the pointing barrel, inside.

When I looked up, Verlaine had passed out.

The crowd had dispersed amongst the stalls, under the awnings, arms waving, voices shouting. Business had restarted. Slowly Rimbaud kicked his feet out from under the bedclothes. He replaced Vardy's pistol under his bed and then heaved himself onto the chair by his desk. As he sat, grim-faced, gritting his teeth, his eyes floated vaguely over the scattered notes on his desk. Then suddenly he found these images flooding into his mind. The occult formulas. Linked symbols tracing the paths of the magical processes. He picked up his pen. Shakily his hand copied as his mind dictated, and the resurrected mysteries became words.

Whose secret he now knew how to use.

He watched as his hand copied, the scar of his old wrist wound rasping across the blank face of the paper.

When night came, and my eyes began to tire, I got up and began mixing the chemicals which Grimes had left me, pouring the fluids into the appropriate vats. My strength was returning, and I could stand now for minutes at a time. I blocked out the light from the lamp and started developing the negative plate. I must have dozed off and woken several times; I remember lying back on the bed and listening to the distant roar of a lion (which somehow didn't disturb the prowling of the dogs on the ramparts) while I waited as the developing and fixing processes took place. Finally, when the stars outside the window had begun to dim with the coming light of day, I found myself holding up before me this curiously anonymous image of a man standing on some rocks, his hand resting on his hip, his bronzed hollow-cheeked deep-eyed face staring out of the picture, slightly sullen, but otherwise expressionless. Behind the small nondescript figure in his white cotton native smock and trousers, rose a tangle of brambles. The figure was completely dominated by the surroundings. As my tired eyes tried to focus, I kept seeing these shapes forming in the tangle of brambles, faint shadowy presences emerging out of the dim grey solidity of the rocks. And as soon as I had deciphered them, I found no matter how hard I tried to refocus my vision that I was no longer able to see this as just a picture of some dour forlorn figure standing in this nondescript landscape. It was so much more. There were so many other things. Forms, patterns, presences, images, which simply weren't there, but which I could see nonetheless, even as I told myself that it was just my imagination.

Rimbaud sank back, laying aside the photograph, his head resting against the pillow as his eyes flickered closed. The light had already grown over the sky. Within moments he was asleep, the distant mounting chant from the caravaners and refugees outside the gate mingling with the first liberated images of his troubled dreams.

Enter Badjian and Ras Makonen.

The patient greets his friends with a show of enthusiasm: the affability of a lonely worried man.

Pleasantries are exchanged concerning the patient's health. 'My friend, you are looking *much* better.'

And concerning the patient's business affairs. 'But you must be making a fortune!'

Thus, evidence of the patient's ruin (both physical and financial) are dismissed, and the real purpose of the visit emerges: 'The war's taken its expected turn. I have it on good authority – the Egyptians are pulling out, my friend' explained Badjian, leaning forward conspiratorially over the bedcovers. 'The Emir is going to be re-appointed. You will be all right, Arthur. But I am afraid I cannot guarantee the safety of the other Europeans. Especially this clerk of yours.'

Rimbaud muses over this news, without comment.

Ras Makonen, seated on the chair at the other side of the room, casts a casual eye over the scattered papers on Rimbaud's desk. 'So you are dabbling in magic, I see.'

'What? . . . Oh, yes. Just looking for a cure in case things take a turn for the worse and Dr Badjian isn't available.'

Ras Makonen smiled deferentially, as Badjian guffawed. Rocking on the bed, slapping his gold braid. Ham. Lapsing abruptly into earnestness. 'The others must leave at once. You must warn them, Arthur.'

'But what about me? Are you sure I'll be all right?'

Badjian beamed, furtive, knowing. An expression of trust which froze all trust. 'My friend, it is time for you to revive your partnership with one of the Emir's closest advisers. Our opportunity has come at last. With a closed city we'll be able to clear the market. We'll have a monopoly.'

Rimbaud glanced across at Ras Makonen: he showed no signs of surprise at Badjian's disclosures. 'You mean you know about Badjian and the Emir?' I asked.

'*Please*, Arthur,' Badjian eyed me sternly as he rested his hand on my knee, turning his back to Ras, '*everyone* knows Badjian is the Emir's friend. Wouldn't the Emir be impotent without the professional advice of his doctor?'

Badjian continued to hold Rimbaud's eye during the ensuing pause.

'And what kind of magic is this?' asked Ras Makonen eventually, holding up my developed photograph.

Badjian immediately rose and began taking an exaggerated interest.

'Ah, daguerreotype. A fine likeness, Arthur.'

'But I do not understand,' replied Ras.

'It's a picture, Ras,' explained Badjian, running his finger over the print. 'This is Arthur. Don't you see?'

'And this?' asked Ras, still perplexed.

'Why, that appears to be rocks. And some kind of tangle. Just outside the walls, isn't it Arthur?'

Ras frowned, still unable to decipher the picture. He'd evidently never seen a photograph before.

'His head, his arms, his clothes,' Badjian traced, as Ras shook his head disbelievingly.

'In our religion we do not have such things,' Ras explained, eventually, after he had reluctantly been persuaded into recognition. 'We are allowed no images. Except God. And Him we worship in the spirit alone,' he added gravely.

'In case the people start worshipping idols,' added Badjian, who now appeared somewhat embarrassed once more. As a professed co-member of Ras's religion, he had evidently displayed a little too wide a knowledge of images.

Which brought to Rimbaud's mind the nagging topic he had tried so often to forget during the long days of his illness. There were so many ways of worshipping false gods, Rimbaud began explaining (to Badjian's acute discomfort). Rimbaud had a friend who had actually become a god. Confident of his wit in rescuing the situation, Rimbaud started to elaborate on Yarousseau's plight with various ironic observations.

Which neither Ras nor Badjian appeared to find in the least bit funny.

'And at night they laid him down and listened to his stomach. For evidence of rain-bearing wind, as far as I could make out.'

The punch line was a total flop.

'I'm sorry. Have I said something?'

With a face devoid of all expression, Badjian rested his hand on Rimbaud's knee once more. 'Your friend who became a god is dead, my friend.'

'What, have you heard something?' demanded Rimbaud, a sudden chill freezing his guts. 'Why the hell didn't you tell me?'

There was nothing to tell, continued Badjian gravely as Ras began fingering the photograph with an unsettlingly detached air, except that Arthur obviously didn't understand what it meant to be a man-god. Didn't understand his true nature. If this rain-god did not fulfil his function within the appointed time, Badjian went on, it was known that he was a selfish god and that he was keeping the rains to himself. Consequently the rains had to be liberated from his body. 'Do you really want to know what happens?' asked Badjian.

Rimbaud nodded, tense with foreboding.

And Badjian explained Yarousseau's fate as a god. To fulfil his purpose, the rain-god was ceremonially disembowelled and his innards spread over the dry land so that the rains could at last be free.

Rimbaud gazed in distracted silence down at the bed-covers, the fluid horrors of his worst nightmares at last given form.

'Ah, here is your clerk,' began Ras, who had at last got up and moved over to the window. 'I see he has become a very important man indeed now.'

Rimbaud turned to look down out of the window. There was Sottiro being carried out into the market place in the old wicker chair from the cellars. To the sides of the chair had been strapped two poles which were supported by four of the old man's sons. While the fifth held above the chair a makeshift sunshade, made out of what Rimbaud recognised to be none other than the frayed material of the panniers which he had used to store his ore samples in while they lay unanalysed in the cellars.

'*The bastard!*' – the mounting charge of Rimbaud's feelings at last found their outlet – '*he must have broken into that cellar where I locked up my chemicals!*'

Rimbaud's fists clenched, trembling. 'My God, just you wait till I've got my strength back!' Rimbaud would break that bloody wicker chair over his fucking clerk's head.

But for the moment Rimbaud had to reserve his strength for

other matters. Such as hobbling to the club room to tell Vardy about the dangerous turn the war had taken.

Vardy, however, seemed unconcerned. 'Oh no, Arthur. Badjian won't get rid of us that easily.'

'But the Egyptians are pulling out!'

'It's a plot, Arthur. Can't you see? Badjian's trying to take over the market place for himself.'

Between them, Vardy and Grimes had come to one or two conclusions regarding Badjian's latest behaviour.

European Conclusions on the Nature of Our Caucasian Character's recent activities.

He had encouraged Sottiro in his outrageous behaviour in the hope of getting all Europeans barred from the market place. Also, Grimes had uncovered 'incontrovertible evidence' that Badjian was indulging in certain practices which were now barred by International Convention wherever civilisation existed.

'What activities?'

'I'm sworn to secrecy at present, Arthur.'

'Slave trading? Is that it?'

'All I can tell you is that Grimes is planning to see the Governor.'

'Don't be a fool, Vardy. Clear out while you can. There won't *be* a Governor if the Egyptians pull out. Only the Emir.'

'You don't honestly believe all that rubbish, do you Arthur?'

'The Emir's going to be re-appointed. And you know what that means.'

Vardy shook his head, grinning complacently. 'You've been made a fool of again, Arthur.'

But Rimbaud, in his present state of health, was in no mood to be reminded of his follies, either past or present.

'Get out! You bloody idiot! . . .'

Five minutes later, Rimbaud was being helped back to his room by his fellow European, speechless with exhaustion.

Next day nothing happened.

Rimbaud sat at his desk, distracting himself with his alchemy notes, gathering his energies for the trials which presumably lay ahead.

Rehearsing his lines for his confrontation with his clerk.

Pondering his guilt and his sadness over the loss of Yarousseau.

Unthreading the intricacies of Badjian's motives.

Should he warn Badjian?

As night came on, Rimbaud sat glowering in his bed, horrified at the extent of his revealed weakness.

Early next morning, as Rimbaud lay waking to the calls from outside the city gate, the door to his room opened, silently.

This shadowy form stood there, motionless.

Rimbaud stared, aghast, at the hunched abject form of the figure he saw before him.

'Tahira!'

Rimbaud leapt out of bed, stumbling forward and taking her in his arms. She neither resisted nor responded. I led her into the room, whereupon she immediately subsided onto the bed, shivering, her arms still clasped about her stomach.

'Tahira! Tahira, what's the matter?' I sank down on the bed beside her. 'You're ill!'

She continued to stare up at me, her face blank, her eyes glazed.

'Tahira ill?' In my agitation I was shaking her shoulders. 'Tahira bad? Tahira bad?'

'Tahira bad,' she repeated, her voice flat, wavering. Then she grimaced, shivering inside her skin. 'Tahira emelia Arthur.' She tried to smile, but it became something else, and she fell onto the pillow with a sob. I laid my hand on her shoulder, but she merely gathered herself up into a ball, refusing to uncover her face. Silent. Suppressed.

As his feelings welled within him, Rimbaud covered his blurred eyes with his hand.

From the distance of another continent and another

decade, the feelings of an aging man (whose lifetime has been spent brutalising his feelings), sharpens, subtly diversifying. The chemistry of time corroding the surface of the crass responses of immediacy.

While the brutal protagonist on the spot merely contemplated his course of action.

'Those fucking bastards! The minute I'm up and about again, I'll *throw* them out. Kick them back to their goddam oasis. Famine or no bloody famine!'

Grimes, inevitably, objected.

'But you can't just have her back like that, Arthur. I know how you must feel, but you never know what she might have gone and picked up.' Tahira, mercifully, slept.

'Don't worry, I'll get Badjian to give her a thorough checkup.'

'Not if I can help it, Arthur. After what I've discovered about him, that character's going to be behind bars for a long time. Or perhaps something even more drastic. He's got it coming, all right.'

'What exactly have you discovered, Grimes?'

'All in good time, Arthur. I've delivered a note to the Governor. He should be sending for me soon.'

In order to put an end to this uncomfortable topic, Rimbaud simply handed Grimes the developed photograph. Grimes was most impressed. The photograph would take pride of place in the club room, he assured Rimbaud.

When Grimes had left, Rimbaud sat at his desk and began to write a note. It was now imperative that he get word to Badjian. But how? Sottiro was his only hope, Rimbaud eventually decided. It was time for Rimbaud to reassert his authority over his clerk, to have it out with him, once and for all.

As soon as Sottiro returned to his room, Rimbaud got up and knocked on the door.

'Ah, so you're better, Arthur. Come in.' He didn't seem in the least apprehensive.

Rimbaud sat down on the bed and Sottiro ordered his slave girl off to the kitchens, demonstrating his mispronounced Harari with a proud flourish.

'Let's come straight to the point, Sottiro. How much have you spent?'

'Spent? What do you mean? I haven't spent anything.'

And so the confrontation begins, with the usual obligatory misunderstandings.

As the exchanges continue, Rimbaud's self-control soon ebbs (along with his strength).

'You've ruined me! You've been cheating me, you bastard!'

'But we've made a tremendous profit. I haven't been cheating you, I promise.'

Rimbaud states his evidence:–
   –Sottiro had broken every contact Rimbaud ever had in the market place.
   –Sottiro had broken into the locked cellar.
   –Sottiro had been trading on credit.

Sottiro's defence:–
   –He had not been trading on credit.
   –He had broken into the cellar because he needed every inch of cellar space they had to store their merchandise.
   –He had been hard in his bargaining with the traders because Badjian had told him that the market was wide open and that he should hold out for the best price.
   –He had made Arthur a fortune.

'How much?'

Sottiro begins a rapid mental calculation. And finally names a sum. A fantastic sum. More than Arthur has made during all his time in Africa.

'Lies! How could you? That's an impossible figure!'

Sottiro begins a second series of mental calculations. And finally names an even larger sum. Rimbaud listens, barely able to contain himself, as Sottiro attempts to justify his mental calculations.

'You realise I can check all this, Sottiro. Have you been keeping any accounts?'

'Yes, it's all written down.'

Rimbaud hesitates, frowning uncertainly. 'You mean this is the sum total according to the accounts? . . . How much did you say?'

Sottiro repeats the larger sum, more confidently this time.

'If that's correct, you're a bloody genius, Sottiro. My God, we're rich!' Rimbaud pauses, visibly repressing his mounting feelings. 'I want to see the accounts, all of them, first thing in the morning.'

Still more than a little uncertain, Rimbaud hands Sottiro his note for Badjian. 'Now get this delivered. And make sure you put it into his hands, personally. It's vital Badjian gets this message.'

'Right you are, Arthur!'

Next morning I checked through the accounts with Sottiro. Eagerly he deciphered the Sanskrit columns, running his fingers down the rows of hieroglyphics. Page by page the magic unfolded, and the chemistry of errors emerged. Sottiro in his prime had transcended the banality of mere mathematics.

'These accounts are worthless, Sottiro.'

'I was in a hurry,' he explained cautiously. I could see him surreptitiously studying my every expression. 'But it's all there.'

'But there's *nothing* here!'

He fingered his chin, furtively. 'Don't you believe me?'

'Belief doesn't enter into it, Sottiro. *I* can see you've made us a fortune, but for the life of me I don't see how anyone else will be able to. How much did you say you'd made?'

'This line here,' he pointed to a row of exploded scratches, 'is the profit.'

'But what about all the gum?'

He frowned, peered, and then looked up open-mouthed. 'Oh, I forgot all about that.'

Rimbaud trembled, barely able to contain his feelings. 'From the look of this coded masterpiece, it appears you've cleared twice as much as I've made during my entire time in Africa.'

'Really?'

'Get out there and hire every camel you can lay your hands on. We've got to get this stuff to Aden before anything happens up here. I'll see if I can sort out these books enough to give Old Man Vardy some idea of what you've been up to.'

For the rest of the day, Rimbaud sat pouring over Sottiro's figures. While Tahira lay in bed. Wan, silent.

As evening came on, Tahira brightened a little, smiling when Arthur finally turned from his desk. Arthur went and sat down on the bed beside her, taking her hand. Did she want anything at all, Arthur asked her. She would like one thing, she told him, more than anything else. She would like to learn to speak again. To speak like Arthur spoke. But she was much too ill for that, Arthur told her. This appeared to disappoint her so much that Arthur finally relented and they started going over the old phrases together. Surprisingly, she'd remembered almost all that he'd previously taught her. In no time they were covering new ground.

'Tahira *has* done. Tahira *will* do,' Rimbaud explained as he attempted to convey the idea of past and future tenses. 'Repeat. Tahira *has* done . . .'

'Tahira *has* done . . . Oasis. Husband. Ride back to Harar on mule with Arthur . . .' (Smirk) 'Emelia Arthur.'

'That's it! . . . Now. Tahira *will* do . . .'

'Tahira *will* do . . .' She frowned, and then her expression gradually intensified. 'Arthur! Tahira bad! Tahira bad!' She clutched at her stomach; and then, as Arthur soothed her, she rolled into a ball once more and silently covered herself with the bedclothes.

She needed a doctor. Where the hell had Badjian got to?

Rimbaud sat watching through the night, working at his

alchemy notes, as Tahira slept. And then woke.

Smiling weakly. 'Tahira will. Tahira will...'

'No, no. Not now. Tomorrow.'

Badjian. Badjian. What on earth are you up to?

I returned to my desk to continue with my notes. *A black E white I red U green O blue*, I wrote. It was all coming back. *The seven stages in the production of gold: — : calcination: solution: distillation: — : conjunction*, and last of all: *fixation*.

Fixation, yes that was it. But there were still two missing. A E I U O. How had that old poem of mine continued? *A, black velvet jacket of brilliant flies which buzz around cruel smells*, I wrote. Shit, this was sickening; already my notes were riddled with blank passages which I'd had to fill in with poetry as best I could. Poetry I had written which had used the magic I could no longer remember. *Gulfs of shadows*, I continued, scribbling in the margin, *E, whiteness of vapours and of tents, lances of proud glaciers, white kings...*

But what the hell did all this mean?

Black velvet, brilliant flies, cruel smells...? Of course, that was what was missing. *Putrefaction*, I wrote on the first blank.

Now: *Vapours, proud glaciers...?* In the blank between distillation and conjunction, I wrote: *sublimation*. Ah, Rimbaud found himself shaking his fists with joy. Sublimation! Of course! At last the picture was complete. All I had to do now was divide each of those notes taken from memory into the appropriate stages, and then I was ready to begin. Only one thing further I needed – Mendeleyev's Table: the order of the elements. Then I could match the two. To each element its own fundamental properties. Each gap bridged by the old alchemical process. I flicked back through my notes.

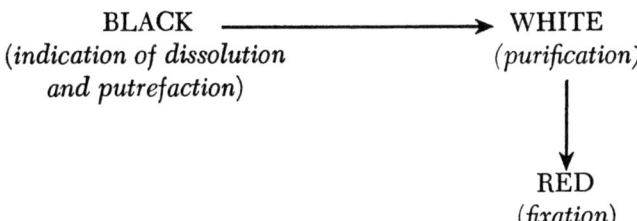

(With RED turning BLUE and then BLACK again to indicate degeneration in cases where the dialectic has not been properly fulfilled.)

Mother must have received my letter by now. Perhaps that book of elements was already on its way.

16

Next day, Rimbaud sat in the sun in the loading yard going over the accounts while Sottiro went off to hire the camels. As Rimbaud looked up, a shadow fell over his shoulder onto the ledger.

'Yarousseau!' Rimbaud leapt to his feet, the ledger spilling from his lap. 'How on earth! . . .'

Yarousseau's robes were in shreds and bleached by the sun; he'd lost his hat and his face was gaunt and bearded. He stood, half in the shade, half in the light, without moving, his hands extended.

The long lost friends embraced.

Rimbaud muttering about a ghost. From the dead. Looking in a terrible state. '. . . how the hell did you escape?'

Yarousseau replying: Ghost yourself. None too good yourself. '. . . what on earth's been the matter, Arthur?'

'Nothing. Nothing, really . . . You clod! My God, it's good to see you! You old bastard! . . .' etc.

This called for a celebration. Rimbaud led his unexpected guest up to the club room. As there was no one there, he simply took down the sacred bottle of absinthe (dusty, unopened, in its place of honour under the photograph of the first European inhabitant of Harar, explorer of Lower Abyssinia etc) and poured them both a drink.

'Are you sure you should be opening that, Arthur? They might be keeping it for an occasion.'

'I should have thought coming back from the dead was occasion enough.'

'Please, Arthur. There's no need to blaspheme.

Yarousseau accepted his drink and sank into a chair.

And how the hell had the local god escaped with his life, demanded Rimbaud, pulling up a stool at his friend's feet. Unable to restrain an involuntary grimace: Yarousseau's feet, caked with filth in his old sandals, smelt as if they were putrefying.

Yarousseau sipped at his drink thoughtfully, before proceeding to explain.

The Circumstances of the Local God's Miraculous Escape
He had been deposed, driven out. He had failed in his capacity as a man-god. (Yarousseau spluttered involuntarily as he swallowed and the undiluted spirit caught in his throat.)

'This is firewater!'

'But you're safe! That's what matters! Why, it's a bloody miracle!'

However, it appeared that Yarousseau found his own personal safety more of a goad than a miracle. 'Those people were dying, Arthur. Dying like flies. Rotting even before we could gather enough strength to bury them. The whole valley stank of death. And yet still they gave me a mule and food for the journey . . . They drove me away in the end. Because I'd failed them.' He shook his head, heavy with self-reproach.

Then he didn't know the truth, Rimbaud realised. Holding his glass to his nose so that the heady odour of absinthe rose into his nostrils to counteract the increasingly pervasive stench of Yarousseau's feet, Rimbaud proceeded to enlighten his friend with the truth, according to Badjian's account.

'Really, Arthur?' A faint smile of disbelief played over Yarousseau's features as Rimbaud came to the end of his diverting theological anecdote.

'Disembowelled. Scattered over the land,' added Rimbaud curtly, forcefully. 'If you don't believe me . . .' But there was nothing he could say. Rimbaud grunted at the lack of response from his audience. He had exaggerated Yarousseau's likely fate too often in the past, he realised, even to the point of childishly dramatising what had then turned out to be a false death. 'Believe me, this isn't just material for another joke letter to your superiors.'

But Yarousseau merely sipped at his absinthe.

'And how *is* friend Badjian these days?' enquired Yarousseau after a short silence, in a simple matter of fact tone.

Badjian was in trouble. Deep trouble, Rimbaud explained, sparing no details or conjecture in his belated efforts to rouse his unresponsive audience. Realising only as he told his tale that Yarousseau was the very man he'd been looking for. Yarousseau could save Badjian.

'Slave trading, you say?' replied Yarousseau.

'That's how it looks to me.'

'So he's fighting for his life.'

'Do you really think so?' Rimbaud drained his glass in agitation. The ham actor's mannerism blurring the true response.

'You know the Convention, Arthur. Slave trading carries the death penalty out here.'

'Unless he's only dealing in tribal girls for the bazaar,' offered Rimbaud hopefully. The authorities traditionally turned a blind eye to the local domestic servant market.

'It doesn't sound to me as if he's only dealing in tribal girls.'

'Then you must help me!'

'Help you?'

'Help Badjian.'

'How?'

Only Yarousseau's word could possibly prevail, Rimbaud explained. Grimes just wouldn't listen to anyone else. Yarousseau could talk to him. Reason with him. See the Governor.

But Yarousseau merely shook his head. He wasn't going to become involved in local politics, he replied. Long ago, he had made a vow: he would never interfere in such matters. The moment the man of God started taking a part in the affairs of man, he compromised the spirit. 'It's not for me to take sides, no matter how noble the cause.'

'You mean you're willing just to sit back and wash your hands of the whole business?'

Yarousseau shook his head again, smiling at Rimbaud's little trap.

'It is they who have washed their hands of me, Arthur.'

'But you haven't been here!'

'Don't take refuge in the literal, Arthur. You know what I mean. And there's no need to pull that face.'

'Your feet stink!' Rimbaud told him bluntly, getting up to pour himself another glass.

But the man of God was not to be put off by such objections. He wanted to make himself perfectly clear. Badjian could come to see him at any time. He would receive Badjian with open arms, and protect him as best he could. But he would never seek Badjian out, or champion his cause, even if it be against death itself – this was not his duty.

'And if Badjian came to you? And they sent the guards to collect him?'

'They would have to take me as well. He would have placed himself under my protection then.'

Rimbaud however, was unimpressed by such sophistries of the seminary. 'You and your bloody martyrdom kick! It always has to be you, doesn't it? You who suffer with the others. You who suffer for all men. You who . . .'

'I claim no monopoly on suffering. Haven't I just left a valley full of it?' Yarousseau's voice was becoming harder now, his cheeks flushing.

'Because they drove you out! Because they preferred to suffer on their own! Because you could do bugger all about it!'

'Suffering is necessary, Arthur. Only through suffering the ills of this earth, by taking them on our shoulders, can we come to the spirit.'

'So you're quite willing to do fuck all about it. That's all that means.'

'There's no need to be so violent, Arthur. Sit down.' His

tone, which had become even with suppression, now appeared to take on its former gentle tone: now that he had got Rimbaud properly worked up. 'What I meant was that if a man comes to me, he can forswear the ills of the world. I would teach him to overcome such suffering.'

'And how would you get Badjian's neck out of the noose? How would you cure them of starvation in your little valley of death? Don't make me sick, Yarousseau.'

'I would ask them to renounce everything and live the life of the spirit, Arthur. For there alone is the truth. In the spirit lies all truth, all real strength, all absolute certainty.' He paused, staring up at Rimbaud with his inane saintly grin, like a lamb offering itself for the slaughter. 'You know all this as well as I do, my good man.'

'Like hell, I do.' Rimbaud banged the cork back into the bottle and strode over to the door. For the first time since his illness he felt fully recovered, his strength returned. 'There's only one life, Yarousseau. As far as I'm concerned. *This* life. Make of it what you will.'

'It is possible to make this life into something more than simply what you will, Arthur.'

Rimbaud hesitated, in spite of himself, his hand on the doorknob. 'What? Make it into what, precisely?'

'You can transcend it. Overcome the ills of the world with the strength of the spirit. In such a way you can transform the very elements of life itself. It is possible to do such a thing, Arthur. God willing.'

'I will, I will,' Rimbaud replied, 'do just that. *And* I'll cure the ills too. You see if I don't, Yarousseau.'

Next morning I was up before dawn. I went round with a lamp checking every one of my cellars. They were all empty now. The consignments were up ready to be loaded in the caravan yard. All that remained was the old wicker chair (withdrawn from public service now) and the flattened rubble of my old ore samples in the end cellar (its lock smashed, hanging loose from the door).

By the time the porters were lighting their fires, I was up in the market place. If I was going to send the old man and his sons packing back to their oasis, I was going to need some porters to help me load up the caravan.

I squatted down by one of the fires as the flames hissed and crackled through the ball of brambles. One by one the ring of shadows grew around me, each man hunching his shoulders to the flames. The air of the market place was icy and still. For several minutes I simply watched, squatting there, listening to the porters mutter across the fire around me. The flames flickered free from the knotted tangle of thorns, detaching themselves in twisting lurid tongues before consuming themselves in the fading upper darkness amongst the fanning clouds of smoke. Soon the skin of my face was scorched and my eyes streaming, although the outer extremities of my body remained taut and frigid, shuddering with the occasional spasm. In the distance a solitary cry rose from the caravaners outside the gate. It was early yet, but there obviously weren't many traders out there. I hugged my knees, and called out across the fire: 'I have much work to do. Is any man free?'

There was no reply. I was aware that my accent had deteriorated through lack of practice, but I knew they understood me, all right.

'No man free?'

The faces loomed, silent, in the flickering watery light, their damp cheeks glistening against the flames. Still not a word. Only the splintering crackle of flames and a single distant plaintive call from outside the gate broke the silence.

All right, bugger them. I'd have to keep the old man's sons. Rimbaud got up and walked away across the square.

After spending all day getting the caravan ready to leave next morning, I went round to Yarousseau's lodgings to see if he could come and have a look at Tahira. But Yarousseau was out tending the sick in one of the tribal quarters, apparently. In a foul temper, Rimbaud returned to his room to find a letter on his desk.

                          Société de Géographie
                          Paris

Dear M. Rimbaud,

We received with great pleasure your account of your travels in the Abyssinian Ogaden. As you must be aware, we have no records of these parts. Your descriptions will be of immense value to us in our efforts to piece together a picture of the true nature of the Interior of Africa, and we would be only too glad if you could send us further details of what you have seen. Have you ventured beyond this territory? If not, should the occasion arise would you be willing to do so?

Also, we would be very pleased to hear of the position you hold in Africa, and your personal interests – social, religious, family etc. To put it simply, if you will pardon the forthrightness of our enquiries, who are you? Have you any photographs of yourself – preferably in some local setting? You may like to know that your name has already been added to our list of famous explorers, and your report has attracted attention in certain influential quarters.

We apologise for the brevity of this note. A further communication will follow. However, we await impatiently your picture and an outline of your life for our annals. Please do not disappoint us. I would like to add, in strictest confidence, that should these biographical details show you to be of suitable moral and social standing (as I am sure they will; your prose alone indicates your scrupulous integrity) then your speedy reply may well prove worth your while in the future.

                Yours faithfully,
                  M. Duchamp.
                  Secretary to the Society.

Rimbaud looked up. The dogs were howling on the ramparts. He listened, craning intently . . . No, nothing else. It must have been his imagination.

He turned back to his paper-strewn desk and took up his pen.

To the Société de Géographie, Paris.
Dear Sirs,
As far as I can gather from my latest communication from the celebrated M. Verlaine, I am now regarded in Paris as the poet of the future by the poets. As well as being a famous explorer to your learned selves. Revered by both, and at the same time anathema to both. To hell with you all! You might like to know that I also intend to become a celebrated alchemist (in magical circles) as well as a revolutionary chemist (for the world of science). I also intend to make myself rich beyond the dreams of avarice. In fact, gentlemen, I intend to become all things to all men.

At the same time, you cultured apes, I would like you to know that I am in my own eyes a complete failure. I am disgusted by myself even more than I am disgusted by you. Keep your impertinent enquiries to yourself. If you are impressed by that fantastic jargonoid nonsense which I have been such a fool as to put my name to, then you may as well know that I don't give a fart for your admiration. However, be sure to send me details of your worthy existences, including all personal deformities, religions, quirks, ideologies, moralities, junior school prizes, peculiarities of etiquette, scatological habits and pornographic preferences. A photograph, preferably in some local setting, would also be much appreciated. Along with the assembled citizens of Harar, I await with bated breath these revelations of your identity. Who are you? Who have you become, away there in deepest civilisation? Are you at war, are you making peace, are you revolting, or are you simply snoozing in practice for the perpetual sleep to come? Please do not disappoint me. These details may well prove worth your while in the future.

> Yours, whoever we may be,
> Arthur Rimbaud.

As Rimbaud laid down his pen, he heard footsteps approaching along the corridor.

Knock- knock!

Yarousseau at last! 'Come in!'

Enter Badjian, black suit glistening in the lamplight, gold braid looming.

'Ah, just the man I need.'

But Dr Badjian had not come to offer his medical services.

'Listen Arthur.' He raised his hand, silencing Rimbaud. 'Turn down the lamp.'

They stood, listening, as the light quickly dimmed. A dog howled on the ramparts; Tahira's fitful breathing sounded from the bed. And then came some unplaceable sound: similar to the one Rimbaud had thought he'd heard earlier. Badjian crossed the room, leaning over Tahira, and opened the window. Immediately Rimbaud heard the muffled tramp of marching feet rising from across the market place.

'The garrison is pulling out, my friend,' announced Badjian with due solemnity.

Rimbaud strained his eyes, peering into the darkness as the cold night air flooded into the room. Gradually he made out the rows of dim shapes. A line of camels was being led in through the side gate.

'The Emir has been re-appointed. You must tell the others to leave at once.'

As Rimbaud leaned on the sill, the warmth of Badjian's breath passed over his cheek. In the chill air Rimbaud could smell that conjunction of odours which had always meant just one thing: Badjian. The sharp tang of body sweat masked by his own peculiar clove-scented perfume, the oiled leather of his boots, the winsome exhalation of dental decay.

Tahira suddenly sat up. And screamed at the solid darkness leaning over her.

Comic sequence. Flounderings. Window closes. Lamp finally turned up. The hard-bitten European trader soothing his terrified concubine as the dark stranger looks on, his dignity ruffled, embarrassed.

'Calm, Tahira. Arthur is here . . . This, Badjian. Badjian good.' She cowered suspiciously.

'Badjian come to make Tahira good.'

'My friend, this is no passing matter. You must act at once.'

Rimbaud appealed to his friend. 'She's sick, Badjian. Can't you just look her over? Tell me what's wrong?'

Reluctantly, Dr Badjian was persuaded to examine the patient.

'Calm, Tahira. Badjian make Tahira good.'

With equal reluctance, the patient submitted to her examination.

'Menelek is advancing from the north. Ras has gone into hiding,' explained the doctor as he examined the patient's throat, feeling her glands. While Tahira stared wide-eyed at Rimbaud. 'Are you still willing to go into partnership, my friend? This is our big chance.' The doctor muttered a few words to the patient in Harari and she drew back the bedclothes. He lifted her robe.

'What are your terms?' asked Rimbaud.

'Fifty-fifty. Gain or loss. You work under my protection. You'll have a monopoly on all trade to the coast. Guaranteed by the Emir.'

As Badjian's sausage fingers began to probe, Tahira started to weep silently.

'Calm, Tahira. Badjian good.'

'So you agree?'

'I haven't got much option, have I?'

'You can always leave with the others. It will be dangerous up here. There will be many changes.'

'All right. I'm willing to risk it, as long at you're absolutely sure we can make something out of it.'

'My friend, I have never been more sure in my life. For over seven years, now, I have been waiting for an opportunity like this.'

The doctor questioned the patient once more. Weeping, abject, the patient replied. Burying her face in her robe.

'What is this medicine you have been giving her, Arthur?'

'Medicine? I haven't given her anything.'

The doctor turned to the patient. Demanding, gruffly. The patient whimpered.

And then the doctor was struggling with the patient. Who appeared to have something hidden in the folds of her robe.

'Badjian! For Christ's sake!'

After a short sharp tussle, Badjian produced a bottle. Which Rimbaud immediately recognised as one of Grimes' photographic solutions. A mixture he'd botched. Developing and fixing fluids, which had all been magic to Grimes.

Badjian sniffed at the bottle, then looked up, horrified. 'Arthur! You could have killed her!'

'But I never gave her that stuff.'

Badjian eyed Rimbaud suspiciously as he handed him the bottle. 'Do you honestly mean to tell me that you haven't been aware of what's been going on – under you very nose?'

'She must have stolen it. I thought I'd thrown away all that old stuff.'

Tahira's sobs fractured the silence as Badjian pulled the covers over her hunched figure.

'You didn't know what was the matter?'

'Why the hell do you think I asked you to examine her?'

Badjian leaned forward and took me by the arm, his other hand still resting on the sobbing heap at his side. 'In which case, my friend, I have more news for you.' It was all a huge joke now, it seemed. 'You are to be a father.'

Rimbaud stared, aghast.

'I thought perhaps you'd given her the stuff to try and get rid of it.'

'Oh my God, what on earth was she thinking?' Rimbaud

sank down on the bed beside Tahira, laying his hands gently on her shuddering shoulders. 'Tahira!'

But even as his lips found hers, and her eyes, pleading at last through the swollen ravages of her tears (no deeper transparency than the tear-blurred eye, smiling – ultimately – through) Rimbaud became aware of Badjian's hand on his shoulder, shaking it. 'My friend, we have business to do. You must act at once, before it is too late.' Badjian's hand persisted, urgently.

Arthur slowly began to disengage himself.

'Tahira sleep now.'

'Tahira emelia Arthur. Tahira will. Tahira will,' she implored, tearful once more.

'Oh yes, Tahira. Arthur will too. But Tahira sleep now. Please!'

'Come *on*, Arthur!' Badjian was already at the door.

Rimbaud picked up the lamp, slipping the bottle of mixed chemicals into his pocket, and followed Badjian out of the room down the passage. Tahira's wavering sobs receded behind him.

As Rimbaud led Badjian down the passage he could hear the sound of Grimes' voice in the club room. Grimes was singing, he realised, only after he had started forward at this further evidence of a seemingly universal agony.

Grimes paused, open-mouthed, in mid lyric, as Rimbaud burst into the room.

'*Hello* there, Arthur!' he craned forward, his hands gripping the edge of the table, beaming blearily. Vardy and Sottiro were sitting opposite him. They'd obviously just finished their meal. Amongst the uncleared dishes was the bottle of absinthe, empty.

Grimes' face suddenly clouded as he saw Badjian come in behind Rimbaud. The other two settled back in their chairs, visibly withdrawing.

'What's this, Arthur?' began Grimes, rising to his feet, bellicose: the gorilla disturbed in his lair. 'You're not thinking of introducing this character to the club, I hope? Not at this stage.'

'You all know Badjian.' Rimbaud took Badjian's arm, addressing himself to the company in general. Expressly ignoring the particularity of Grimes' demanding presence. 'Badjian has something important . . .'

'You're arrested. I arrest you, Badjian,' Grimes stumbled drunkenly forward.

'Stay where you are, Grimes!' Rimbaud moved towards him, menacingly. Grimes reeled, glowering morosely, blinking at the lamp in Rimbaud's hand.

'You don't seem to realise, Arthur,' began Grimes, propping himself, grasping the back of Vardy's chair for support. 'I've seen the Governor. Badjian's under arrest. S'what we're celebrating. With the precious little you left us out of that damn bottle of yours. Bad form, you know. Do wish you'd have told us you'd broken into it. Can't give a thing, n'then just take it back, y'know. Can he, Vardy? . . .' Grimes' voice wavered, uncertain of its tone or train of argument as he assembled his scattered wits to face this monstrous invasion.

Badjian meanwhile had moved over to the window.

'Gentlemen,' he announced theatrically, taking advantage of Grimes' temporary incapacity. 'The garrison is pulling out. You will have to leave at once.' He opened the window, nodding down to the market square.

The call of muttered orders rose into the room on a gust of freezing air.

'Shut that damn window!' yelled Grimes.

Badjian immediately closed it, withdrawing quickly into the centre of the room. 'You must be quiet.' he demanded, urgently, in a low voice. Possessed with the melodrama of his role.

'You don't fool me,' replied Grimes, his voice as loud as ever. 'I saw them out there hours ago. They're going on manoeuvres.'

'They're pulling out, you bloody oaf!' snapped Rimbaud, aggressive now. The charge of his contradictory feelings exploding. Quickly. Violently. 'You great clown! Menelek's advancing from the North. The Emir's taken over.'

'Don't believe a word of it, Arthur! This man's a charlatan and a rogue. Why, the Governor himself told me he was a quack.'

'Is that so?' Rimbaud advanced to the table, setting down the lamp with a clatter amongst the dishes. Sottiro reached forward quickly, balancing it. 'Well, you might like to know,' Rimbaud leaned forward belligerently, 'that this quack, as you call him, once cured me of syphilis.'

Vardy paled, grimacing viciously across at me as Grimes hauled himself upright to face Rimbaud.

'Then y'even more of a bloody fool n'I thought, Arthur. S'no cure for syphilis. Didn't y'know that?'

'I can assure you there are cures,' began Dr Badjian coolly, in a severe precise tone. Badjian's dignity was deeply offended, Rimbaud saw. Grimes had evidently touched a raw spot. 'In Germany, my friend, many cases have been treated. I know this for a fact.'

'Heard all about that one,' replied Grimes dismissively. 'Y'know what happened afterwards? . . . Well, *do you*?'

'No,' answered Badjian, flatly.

'New strain developed. More malignant. Heard all about that one in Aden. Hideous death. Can't pull the wool over my eyes.'

So, even in the face of mortal danger, will men insist upon defining their terms, self-assertively. For as long as the inevitable impulsive action can be avoided.

'There are other cures,' Badjian was not to be put out. 'My method, for instance.'

'And whassat?'

'Men at sea were cured by a sea-going ship's doctor. And there was no malignant strain there, I can assure you, my friend.'

'Sea-going ships' doctors!' Grimes scoffed. 'What next!'

Silence. And then, surprisingly, it was Vardy who spoke. 'Darwin was a ship's doctor too, I believe, wasn't he?'

Grimes grunted. Badjian smirked, faintly. Even Vardy appeared relieved by his own astonishing contribution.

Once more Badjian took up his part: the dashing declaimer of bad tidings. 'Gentlemen, you *must* leave! You are in danger!' Badjian turned back to the window, cupping his face against the glass as he peered. 'There is no time to lose. The last of the garrison will be on its way in a matter of hours.'

The other two rose from their seats, leaving Grimes propped against the empty chair. As they all peered through the window, they could see below them strings of pack mules assembling along the walls and lines of soldiers filing through the gate across the square into shadowy platoons.

'He's right, Grimes,' began Vardy, turning away from the breath-misted glass. 'It isn't just manoeuvres. They're taking everything.'

Grimes blundered forward from his perch. Everyone watched as he rubbed the glass and cupped his hands against the window, peering. He snuffled, sharply, and then stood upright, glowering at Badjian.

'So you've succeeded at last,' remarked Grimes, allowing the company the benefit of his own conclusion. To his own undivulged thought processes.

By the time the first light of day was beginning to grow over the ramparts, all was ready. Vardy and Grimes had loaded up their possessions on pack horses. They appeared to be abandoning their consignments. Rimbaud's long string of camels was strung out across the yard, each loaded high with merchandise.

'Where are your personal things, Arthur?' demanded Vardy.

'I'm staying behind,' replied Rimbaud.

'*What!*' exclaimed Vardy.

'What's this I hear, Arthur?' Grimes staggered up, haggard-faced.

Grimes and Vardy exchanged knowing glances.

'But you can't possibly stay behind!' expostulated Grimes.
'You just watch me.'

And so, after the traditional opening declaration of opposed standpoints, the inevitable bargaining began.

Grimes was all for pressurising Arthur into joining them. By force, if necessary.

'For your own good, Arthur!' pleaded Vardy.

Rimbaud motioned for the camel leader to start off with his loaded camels.

Grimes and Vardy remonstrated as the camels slowly loped past out of the yard into the market place.

But Rimbaud was prepared.

Rimbaud's declared reasons for remaining in Harar:
- To maintain a European presence. (Grimes purses his lips contemplatively. Vardy shakes his head.)
- To maintain a commercial presence. (Both 'mm'.)
- This place was his only home now. (Grimes nods seriously. Vardy puzzles.)
- Badjian had guaranteed his safety. (No comment, visible or verbal.)

Vardy and Grimes show signs of relenting, albeit sceptically.

Rimbaud's trump card: for 20 per cent of the profit he would have all their abandoned merchandise shipped down to Zeyla within a fortnight.

Grimes: 'I suppose it's better than nothing . . . ⎱ All right,
Vardy: 'That's hardly fair, Arthur . . . ⎰ done!'

Thus Vardy and Grimes allowed themselves to be persuaded (persuaded themselves?) by the unassailable strength of Rimbaud's arguments (commercial, ethical, sentimental, self-interested, unspoken) and took their leave of him. Boisterously. With a show of appropriate affection. (Saving the tortuous details of their recriminations and self-justifications for the tortuous journey.)

The last of Rimbaud's camels loped past, Sottiro's horse bringing up the rear. Already its rider appeared to have sunk into his habitual travelling coma.

'Here, wake up!' Rimbaud shook Sottiro's thigh. Sullenly Sottiro reached down and accepted the letter Rimbaud handed up to him. 'This is for you.'

'But it's addressed to you.' Sottiro frowned casually at the envelope in his hand.

'Tell them it should have been addressed to you. It's from the Société de Géographie, about our little expedition to the Ogaden.'

Rimbaud was having to walk faster now, to keep up with Sottiro's horse. 'As far as I'm concerned, you were the leader of that expedition. You can say I only took down the report. In your words.'

Sottiro scanned the letter as Rimbaud stumbled along beside him. 'You've made yourself a good bit of cash,' continued Rimbaud. 'But it's not the fortune I promised you, I know. I'm sure you won't mind making do with fame instead.'

Sottiro was gasping as he finished the letter. 'But this is great Arthur! Are you sure you don't want to use it?'

'It's all yours.'

Sottiro, ecstatic. He'd make something out of this, all right. Maybe even a fortune as well. Sottiro rode on, commenting enthusiastically as he re-read the letter, for all the world unaware that Rimbaud was no longer beside him. Rimbaud turned back to the palace. His palace.

'Goodbye, Sottiro!' Rimbaud gave a final cursory wave, without even bothering to look round.

So much for being all things to all men.

17

It wasn't till I was back in the yard that I realised we'd all forgotten about Yarousseau. Immediately, I set off at a run for his lodgings. If he started out within the hour, he'd easily catch up with the others. But Yarousseau still hadn't returned from visiting the sick in the tribal quarters, according to the women in the courtyard. He'd been out all night.

Taking a chance, I set off for the narrow lanes of the district behind the palace. Perhaps fallen women were still his main preoccupation. The alleys were silent, except for the yapping dogs. No one was opening up today, it seemed. The brothels were all closed, and even the little coffee dens were still barred and shuttered. The whole town was ominously quiet as I ran from deserted alleyway to deserted alleyway. Even the beggars had vanished. Only the occasional bundle outside a doorway showed that, come what may, Harar still looked after its sick in the time-honoured fashion.

Although the sunlight was already falling onto the alleyways the air was still cold; yet within half an hour I was exhausted and running with sweat. I'd been up and down every alleyway in the quarter and not seen a soul. Eventually I came to the little square by the quarter's public well. Under the shade in the corner a figure lay huddled against the mud wall. I stopped in my tracks – it was Yarousseau! As I approached I saw the flies humming in a cloud above the folds of his robe. Then I saw the blood stains. I took a few steps closer and I made out a gash in the robe. The blood had dribbled along a thin, twisting trail to the gutter, where it lay in a dust-scummed pool; and spilling out over the frayed worn blackness of Yarousseau's robe was a shiny convoluted mess of white entrails blotched with puffy viscous blue and yellowy excrescences. The hum of flies rose around me in a mesmerising drone as I knelt down beside the savaged body. I heard a sound from further down the wall in the shadows and looked up to see a mangy cur stumble off, hopping, one of its hind legs lame, a mouthful of glossy, bloodied entrails hanging from between its teeth like some hideous saliva. I retched, and my bile spilled down into the dust at my feet, separating slowly into round globules as it ran down into the hard corrugated ruts. The flies were now batting against my face, settling on the backs of my hands as the sound of their droning pressed in around my ears; it was as if the sound were turning and turning, spinning and uncoiling through my skull. I reached forward and pulled back the shoulder of the robe. The stench rose into my nostrils and my stomach clutched. The lion, or whatever it was that had got him, had torn open his front from his neck to his groin. Between the lacerated strips of skin I made out the occasional whiteness of a rib, and underneath that a glimpse of some sagging cavity of darkness. For several moments I simply stared, aware that my whole body had become numb and distant, as if I were drugged.

Rimbaud reached up and lifted the robe from where it still lay across the corpse's face. His eyes had sunk, and were already running; his thick, yellow skin sagged over his fleshless skull; his mouth lay open, revealing the pink, rough surface of a small tongue and a row of toothless gums. It wasn't Yarousseau . . . Rimbaud looked closer at the frayed worn edges of the robe. The robe was definitely Yarousseau's. Groggily, Rimbaud rose to his feet and staggered away down the alleyway. Where the hell had he got to? Was he running round the streets bollock-naked now?

When Rimbaud arrived back in the market place, he found that trading had come to a halt. The dealers were beginning to dismantle their stalls, and the caravaners were reloading their caravans. The buyers stood about idly, in groups.

Rimbaud's immediate reaction: No market, no profit. No monopoly . . . no reason for staying in Harar . . .

And immediately acted accordingly.

How much for your ivory, he indicated to the first dealer.

The dealer looked at him, uncertainly. He'd already begun to pack up.

What was his price, demanded Rimbaud, making sure that his actions were noticeable to as wide an audience as possible.

Cautiously, the old trader named his price.

And the bargaining began. Slowly. Publicly.

Gradually the dealer's responses awoke to the old familiar phrases.

And as the crowd gathered, the pantomime took on life. His fears temporarily forgotten, Rimbaud's adversary began to submerge himself in the full ritual histrionics of his trade.

And, overcome by the occasion, muffed his responses. Rimbaud secured the consignment of ivory at a price on a par with those which Sottiro had achieved. The crowd murmured with approval.

Rimbaud called across to three nearby porters: three of his regulars. They hesitated, glancing at one another. But immediately three others detached themselves from the crowd and offered their services. By custom, Rimbaud was bound to take them. His three regular porters avoided Rimbaud's persistent gaze.

Rimbaud affixed his credit sign to the trader's leather scroll and called on the crowd in the usual manner to witness his intention to pay, while the porters loaded up the ivory. As he started forward, Rimbaud noticed that the crowd were following him. The other traders were watching, having motioned for their men to stop packing up.

Rimbaud's Dilemma

- The market was at his mercy; he could buy up everything in sight at rock bottom prices.
- His confidence alone could keep the market going.
- He could make a killing in next to no time. Vast profits . . . fortune assured . . . . etc etc.

- Sottiro had used all the barter; Rimbaud could only buy on credit until new stocks arrived.
- But Old Man Vardy might not be willing to risk sending up any more stocks.
- Without trade, the market would simply fade away; the closed city cease to be a trading centre. No profits, no monopoly . . . No reason for staying in Harar . . . ruin . . .

Conclusion: He had no choice.

Never a man to prevaricate, Rimbaud immediately began buying up large stocks of gum, coffee, hides, ivory etc. At the end of each deal Rimbaud affixed his credit sign to the dealer's scroll, turning to the crowd to witness his intention to pay. (By tradition, he had forty days and a sundown in which to pay. If not, he lost the lot – at ruinous interest rates.) If these deals fell through, he'd be lucky to get out of Harar with his life.

By the time Rimbaud was leaving the market place, trade was turning over once more. Even the soothsayers' booths were setting up.

In the palace yard the old man's sons glowered at the triumphal procession. They still hadn't finished clearing the camel dung left by the morning caravan. As soon as the porters had unloaded, Rimbaud called the old man's sons across.

Harar had now become a place of great danger, he explained. He could no longer keep them. They must return to their oasis with their father.

They retired to mutter amongst themselves, and Rimbaud left them. If they didn't leave of their own accord, he'd have to drive them out, he realised. They alone knew the secret of his non-existent credit; they must have seen how Sottiro had run through all the barter.

Once up in his room, Rimbaud began listing his purchases, adding up his debts. Tahira sat in bed watching him quietly, her face blank and submissive. She looked much better – even after only a night off the 'medicine'.

As he continued working over his accounts, Rimbaud soon found himself becoming light-headed from his lack of sleep the previous night, the whistles and tintinabulations rising in his mind whenever he paused to rest his head on his hands. Several times he nodded off over the figures, waking with a start. Each time he was surprised to find that it was daylight, that the paper before him was covered with lists of transactions and invoices. Night, and pages covered with magical hieroglyphics, poetic fragments and esoteric formulae, were what he was accustomed to waking to whenever he nodded into unconsciousness over his desk with that eerie whistling and bird-twitter sounding in his head.

Then, just as he was on the point of nodding off once more, Rimbaud heard the sound of sobbing. He turned; Tahira was asleep, her face peaceful as a death mask. The sobbing was coming from through the wall.

Rimbaud opened the door to Sottiro's room to find it completely bare, except for the bed in the corner. On the bed sat Sottiro's girl, cross-legged, her podgy clenched fists pressed into her face, sobbing in spasmodic shoulder-shrugging convulsions.

Rimbaud's immediate reaction: How much is she worth? If he got a good price for her down at the bazaar he could guarantee some of his credit, or at least make a show of having some money so as to quieten any suspicions.

But to do that he'd have to start up trade in the bazaar single-handed, just as he'd done in the market. When he'd passed through the bazaar on the way to look for Yarousseau that morning the place had been all but deserted.

Rimbaud sat down beside Sottiro's girl and put his arm

around her shoulder.

If he opened up the bazaar, trade would be well and truly on its feet again. But how much credit would that need? Rimbaud felt the tingle in the pit of his guts as he began calculating.

Sottiro's girl had taken Rimbaud's hand and was now kissing it, pressing his palm to her damp cheeks.

But to open the bazaar, he'd have to act now, before it was too late. The weight of Rimbaud's tiredness dragged at the dreamy unreality of his mind . . . If he started with the gold stalls. Then the jewellery booths. Then the worked ivory. Then finally the silver. At each mental transaction the tingle of apprehension grew in his guts.

Sottiro's girl nestled against him as his fingers unthinkingly played over her, soothing her.

Rimbaud's eyes blinked closed as he sank back exhaustedly onto the bed. It all depended on Old Man Vardy. How could he convince him of the urgency of the situation? How could he persuade him to risk sending up all that barter?

Rimbaud's hand smoothed over Sottiro's girl as he instinctively drew himself up against her. His heart was thumping now, his throat dry. It was all or nothing. He was staking his very life in Harar now. Dreamily his lips played over her as his prick hardened between her coaxing fingers. And then her thighs were parting as she eased him on top of her, sighing languorously.

All or nothing! His eyes were open. He was pressing himself into her, his hands clutching her shoulders, his hips thrusting. Awake. Enlivened by this deep clawing sensation of sheer fright. Rimbaud began driving himself on, with all his strength, faster, faster, as her tremulous cries rose beneath him. The power surged through his limbs. His energy was limitless. He could do anything! He'd open the bazaar, he'd keep the market going. Single-handed. He'd even force Old Man Vardy to send up that caravan of barter.

Her neck arched beneath him as she cried out, in a long

wavering dying whimper, her face taut, as if she were on a rack with the screws slowly tightening to the ultimate limits she could endure.

Emelia Vardy, Rimbaud drove himself on, his energies mounting, pressing, that's how he'd get Old Man Vardy to send that stuff up. A silver trinket for Emelia Vardy.

Rimbaud pressed himself against the softness of her breasts as he forced himself on towards his climax. A silver trinket, with just a few words. The wild man of Harar is coming. Soon. Rimbaud murmured, hugging Sottiro's girl to him as the charge burst and flowed out of him.

Now nothing on earth could stop him.

Scene: The bazaar at Harar (echoing, empty).

Enter the European trader, followed by one of his slave girls (the little tubby one) and his five personal porters (previously dismissed, but still apparently faithful to their former master – where they perhaps owed back wages?)

And a large crowd.

The European trader orders the gold stalls to open. He wants to do business.

Within half an hour he has opened up the gold stalls, the jewellery booths, the worked ivory stalls and the silver stalls, buying up large quantities of merchandise on credit, all at extremely low prices. Tempted by the sight of such unaccustomed prices, speculators start snapping up bargains at the stalls in his wake. Business is soon almost back to normal.

Finally the European trader passes on to the slave bazaar, his slave girl and his previously dismissed porters following behind him, carrying his purchases. But now the European trader's movements have become curiously sluggish. He appears to be drunk, or drugged. Half asleep. Fighting against some increasingly overwhelming lethargy, as the crowds part about him. The slave booths open in anticipation, tribal girls ushered out onto the platforms. The European, obviously in some confusion, appears to be trying to *sell* his now tearful slave girl. The dealers are demonstratively not interested. But frantic to sell, nonetheless. They plead with him. They have fine tribal girls. Very cheap. The slave dealers are desperate, for theirs is the most precarious situation of all in the city.

The Slave Traders' Precarious Position in Harar

Under the Egytians, slave trading on a strictly limited scale had been tolerated, for a domestic market only. To provide servants, concubines, replacements for the brothels etc. The lucrative trade of providing for the harems of Jeddah, Damascus and even Istanbul was carried out under pain of death. Should the slave market fold up in Harar, this more hazardous market would be the only outlet by which the traders could recoup their losses. All this had been explained to Arthur long ago by Badjian (who seemed to be well versed in these matters) while he had been elaborating on the nature of the closed city and how it would affect trade.

The Nature of the Closed City and how it affected the Traders

The closed city was by tradition a law unto itself, cut off from all outside influence. When a city became closed, things remained exactly as they were, and nothing new was allowed. The elements of its way of life then waxed and waned in response to popular demand; and whatever passed out of practice of its own accord was allowed to die, never to be replaced. This was the time-honoured manner of purifying the city of all that was not necessary. This way there was never any popular disturbance, but the effects were more lasting and more ruthless than any imposed ideology.

Thus, should the slave market fold, slavery (even of the tolerated domestic variety) would vanish forever from Harar.

A source of possible profit eliminated, realised Rimbaud.

But what the hell was I to do? I only had tokens enough to feed Bomba, Tahira and myself for the next month until the caravan arrived. If I bought any slave girls, I'd have to ask for credit in the vegetable market. They'd soon realise then that I had nothing. Nothing! I'd be lynched!

Yet with the slave market turning over, and the Egyptians gone, Harar would be wide open. Regular caravans could be shipped North to the harems, evading the Convention. No danger. Vast profits etc . . . (This was obviously what Badjian had been up to, what Grimes had found out.)

Yawning, Rimbaud gazed blearily before him.

Bring me three good tribal virgins, the best you have, he indicated. Three specimens were immediately produced for Rimbaud's approval.

Rimbaud, wide-eyed in an effort to stop blinking, stared. The crowd jostled around him. (This European trader was obviously some man. Sleepless with exhaustion after satisfying himself with the two slave girls he'd already got, he now appeared to want to take on three more. And such girls, too!)

Rimbaud peered, his eyes puckering. Were these the very best?

The very best.

Before him, stood three fat frightened wobbling fourteen-year-old tribal virgins with dyed hair. (If these were the best, then a fat-arsed butter-fed Dutch girl weighing anything up to sixteen stone and just emerging from puberty would obviously have been the embodiment of the Harari ideal of womanhood.)

Yawning once again, as the whistles grew in his head, Rimbaud accepted. With a lackadaisical gesture. Marking down his credit sign.

And stumbled on.

While the renewed bargaining began around him.

And a wave of utter fatigue swept over him, buckling his knees.

The European trader stumbled to a halt, shaking his head, as the crowd peered at him curiously.

All heads suddenly swivelling.

Shouts. Uproar.

Through the flickering dusk of his half-closed eyes, Rimbaud saw the old man's sons were fighting over something. Pulling at the slave girls he had just bought. Wrestling with Sottiro's girl.

Five men, and only four girls, Rimbaud realised, in a daze. They must have thought he'd bought the girls for them!

The girls were screaming, clawing at the faces of their attackers. A distant nightmare at the end of a dim receding funnel of vision. Rimbaud sagged, staggering. Fumbling under his smock, he pulled out Vardy's pistol. His eyelids were slipping closed as he placed one foot in front of the other, knees folding.

Rimbaud raised his hand above his head, waveringly, and pulled the trigger.

The sound of the explosion sliced through his skull, resounding giddily. At the frayed edges of his blink, the crowd scattered.

'They're mine . . . They're all mine! *I* bought them . . . for me!'

The second shot banged, and whined. Ricochetting among the rooftops.

As the darkness swivelled.

Roaring.

Forwards . . .

And the European trader fell to the ground, asleep on his feet.

Only the sound of my breath. And the night. As I drag on my artificial leg over my stump.

Pain I understand. Pain I long for. Pain I live.

To dull the unending isolation of the darkness.

My nerves sleepless. Jiggering membranes of fire. Remembering fire.

Jiggering. Bared . . .

Bared still. Even as the first light looms faintly at the edges of the pane. Or is it my eyes? The optic nerve flicker-

ing? . . .

Undeterred in his efforts to get himself into a fit state to return to his beloved Africa, the invalid tugs at his metal leg in the gloom. Fumbling. His nerves, detonated into disarray by his daily electric shock treatment (which he insists upon, vehemently), now blurring, now overemphasising, now responding – too much! too late! too early! – to the numbed unceasing insistence of his locked will as he fumbles in the dark.

'Arthur! Arthur!'

It was night. Tahira heavy and warm in bed beside me. But awake, I could sense it. On the ramparts the dogs were howling. The sound of distant shouting voices on the end of a gust of wind. Then the sharp heartstopping rattle began again, and I recognised the sound that had ended my dream. Someone was trying to break in through the bolted front door of the palace.

Through the window, the dome of the mosque. Pink. Tremblingly reflecting some invisible light.

The downwind cry of voices rose, and then receded.

'Arthur!' Badjian's voice, from below. '*Arthur!*' The voice that had been calling into my dream.

I padded down the stone stairs in my bare feet as Badjian battered the door impatiently.

'Are you deaf or something?' Badjian angrily pushed in the door as I unbolted it.

A gust of chill wind whined into the empty darkness of the hallway as I pressed the door closed, slamming the bolts.

'Watch out for the steps.' I guided Badjian's arm.

His cautious footsteps hissed up through the darkness beside me, echoing around the high stone walls of the hallway.

Tahira had already lit the lamp and was sitting up in bed, staring out of the window.

'Put out that light!' ordered Badjian sharply.

Still thick-headed with sleep, my limbs shaking more from

lack of co-ordination than the numbing cold, I began fumbling with the lamp. Badjian leaned over my shoulder and blew it out. 'Any light might attract them!'

I leaned over the bed, following Tahira's gaze out of the window. The dome of the mosque was still pink in the night, flickering.

'Who? What's happening?' I asked, my thoughts stumbling, doped, bewildered.

'Have you heard *nothing*?'

'The voices?' My thoughts were blundering on towards this vaguely apprehended objective.

'The curfew has been broken, my friend.' He took my arm and led me to the door. 'It is not visible from here. This way. You will see from the other side.'

'Arthur!' I heard Tahira's call. And then she was a presence at my side, clinging to my other arm.

As we rounded the corner in the passage, I saw, through the open door of the old man's room, the jagged brilliant teeth of a line of flames. The room was on fire! Breaking free of Badjian's leading hand and Tahira's clinging arm I ran ahead down the corridor.

The room was empty, stripped and bare, with the twisting garish light of flames playing over the ceiling and the upper corners of the walls. The fire was outside. The garrison was ablaze. Below the sheets of rising flame, the ant figures of the crowd scurried in and out of the shadows. Above in the sky, the low pall of drifting smoke flickered with a dull orange glow, as if containing some higher unrevealed conflagration.

'It started in the bazaars this afternoon,' began Badjian. The cries of the distant crowd were sharper now, distinguishable as individual yells and higher-pitched wails of lamentation, dying in the wind. 'Accounts differ,' continued Badjian, 'but it seems some shots were fired and there was a brawl over some slaves. Then the rioting just spread.'

The old man and his five sons had decamped, I realised as I stared about the room in the flickering gloom. They must have taken the slave girls with them, too. (*And the jewellery? The gold? The worked ivory? The silver trinket for Emelia Vardy? . . . No!*)

Beside me, Tahira's face, statuesque in the flickering light. Her eyes blank shadows. I watched as a heightened flare of light illuminated her closed eyelids, and then I noticed her lips were trembling. Either she was praying to herself, or she was still sick. I ran the back of my hand over her cheek and she turned into the darkness to face me. Her skin was as cold as stone.

'Go back. Tahira sleep,' I told her gently, taking her arm and leading her to the door. Limply she obeyed, and I heard the rustle of her robes recede along the darkened corridor as I turned back to the fire.

'If what you just said is true, then I think I'm the one who's responsible for all this,' I told Badjian. 'I fired those shots in the bazaar.'

This admission didn't appear to astonish Badjian at all.

'Anything could have sparked it off, my friend. No one is responsible.'

'But why are they sacking the garrison? There's no one there any more, is there?'

Badjian sighed, and shrugged. 'Why did they sack the Bastille, my friend?'

'To release the prisoners, of course.'

'You really think so? . . . Didn't you know? All they found in the Bastille were four forgers, a couple of beggars, and the local rake. All that trouble, just for seven old deadbeats.' He laughed, gently, without feeling.

'Then what's this for?'

'Guns. They're looking for the arsenal. But they're too late. The Emir has beaten them to it.'

'How do you know all this?'

'I was there this afternoon, supervising. Half the men loading up the stuff were Ras's men. It was so dark down in those dungeons no one knew what was going on. For all I know, Ras was there himself.'

'So there's going to be a civil war as well?'

'No.' Badjian was quite adamant.

'Then what's going to happen?' Badjian alone appeared to possess the key to this barbarous sideshow unfolding in miniature beyond the window. 'Is Menelek still advancing?'

'No. He'll wait now.'

'But why?'

'If a man can take a city which has destroyed itself, why should he bother to waste his energies fighting for it?'

'So this is where we make our grand killing on the market, is it? What the hell kind of a market do you think there's going to be in the morning after all this?'

'A speculator's market, my friend. The traders will be getting rid of all they can.'

'But if there's no civil order?' I remonstrated. 'Do you realise I had to get the market turning over single-handed this morning? There wouldn't have *been* a market but for me.'

'So I heard, my friend. You are indeed a good partner. Don't worry, I shall fulfil my half of the partnership.'

'And what's that?'

'The Emir will decree that the market remains inviolate. On pain of death. He will station guards. I am to be his personal superviser of internal trade.'

'On your own head be it. I'm clearing out as soon as they open the gates in the morning.'

'Don't be a fool!' Badjian gripped Rimbaud's arm, his face pressing earnestly. Beyond the silhouette of his skull the night flickered fitfully. 'If you leave now, you'll never get back. This is a closed city now, my friend. Don't you realise what that means?'

'The place destroying itself, while Menelek stands by and watches. You said as much yourself.'

But even the forces of self-destruction had processes, apparently. Predictable formulas – which were open to calculation, according to Badjian.

Badjian's View of the Pattern of Events to Come

At present the mob were merely satisfying themselves. Venting their fears in purposeless anarchic rage. In the morning there would be a call from the mosque for thanksgiving for the deliverance of the city from the Egyptians. By tomorrow night this madness would be transformed into partisan religious fervour. There would still be rape and pillage, but it would gradually be channelled. Only people who had fraternised with the Egyptians would suffer. (Except, of course, for those fortunate few under the Emir's personal protection.)

For the Emir, this period of madness was merely the inevitable prelude. This was the city purifying itself, destroying all alien influences. Within a few days Harar would already be well on its way to becoming the closed city of former history, as it had been since time immemorial, all this madness devoted in a frenzy of worship to the One True God. With the Emir in complete command, and the old rule firmly established. With no disturbing novelties, no uncertainties – every question answered by previous centuries of precedence and custom.

'But what about Menelek? And Ras and his men?'

The Coming of Menelek to the Closed City (Badjian's View)
Menelek was the people's hero, the modern hero. And the Emir was only practised in the old ways. But he too had had his taste of freedom, even in his luxurious captivity. (Witness his call for Dr Badjian's services.) What the Emir was now establishing would be a far more austere form of captivity – for himself perhaps too austere. Human nature being what it was, he would find it difficult to change his personal ways; and as rumour of his corruption spread – 'as it will, my friend, I can assure you' – the people would begin to look about for a more reliable master. One who was capable of conforming to his own standards. Menelek, the people's hero in his fight against the Egyptians, would eventually be welcomed with open arms. And once established, he would leave Ras in command – with orders that the city should gradually be re-

opened once more.

'So you see the whole thing as just one continuous cycle?' I asked.

Badjian chuckled hollowly, his face only dimly visible in the flames, which were now dying down, receding into the burnt-out shell of the garrison. 'If only it were all as simple as that, my friend.'

'I know. It isn't. And that's why I don't believe you, Badjian. You can't control human nature that easily. I've seen it before. I was in Paris at the time of The Commune, remember.'

'Harar is no Commune, Arthur. These people are still primitive. They answer to the call of their God.'

'And civilised Paris was merely answering to the call of more human needs, is that it?'

'Perhaps.'

'Then what do you think's going to interfere with your simple cycle, if the mob can be controlled? And fed, presumably.'

'Why, you, of course, Arthur.' Badjian turned to study the effect of his grand revelation. 'That is why we are partners. Abyssinia is not the world, unfortunately. Its ideas may well do for itself – but there will always be outsiders who have their own ideas. In Paris, in London, in Rome. And even closer at hand. What, for instance, are your ideas for this place?'

'I'm here to get what I can, you know that. The same as you are.'

Badjian nodded. 'And if we succeed, others are bound to follow us. Other conquering Meneleks perhaps, but with European ideas. And then Harar will become just another little process in a far larger, far more complicated cycle. And for the people of Harar, the will of God will be controlled by a man in some distant foreign office.'

'And you think *he'll* be in control of the cycle? No, Badjian, it's not even as simple as that. He'll merely be another man doing his best to make what he will out of the drift of circumstances.'

'Which constantly threaten to overwhelm him. Yes, my friend, I expect he will be no different.'

'Exactly. A man like us, in fact.'

Rimbaud and Badjian stood at the window, looking up at the now darkened sky. 'So you think you will be leaving us, my friend?'

'With all that merchandise stuck down in the cellars? Surely you know me better than that, Badjian.'

The invalid, his metal leg at last strapped to his stump, begins once more to rehearse his recovery. Tottering forward, blundering away from the bed. Whinnying with pain as he feels his way along the wall of his silent dawnlit hospital room.

For him there is no going back now, there is no alternative. The decision is inevitable. Just one further turn – he feels his way past the door, heaving his clanking leg across the floor – in some infinitely complex cycle, which for the moment he has reduced in his mind to the one cycle he is willing himself to complete. Determined to complete. Past the window, panting. Treading the night-fallen petals of Bougainvillea. Groping through the scent-cloyed air for the bed once more.

He heaves himself back onto the bed, wincing. He has made it.

And while the sweat dribbles from his face, he smiles as he returns once more to the beloved Africa of all his hopes.

In the morning, life was much as Badjian had predicted. A large, slightly more subdued gathering around the mosque, and guards placed at the gates to the market.

In the market itself, prices tumbled as the merchants broached their cellars and began unloading their stocks. Then, with the appearance of the morning caravans, prices rose again, sharply. Speculators, or perhaps simply those who by habit were unable to restrain themselves at the sight of such bargains, had begun buying up merchandise in large quantities. By mid-afternoon, when the prices had fallen for the second time, Rimbaud could stand it no longer. With an electric tingle playing in his loins, he started snapping up one bargain after another: only the best quality, and all at lower than Sottiro's lowest prices. By the time he had finished, the market was rising steeply again, price after price leaping up, often doubling itself. As Rimbaud watched this immediate vindication of his afternoon's purchasing, his guts dissolved. This was his work; he alone was in control now.

But how? Operating solely on credit. Bargaining with something he simply didn't possess. And each day's business would bring the day of reckoning closer, as well as increasing its consequences. It was all very well for Badjian to go on with his grand historical predictions, what he didn't seem to realise was the utter precariousness of simple day to day living.

Which depended on me.

And yet at the same time was being undermined by me. Utterly. In ever increasing proportions.

Not surprisingly, Rimbaud had forgotten about Yarousseau. At the end of the day, as Rimbaud led his porters towards the palace, each loaded down with the day's spoils, he saw Yarousseau approaching across the rubbish-strewn square. Around him the booths were subsiding, their loosened awnings fluttering to the ground. Directing his porters to unload the merchandise in the palace courtyard, Rimbaud started across to meet Yarousseau. Who'd found himself a new white robe, Rimbaud noticed.

'Look, you've got to get out of here! Pack up your things and start off before they close the gate. If you travel overnight, you might be able to catch up with the others in a couple of days.'

Yarousseau heard out his agitated friend with an air of unconcerned benevolence.

'Calm down, Arthur. I'm not leaving yet.'

'You clod. Don't you realise, you're playing with your life!'

'And what may I ask are you doing?'

Already the porters were raking up the refuse into piles as the scavengers moved across the square.

'So you're up to your bloody martyrdom tricks again, are you? You know how the Emir feels about missionaries.'

'I have my orders, Arthur. And these I must obey.' He tucked his hands into his sleeves as he started forward slowly towards the palace at Rimbaud's side.

'What orders?'

'My superiors have decided that I should stay in Harar. To build a church here.'

'Are you mad?'

Around them the porters were setting fire to the piles of refuse, the smoke drifting in feathered trails as it was caught in the snatches of breeze.

'Yarousseau, are you trying to ruin me? Because that's what you're doing, you realise that, don't you? My position up here is precarious enough, without you going and getting yourself stoned by some religious mob. You're just being bloody selfish!'

'I suppose it is inevitable that in your eyes my actions can only be seen as selfish.'

'None more selfish than those who are convinced of their own selflessness, Yarousseau.'

'Only if they are without spirit, Arthur.'

'Of course. The voice of the spirit. Who speaks to Yarousseau alone. Who alone Yarousseau will obey.'

'Don't mock me, Arthur.'

'Well, isn't that how you see yourself?'

'No, Arthur. To tell you the truth, not any more.' He shook his head, seriously. 'I too have fallen from grace in these difficult times. In myself, I am deeply divided. Your words hurt me, Arthur. More than you perhaps realise. I know their meaning. I have found myself much troubled by heresies during these last few months.'

'What heresies?' Perhaps Rimbaud could persuade this obstinate clod to leave on some theological quibble.

'I have come to the point, during my travels here in Abyssinia,' continued Yarousseau earnestly, 'where I can see little purpose in hell, or even in heaven for that matter, after what I have seen of life on this earth.' The admission obviously disturbed him deeply.

'Is that why you won't leave? Are you afraid of what your beloved Authorities might have in store for you? Watch out, you're going to catch fire!' Rimbaud pulled his companion aside as the flames leapt on the wind from a nearby pile of refuse. But for my helping hand, the bumpkin would probably have burnt himself to a cinder. The market at clearing up time was no place to go wandering about in flowing robes, especially with one's mind attuned to more pentecostal bonfires.

'Thank you, Arthur.' Yarousseau leant down, beating at the hem of his robe. 'Perhaps we'd better go into the palace.'

'No,' Rimbaud told him firmly. 'We're going to have this out here and now. Once and for all. Are you going to leave Harar, or do I have to drive you out?'

'No, Arthur. You can't drive me out.' Yarousseau stopped, his eyes narrowing against the smoke-filled wind. In the distance the curfew warning bell had begun to toll.

Arthur's Plan of Action

He'd knock Yarousseau unconscious there and then. Hire some porters to tie him up. And then bribe one of the caravaners to get him out of the city before the gates shut. He'd make sure Yarousseau had a mule and enough food for him to catch up with the others. Once outside the city walls, Yarousseau would never be allowed back in again while the Emir was in control.

But even as Rimbaud drew back his fist in preparation for stage one of his rapidly conceived plan, Yarousseau began to explain the true nature of his position in Harar.

Yarousseau's position in Harar

Yarousseau was also under the Emir's protection. He was being held as a hostage by the Emir, for the Emir's own protection. Many of Menelek's men were Christians; and the Emir had sent word to Menelek that if he besieged the city, Yarousseau would be killed. This event, both the Emir and King Menelek knew, would bring about even more far-reaching reprisals than a mere revolt in the ranks; reprisals which would mean the end of any purely Abyssinian power in Harar, whether it be the Emir's or Menelek's. For the two of them had heard that both the Italians and the French were apparently just waiting for any excuse to send in their own force to take over Harar for themselves – now that it was no longer under Egyptian rule (and thus, theoretically, the British sphere of influence). The martyrdom of Yarousseau would provide just such an excuse. For this same reason, Yarousseau had not been actually imprisoned, even though he was being held a hostage.

'Everywhere I go I am followed. To make sure of my presence, as well as my safety.'

'Where?' Rimbaud lowered his fist, peering round amongst the last shredded clouds of smoke. There behind them, not half a dozen paces away, Rimbaud saw two tall figures emerging from the smoke. He immediately recnised the red and black turbans of the Emir's personal guard; they both had rifles with fixed bayonets slung over their shoulders.

'So now I am involved in local politics whether I like it or not,' commented Yarousseau ruefully.

'Oh, go and build your damned church and leave me in peace!' Rimbaud strode away across the ash-strewn market place. So even here, now, with his world on the point of crashing about his ears, Rimbaud still wouldn't be able to do as he pleased without someone watching him. Judging his every action.

19

Within a few days Rimbaud had broached both Grimes' and Vardy's stocks and was using their merchandise to keep the market circulating. He would sell at a heavy loss, in the hope that he would recover in another commodity before the day was out. With his nerves inducing in him an almost ethereal state of lucidity, Rimbaud would calculate his purchases with split-second timing. His band of permanently hired porters would follow in his wake, unloading or loading the appropriate merchandise. No one knew exactly how much Rimbaud had taken on or unloaded, and by the end of the day he would only have a vague idea himself, although he would know to within a token or two the exact extent of his profit – according to the latest outside prices he had received from Aden.

Well before the end of the week, he had accumulated enough profit to cover the price of the three slave girls and all the jewellery with which the old man and his five sons had decamped. The thieving bastards! To hell with them all. He was well rid of them. Rimbaud began to realise that perhaps he'd got off quite cheaply without realising it. The old man and his sons would never bother him again after that: he was free of all Tahira's relatives now for ever. To keep things ticking over in the bazaar, Rimbaud decided to repay some of his jeweller's debts with one of Grimes' consignments of musk. Only one problem remained as far as keeping the markets open was concerned. Slaves. Rimbaud didn't dare take on any more after his first disastrous attempt – he knew he just wouldn't have enough to feed them with if he did. Each day during the mid-afternoon lull, he would go down to the bazaar to see how the slave market was moving. As long as trading continued in the main markets, it appeared to remain at a little below its usual turn-over. This was encouraging enough. Yet whenever trading ceased for even an hour or two in the main markets, another of the slave merchants would leave, he noticed. For good, he realised. He'd have to keep the market turning over all the time now, come what may.

This, compared with Rimbaud's dealings with Aden, was sophistication itself. How does one convey necessity in the poetry of commercial jargon? Rimbaud pondered, pen in hand. As he composed his letter to Old Man Vardy.

Menelek's advance has been halted a long way to the North. Send all available stocks at once. The market is mine. The possibilities for immediate profit are unlimited. However, this state of affairs will not last. For the present, the Emir himself has guaranteed trade. He is most anxious to establish himself in my eyes, and is offering me a chance which will surely never be repeated.

I enclose a trinket for your dear wife which comes from the Emir himself. Do not disappoint him. This is the opportunity we have all been waiting for.

Three days later, on the next caravan leaving for Zeyla, he sent a further note:

I am holding all stocks, including those of your brother and our fellow trader Grimes, until I receive the large consignment of barter which I trust you have already despatched. I intend to make up a vast caravan which I myself will accompany to the coast. The profits on this caravan will certainly exceed those for all our trading so far in Harar. Enclosed is another small trinket for your dear wife. The Emir's favours have exceeded all expectation, but he will require an immediate and large response on your behalf if our position is to be assured. I have further gifts for your dear wife – sundry set jewels which I myself will bring to you as soon as I have received your large consignment of barter. Please despatch all you have, at once – for the Emir, I can see, may well grow restless if I do not take advantage of the opportunities he is offering.

A week later Rimbaud despatched a single messenger posthaste for the coast.

> I have heard no word from you. If the consignment of barter is not forthcoming, I am afraid I will be forced to start disposing of your wife's jewellery on the market. I have traded all I have. The survival of the good name of Vardy stands in dire jeopardy unless your consignment is forthcoming . . .

By now Rimbaud's time of credit had run more than half its course, and several of the traders were becoming reluctant to do business with him. Avarice alone prevented the market from grinding to a halt as Rimbaud slashed his re-sale prices to the minimum.

Next day, Rimbaud met Badjian in the market place. Badjian asked him if he could move into the palace. His position as supervisor of internal trade required his constant presence in the market place, apparently.

'But I haven't seen you near the place for days!'

Rimbaud searched Badjian's face enquiringly. The strain of office seemed to be telling. Badjian's eyes were staring with fatigue, yet at the same time more shifty than ever.

'You want to keep a watch on me, is that it?' suggested Rimbaud. 'Afraid I might run out on you with all the profits?'

'This is no time for joking, my friend. Matters have taken a serious turn. The traders have been pressing the Emir for an immediate recall of all credit.'

'In which case you can move into the palace right away.

I'm leaving.'

Badjian caught Rimbaud's arm firmly, his grip closing like a tourniquet around Rimbaud's bicep as he led him with a forced sickly smile towards the palace. They were the centre of attention in the market place. 'Out of the question, Arthur. You wouldn't get more than a day's ride down the road,' he continued, beaming, bowing courteously: the Market Supervisor and the European trader exchanging pleasantries as they ambled between the stalls.

'Then what are we going to do? You're hurting me!'

'Put a good face on it, Arthur. All is well. We don't want the market upset by any rash displays of emotion.'

'Then how the hell are we going to get out of this mess?' Rimbaud grimaced nodding inanely. 'They won't accept my credit much longer. I'm pretty sure some of them have guessed what I'm up to already.'

'Don't worry, I have access to funds, my friend.'

This time Rimbaud's joy needed no feigning. 'Why the hell didn't you tell me! My God, we're saved! That's all we needed. We've got it made now.'

Badjian's smile remained false, however.

'They are funds entrusted me by Ras Makonen, for safe keeping. If he learns I've touched them, my life won't be worth living. And if the Emir should ever suspect where they came from . . .' Badjian left this particular possibility to Rimbaud's imagination, as he stepped aside to follow him in through the palace door.

Rimbaud closed the door behind them, and slammed the bolt to.

'Give me those funds, Badjian. Every penny of them. I don't care where they came from, that's your look-out. I don't even care about the market any more. All I'm interested in is my own skin.'

'Quite right, my friend.' Badjian placed his hand on Rimbaud's shoulder, his narrowed eyes smiling into Rimbaud's for a moment, before blinking away into some more calculating middle distance. 'So now we are forced to trust one another. For the sake of survival.'

On the following afternoon, the European trader had his porters carry a large consignment of gum in barrels up to the Market Supervisor's house. He had arranged to sell the gum to the Market Supervisor, and then help him to remove his belongings to the palace.

But when they arrived at the Market Supervisor's house, the Market Supervisor had decided that he didn't want to buy the gum after all. The European trader began to remonstrate, heatedly. The Market Supervisor replied that he wasn't willing to stand there and argue in front of the European trader's porters like some common beggar in the market place. With a gesture of annoyance, the European trader dismissed his porters and told them to come back in an hour's time. (As soon as the gates had closed behind them, Rimbaud and Badjian began quickly unloading the gum barrels, carrying the gum bales down to the cellars, and refilling the barrels with quantities of padding and boxes of tokens.)

When the porters returned, they found that the European trader had apparently lost his temper and was hardly on speaking terms with the Market Supervisor. The European trader told his porters to load up the gum, and then took his leave of the Market Supervisor, coldly, but with a show of courtesy. This European trader knew what he was doing all right. He knew he had to keep on the right side of the Market Supervisor, especially as the Market Supervisor was moving into the palace.

The porters carried back the barrels of gum and restacked them in the end palace cellar under the direction of the silently fuming European trader. (That night, Rimbaud mended the lock on the door of his end cellar and then began unpacking some of the tokens into coffee chests.)

Two days later, in spite of all the European trader's efforts, the market finally ground to a halt. No one would trade with him on credit any more. They wanted tokens.

Shaking with rage, the European trader returned to his palace, only to emerge several minutes later with his porters carrying several coffee chests behind him.

Addressing the assembled crowd, the European trader indicated that these chests were filled with tokens. He even flung a few to the crowd, just to show them. Any trader who did not trust the European trader and who wished to claim his debts before he was legally entitled to them, explained the European trader, could do so now. *On one condition.* The European trader would never under any circumstances trade with this man ever again. He wished to trade only with men who trusted him; such men as he knew he too could trust.

The traders began to retire, muttering amongst themselves in groups. After waiting for several minutes, the European trader beckoned them across. He realised that most of the merchants were men he could trust, he told them. But just to show those few weaker brethren who threatened to undermine all trust in the market place, he wished to demonstrate once and for all that he was a man of good faith. He had decided that he would relent – just this once – and for the rest of the day, until sunset, he would trade in tokens. He asked for forgiveness in advance from those honest traders who had trusted him for so long. He did not wish to offend them by trading in such a primitive manner, but he was sure they would understand that in these troubled times some of the weaker, less trustworthy brethren amongst them needed this childish demonstration of good faith.

As the curfew trumpet sounded, Rimbaud left the market place followed by five strings of porters, each loaded down with merchandise. Around him the market was a hive of activity, trade booming, making up for all the time that had been lost.

From his window Rimbaud watched the sun set behind the mosque, rise again, and then set for the last time behind the ramparts. As dusk descended trade was still continuing. Several of the stalls were pinpointed with lamps and the crowds seethed between the booths. Eventually, after nearly an hour of pitch darkness, the Emir's guard began clearing the market place, herding the crowds out through the gates with their rifle butts amidst howls of protest.

In the morning, Rimbaud's credit was as good as ever.

How long can this go on? Or do they know already?

'Forward . . . Remember . . . Forward . . . Remember . . .'

The patient stumbles forward, propped between his sister and the doctor, his metal leg clanking as it drags, rises, drags across the floor.

There must be some hope. They wouldn't be putting me through all this if they knew I was just going to die.

'Enough for today, I think, Arthur.'

'Yes, Arthur dear. You are looking tired.'

'All right, doctor. Time for the treatment.'

'Are you sure you still want to go through with it?'

'Bring it on, man! We're not children playing games.'

The patient lies on his bed as his sister Isabelle gently unstraps his leg. The doctor wheels in the apparatus and begins silently fixing the electrodes to the patient's paralysed limbs.

'Ready?'

The patient nods curtly, while his sister, her face pained, takes hold of his shoulders, pressing them to the pillows.

As the charge runs through him, the air jiggering in his lungs, his voice whimpering its plaintive guttural rhetoric, the patient watches his paralysed limbs dance.

Safe, even as the excruciating pulse slices razor-fingered through the innermost membranes of his skull, in the certain knowledge that I is another.

He is dancing now. His limbs leaping in their sockets with Dionysian ecstasy.

He understands only this pain. Which is life.

With this life he will walk again in the Africa of his obsession.

I will!

So trading continued in the market. All day, without even the need for Rimbaud's active participation. That night, however, rioting broke out once more.

Rimbaud stood at the window of the old man's empty room with Badjian, while they listened to the mob running through the streets over near the garrison ruins.

'They are killing the last of the Egyptian sympathisers,' explained Badjian, not without a note of nervousness in his voice.

Soon the flames began rising from the brothel quarter beyond the palace walls as various isolated fires started up. Then Rimbaud saw flares moving through the alleyways towards the garrison ruins. A necklace of dancing lights had soon surrounded what used to be the parade ground, and the crowd began yelling, their voices surging and falling on the wind. But this time there seemed to be nothing more to burn, for the little ring of lights simply remained, as the crowd howled and roared. After half an hour or so, there were several shots fired. The ring burst outwards, the pinpoints of light scattering through the alleyways while the sound of running and cries spread through the city. Rimbaud watched as several lights approached the palace walls. The men carrying the flares were alone, or in groups of two or three, he noticed. It was only when they passed directly under the walls by the market place that he recognised their turbans. They were men from the Emir's guard.

Gradually calm settled over the alleyways, and only the howling of the dogs on the ramparts and the regular distant roar of a starving lion disturbed the night. Outside the walls there was still famine.

After some time Rimbaud noticed the flares had begun to move back along the alleyways again. Slowly they approached the garrison ruins once more, this time silently. Then they formed a ring around the old parade ground, exactly as before. Rimbaud and Badjian stood watching in silence, but still the twinkling flares remained, unmoved.

'They look as if they're guarding something,' remarked

Rimbaud.

'For once, I do not know, my friend,' replied Badjian. 'This I have not heard about.'

Eventually, Rimbaud returned to his room. In an effort to restore his nerves he had started reworking his magic notes. Occasionally, as he turned over the pages, his memory would pick up something that he had previously forgotten, and some new formula would begin to emerge, or some old one become complete. Over on the bed, Tahira slept. She appeared to have completely recovered during the last few days, and already her belly had begun to swell slightly. As she had proudly demonstrated to me, with much 'Tahira will, Tahira will,' and shy giggles whenever I laid my hand on the taut skin of her navel.

Was this her first child, I found myself wondering. And then, sickened at my own thoughts, hugged her to me. Those nightmare days of disease and suspicion were a thing of the past. Over and done with. Gone, like the old man and his sons. If I was going to make anything out of my life with Tahira, then I was going to have to learn to forget those old rankling memories.

Rimbaud laid down his pen on top of his growing pile of notes and went over and kissed Tahira gently on her forehead. Out of curiosity, after he'd blown out the lamp he walked down the passage again to what had once been the room shared by the old man and his sons. The ring of tiny flares still remained exactly as before, their distant tongues of flame dancing in the wind around this central dark patch, which appeared to be in the region of the old parade ground, as far as he could calculate through the darkness. Rimbaud grunted and started back down the passage to bed. Badjian's light was still on in the club room, he noticed. He obviously couldn't sleep either.

Next morning, still no news from Aden. And trade in the market was at a standstill once more. With a feeling of hollow dread lying in the pit of his stomach, Rimbaud started out of the palace to begin trade. There was a consignment of hides in fresh from the South. Rimbaud inspected the bales while the emaciated hollow-eyed trader stood at his side. Anything from the South now was invariably of good quality, in pitiful contrast to the mangey skeletal mules of the caravans and ragged sunken-cheeked traders. Each caravan brought further news of the spreading famine.

Rimbaud watched as the hollow-eyed trader started to bargain, his gnarled fleshless hand gesticulating. Half-heartedly Rimbaud began his responses, savagely cutting the price. He'd made a mistake choosing this particular trader, he realised. But it was too late now – this was his showpiece: his demonstration of his faith in the market. He couldn't let the man get a fair price, or the whole object of the exercise would be defeated. With a dull sensation of malaise, Rimbaud completed the deal and affixed his credit sign to the hollow-eyed dealer's scroll. He left the porters to carry the stuff back to the cellars and walked away, his limbs leaden, overcome by this deadening weight of self-disgust. For a while he wandered amongst the stalls, completing one or two small purchases to get the other commodities turning over. His time was running out. This was the end, he realised. But even this knowledge of his own personal danger hardly inspired any freshness of feeling in him. He merely felt his will sapped by this negative oppression which seemed gradually to be draining him of all his energies.

In Paris as the Commune had been crushed, street by street, with the soldiers systematically putting every house to the fire, raping and butchering the communards at will, or simply torturing them to death with a callous disregard for lives which were no longer considered to be human, whole houses had been found with their communard defenders snoozing at their sniper posts, their heads bowed, open-mouthed and snoring over their rifle butts. They had not been tired apparently, merely overcome by some mysterious insurmountable malaise from which even the bayonets hardly awoke them. In much the same way, as the time of Rimbaud's credit inexorably decreased, he found himself becoming more and more numbed by this all-pervasive cocoon of enervating lethargy which even the sensation of danger inspired by the nightly riots hardly penetrated.

In an effort to rouse himself, Rimbaud took to strolling through the alleyways during the afternoons. One day (how many days later?), wandering amongst the blackened ruins of the garrison, he came across Yarousseau. With his robes tucked up in his belt, the sweating priest was prising the smoke-blackened stones free of the rubble. The clod was building his church in the old parade ground.

'And it's under the Emir's protection as well, Arthur. They even mount a guard each night to see that no one interferes with my work.'

The ring of flares in the dark, Rimbaud realised as he sat in the only spot of shade, his head propped in his hands.

In future his walks would be in the opposite direction, he promised himself, as he heard out his compatriot's gasping enthusiasm.

With a cursory wave, Rimbaud hauled himself to his feet and stumbled away across the parade ground. There, neatly marked out with pegs and string, was a shallow rectangular trench amidst the cleared, heaped rubble of the garrison billets. Along the edges of the trench were regular piles of rectangular stones: the foundations for the first church of Harar.

In spite of himself, Rimbaud found himself returning next day – after making some pathetically easy killing on the market. Already the foundations were laid along the trenches, and in one corner this little stone igloo had started to grow above ground level. Rimbaud sat down in the shade behind the rubble of the garrison, out of sight, watching bemusedly as Yarousseau heaved the stones into place. Yawning, Rimbaud rested his head on his hands. He had a week now (or was it five days? – or perhaps nine?) until the day of reckoning. If Yarousseau went on at his present rate the walls would be all but built by then.

The opening ceremony: the consecration of the first church of Harar. Father Yarousseau officiating. Alone. Over the coffin of the first European inhabitant of Harar, explorer of Lower Abyssinia etc. His dying wish would be for rain, Rimbaud told himself. With no roof on it, perhaps the unfinished church would be washed away and he'd be buried – an act of God, none less! – in some absurd miniature cataclysm. A fitting end.

Over in the parade ground Yarousseau sat down, mopping his brow.

'Get on with it, you clod! You'll never be finished in time just sitting there!'

Yarousseau leapt to his feet, looking about him.

'Oh, it's you, Arthur! You gave me quite a start.'

Rimbaud stumbled forward into the parade ground. 'I'll give you a hand.'

The clod was overwhelmed.

And so, for the next few afternoons, after his grand killing in the market place Rimbaud would wander down and help Yarousseau set up his stones.

'I can't tell you how much I appreciate your gesture, Arthur,' Yarousseau would repeat, with sickening frequency, as Rimbaud encouraged him on. There were no breaks while Rimbaud was on the scene; as long as he was there they worked non-stop.

With two days to go (yes, two days – according to the one-eyed gold merchant in the bazaar), Rimbaud discovered, while he was shifting some merchandise in the cellars, that the door to the end cellar containing the old wicker chair and the tokens (some still in their gum barrels) was ajar. The lock broken. Rimbaud stood at the cellar doorway, yawning, pondering. A few handfuls of tokens were missing, but that was all.

Then he realised. It could only have been one of his regular porters. In which case his secret was out. Any one of his regular gang seeing those gum barrels filled with tokens would immediately have understood about that trick deal with Badjian.

Stumbling dreamily up the cellar stairs and out into the yard, Rimbaud began lethargically, methodically, barring the gates of the palace, finally bolting the front door.

Breathing heavily, he mounted the steps to his room, and then stood at the window looking out through glazed eyes over the market place. Gradually trade came to a halt, and the mob gathered in front of the palace.

After some time, I was aware of Tahira standing at my side. The mob was yelling, chanting. She looked terrified. Lazily I slipped my arm around her shoulder, turning to her with half-closed eyes. At the same moment a stone crashed through the window. The slivers of glass tinkled over the windowsill, the stone clunking against the wall behind us and then clattering onto the floorboards.

Next moment I heard a voice, bellowing stridently above the others. Badjian was down there! I stumbled forward, and with an immense effort began fumbling under the bed for Vardy's pistol. Pushing myself to my feet, I moved over towards the window, propping myself against the wall, looking down.

Scene: Background: the sunlit market place of Harar, rows of deserted stalls.

Middleground: the mob, fists shaking, sticks waving, the occasional knife glinting, yelling, discordantly.

Foreground: the Market Supervisor (black shiny uniform, gold epaulets) arms raised imperiously, a whip in his right hand.

Inner foreground (audience): the fatigue-stricken European trader, fiddling with his pistol. And three bullets.

One for Badjian.

One for Tahira.

One, presumably, for himself.

Below, the crowd backing as the Market Supervisor

advances, cracking his whip above their heads . . . waving sticks, knives, hands.
Clawing.
The whip raised.
As they cower, backing, snarling, baring their teeth, while the ringmaster advances, cracking his whip above the heads of the lions.
Young Arthur Rimbaud standing behind the ringmaster, petrified, immobile . . .
Scene: Hamburg, the circus.
(*Verlaine still in jail after the Brussels shooting – Arthur Rimbaud, in despair, finally burns all his poems in the granary back at home and sets out on his travels once more. This time with only one aim in mind. A new one. To make money. In Hamburg, the old circus manager – who doubled as ringmaster, lion tamer, impresario, carpenter and general Svengali – had taken on the former boy poet, drug addict, vagabond, visionary and devil's advocate, as his clerical assistant, tent erector, publicity agent, box office man and general factotum.*)
Scene: The big top, the circus's last night in Hamburg.
A full house. Holiday crowd. The ringmaster (*battered top hat, floppy green cravat already coming undone, threadbare red jerkin straining to contain the white flannelled trousers drawn up over his pot belly*) waddles on to receive the applause as the performing bears stagger out, sailor-jaunty, on two legs, led by their somersaulting trainer in his baggy silk Turkish pantaloons.
In the front row, Arthur Rimbaud sits totting up the night's takings.
The tired three-piece band wheezes through another number. The ringmaster continues bowing, smile set, as the applause filters away.
Catcalls. Whistles.
Stamping.
Gaining momentum.
Where are the clowns?

Ringmaster gesticulating earnestly to Arthur, mopping his brow with his sky blue silk handkerchief. As the dissonant yells and stamping settle to a regular resonant roar.

Young Arthur dashes across the ring, tin money box clanking under his arm, the stench of animal sweat and exploded fireworks catching in his nostrils. As he enters the tunnel he becomes aware of another sound beside the rattle of coins in the money box and the steady thump of the barracking crowd. The lions, roaring. And beyond, the high glissando blare of the elephants, trumpeting. Two dishevelled clowns rush towards him out of the darkness, past him, followed by the poodle woman dragging a flotilla of trotting yapping poodles.

Outside, where the canvas tunnel gives way to the cool outer dome of the night, there are flickers of hidden light.

Fire!

The ringmaster at Arthur's side, breathless. 'The lions are loose, Arthur! . . . The clowns are clearing the crowd . . . You stay here!'

Flames begin licking out of the windows of Samson's painted caravan.

The ringmaster stands, panting into the darkness.

'Arthur, whatever you do, don't let anyone out here . . . My lions, my lions! They'll shoot them! My prize lions, Arthur . . . And I've only paid the deposit on Leo!'

The ringmaster advances tentatively into the darkness, holding out his whip.

As Arthur freezes, his eyes starting, the hair at the back of his head frizzing.

At the edges of the dim light, there are three pairs of gleaming eyes, advancing. A low rasping snarl as the whip cracks. One by one the lions emerge into the light, circling, paws clawing the air, snapping, as the whip cracks and double-cracks around them, marshalling them.

Beyond the caravans, the trumpeting of the elephants sirening into the night. The regular splintering cracks as the horses kick through the walls of their boxes. Behind in the big top, howls of panic, thunder of feet.

Arthur stares, his knuckles white around the clutched cashbox.

As the ringmaster advances, barking, peering, his arm waving a constant fusillade of cracks into the snaking whip. The vague shifting blurs of fur, edging first one way and then the other as the ringmaster forces them back between the caravans.

Back, into the darkness, away from the flame-sheathed inferno of Samson's caravan. Barking gutteral orders. Against the quick, snapping snarls.

Badjian's voice echoed over the silent market place as he stood, whip raised, facing the crowd. While at the back of the crowd the Emir's guards filed in along the walls.

'There is no cause for alarm. The European Trader has his credit guaranteed by the Emir . . . For the good of Harar, the market must continue!'

Rimbaud yawned, his chin juddering, as he emptied the three bullets out into his palm. With a long sigh he laid the pistol and the bullets on the table amongst his notes. Then, pulling back the rug from the bed so that the slivers of broken glass from the window fell in a tinkling avalanche onto the floorboards, he laid himself down and almost immediately fell asleep.

Next morning the merchants began setting up their stalls amongst the piles of refuse. The porters appeared to have given up clearing the market place now. As the heat of the day rose, the air became filled with the stench of rotting refuse.

Rimbaud lay in his bed, propped up on a pillow, gazing down. Snoozing. Waking . .

As Badjian patrolled the stalls, kicking through the refuse, two guards at his elbows. A charade of bargaining wakens to life amongst the various scattered groups as he passes by. Dying as he passes on . . .

Rimbaud staggered to his feet and started down the

passage. Across in the parade ground Yarousseau was at work, mounting a ladder, laying the stones one by one. Disappearing from view behind the walls as he went to pick up the next stone. At the edge of the parade ground, a knot of curious onlookers. In the shade of the heaped rubble which had once been the barracks, one of the Emir's guards, propped on his rifle. Rimbaud yawned and returned to bed ... Waking to find Tahira offering him a bowl of rice hash. Rimbaud ate a few mouthfuls and then handed back the bowl, ignoring Tahira's worried tentative attempts at conversation.

Rimbaud turned over and lay dreamily studying the bare wall. Beyond, the occasional murmur from the sunlit market place. He had till sundown next day.

Later, he sat up, yawning. Casually he reached over and picked up the pistol on his desk. He slipped the bullets into the chamber, and cocked the firing pin. Then he sighed, yawning again, and emptied the bullets out onto his desk once more.

He lay back, his eyelids flicking closed. In my dreams I followed the meandering trail across the rolling plateau where the grass whispered in the breeze. The distant grazing herd of antelopes looked up as they caught my scent on the breeze. Lazily the elephants trundled out of my path. The lions stared and then slunk into the grass; the herds of antelope fled, changing direction in sudden unison like frightened shoals of fish ...

Dusk. A putrifying stench mingled with the acrid tang of smoke rising from the empty market place. Groggily Rimbaud pulled back the covers and got up. Beyond the icicle slivers at the edges of the shattered window, a silent city. As he started down the dim passageway he heard the distant tolling of the curfew bell.

Rimbaud stood by the open window in the empty room at the end of the passage, gazing out. The little black walls of the church were almost complete. Rimbaud watched as gradually the dim rubble of the surrounding ruins imperceptibly faded into the dusk, and then he made out the lights of the torches, approaching through the alleyways. The Emir's guard took up their positions in a flaming ring around the parade ground. From the outer walls by the main gate the released dogs began to yap furiously, separating, spreading around the city, along the ramparts. Rimbaud stood, motionless, as the darkness increased. The tiny crescent sliver of the moon slipped free of the horizon and slowly began climbing into the sky. Methodically, Rimbaud reached into his pocket and took out the bullets, one by one. The chill of the freezing night air had slowly begun to penetrate the leaden malaise of his thoughts. Outside, the night was silent now, with only the occasional long howl from the ramparts. Raising his hand and taking aim, Rimbaud pulled the trigger.

The explosion flared through the night, its echo receding obliquely amongst the alleyways below. Immediately the tight circle of flares began to scatter. Rimbaud took aim and fired again. And again. This time, as the explosions resonated over the outer edges of the city, he heard calls in the distance. The guards were yelling to one another. The smell of gunsmoke started to prickle in Rimbaud's nostrils, and he turned and walked slowly down the passage, a shiver passing momentarily through his body. At the end of the passage he saw a lamp, approaching. There was a cry, and then the lamp fell, shattering on the floorboard. The blue flames danced along the spilling trickles of oil, catching at the edges of a switching robe.

In the sudden flare of light – Tahira's face!

She screamed as I ran forward, struggling frantically while I pulled her free of the flames.

'Tahira! It's Arthur!'

Still she screamed, flat, hysterical – not struggling now. A dead weight in my arms as I smothered myself against her flaming robe.

Then Badjian was with us. Stamping at the flames which were licking along the corners and dancing ahead into the darkness down the passage. Bomba came running with a lamp. By now the passageway down to the empty end room was blocked by a sheet of flame. Tahira subsided in my arms, the hem of her robe suddenly flickering alive with flame again. Next moment Badjian was wrapping his jacket around her flaming hem while I supported her. She appeared to have fainted.

'Get her out of here, Arthur!'

Tahira moaned as I dragged her upright, and then, cupping my hands under her bent knees, carried her off, pressing Badjian's jacket around her. I ran down the corridor and laid her out on my bed. She was unconscious, but there was no sign of any fire in her robes. I pulled the bedclothes up around her and ran out into the passage.

Badjian was silhouetted against the sheet of flame, cowering, backing, his arms raised against the light. And then Bomba was running past me. I felt the slop of cold water through my trouser leg. Badjian took the pail and swung it at the flames. The veil suddenly parted in a hiss, and then Bomba was running back for more water. I followed him, shouting to Badjian to stay where he was. In the kitchen quarters, I found another wooden bucket and scraped it into the rustling darkness of the large stone water pitcher in the corner. Then I was running along the passage again after Bomba, who was jabbering, excitedly, while Badjian yelled for us up ahead. Bomba's bucket of water dampened the flames along the wall on one side, and mine plunged the passage into hissing darkness. Several little patches of twisting flame grew up along the floorboards and I tipped the last drips of my bucket over them. The flames spat, leaping, scorching the side of my arm, and then Bomba was back with more water. Badjian took the bucket from him and doused the last of the flames. The dark air was full of the rich tang of burnt wood. Behind us, Bomba's lamp glowed dimly from down by the door to my room.

'And what was all that damn business about?' demanded Badjian sharply.

'Tahira dropped a lamp.'

'But I heard shots. Three of them. From inside here somewhere.' He paused, breathing heavily. From the end of the passage I could hear the shouts out in the street.

'There's a riot going on,' I began. 'Listen!'

'But I heard shots,' Badjian insisted, as we started down the passage. His feet scrunched over the broken glass of Tahira's lamp. Where the hell had I dropped that pistol?

'I definitely heard shots . . . What are you doing?' Badjian called back.

'Looking for the remains of the lamp. In case there's any more oil . . . Can you see what's happening?'

I fumbled desperately along the warm damp velvet of the charred floorboards, feeling the occasional sharp prick as a piece of glass cut into my fingers. Badjian was at the window in the end room. I stumbled forward. The floorboards became drier, with dusty patches, and I felt the sliminess of blood between my fingers become tacky. I ran my hands along one wall, and then the other. Just before the door, my fingers fumbled against it, withdrawing instinctively at its cold reptilean solidity. I picked up the pistol and shoved it into my trousers under my smock.

'What's happening?' I asked Badjian as I stumbled up beside him.

The lights were passing through the alleyways, dispersed, moving apparently at random. The guards were shouting to one another, and various other voices had begun calling across the night.

'The guards have been called out. They must be looking for whoever fired those shots.'

'Why?'

'This city's like gunpowder, my friend. Anything may set it off. Especially with the way things are in the market.' He turned, suddenly grabbing my smock up under my chin. 'My friend, you are a fool! I don't care if *you* want to commit suicide . . .' His hand was shaking, and I could feel his breath on my face, warm, repellent, heavy with the odour of decay. 'Why did you do it?' demanded Badjian vehemently.

Rimbaud hung, limp, under Badjian's shaking grasp, the yawn barely suppressed in his throat.

'Give me that gun!'

'No, Badjian,' Rimbaud heard his voice drift away from him, dreamily. 'It isn't mine to give . . . It's Vardy's.'

Badjian immediately began running his hands over Rimbaud's body, feverishly searching. With a feeble effort at resistance, Rimbaud stumbled back against the wall.

'No, Badjian.'

'Give it to me!' demanded Badjian angrily, standing his ground. Rimbaud could see the outline of Badjian's hunched shoulders against the window. Half-closed, Rimbaud's eyes followed one of the torches as it passed along an alleyway, disappearing into Badjian's head.

'No!' Rimbaud's voice sounded, surprisingly adamant, through the hollowness of the empty room.

Badjian grunted, sharply.

And then they were both listening in the dark.

From down the passage, Rimbaud could hear Tahira crying out, whimpering, calling his name.

Dragging at the overwhelming weight of his limbs, Rimbaud started forward. Tahira was calling, frantic (in pain?), in her own tribal language now. Rimbaud's mind fumbled after some elusive meaning as he trudged down the passage. Badjian was already scrunching through the glass ahead of him.

'Get a lamp, Arthur!'

Blearily, Rimbaud stopped in his tracks. Lamp. Lamp? *Lamp!* 'Where?'

'From my room! Hurry *up!*'

Badjian's voice was already inside Rimbaud's room. He was talking to Tahira, soothing her. Rimbaud blundered on down the passage, wading through the rubbery weight of inertia that encased him. And came to this light. Which he lifted in his hand. His head lolled onto his chest as he started forward on the return journey. His fingers were coated in blood, the backs of his hands streaked. Blotches and smears on his smock.

'Hurry up, damn you!'

Badjian's voice was there ahead. Beyond these webbed shadows.

Rimbaud stood at the door to his room, looking ahead of him, fixedly, blankly. Badjian rose from the bed and snatched the lamp. The shadows scattered as it withdrew, at speed. Tahira was moaning.

'Get out!' ordered Badjian.

Rimbaud turned, placing one foot clumsily in front of the other. The light had receded to the end of some plunging tunnel of darkness. Tahira was screaming. Rimbaud floundered, leaden-limbed, out of the door. Which he heard close behind him. The lock clicking.

Unable to move another step, Rimbaud subsided against the wall, his knees folding beneath him. There was this noise. It was screaming. To someone, from somewhere. At the end of some infinite corridor. Smelling of burnt wood. Black. As I glided through this sea of grass with the antelopes scattering languidly about me, leaping meltingly . . .

20

I woke, shivering with the cold, to a grey bleak underwater light. The sky was white through the window of the old man's room at the end of the passage. Out of the silence I heard a muffled cough, followed by a grunt, and then footsteps. The door to my room opened and I recognised the shape of Badjian, looming.

'My friend?' he called down to me, hesitantly, a flat whisper. 'My friend, are you awake?'

In answer, I pushed myself wearily to my feet. My limbs were numb with cold and my clothes felt slightly damp.

I could just make out Badjian's haggard face. Without speaking he unfolded his jacket, which he was holding cupped in his arm. Nestling among the black folds and splayed golden suns of the epaulets was a bloated leprous tadpole. Which I recognised, after several moments, as a foetus. The spasm of nausea clutched at my empty stomach.

'Oh my God,' I exclaimed involuntarily, the expression rising from the heart of this dead weight of weariness which still possessed me.

Badjian rested his hand on my shoulder, gazing intently into my face as I raised my eyes. In the grainy light, the tiny foetus's skin now appeared a lustreless ivory colour – almost as if it were some tiny carved ornament.

'She is all right,' Badjian said, his voice gravelly, but drained of all emotion. 'Leave her to sleep.'

'It's my fault, isn't it?' I began, in a desperate attempt to rouse myself from this stupefying torpor.

Badjian lifted his arm from my shoulder and covered the

bundle once more. 'If it means you will torture yourself, no, it is not your fault.'

I breathed, heavily. 'Then whose is it?' I asked. Life returning with a flicker of repulsion.

'It was bound to happen, I think, my friend,' he continued, his voice cracking, at the edge of a dry whisper. 'She does not appear to be made to bear children.'

I sighed, as my guts trembled.

'It may even have happened before,' he continued, 'if that is any consolation.'

'She told you?'

'She told me nothing.'

I watched, bleary-eyed, as Badjian trudged wearily down the passage towards the club room. Then I started to walk towards the daylight at the far end of the passage. I felt the pistol in my belt cut into my skin. As I withdrew it from my trousers I noticed that it had pressed its design into my stomach. My skin was mottled and chafed. I opened the door to what had been Sottiro's room and went to lie down on the stripped bed. Outside, I heard a single solitary call from beyond the walls at the main gate. Tossing down the gun onto the bed, I went over to the window. The market square was covered in a low swathing strand of white mist. The call sounded again from outside the gate. Could it be Old Man Vardy's caravan, arrived at last? I listened, and over the silent mist-shrouded roofs of the city the call sounded once more. No, that wasn't a caravan, just some poor trader.

I left the room, went downstairs and opened the front door into the market place.

So this was my last day. From over by the far corner under the walls I heard several voices muttering, and as I approached I saw the orange glow of one of the porters' fires flickering through the misty dimness. The chill muffling air choked in my lungs, and I coughed. Then I felt the warmth of the fire on my face. I squatted by the fire, putting my hands up towards the flames, and the voices stopped. There were three other shapes around the ball of glinting, crackling brambles, and as the mist parted, swirling in the rising heat of the fire, the dull featureless shade beside me became a face I recognised. The leader of my regular gang of porters.

I nodded to him, but he showed no sign of recognition. The voice called out again, plaintively, from beyond the main gate.

'What will happen to me?' I asked him, eventually, my voice barely sounding above the crackle of the flames. 'I did not intend it to be like this,' I added. 'I have been let down.'

Still he simply faced the fire, showing no sign that he'd even heard my words.

'What can I do?' I asked.

'Flee with your life,' he replied, without even bothering to look round, as if muttering to himself.

'No!'

He turned, in his own time, to face me. 'What more do you want from us? Leave Harar, and go back to your own people.'

'What, start my life again?' I sighed. '*Again?* With what?' I was talking my own tongue, I realised.

Then, out of the crackle of the flames, I heard the sound of a horse's hooves galloping through the side gate across the square. I heard the horse snort as it drew up on the far side, then the sound of someone hammering on the palace door resounded dully through the mist.

I leapt to my feet and ran, blundering through the piles of rubbish towards the palace. My head began throbbing at the base of my neck as I forced my limbs to break through the armour weight of my inertia. I heard the horse snort and shake itself, its reins clinking, and stumbled to my right. I was way off course. Eventually the knocking sounded once more, and then I saw him, stamping impatiently in front of the door to the palace, chafing his limbs. He was a tribesman, one of the men who worked on the regular caravans to Zeyla. As soon as he saw me, he handed me the bundle he was carrying under his arm.

'The caravan?' I demanded, as I tore at the bundle.

'It is coming.'

'When? How many days away?'

'Some days.' He tilted his head indecisively. 'I do not know. I left Zeyla before them.'

'*How many days?*' I insisted, tearing frantically through the seemingly endless paper wrappings.

'I do not know,' he replied irritatedly. 'Maybe they have not started yet.'

There was a note, I saw, as I pulled free the last of the wrappings. '*For the future, love Emelia.*' I turned it over. Nothing more. I pulled open the paper bag. The motley of clothes spilled out between my grasping hands. It wasn't till I leaned down to pick them up that I saw that they were all baby clothes.

I sank to my knees amongst the rubbish, staring. And then, with a sudden upsurge of violent agitation, I leaned forward with my arms extended and gathered up as much refuse as I could, pulling it towards me over the pile of coloured baby clothes. The next moment I was on my feet, stamping on top of the heap, jumping with the fury I felt bursting through me.

The tribesman was staring at me, narrow-eyed.

'The caravan!' I lunged towards him, grabbing at his front. 'Where is it?'

I saw his hand go for his knife and threw him away from me. He sprawled against the wall, pulling out his knife from its sheath.

Hardly aware of what I was doing, I leapt up onto his horse and dug my heels into its flanks. The horse lurched forward, and by the time I had my feet in the stirrups we were galloping full tilt through the mist. Desperately I yanked at the reins. The horse's neck arched, its hind legs skidding on some refuse as I dug my fingers into its mane and clung with my thighs to the saddle. It whinnied, kicked, and then leapt forward, as if trying to jump some obstacle.

For a moment I was tempted to let myself fall, but it had started into a gallop before I could release my grip. I simply watched, grappling for the reins as we passed through the main gate of the market place into the alleyways.

Here the mist had cleared and only the yapping dogs on the ends of their tethers at the courtyard gates dictated the direction of the horse's mad flight. Eventually we rode into a *cul-de-sac*, and then the horse reared up once more. By this stage I had a hold of the reins. I yanked the horse round as it reared, and then let it gallop on down the lane, turning it at the next corner towards the main gate. The customs officers scattered at my approach, and the horse jumped, with surprising grace, clear over the tables. The pit of my stomach rose as we fell through the air, and then we were out on the trail, galloping up the hillside beyond the walls.

The horse now settled to a regular pace and I bowed, pressing my cheek to its mane as it pounded on up the trail, its hooves ringing against the stones. We passed a couple of traders, who yanked their loaded mules aside into the ditch as we galloped on; and then the horse slowed to a jogging canter. My arse bumped unevenly in the saddle as I righted myself, slowly drawing in the reins. Finally the horse shook its head and snorted, breaking into a trot, and then walking. I drew it to a halt and dismounted, tethering the reins to a bush.

My heart was still thumping as I sat down on a rock above the trail. Below lay Harar, its roofs swathed in long thick strands of mist. The upper storey of the palace loomed above the opaque market place. Beyond were the blackened ruins of the garrison, and to the left the higher white dome of the mosque. It was all so close and intricate, and yet so small. Like a painting touched out in delicate watery tones, complete in every detail in those parts which had been painted. At random. On this broad white grainless canvas... Then, as I gazed, I became aware that the mist was not flat, but had this curious multi-dimensional effect of depth, making the visible parts of the city appear somehow thin and insubstantial, for all the world like some precisely painted twists of ribbon drawn across the still unending whiteness of the sky.

As my eyes settled tiredly into first one focus and then the other, I found I could transpose either picture at will. The city as ribbons of faint colour trailing across a windless abyss of sky – and then this *trompe l'oeil* betrayed only by the incomplete stretches of canvas. I no longer had the strength of mind to bring myself to focus on the reality. I could see beyond it too easily. The ribbons would eventually flutter away, leaving this misty all-embracing sky unblemished once more. The artist, dissatisfied with his work, would paint over these self-contained vignettes of meaningless intricacy with a few cursory swabs of distemper.

I watched as the two solitary traders moved down the trail below me with their loaded mules, disappearing into the pit of mist. I was on the southern trail. Over there to my right, two weeks away, was the coast. The rocky scrub-covered hills curved along the trail to the east, giving way on the horizon to the distant blur of the desert plateau. The occasional patches of cleared farmland on the hillside were brown and barren under the cloudless blue sky. As I watched, I saw one or two figures moving around the nearest farm huts. A herd of goats slid like a mottled carpet over the scrub on the far hillside above the high eastern trail. Then I made out something moving up the trail. A camel. A string of camels. One by one, at regular intervals along the trail, I made out their slowly moving shapes, their brown skins hardly visible against the pressing backcloth of sunburnt scrubbery and brown rocks as they plodded forward. And behind them was another string.

And a third!

'Why, Arthur, you're crying! Is anything the matter?' Isabelle puts down her knitting and crosses over to the patient's bedside. 'Are you sure nothing's the matter, dear?'

The patient gazes silently up at the blank white wall of

his hospital room. As his vision blurs, the wall fractures, taking on twists of fluid colour.

He blinks.

'What is it, Arthur dear?' Isabelle dabs at the patient's cheeks. 'Africa, still?'

He twists his head.

'I'm only trying to wipe your eyes, Arthur. Please keep still!'

The patient raises his hand and grasps his sister's wrist, pulling it slowly away from his face.

'That's better, Arthur. I do believe you're smiling!'

After riding down to meet his caravan, the European trader escorted it up the trail towards the city, occasionally turning in his saddle to gaze silently at the strings of camels which wound in a long regular arc down the trail behind him.

'Are you sure nothing is the matter, Arthur?'

In the market place the crowds gathered to watch as Rimbaud led his gigantic caravan of barter in through the palace gate.

'My friend. My dear, dear friend!' Badjian clasped me to him.

Three days later, as the curfew bell began to toll, I helped Tahira up onto her mule in the palace courtyard. Already the last of the caravan camels was loping out through the palace gate. In the dying light, as the flames flickered from the piles of refuse, I led Tahira across the market place, down along the alleyways towards the main gate. There, strung out in lines across the gateway square before the lamplit customs table, was my caravan carrying all my merchandise for Zeyla.

Badjian approached through the gloom from the customs table, taking my arm. 'For you my friend, we keep the gates open. For you, my dear friend, the gates of Harar will always be open. Now get this lot out quickly, Arthur. The customs officer is under the delusion that there's no duty to pay.

Emir's orders.'

Badjian squeezed my arm and I nodded the caravan leader forward.

'Quickly!' Badjian hissed across to him. And then: 'Farewell, my friend.'

Rimbaud took his leave of his faithful partner. Placing in his outstretched hand two bags of coins containing 50 per cent of the sum he had set aside to pay the customs due.

As we descended the slope and the darkness grew around us, I heard the yapping of the dogs begin on the city ramparts. Within a few hours we'd reached the lower slopes of the mountains. The air was still and bitterly cold. The light from the stars and the tiny silver crescent of the moon lit up the barren rocky trail ahead. And then, as we ascended into the mountains, it gradually became darker. There were clouds obscuring the stars to the south. Slowly the clouds moved between the mountain peaks, until they were overhead, and then I felt the first soft flakes on my cheek. It was snowing. I called across through the darkness for the caravan leader to halt, and then helped Tahira down from her mule. We rested beneath an overhang of rock while the snow began to settle over the surrounding boulders and lines of standing camels. The rains had come at last!

I watched as the looming flakes flurried thicker and thicker through the night. Tahira was already asleep beside me, and I laid my head wearily on her lap. When I woke, the snowfall had stopped and the valley was covered in an unbroken carpet of whiteness. The sharp sides of the mountains rose around us like the landscape of some silent frozen planet.

Instinctively, Arthur looked up into the black sky.

There, fluttering silently through the heavens, was this speckled shimmering luminescence – the Northern Lights. Arthur hugged himself deeper into his fur coat, edging closer to the glowing embers of the fire, pinning his rifle across his chest with his muffled hands. Behind him, inside the mouth of the cave, the snores of the old circus manager resounded through the distant inner caverns. (After the fire at the circus in Hamburg, Arthur had received a letter from Verlaine. By then Verlaine had just been freed from jail, converted to the One True Church. He wanted to see Arthur before he went to join a monastery. To hell with that; Arthur had shipped out to Spitzbergen with the old circus manager, this time as his sole assistant. The old circus manager had disbanded the circus, getting rid of the tearful poodle lady, paying off the sullen clowns, selling the remaining animals to the zoo and the knacker's yard, and issuing a writ against Samson for starting the fire. He was going to drag that boneheaded strongman through every court in the land. But first he had this plan. The zoos of Europe would pay highly for good quality young polar bears . . .

He and Arthur had left Hamburg on the packet for Spitzbergen with three large cages, several crates of salted horsemeat, and two rifles with veterinary bullets. For three weeks the two of them had roamed the icefields, sheltering at night in caves as the wind howled, whipping up the ice dust.)

On look-out by the fire at the mouth of the cave, Arthur stared up into the darkness, watching while the Northern Lights drifted and undulated through the night sky, a speckled indeterminate green veil. It would flutter, as if some gentle breeze was passing through the upper heavens, and then it would sink back into the absolute darkness of the night, reappearing at random, bellying out from nowhere like some silken sail. Sometimes it would light up the whole sky, and then occasionally it would vanish for minutes on end so that the exact icescape below receded into a blur of dull indistinguishable shapes.

Rimbaud gazed up at the utter darkness of the Abyssinian sky.

Remembering.
Is there to be no end to all this?
Am I simply to die?
The ships are hooting down below in the harbour. Isabelle

knits in the corner, subdued.

She won't speak. I am 'too uncivilised' to carry on a conversation with now, apparently.

All that swearing, this morning.

So she sits, knitting, silently.

That same rats-tail braid in her hair. That same black dress. Even the same freckled horny hands. Mother! . . .

Knitting by the fire as I pored over my school books, waiting to test me on my homework.

'Have you done your sums, Arthur?'

'Nearly, Mother.'

'Right. You can finish them before you have your breakfast in the morning. Now, what else did you have to learn this evening?'

'Geography, mother. About Africa.'

'What about Africa, Arthur? No looking. Hand me your book.'

(Pause, posture, arms behind back, eyes to ceiling:) 'Little is known about the Interior of Africa. In the northeast of Africa lies Egypt. Egypt was one of the cradles of the history of mankind. In 3000 BC the Upper and Lower regions were united and Egyptian civilisation began under the rule of the Pharaohs. At its greatest, the Egyptian empire extended in Africa as far as Libya and Abyssinia, but these possessions would often be lost as this civilisation's fortunes fluctuated . . .'

'Good, Arthur. That's enough for now. What next? Is there anything more?'

(Eyes raised to the ceiling once more:) 'To the south lies Abyssinia. Abyssinia is a mountainous inland kingdom which has hardly been explored. Since earliest times it has had little contact with the outside world. . .'

But now Mother is far away. Back on the farm. An old, crabbed peasant woman gathering in her harvest. Mother! . . .

'Do you want me to go on now, Isabelle?'

She looks up, her face pained, pinched.

'With what, dear?'

'Why, my life. About Africa. All those things I've been telling you . . .'

'All I've heard is filth, Arthur. Pure filth.'

'But what about Harar? . . . Don't you want to know what's going to happen? It isn't finished yet.'

'Another day, Arthur.' Isabelle lays down her knitting and comes and sits on the bed beside me, her cold hand raising vague scribbles of pain in my forehead as she smoothes my brow. 'There's all the time in the world for that. Another day.'

'Are there going to be other days, Isabelle?'

'We shall see, my dear . . . Calm yourself. It's no good fretting.'

'Has all this been for nothing, then? All this suffering? . . . I'm not just going to die, am I? I'm not. I won't. I will not!'